the
wrong
daughter

Turn the page for an exclusive extract from

The Wedding Vow . . .

Prologue

The Wife

My husband isn't answering his phone. While not entirely out of character, it still makes anxiety flutter in my chest. On the train, I scroll back through our messages; Linden hasn't responded since I left for Oakleaf Yoga Retreat yesterday morning. He's supposed to collect me from the station when I arrive but, as the connecting train from Oxford to Bath was delayed by fifty minutes, I'll be getting in much later than planned. Linden has no idea though, and all my calls are going unanswered. I'd be agitated if I had to wait around for him for an unknown stretch, but my husband has a more laissez-faire approach to life. I try not to worry; he'd usually pop into the coffee shop across the road and settle himself down with a newspaper. I don't know anyone else under forty who still buys the paper, but before his death, Linden's uncle was a reporter for one of the big internationals, and the smell of ink reminds Linden of his childhood. Still, I try his number one more time. Again, he doesn't answer.

'Verity, is everything OK?' asks Flora. She's sitting across from me, surrounded by pamphlets for Oakleaf Yoga Retreat and all the notes she wrote during our visit. Being so young, I expected she'd work from her phone, but, like Linden, she's an old soul, preferring pens and paper.

'All good,' I tell her with a too-bright smile. I fire off one last message to Linden before sliding my phone onto the little table between us.

The carriage isn't as busy as expected, but then, it's a Sunday in first class. In the seat adjacent to us is a man with polished leather shoes and a heavy, expensive watch, engrossed in his Kindle. A little further up is a rosy-cheeked, mousy-haired woman minding two immaculately behaved children, both dressed head to toe in Boden's latest autumn collection. When she sees me looking, she smiles, and I smile back before picking up my phone to check for a reply from my husband. 'Nothing,' I say out loud. 'Brilliant.'

'Sorry?' says Flora.

I give her a distracted smile. 'Just . . . Linden.'

'Oh.' She looks away and I put my phone down again, feeling restless. 'So,' she says, 'are we going ahead with the Oakleaf collaboration?'

I force the whirling anxiety to the back of my mind and concentrate on the task at hand. 'I think so, yes. They're a good fit. Their technology ban is on trend for the burnt-out millennial.' When I arrived at the retreat yesterday morning, I'm ashamed to say I felt naked without my mobile and, heart racing, kept patting myself down for it. Heidi, our in-house graphic designer, eagerly handed over her devices. She's been talking about this retreat for weeks. Though, as a mother of three, it's a rare break from her hectic home life. 'Let's feature them on the website in November. See if we can get a Christmas discount for our subscribers.'

We're only half an hour from Bath now. Unusually, Linden hasn't called to find out where I am and how long I've been delayed. I should've taken Heidi up on her offer of a lift since we're all headed back to Somerset but as I live in Bath and she lives in Frome, she'd have had to drive twenty minutes out of her way. That, and her car is always littered with children's toys and stray socks, and once, there was a bottle of curdled breast milk forgotten under the passenger's seat in the height of summer.

'Thanks again for inviting me to join you this morning,' says Flora.

I pull a face. 'Sorry I couldn't get you in for the entire weekend. I needed Heidi with me to take the photographs.'

'Oh, no worries. I had plans last night anyway.' Before I can enquire, she adds, 'My skin feels incredible after that Oakleaf mud bath.'

'Still happy to write up a review of their treatments?' She nods. 'Absolutely.'

'Do you think you can get the first draft to me by Friday?' Another enthusiastic nod.

Flora has been my assistant for the last year but her ambition lies in content creation. It's a shame; I don't know what I'd do without her as an assistant but if I want to keep her at Verity Rose at all, I need to let her branch out. Still, my head aches with the prospect of finding a replacement – all those awkward interviews and sweaty, overly eager candidates.

Flora goes back to scribbling in her notebook. Her teeth bite into her full lower lip as she writes. She's attractive, with her long red hair and pretty green eyes. She's self-assured, but inexperienced. Idealistic, but talented. And twenty-three. So young. Though I am only seven years her senior, I feel old around her. Out of step. She is the sort of young that can drink cheap tequila and even cheaper wine, crawl home at four in the morning and wake up a few hours later, fresh-faced and hangover-free. So young that finding The One isn't important. So young that there is enough time to fall in love again and again and make mistakes because, at twenty-three, no decision will ever leave you stuck, *truly* stuck, on a path you no longer want to walk.

I think about the girl I was at twenty-three, so different from the woman I am now.

Flora is bright. Brighter than I was at her age. She's Oxbridge-educated but, unfortunately, that isn't what will open doors for her in life. It's her shapely legs and smooth, dewy skin, because whether we like it or not, sex still sells. Of course, being a young, attractive woman in the workplace isn't always easy. It can breed jealousy among the older women who eye your bare legs in a heatwave and still make comments like, 'Just looking at you makes me feel cold.' Not because they are concerned, but because they are jealous, threatened by someone they feel is more desirable. And the men are worse. The ones who patronise. Who lean in a little too close. Who leer at your bare legs, not with jealousy, but with something darker and stickier. Then blame you for their unwanted attention because you had the audacity to wear a skirt in summer. Flora doesn't realise how lucky she is to work for a website run *by* women, *for* women.

When I started my lifestyle blog from my bedroom six years ago, I never imagined it would grow into a household name. What was once interior design tips and smoothie recipes read by only a handful of people and solely managed by me, is now a global well-being and lifestyle website, dealing in topics from home decor to sex and relationships, from culture to health and beauty. I still do the bulk of the writing, but we've worked with renowned guest writers and partnered with huge brands. Verity Rose expanded so quickly that two years ago, I had to put together a small team: a marketing manager, a graphic designer, an assistant.

I look out at the darkening, rain-laden clouds. It's mid-September. The summer heat has waned quickly and there's a chill in the air. Without Linden to collect me, I'll be stuck waiting for a taxi without a coat. I pull my phone towards me. As anticipated, no call.

'Sure you're all right?' presses Flora.

I stare at my seven unanswered messages and finally, I shake my head. 'Linden isn't responding. It's just . . . unusual.'

She wrinkles her nose. 'Oh. Well, maybe he fell asleep?' 'Perhaps,' I say, even though at 6 p.m. it's unlikely.

'Could someone check on him? If he's taking a nap, the doorbell might be enough to wake him.'

I nod, thinking of Mimi. We live on a private road, set back from the main thoroughfare, separated by a low stone wall and a row of tall evergreen trees. There are only two houses on Rook Lane. Windermere, which is ours, and Ullswater, which is Mimi's. As a freelance book translator, she works from home. If it were a weekday, I'd be confident she'd be there, but Mimi fills her weekends with an eclectic mix of hobbies, from pottery classes to archery. She says it's because she has a broad spectrum of interests, but the death of her mother three years ago and the breakdown of a long-term relationship a few months before that has left her with a void.

I'm surprised when she answers on the fifth ring. 'I'm just coming back from this fantastic cooking class,' she enthuses, as though we are mid-conversation. 'When you come over for supper tomorrow, you're going to dine on the most incredible gnocchi you've ever eaten. It's so good, you'll think you're in northern Italy.'

Despite my churning unease, I smile. 'You *are* Italian. Didn't you already know how to make gnocchi?'

'Half Italian, and yes, but the teacher didn't know that and now I am the star of the class,' she sing-songs.

'Naturally,' I say. 'Look, Mimi, can you do me a favour and please pop round to check on Linden?'

She's driving. I hear the rhythmic clicking of her indicator. 'Why?'
'He isn't picking up his phone and he's supposed to collect me from the station. I'm delayed.'

Silence. 'You mean . . . you aren't home?'

'No. I've been at Oakleaf Yoga Retreat since Saturday morning. Why?'

'Oh. I thought . . .' She trails off. My pulse kicks. 'Thought what?'

'Nothing. I just . . . I didn't realise Linden was home alone.' 'Well, at thirty-seven, I tend to trust him not to run with scissors or open the door to strangers late at night,' I deadpan.

'There's that Verity Lockwood charm,' she teases. 'Maybe he left his phone behind when he drove out to get you? He's probably waiting at Café au Lait with a newspaper.'

'Left his phone at home . . . of course,' I say, unconvinced. He's a perpetual scroller and wouldn't last five minutes without his phone in his hand. 'I didn't even think of that.'

More silence.

'You're worrying, aren't you?' she asks. 'No,' I lie.

'You are, aren't you?' she presses.

'I mean, Linden's fit. He takes care of himself. It's not as though he'd have suffered a heart attack or stroke. But a fall down the stairs or slipping in the shower . . .' I wince.

She sighs. 'I'll be home in ten and then I'll head over.' Relief sweeps through me. 'You sure?'

'I've got a key. It will only take a couple of minutes.' 'Thank you.'

'But Verity? Text him so he knows I'm coming round. I don't want him jumping down my throat the second he sees me.'

When I ring off, I send Linden another message, warning him to expect Mimi. He doesn't like that she has a key. Just as he doesn't like how much time Mimi and I spend together. For the most part, my husband is effusive; just occasionally though, he is sullen, borderline sulky. Quality time is important to him, important to any successful relationship, but lately, between running Verity Rose, keeping on top of the house, exercising and juggling a busy social life, it's a tight schedule, and Linden feels he doesn't get a large enough portion of it. He wasn't overjoyed about me going away to Oakleaf for the weekend, but it's a big brand and I needed to check it out for myself before recommending it to our audience. It's not that I don't trust my team's opinion, it's just . . . Verity Rose is my baby. My only baby. And, as expected, handing it over to others is challenging. Like I've told Linden, one day, in the next few years, I can step back a little more.

By the time we disembark, I still haven't heard from Linden or from Mimi.

Distracted, I wheel my suitcase through the crowd, catching people's heels as I weave in and out. Flora jogs to keep up. I can't slow. Can't shake the crawling sense of disquiet. Just as I thought, Linden isn't milling in the foyer and he isn't standing outside on the street either.

People scuttle along the pavement in a steady stream. I stand on my tiptoes, scanning the crowd for his golden head, his tall, lean frame. He isn't here. Still, I decide to duck into Café au Lait. Too impatient to wait for the green light, I stride into the flow of slow-moving traffic. A cyclist slams on his brakes and yells at me. I don't so much as glance his way. Flora staggers after me. She's talking, but I can't hear her over the rush of blood in my ears as I stand in the café and see that Linden isn't at a table with a newspaper.

'Shall we share a taxi?' asks Flora. 'It will be quicker than the bus.' As we approach the house, I feel sick with dread. Flora is wittering on about Oakleaf, probably to distract me, and I fight down the urge to snap at her. Mimi should've been in touch by now. 'Left,' I instruct the driver. 'Just here.'

It's a tight turn, missed by most. He swings onto our road. Our house is a double-fronted Georgian affair in Bath's signature cream stone. Far too big for just the two of us, but Linden was really taken with it. It looms into view. Its large bay windows like two wide, petrified eyes. The black front door like an open, screaming mouth.

We pull up and I pay the driver. I'm just climbing out of the taxi when the front door of my house is flung wide. Mimi hurtles onto the driveway, shrieking. A continuous, high-pitched, blood-curdling cry of fear. I stumble towards her. Mimi crashes into me, her dark curls coming loose from her bun.

'What is it? What's happened?'

Her huge hazel eyes find mine. They are glazed over in horror. She is trembling. Violently trembling. 'Police!' she manages. Then louder, 'Police!'

I am vaguely aware of people behind me. A man's voice at my back. 'I'll call them, love. What's happened?'

Mimi starts sobbing. Thick, clotted cries of terror. I grab her arm. 'Mimi, what is it?'

But she bends over double and retches. Then she is on her knees, vomiting onto the pavement. I look towards the house.

Linden.

I dart around her. 'Verity, no!' shouts Flora.

Ignoring her, I race along the path, up the stone steps and tumble into the house through the open front door. I skid to a halt in the foyer. I stop and listen. Silence. The kind that settles over mouldering bones in a graveyard. To my left is his study. To my right is the lounge. Ahead of me is the entrance to the kitchen. Only one of the doors is open. I pivot slowly towards the lounge. I feel my pulse in my fingertips as I step inside.

Something squelches underfoot. I look down. My black leather boot is in a puddle of dark, sticky blood. With a hot rush of horror, my gaze lands on Linden. He's in a heap on the wooden floor in front of the fireplace. One arm is down by his side, the other stretched out in front of him, as though reaching for the door. I stare at that hand. It takes me a moment to realise there is a hole in his palm. Raw and bloodied. Something has been stabbed through it. Blood is spattered up the walls and matts his golden hair, pooling beneath him. His face is turned to one side. His head littered with ugly gashes. His nose broken, bent at an unusual angle, and swollen like a pig's snout. The truth sinks in slowly, like a blade into my chest: he's dead.

My husband has been murdered.

Also by Dandy Smith

'Heart pounding gripping book. It's a great story.'

'Kept me enthralled and entertained.'

'I could not put this book down . . . will grip you like a vice.'

'This book made me realise that maybe my fave genre is psychological thrillers.'

'OMG this book is so good!'

'Loved, loved, loved! Lots of twists, turns and shock! Kept me gripped and unable to put down. Not one to miss.'

'Wow!!!!! That ending pulled on all my heartstrings . . . I was left totally speechless and in shock.'

'I completely devoured this in one sitting and cannot wait for the next.'

'Captivating plot and characters, love this author.'

'Excellent from start to finish.'

'This book is beautifully written, a brilliant book, that I have thought about since reading it.'

'Fantastic . . . a must read book.'

About Embla Books

Embla Books is a digital-first publisher of standout commercial adult fiction. Passionate about storytelling, the team at Embla publish books that will make you 'laugh, love, look over your shoulder and lose sleep'. Launched by Bonnier Books UK in 2021, the imprint is named after the first woman from the creation myth in Norse mythology, who was carved by the gods from a tree trunk found on the seashore – an image of the kind of creative work and crafting that writers do, and a symbol of how stories shape our lives.

Find out about some of our other books and stay in touch:

X, Facebook, Instagram: @emblabooks
Newsletter: https://bit.ly/emblanewsletter

About the Author

Dandy Smith lives in the Somerset market town of Frome with her husband and two cocker spaniels. She has an undergraduate and master's degree in Creative Writing from Bath Spa University, and enjoys all things aerial fitness, true-crime and *Gilmore Girls*. *The Wrong Daughter* is her third novel.

the
wrong
daughter

DANDY SMITH

First published in Great Britain in 2024 by

Bonnier Books UK Limited
HYLO, 5th Floor, 103–105 Bunhill Row, London, EC1Y 8LZ
Owned by Bonnier Books
Sveavägen 56, Stockholm, Sweden

This edition published in 2025.

A CIP catalogue record for this book is available from the British Library.

3

ISBN: 9781471418402

This book is typeset using IDSUK (Data Connection) Ltd

Printed and bound in Great Britain by Clays Ltd, Elcograf S.p.A.

Embla Books is an imprint of Bonnier Books UK
www.bonnierbooks.co.uk

For Mel Neville (née Monteath)
May the wings of your eyeliner always be even.

Prologue

They are sisters. They are aged ten and thirteen years old. They are home alone. Neither girl notices the man who watches them from the woods behind their house.

The eldest, Olivia, is in charge while their parents are out. There is money for pizza on the kitchen counter and a list of emergency phone numbers pinned to the fridge. Olivia doesn't even glance at them; Blossom Hill House is in Stonemill, an idyllic market town in the heart of Somerset, a place where people feel safe enough to leave their doors unlocked.

At six in the evening, the girls slip on their shoes. Despite instructions to be in bed by nine, Olivia has decided she will let Caitlin stay up half an hour later and, as she takes her sister's hand and walks out into the summer sunshine, her parents' warnings to stay inside are blown from her mind like dandelion clocks.

The girls close the navy-blue front door with the brass-bee knocker, but do not lock it. Caitlin glances up, missing the pretty pink petals that drift down from the cherry blossom tree in their garden during spring. They turn right out of the gate, then left onto the road that leads to the farm shop. They use the pizza money to buy sandwiches; thick, crusty bread, smoked ham and strong cheese. Next door, at the bakery, they buy rich, dark chocolate brownies and icy bottles of lemonade. They leave with their haul and race to the wildflower meadow. Here, among baby-blue forget-me-nots and bright bursts of yellow buttercups, they while away hours on sun-warmed grass. The summer stretches out before them, a blank canvas, waiting to be painted with possibility and adventure.

Olivia turns her face to the sky and loosens her thick, golden

1

braid. She combs her fingers through her hair until it falls in a flaxen cascade down her back. Caitlin picks at a lock of her own hair; dark brown and, in her opinion, boring compared to the sunset glory of her sister's. Noticing the derisive look on Caitlin's face, Olivia says, 'Your hair is so shiny; fox red when the light hits it, Kitty-Cate.'

She beams at Olivia, catching the compliment and clutching it hard to her chest.

The girls sit and make daisy-chain jewellery. They polish off the last of their now sun-warmed picnic and drink the last of their lemonade. In the balmy glow of the evening light, Olivia performs a perfect cartwheel across the meadow. She is all long, tanned limbs and flawless symmetry. She offers to teach Caitlin. Caitlin who is clumsy and uncoordinated and afraid of failure. Caitlin fibs, feigning a sore ankle because she knows she will never be able to imitate Olivia's effortless poise. She lives contentedly in the long shadow of her sister. Not in the sense that she is loved any less by their parents because the girls are adored equally. Rather, Olivia is older, she was the first to talk and walk and cartwheel. Caitlin is forever following a little way behind. She's happy, safe in the shadow of her sister.

The girls lie on the grass and gaze up at the milk-white clouds in the endless blue sky – they point out shapes they see: a leaping hare, a witch's hat, a ballet slipper. If they knew of the horrors of tonight, or the savage reality of tomorrow, they would want to pause time, to burrow down into this warm, July afternoon. In this moment, they are young and carefree, their futures as organic and as wild as the meadow around them. And though they don't yet know it, this is the very last perfect afternoon the sisters will share.

The girls walk the long way home, breathing in the fresh smell of cut grass and listening to the far-off sound of an ice-cream van. They pass Florence's house. The willowy girl with her inky, Parisian bob, sits in her bedroom window, staring out apathetically, her head on her knees. She had detention today, on the last day of school, for rolling her skirt too short. Olivia and Florence are best friends. They are the queen bees of Southfield School for Girls. They have the kind of easy, effortless friendship Caitlin craves. When Florence notices the Arden sisters lingering at her front gate, she brightens, removing her MP3 player headphones. She waves but stays quiet in case her mother is lurking nearby. The sisters wave back. Later, Florence will be asked over and over by the police what time, exactly, she saw the girls pass by her house. Her answer will change and change again because she isn't sure. For the rest of her life, she will pay close attention to the time.

At home, the girls wear matching cotton pyjamas. They settle down on the large sofa in front of the TV, a bucket of popcorn between them. They are oblivious to the stranger that lurks in their back garden, watching them.

Later, Caitlin goes upstairs to use the bathroom and stops at the door of her sister's bedroom. Inside Olivia's room, Caitlin notices a forest-green diary on the dressing table. She picks it up. She can tell from the soft velvet and the gold bee embroidered on the front that it is expensive. Nothing like the flimsy diaries from the old stationery shop in town. Caitlin is about to open it to the first page when her sister appears in the doorway.

Olivia halts, eyes narrowing as she catches Caitlin. She isn't angry; Olivia doesn't get angry. She is confidence and compassion. Determination and sugar. Wordlessly, she holds out her hand, palm up. Cheeks flaming and guilt swirling in Caitlin's stomach along with the picnic and popcorn, she relinquishes the diary, but works up the courage to ask where it came from.

'It's not a diary, it's a journal,' corrects Olivia because diaries are for girls. Journals are for young women. 'A boy gave it to me,' she elaborates, carefully placing it back on her dressing table. 'The boy on the bus.'

This doesn't surprise Caitlin. On occasion, as Olivia walks home from the bus stop after school, she will duck into the florist on Honeysuckle Avenue and buy a small bunch of flowers for their mother. Sometimes, because she is beautiful, she is given them for free. A lesson Caitlin has learned early on, is that beautiful people are often gifted beautiful things. Like flowers. Or journals.

'He told me to write it all down,' says Olivia.

Caitlin wrinkles her nose. 'Write what down?'

'All of it.'

She asks who the boy is.

'Just a boy.' Olivia's smile is secretive. 'Just the boy on the bus.'

After, the police will search for The Boy on the Bus. They will never find him. But they will look.

In bed, as sleep tugs at her, Caitlin wishes for a journal of her own. One exactly like Olivia's. She does not hear the excited pant of the man's breath at the unlocked French doors downstairs, or smell his cologne as he slips silently into the house. She drifts off.

Moments later, Caitlin jolts awake, ripped too abruptly from her dreams. The night is deepest black and all around her. She can't be certain what had woken her. She sits up in bed and listens.

Silence.

She knows something is wrong. It is an instinct she cannot fathom but it is as real to her as the heart that canters in her chest. Slowly, silently, she slips from her bed and pads across the hardwood floor. She stands statue-still by the door. It is open half a foot. Though her bedroom is plunged into blackness, the moonlight shut out by the heavy curtains, there is a high, round, stained-glass window on the landing which casts the space beyond her room in an eerie silver glow.

She holds her breath and listens. Beneath the sound of blood rushing in her ears, she hears her sister's bedroom door yawning open down the hall. Caitlin's fingers curl around the cool, brass knob but another instinct stops her from opening the door wider. Heavy, even footsteps cut through the quiet. They do not belong to her sister. Caitlin does not move. Does not make a sound. Does not blink as her sister drifts into view. And then so does a figure – tall and broad – too tall and too broad to be anything other than a man. Horror is a roaring inferno in Caitlin's gut. She cannot see his face; it is obscured by a Venetian mask with a long nose and furrowed brow. It is grotesque and surreal, like something from the circus. It's only as he guides Olivia to the top of the stairs that the knife pressed to her sister's throat catches the moonlight.

Fear flares in Caitlin's chest – a flame threatening to lick up her throat and out of her mouth on a fevered scream. Momentarily, the knife disappears into his black shoulder bag. The masked man curls a gloved hand around the back of Olivia's neck and turns her slightly. She is facing Caitlin's bedroom door. Olivia looks up. Their gazes lock. Taking advantage of his lapse in focus, Olivia lifts a trembling finger and presses it to her lips, willing her sister to stay silent. Caitlin's own hands fly to her mouth, containing the scream that has surged like bile. In muted dread, she watches the man produce a second Venetian mask from the bag and place it over Olivia's face. It is patterned, dark green and gold, just like the journal. The knife back to her throat, Olivia is led away, down the stairs. Caitlin thinks of the setting sun, sinking beneath the horizon. Disappearing into the dark.

Moments later, she hears the back door open and then shut. She feels the finality of it in her blood. She stands a while longer, replaying the image of her sister pressing a finger to her lips. She isn't sure how long she is paralysed in the doorway before the spell is finally broken and she shrinks back into the shattered safety of her bedroom. Beneath the covers of her bed, she cowers, shaking like an abandoned dog.

She is alone.

She doesn't really understand what alone is. But she will. In the coming months and years, she will come to understand *alone* all too well.

It is hours before their parents return. They are merry, their night a whirlwind of red wine and rich food and good conversation. It is almost one in the morning when they stumble up the stairs to check on their girls. Even though Olivia's room is furthest, it's her room their mother looks in on first. She is unconcerned to find the bed empty, convinced her daughters are tucked up together, limbs intertwined, in Caitlin's room.

She checks. What she finds is her youngest, and only her youngest; pale and quaking. Caitlin's tale of a masked man with a long nose, of a knife, of a secret journal and The Boy on the Bus, of a setting sun and Olivia being stolen away into the night, is garbled and too fast. If it weren't for the empty bed of her first born, their mother would not believe it.

What comes after is a blur of noise and artificial light and the police crowding their house, skittering all over like ants. Olivia is gone. Her journal is gone, too. Their father promises Caitlin that Olivia will return. That her mother will stop making those broken, animal noises. That everything will be alright. Caitlin doesn't reply. She doesn't reply because she knows the truth, she feels it in each beat of her heart, in every breath, even in the bright red of her blood: her sister is never coming home.

1

Summer

Caitlin Arden

It's the last day of the school year. The children have left in a gaggle of summer-holiday giddiness. Only one of my Year 5 pupils remains. I glance at the clock. Her mother is forty minutes late. The lady who oversees afterschool club has complained before that Natalie's family take advantage and never arrive on time to collect their daughter. As afterschool club doesn't run on the last day of term, it's just me and Natalie, and Miss Jones in the classroom next door.

Natalie is drawing and doesn't seem at all fazed by her mother's absence. I kneel beside the little girl and give her my widest smile; she isn't to blame for her parents' constant tardiness. 'That's a lovely picture,' I tell her.

She beams at me. 'It's my family at the beach. We're going to Greece this summer.'

In her drawing, there are two large stick figures and two small ones. The smallest of them, with her pink skirt and red hair, is all alone, set aside on the farthest corner of the page. I point to her. 'And who is that?'

'My little sister, Charlotte,' She sighs and picks up a blue pencil to colour in the sea. 'She's *really* annoying.'

I stare at the picture, and even though it's just a child's drawing, I feel a pang of sadness for the figure alone on the sand. It's unavoidable that sisters bicker, especially at this age. I probably shouldn't comment, but the words rise from some melancholy place in my chest. 'You know,' I say quietly, so she has to stop what she's doing to listen. 'Being a big sister is very important.'

Her eyes narrow. 'Why?'

'Your little sister looks up to you. She loves you so much.' I take a breath. I think of Olivia. 'You're probably the bestest friend she'll ever have.'

Her little nose scrunches up in thought. She glances down at her drawing and gently strokes a finger over her sad, lone sister. When she looks up again, her face is bright with intrigue. 'Do you have a sister, Miss Fairview?'

Her question, in all its buttery innocence, slices through me, and the answer catches in my throat. It isn't as simple as yes or no. It hasn't been since the day Olivia was taken.

'Sorry I'm late. Sorry!' I jump at the sound of a woman's voice and turn towards it. She's striding across the classroom. As Natalie was a late joiner, this is the first time I've met her mother. She's wearing Lululemon yoga leggings, her red hair swept up in a short ponytail. 'And on the last day of term, too. Apologies!'

As she comes closer, I get an itch of recognition I can't quite scratch. I know her. *How* do I know her?

'Hope I haven't kept you too long?' she asks.

I stand. 'Not at all,' I say, even though she should've collected her child forty-five minutes ago.

'Great!' She turns to her daughter who has discarded her original drawing and has started another on a clean sheet. 'Did you give Miss . . .' She glances at me and pulls a face which I think is meant as some sort of apology for forgetting my name.

'Fairview,' I offer.

'Fairview!' she repeats loudly, as though she's shouting bingo at a Gala. She rests her hand on her daughter's head and runs it down her long, pale blonde plait. 'Did you give Miss Fairview her gift?'

Natalie nods, but doesn't glance up.

'She did. It's lovely. Thank you,' I say, thinking of the tasteful, cream stoneware mug and Belgian chocolates. I have so many mugs – at Christmas and the end of every school year, I'm gifted dozens, most with 'World's Best Teacher' printed on the front. I feel guilty they can't all be kept, but at least the local charity shop is well stocked.

'You're welcome,' she says, her gaze boring into mine as though she's trying to place me too. 'I'm Laura.'

And the itch is suddenly scratched. Laura was one of Olivia's close friends at Southfields School for Girls. It's been fifteen years since I saw her last, at the vigil for the one-year anniversary of Olivia's disappearance. Laura's family moved away after that. She is a piece of our past, plonked into the middle of my new present.

'It's nice to meet you,' I say, praying she won't recognise me too.

She smiles, her eyes questioning. I want her to leave my classroom. Today, so close to the sixteenth anniversary, I can't bear to dredge it all up with a practical stranger who will act as though the hole Olivia left in her life is as big as the one she left in mine.

'That's a great little sketch,' says Laura to her daughter.

I glance down, grateful for the distraction. In this drawing, two girls play hopscotch together in a park.

'Is that you?' Laura asks Natalie, pointing to the stick figure with yellow-crayon hair.

She nods. 'And this is Charlotte,' she says, reaching for the orange pencil.

A smile spreads across my face like warm honey.

Laura smiles too. 'Oh, darling, that's wonderful. What a brilliant surprise.' Then to me, she says, 'You know how it is, sisters always squabble, don't they? Whenever they're awful to one another, I remind myself when they grow up they'll be best friends.'

My smile falters as a wave of longing for Olivia surges. Not trusting myself to speak, I nod instead. I'm usually very good at fighting the swell of emotion whenever I think of Olivia but today, the day before the anniversary, I am crumbling like pastry, bits of me flaking off at the slightest touch.

'Miss Fairview said being a big sister is very important because I'm the bestest friend Charlotte will ever have,' sing-songs Natalie.

Laura stares at me. She's stopped stroking Natalie's hair. Because now she sees me. *Really* sees me. She's followed the trail of breadcrumbs through the thorny forest and arrived at the gingerbread house.

'Caitlin?' she says quietly. 'Caitlin Arden?'

Great.

My gaze darts down to Natalie. But she isn't paying attention now. To her, this conversation is painfully dull, happening between painfully dull adults, high above her head. Still, I move away from her and over to my desk, not wanting her to use that name in front of other pupils in case it gets back to parents. Here, at the school, I am Miss Fairview, class five teacher. Everywhere else, I can't escape that I am Caitlin Arden, sister of the missing Arden girl. I start arranging exercise books into a neat pile so Laura can't see how my hands tremble.

'It is Caitlin, isn't it?' she presses.

'Yes.'

She's shocked. 'I'm Laura, I knew your—'

'I know.'

Silence.

It takes all my will not to turn and walk briskly from the room. I can't do this. I need a reason to get away. Now.

'I'm so sorry I didn't recognise you,' she says, examining me as though I'm a particularly unusual exhibition in a museum. Something fascinating from long ago. 'Your name . . . You're married?' She glances down at my left hand. At the solitaire diamond that's never felt like it belongs to me. No wedding band.

'Engaged,' I correct. 'Fairview is my fiancé's name.'

She frowns, confused that I'm using his name before we've walked down the aisle.

'Bath is a small city,' I offer, and let my words hang.

She catches them. Inspects them. Realises that the Arden name is intrinsically linked to the disappearance at Blossom Hill House. 'I see. Well, I won't say anything to the other parents. It's no one's business.'

But for the longest time, the media made it the nation's business. They took the story and feasted on its carcass, sucking meat from bone until there was nothing left. 'Thank you.'

We fall quiet again. All that can be heard is the scratch of Natalie's pencil on paper. I really don't want to reminisce about my disappeared sister with a near-stranger but I'm not sure how to shut this conversation down without being rude. After all, this is my place of work. I must remain professional.

'Do *you* still draw?' asks Laura.

Her question catches me off guard. I don't know why, but my pulse quickens. 'How do you know . . .'

'Olivia, she was always telling us how talented you were. *Are*, I suppose.' She smiles encouragingly. 'So, are you still drawing?'

'No, I'm not,' I lie. Her smile falters. I am not making this easy for her. I am all spikes and rough edges. I try to smooth myself out. 'But thank you for asking. It means a lot to hear that Olivia . . .' I stumble over her name. It's not very often I speak it out loud anymore. When she was first taken, it was said a thousand times a day in our house, whispered with all the reverence of a prayer. I swallow. Then smile and start over. 'It's nice to hear Olivia talked about me.'

'Oh, yes, all the time. She—'

'Mummy!' calls Natalie, scraping her chair back and running over, waving her drawing above her head. 'Finished!' She thrusts it at Laura. Then pushes the loose tendrils of hair back from her face. 'Can I have a snack now, please?'

They leave soon after that. Laura gives me her number and says we must meet up. I smile and agree, even though I have no intention of seeing her outside of school. It sounds cruel. Maybe it is. But too many times I've sought comfort in others who knew Olivia, trying to gather the pieces of her they hold, only to discover they're fool's gold because no one knew her like I did. Not even Florence. I have the shiniest, most precious pieces of who Olivia was. It's true that over time they have become marked and dented, but I still have them. And then there are the questions I don't want to answer. The morbid curiosity of *that* night. Of what I saw. Of how it happened. Of what I did, or *didn't* do, to stop it. I am dragged back into the past over and over. No. I won't see Laura again. I take out my phone and delete her number. Then I perch on my desk at the front of the class. I have a message from Mum.

11

How are you, sweetheart? Home yet? x

I get one of these messages every day. She worries. She is always worrying. Convinced that fate is vicious enough to take me, too. I reply before I receive the habitual, firm follow up from Dad – these are the rare occasions he breaks his silence – instructing me to answer my mother immediately. I tell her I'm fine. That I am staying on at school to do paperwork before I drive home to Oscar. I don't tell her I'm meeting Florence in town for cocktails. That I'm catching the last bus home. She will only mither, and I can't bear to cause her any more anxiety.

Still in my classroom, I change out of my work clothes and slip into the red polka-dot dress I brought with me. Then I stash my blouse and culottes under my desk. I have six weeks off this summer, but I'll return before then to prepare for September.

With time to kill before I have to leave, I sit at one of the desks and slide my white heeled sandals onto my feet. Then I take my phone and log into my socials for Wanderlust Illustrations. Last week, I hit 41k followers. Since then, my secret project has gained another 300. I've been lucky, a few larger online accounts and arty news outlets have shared my work: hand-drawn illustrations of local landmarks with collaged vintage fabrics. A little of the past brought into the present.

I click on my latest post – it's of my best-selling print – *Bath Pulteney Bridge at Sunset*; the sky, a vintage, floral fabric in mustard yellow. In the photograph, my print is blown up to A3 and held up in front of the bridge itself – my hand just visible in the bottom right corner. I keep my identity a secret. I want people to buy my art because they love it, not because I am the sister of that missing Arden girl. The one whose face was plastered on the news for weeks after her disappearance. I scroll to the comments. They are glowing and full of praise. Happiness slides through me like butter on hot toast.

Oscar knows about Wanderlust. He's the only one who does. Sometimes, I want to share it with my parents. They'd be proud. I know they would. But Mum would be concerned, too. Afraid I'd abandon my teaching career to be an artist. She didn't exactly say I *couldn't* study art at university, but she did question what I'd do with a degree like that. I refrained from saying 'be happy'. Because of course she wants me to be happy. But, more than that, she wants a safe, stable, reliable career for her remaining daughter. One less thing to worry about. And she brightened so much when I showed a flicker of interest in English Literature – the degree she'd done. She ordered brochures from local universities and laid them out on the dining table. I'd wanted to study abroad. To see the world. But I knew she'd start slipping if I left. Free falling into that dark, serrated place that took her years to claw out of after Olivia was taken. So I stayed local, studied English Literature at Bristol and went on the following year to do my PGCE. I think Olivia mentioned to her *once* that she'd like to teach. Mum would never admit it, not even to herself, but that's part of the reason she encouraged me to follow that path. In the ghost of Olivia's footsteps.

Truthfully, I can't imagine my sister would ever have shackled herself to the mundanity of teaching. Sure, she liked to show me how to do things when we were children: how to ride a bike, to cartwheel, to brush my own hair, but I think, if she'd had the chance, she'd have *been* more. *Done* more. *Seen* more.

I take one last look at Wanderlust Illustrations and the community I've built, wishing I was brave enough to chase what I want. Or callous enough not to care what my adoring mother would think if I did. Then I log out of the account, call a taxi, and go to meet the best friend who once belonged to my disappeared sister.

2

Caitlin Arden

Florence has chosen a quirky venue down one of the cobbled side streets in the city centre. It's all high ceilings and Victorian tiled flooring. The circular bar is mahogany and marble, above it are hanging baskets of trailing ivy and strings of fairy lights. A waiter drifts past, carrying a tray of cocktails in plant pots and propagation glasses. It's busy. I move through the crowd, searching for her. Two women brush past me. They are too similar to be anything other than sisters. Elbows hooked, laughing. This time of year, I see sisters everywhere. Pairs of women, safe in the knowledge that at the end of every bad date, or party or day, there is a soul out there born of their blood who will love them always.

Loneliness seeps into me and despite the heat, I am cold. The fact is, most people don't understand what it is to be terrified. Truly terrified. To lose someone to a man with a mask, brandishing a blade. Waxing lyrical won't make them feel it, either. Words are powerful. Experience is more. And because of that, I can be in a crowd of people – strangers or family and friends, even people who've known me my entire life – and feel as though I'm standing by myself. Alone. That word doesn't carry enough gravitas. There isn't a word big enough or wide enough or sturdy enough to bear the weight of its meaning.

Florence is already waiting for me at a table across from the bar, biting her signature, red-painted lips as she scrolls through her phone. I slam the shutters down on all the negative feelings, reminding myself I'm *not* alone. I'm here, now, with my chosen family. Her inky, collarbone-length hair and thick fringe is chic and glossy. She's wearing a black-studded leather jacket over a silk, ivory camisole and a burnt orange skirt with a lace hem. By comparison, my little polka-dot dress and heels feel far too obvious.

'You're late,' she says by way of greeting.

'Only five minutes . . .'

'Seven,' she corrects as I sit down opposite.

'How can you go about your life never being late?'

'The same way you go about yours never being on time.'

We smile at each other. 'Missed you,' I say.

I order us two cocktails and we slip easily into conversation. Florence is filling me in on her latest audition but stops mid-flow, eyes narrowing. I twist in my seat to follow her gaze. My friend Gemma is weaving through the throng towards us, grinning at me. The lavender dress she's wearing is beautiful against her dark skin.

'Happy end of term!' says Gemma, raising her glass.

We met at a little village primary school during my first placement five years ago. As the only staff members under the age of forty-five, we had things in common, bonding over our love of *Gilmore Girls* and our hatred for the emotionally abusive pinnacle of toxic masculinity that is Jess Mariano.

I get up and hug her. 'Here's to six weeks of bliss.'

Gemma turns to Florence and says warmly, 'Good to see you again.'

Florence gives her a cool, barely polite smile in return. They've only met a handful of times but Florence took an immediate dislike to her. The thing is, Gemma is all spontaneity and tarot cards and hot yoga – everything Florence was before she got engaged to Daniel. Now, Florence is all organisation and home decor and weekends spent with Daniel's family in Kensington.

'If I'd known you were coming here for a drink, too, we could've organised something,' says Gemma.

And before I can respond, Florence chimes in, her tone too smug to be charming. 'It's actually an annual gathering. Caitie and I do this every year.'

'Oh . . .' She glances between the two of us. 'Is it a birthday or . . .'

A dark yellow queasiness rises within me. She doesn't know about my missing sister. Or that Florence and I have been meeting up on the eve of The Anniversary for almost a decade. Gemma doesn't know the murkiest, saddest parts of my life.

Silence hangs between the three of us. Realising she isn't clued in, Gemma is awkward and hurt. A child in the playground being told they can't join in. 'I can give you a call tomorrow?' I say, rushing to dispel the tension. 'We could go for brunch this week? Or coffee?'

She glances only briefly at Florence, as though waiting for her to object, before nodding at me. I give her my friendliest smile to make up for Florence's thin-lipped one. Once Gemma's disappeared to rejoin her group, Florence says, 'She doesn't know, does she?' with a look that tells me she's satisfied she's still the *main* friend.

I quickly change the subject. 'Excited for the wedding?' In just seven weeks, Florence will be a married woman. At twenty-six, most of my friends are either married or engaged. It feels like only yesterday we were lamenting about our university deadlines and the pains of a lecture scheduled at the ungodly hour of nine in the morning.

'As long as my mother sticks to wine and you don't make me late to the ceremony, it'll be brilliant.'

I nod solemnly. 'My main duty as maid of honour is to ensure Susan doesn't down bottles of tequila behind the bar.' Florence raises one reproving eyebrow. I try not to smile, keeping my expression as grave as possible. 'And my other pressing duty is to keep excellent time,' I add. She narrows her eyes and I flash her my most magnificent smile. 'Promise.'

Our drinks arrive, served in terracotta pots with smoking dry ice and edible flowers in buttercup yellow and cornflower blue. Just for a moment, I'm back in the wildflower meadow on that last perfect afternoon, watching Olivia cartwheel in the setting sun. I can still smell the sunscreen on my skin, feel the waning heat of the afternoon warming me, hear her tinkling laughter that reminds me so much of windchimes.

A slow-waving hand appears in front of my face, tugging me from my reverie. 'Are you listening?' asks Florence.

'Yes,' I lie, blinking away the memory. But I don't blink it away fast enough; she sees the undercurrent of sadness that threatens to pull me under.

Her face creases with sympathy. 'Caitie—'

'Did you and Daniel settle on double-barrelling?' I say, cutting her off before she can ask me if I'm OK; my missing sister is a wound I don't want to reopen. The conversation with Laura has thrown me, that's all.

She takes a breath, as though she wants to pursue it, but we have a rule that during our anniversary get-together, we don't discuss Olivia, so she leans into my change of subject. 'Absolutely. Though he wants us to be Odell-Fox.' She pulls a face, as though this idea makes as much sense as changing their name to Mr and Mrs Hitler.

I laugh. 'What's wrong with Odell-Fox?'

She lifts her chin. 'Fox-Odell is better.'

I shake my head. 'Nope. Odell-Fox. Definitely. I'm with Daniel on this one.'

Hey eyes glint mischievously. 'Well, I'm going to tell him you agree with me, anyway.'

I raise my drink. 'Best way to start a marriage is with deception.'

She grins.

The evening unwinds. We order two more cocktails and I realise how lucky I am to have Florence. When I was little, I coveted the friendship she and my sister had. They walked around Stonemill arm in arm, their bond as easy as breathing, heads bent close together, laughing louder than anyone else. Then Olivia disappeared and Florence started coming to the house to check on me. Before, I was just Olivia's annoying little sister, but after, we became family. Sometimes, I can't sleep for thinking about Florence disappearing, too.

'And what about you and Oscar?' she asks now. 'Are you still planning on taking his name?'

'I am.'

She rolls her eyes as though I'm betraying all of womankind. The thing is, Arden is so closely tied to The Disappearance at Blossom Hill House and the infamous case of the missing Arden girl, that the name is stained. Changing to Fairview is like shaking up a snow globe so I'm left with neatly covered, untrodden ground. A fresh start.

'So, how're *your* wedding plans coming along?' she asks.

'Great,' I say shortly. 'Fine.'

'So you've finally got a date then? Booked a venue? Chosen a dress?'

At the mention of all the things I've failed to do, anxiety flutters in my chest. I don't examine too closely why I'm dragging my heels and I don't want her to, either, so I say something I know will send her off on a tangent. 'You sound just like my mother.'

She pulls a face. 'Jesus. A fate worse than death.'

Florence and Mum have a complicated relationship. Mum is grateful to her for taking me under her wing after the disappearance. She was glad I had someone close to my age to talk to. Over time, though, she grew jealous that I opened up to Florence more than I did to her. She accused me once, during those difficult teen years, of trying to replace Olivia. Not wanting to hurt my mother the way she hurt me, I bit back the barbed retort, 'Actually, it's *you* who keep trying to replace *me* with Olivia. To erase me completely until all that's left is her.'

'As much as I hate to agree with Clara,' ventures Florence. 'She's right to ask questions. I mean, you've been engaged for nearly three years.'

'That's not long,' I say, defensive.

'I was engaged five minutes when I started googling wedding venues.'

'You're a planner. You like to plan.'

She takes my hand and squeezes. 'I just want you to be happy.'

'I am happy. I *love* Oscar.'

'I know you love him. Everyone knows. The two of you are sickening together . . . So why haven't you set a date?'

I bite the inside of my cheek until it aches, wishing she would drop it but when it's clear she won't, I lie, 'We're going to view a venue next weekend.'

She's sceptical. 'You are?'

'Yes,' I lie again.

'Great! That's exciting. Which one?'

'Priston Mill,' I offer, thinking fast.

She's nodding slowly. I see the cogs turning, trying to work out if I'm telling the truth. The stab of guilt I feel for being dishonest fades as she says, 'Honeymoon plans?'

I close my eyes against a potent mix of foreboding and exhaustion. 'Don't.'

'What?' she says with feigned innocence.

'You already know. I'm *excited* to go to York.'

'Wouldn't you rather go to *New* York?' she enthuses, leaning forward, eyes bright. 'Or the Maldives? Or Greece? Or Italy?'

Yes, I think. 'No,' I lie.

She dismisses my denial with a roll of her eyes. 'It's not like you're on a super-tight budget.'

'Florence, *please*.' I know she cares. I know she just wants the very best for me. But I don't have the emotional reserves for this conversation. Not now.

'It doesn't make any sense,' she goes on, ignoring my plea. 'Clara is so anxious about you travelling, going too far afield, but her daughter was snatched from home. From her own bedroom. So why does it matter if you travel to Mexico or Timbuktu?'

We've had this conversation before, and even though I know my lines, it's an effort to recite them. 'Anxiety is very rarely rational.'

'Your mother is the reason you didn't go away to university. The reason you didn't study what *you* wanted to study. And now you're spending your honeymoon in dreary old England just to placate her.'

'Mum didn't ask me not to go abroad for our honeymoon.'

'She didn't have to. She just worried her bottom lip and you gave in.'

Mostly, Florence understands me better than anyone. She knew Olivia. Loved Olivia. And she thinks she sees me so clearly: my desire to please people, mostly my mother, outweighing my own personal hopes and ambitions. But there are things she doesn't see. Things I force to the very bottom of myself. A truth so ugly, I sometimes struggle to look in the mirror or sit quietly in my own company: it is my fault Olivia has been missing for sixteen years. If I had acted sooner, if I hadn't frozen in that doorway, if I'd run downstairs and called the police or my parents instead of cowering until they returned, Olivia would have been found. The man in the Venetian mask would have been caught. This is the reason I bend to my mother's will. I owe my parents the daughter they lost. That stayed lost because of me.

'Caitie, are you OK?'

I try to blink away my dark thoughts but they linger like black smoke. 'I'm fine.' It sounds forced, even to my ears. 'But you did break our only rule for tonight. You talked about her.'

'Not directly. Not really.' She looks down, stirring her drink with the metal straw so the ice clinks. 'I just want you to be happy. You deserve to be happy, Caitie.' Her eyes find mine. 'You do believe that, don't you?'

And even though I don't, I nod. I'm tempted to confess to her how I truly feel, but she will only comfort me, assure me it wasn't my fault. I don't need her well-intentioned lies. I know the truth. It lives inside me, razor sharp and cutting.

3

Winter

Elinor Ledbury

Elinor wakes up to find he is gone. She rolls onto his side of the bed and breathes in his familiar scent. Her heart is already hammering. She hates when he leaves. Especially when he doesn't tell her he's going. The too-fast buzzing in her chest, like a hive of livid bees, makes her feel sick. At seventeen, she knows she should cope better with being alone for a few hours, Heath has told her so, but she doesn't. The bees won't stop stinging. She wants to claw them from her chest. Instead, she screams into her pillow. No one will hear her anguish. Ledbury Hall is miles from anywhere. A twenty-minute walk to the closest residence and a half-hour drive to the nearest town.

She breathes deeply, telling herself that Heath will return. Naked, she sits up in bed. Without his body warming her own, the winter chill bites at her skin. She wraps the duvet around her shoulders and gazes sullenly at the heavy curtains across the room. It takes her another ten minutes to muster the energy to rise from her bed and open them. The weak, blue light from the watery, winter sun trickles lazily across the hardwood floor. Her bedroom overlooks the garden with the large pond. Though it's more of a lake than a pond. At its centre is a little island with a stone statue of two entwined lovers.

The man is kissing his way up the girl's throat, his hands moving around her bare stomach to cup her breasts.

Heath swims in the pond every summer and always tries to coax Elinor to join him. She doesn't. She's not sure she even knows how to swim. When she was little Uncle Robert tried to teach her, but the second she stepped into the water, she imagined drowning, just as her parents had. She could feel murky water rushing down her throat and filling her lungs until she couldn't breathe. Her heart would beat so furiously, she was sure her ribs would crack and splinter. Sometimes, she dreams of her parents' yacht, sees it bobbing in the middle of the ocean, in the centre of all that vast, empty space. Adrift. That's how she feels in Ledbury Hall without Heath.

She showers and dresses, but by noon he still isn't back. Tomorrow, Uncle Robert is due to return – she dreads his weekend visits and his ability to make the vast, Georgian manor house feel the size of a matchbox. She's fretting, worrying the skin around her fingernails. Only three of the seven bedrooms have fresh linen. Heath was supposed to change them; without him here, she will have to do it alone, because even though Uncle Robert fired the housekeepers years ago, he still expects Ledbury Hall to be spotless. Elinor and Heath started cleaning last night, but they'd grown bored, allowed themselves to become distracted, liberating a bottle of wine or two from the cellar. Elinor wonders if the reason Heath has ventured out is to replace the bottles. Uncle Robert counts the bourbon he keeps in what used to be her father's study, and sometimes, he will venture down into the cellar too.

Once the beds are made and the library is dusted, she allows herself to sit down and read to pass the time. Though she has read *Little Women* before, she reaches for it again. Secretly, she longs for a sister and believes that maybe, in a past life, she had one. Perhaps a writer like Jo or an artist like Amy. Soon, though, Elinor abandons her book and finds herself in the foyer, staring at the grandfather clock. It's four in the afternoon and still she is alone. She starts to catastrophise. She imagines Heath's car skidding across the icy road and into oncoming traffic. She can see in great, clear detail the wreckage. Heath trapped inside. Crushed ribs, splintered like matchsticks, blood pouring from his temple, his wide, unseeing eyes. She shakes her head, trying to dislodge the image. She knows she is being irrational . . . but what if she isn't? Her heart races and her breath comes too fast. She cannot banish the image of Heath's broken body. She paces the front room. He is late. *Why* is he late? Heath told her before that they are the kind of people who will always only have each other. If he never returns, there will be no end to her loneliness.

Fear bleeds into anger. He should be back by now. He could have at least told her where he was going or how long he'd be. She takes hold of that anger and digs her fingernails into it so it cannot escape. It is better to be angry than it is to be abandoned. She goes to the window again and again, hoping to see his headlights coming up the drive. Each time, she is disappointed. She sneaks another bottle of wine from the cellar, deciding a drink will calm her nerves. She sits on his bed and takes slow, medicinal sips until the room blurs. Until she is sucked into the dark.

When she wakes, it is late evening. Never, in her seventeen years, has she been alone this long. Without Heath, she feels as though she is being carved up, piece by piece.

Her world was once made up of four, and in an instant it shrank by half. It could shrink by half again if something has happened to him. Without Heath, where would she be? *What* would she be? This fear that he is gone forever may be irrational, but it is as real to her as the cold floor pressed against her hot cheek. She searches again for that anger. But, like a tide returning to shore, so too does the terror. It is a forceful tsunami that washes over her and fills her ears and her eyes and her lungs until she cannot hear or see or breathe.

Then there are hands around her wrists and she is being pulled to her feet.

'I'm here.' The deep timbre of her Heath's voice forces the tidal wave back. 'Have you been drinking?'

She nods. The buzzing, stinging wasps that were in her chest this morning have migrated to her head. Immediately, she feels ridiculous. She *is* ridiculous. But more than that, she is relieved. All that coiled tension drains from her and she becomes soft, like candlewax, in his hands.

Heath runs her a bath. She undresses and gets in. He sits on the edge of the tub as she soaks. They are quiet. But it's the good kind of quiet. Comfortable and smooth.

'Where were you all day?' she whispers, staring down at the water that ripples with her breath.

'Went into town for supplies. The roads were icy so I waited for them to thaw a little before coming home.'

She doesn't believe him. Knows he is lying. Can smell another woman's floral perfume on him.

'I was alone all day, Heath.'

Silence. Then, 'I can't take you everywhere, Ellie.'

'I know,' she says, even though she doesn't understand. She doesn't leave Ledbury Hall without him. He doesn't like her to. They are always together, until Heath decides they are not. She wants to tell him how unfair it is, but she is glad he is home and doesn't want to ruin it.

'You need to learn to be alone sometimes. To make decisions by yourself.' At his patronising tone, indignation gathers like a dense fog between her eyes. She rubs at her forehead, trying to disperse it, because she doesn't want to drive him away again. 'Robert is coming back this evening,' he says tightly. 'He called early this morning.'

Her stomach knots. 'But it's Thursday.'

He shrugs.

She gets out of the bath and wraps herself in a thick, white towel. She hoped she'd have one more night alone with Heath, a chance to ask who the perfume belongs to, before Uncle Robert invaded Ledbury Hall again.

She busies herself, brushing her hair, but she can feel Heath's eyes on her. She glances over her shoulder. He stands behind her, his expression penetrating. She turns back to her reflection. He comes closer. He takes the brush from her hand and starts to comb her hair. In the mirror, their eyes lock. When her hair is a sleek, golden waterfall, he puts the brush down and runs his fingers through it. It feels good. She tilts her head back, leaning into him. Her entire body tingles, from the wine in her blood and the feel of his fingers in her hair, and the heat of his body against her bare back.

She shivers.

Downstairs, keys jingle in the front door lock. Uncle Robert is home.

Heath's hands linger on her hair and then slide to her shoulders. He kisses the back of her neck, just like the lovers in the garden.

'Don't go down without me,' he instructs before quietly leaving the bathroom. Her skin is still singing as his footsteps fade down the hall.

She dresses hastily. Uncle Robert bellows their names. She hovers at the top of the stairs and glances towards Heath's closed bedroom door.

'Elinor!' Uncle Robert shouts, angry now.

She can't wait for Heath any longer, she rushes down to the foyer to greet her uncle. He doesn't like to be kept waiting. But the irritation on his face quickly shifts into something else. A kind of sad longing. 'You look more and more like your mother every time I see you,' he tells her.

Elinor has the feeling Uncle Robert was far too fond of his brother's wife.

She lowers her gaze and smooths her hands over the hem of her dress. She feels him watching her.

He clears his throat. 'And where's that conniving brother of yours?'

'Good to have you home, dear Uncle.' Heath's voice rolls down the stairs and Elinor can taste the insincerity in it. Uncle Robert can, too. His eyes narrow. Her brother takes his time joining them, which only serves to further irritate Uncle Robert.

The tension between them is immediate. Heath says their uncle is a murderer but, while he's in charge of their inheritance, they must do as he says or risk their silent understanding: as long as they spend the weekends pretending to be the perfect family, Uncle Robert allows them to live their lives undisturbed during the week.

Their uncle takes a threatening step towards Heath. He isn't a small man, but Heath isn't a child anymore. At twenty years old, he is taller and broader than their uncle. Where Heath was once a sapling, he is now a great oak. Uncle Robert frowns and Elinor is sure he is thinking the same thing. 'I collected supper from a restaurant in town,' he announces. 'Bring it in from the car and warm it up. You'll serve it in the dining room.'

Heath bows in an exaggerated show of servitude.

Uncle Robert's hand flexes and Elinor holds her breath. But then he turns on his heel and walks away, his expensive leather shoes tapping against the hard wood.

'Why must you bait him?' she whispers.

Heath's gaze finds hers. 'I told you not to come down without me.'

'But why?'

He places his thumb beneath her chin and tilts her face up to his. 'Because he wants what he can't have.'

She feels her pulse in her lips. 'And what's that?'

'You.'

4

Caitlin Arden

Oscar is working in his study when I return home from the bar. I see the glow of his office lamp down the hall as I close the front door quietly behind me. As a freelance web designer he can set his own hours, and for the last few months he's been working late into the night. It's just after ten now and I really don't want to go to bed alone. I'll lie awake, counting down the hours to the anniversary. Suffocating beneath the memory of Olivia being taken as I hovered uselessly nearby. So I set down my bag and slip off my sandals, then I move barefoot to his door. It's ajar. I peer inside, wondering when he'll be done. He's sitting at his desk, headphones on, his back to me, tapping away at his laptop. Every now and then, he glances at the thick binder of notes on the desk beside him.

I push open the door, but he doesn't hear me. Brushing grief away like dust from a bookshelf, I paste on a smile and move up behind him. Then I lean over his shoulder, playfully covering his eyes with my hands. He yelps like a dog being kicked and leaps from his chair. I jump back, startled by the outburst. He rounds on me, arms raised, ready to fend off his attacker. A giggle rises within me and I clap a hand over my mouth to squash it.

The fear in his eyes burns away. 'Jesus Christ, Caitie,' he breathes, removing his headphones.

'Sorry,' I say around my hand. 'Didn't mean to scare you. You're working late.'

I move towards his laptop, curious about this new project he's been pouring all of himself into, but he catches my wrist and pulls me to him. 'I can stop now you're back.'

I smile, relieved I won't have to coax him up to bed.

'How are you? How are you feeling?' There is a sincerity in his voice that scares me. He doesn't want a mundane and dishonest 'fine', like most people do when they ask. He genuinely wants to know. Tonight though, I don't have the energy to unearth it all. I can't answer with the rawest truth. Can't admit that I feel enraged and guilty, that there's a loneliness so thick and black, it blots out everything else; that this time of year I harbour an irrational and intense anger at all the people with sisters they can see and touch and talk to. So I offer him another, more easily digested truth. 'I really, *really* miss my sister.'

He nods, folding me into him. I bury my head in the crook of his shoulder and breathe him in slowly: shampoo and cologne, citrus and wood, coffee and ink. I ground myself in this moment. In the reassuring pressure of his palms against my back, holding me to his chest. In the safety that comes with his thick, strong arms encircling my body. The heat of him. The hardness.

But then Olivia's face flashes into my mind like a strike of lightning. Her wide, terrified eyes, caught in the eerie silver-blue glow of that night. Her finger pressed to her lips, warning me to stay silent. The horror that starts in the balls of my feet and rushes up through my body like engulfing flames.

'Caitie, you're shaking,' he says. He tries to pull back, to study my face, but I cling to him. Citrus and wood. Safety and strong arms. Heat and hardness. It isn't enough. I can still see her face. Can see that man in the mask with the long nose and furious brow, the blade in his hand tilted towards her throat.

Loneliness threatens to overwhelm me again, coming for me in an enormous barrelling wave. I run from it. I kiss Oscar with so much need, my hands slipping beneath his T-shirt and up his back. Then down, raking my nails across his skin. He groans lustfully into my mouth.

'I want you,' I say because sex is a place I can go where the dark glitter of her disappearance can't follow. He lifts me easily.

I wrap my legs around his waist and kiss him as he carries me upstairs to bed.

After, Oscar falls into a deep, satisfied sleep. I lie awake, my head on his chest, listening to the steady thump of his heart. When we met, I was twenty-one and fresh out of university. Where most of my friends were applying for graduate jobs, I was secretly planning a trip backpacking around Europe. I'd saved enough to travel for at least four months. I was afraid my parents would object so I kept it from them, too. Then I met Oscar at a cheese-and-wine night at the local farm shop. It wasn't my kind of thing. As a student, my taste was limited to Malibu and Coke or cheap vodka, but it felt so sophisticated, so grown up to attend an event like that – and the tickets were free, emailed to me in a competition I hadn't even entered. Oscar was helping his parents run it. Now he says meeting each other was fate.

He took an immediate interest. We ate good cheese and drank good Merlot. I liked that he didn't look down on me when I admitted I knew nothing about wine, which, to people who do, is like confessing you're illiterate. He was handsome, a mop of sandy hair, dark eyes and darker lashes, a taut, lean body. He was charismatic and interesting, but nervous, too. So nervous he spilled his drink on me. He apologised profusely and insisted on taking my number so he could pay for the dry cleaning. I gave it to him, though I'd never had anything dry cleaned in my life. The next day, he asked me on a date. We met at a bar. He was playful, educated, well-travelled. We talked about his adventures. Summers spent in Egypt, Peru; a placement year in Berlin. I told him of my secret plans for the autumn. He was excited for me. Offered to help plan my trip. I didn't mean to fall in love with him. But that summer was a montage of picnics and quirky bars and great sex. Of wild-water swimming and candlelit dinners. Of balmy evening walks and barbecues. Talking to him was easy. It felt like I'd known him all my life. Though he was only vaguely aware of the famous Disappearance at Blossom Hill House. At the time Olivia went missing, she and Oscar were the same age, but his family didn't move to Stonemill until a few months after she was taken. When I told him about my sister he was unwaveringly supportive. Interested without being morbid. He asked questions but didn't push for answers. When I gave them, he listened intently, and could recall what I'd said in great detail. We grew close. Suddenly, the idea of losing him terrified me. I worried if I left to travel, things between us might fizzle out. That, and I was still too cowardly to tell my parents. So I took the easier option: I stayed. Five years on, Oscar and I are engaged. Every year we attend the annual cheese-and-wine night at his parents' farm shop where we met. When fate brought us together.

My engagement ring is on the nightstand. I stare at it. I've always wanted to get married. When we were little, Olivia and I would play Weddings. We'd use the fluffy white bath towels as veils and sneak our mother's white stilettos from her cupboard. We'd liberate flowers from the wild meadow for a colourful bouquet.

I love Oscar. I want to be his wife. Our families want it, too. With Olivia gone, mine is the only wedding either of their children will ever have. Mum is like a racing greyhound in her pen, waiting with barely contained patience for the gun to sound so she can set off. She is desperate to discuss table settings and floral arrangements, entertainment and canapés. To go dress shopping as mother and daughter. To buy the big hat. But who will my mother see as I step into the white gown? Me or Olivia? Will she shed a tear because she's overjoyed that her youngest is getting married, or because her eldest never will? And how will I feel on that day as I walk down the aisle without my sister? Knowing she will never have a happily-ever-after. That she was stripped of it. Of everything. Because I didn't save her the way she saved me.

'I'm so sorry,' I whisper into the dark.

In the early hours of the morning, I'm woken by my ringing phone. Oscar grunts and rolls onto his front. I intend to decline the call and go back to sleep until I see it's my mother. She probably wants to know what time I'm coming over today. In the early years of Olivia's disappearance, the entire town would gather on the anniversary. Journalists and television crews would come to record the event. Close-ups of my mother's red eyes and thin face. Of my father's set jaw and furrowed brow. Shots of flickering candles and bouquets of flowers. I hated the media. Hated the journalists that suggested my parents were involved. Hated the strangers with watery eyes who didn't know my sister but wanted to sink their teeth into our mourning. Still, we got through it for Olivia. The more widely broadcast her story was, the more likely she was to be found. Of course, she never was. I was glad when the annual vigils petered out, replaced by a yearly, more intimate, gathering at my parents' house.

The phone stops vibrating in my hand and I'm relieved. I'll call her back. After coffee. I'm setting my phone down again when it rings for the second time. Only, it isn't my mother. It's my father. He never calls. Never. Pulse racing in trepidation, I sit up in bed and answer.

'Caitlin,' he says with so much authority. 'You need to come to the house.'

I sag against the headboard. Of course, when I didn't pick up Mum's call right away, she asked Dad to phone. 'I will. What time is everyone arriving?'

'No. You need to come now. Right now.' There's a thick tremble to his voice. It makes ice drip down the back of my neck.

'Dad . . .' I say slowly, trying to calm my cantering thoughts. 'What's going on?'

Beside me, Oscar stirs.

'Come to the house.'

'Dad,' I say sharply. So sharply, Oscar props himself on his elbows and mouths, 'You OK?'

Silence. I picture Dad in the kitchen, staring out of the French doors, the frustration he holds only for me starting to blister again. But I don't care. I need to know.

'She's back,' he says.

My breath comes faster. 'Back?' I whisper. 'Who's back?'

'Olivia.'

5

Caitlin Arden

In the bedroom, I yank on an outfit without paying attention. I'm in such a rush, I don't hear Oscar come up behind me. Startled, I jump as he appears in my peripheral vision. 'Christ, Oscar. Make a noise when you come into a room. Jesus.' I am snapping at him even though he hasn't done anything, but tension runs through me like an electrical current and anyone who gets too close will receive a sharp shock.

'I did,' he says softly. 'I called your name.'

I swallow but my throat is tight. He's brought me a cup of tea. It smells floral. Something I'm sure he's hoping will calm me. I take it to be polite but know I don't have time to drink it. I move past him to the door when he says, 'Are you sure I should come?'

What? I spin towards him so fast, tea sloshes onto the floor.

'I don't want to impose,' he says.

This is one of the things I love about him: he's polite and thoughtful. But, even if my parents had banned Oscar from being there, I *need* him with me. The thought of facing everyone alone makes anxiety churn in my stomach like pebbles in a washing machine. 'Of course you should come.' I set the tea down and go to him. 'You aren't a stranger.'

'Sorry?' he says, eyes searching my face.

I blink up at him, confused by his reaction. 'I mean, you're my fiancé.' At this, he relaxes a little. 'You're family, not some stranger off the street.'

Though he's nodding along, I can see from his frown he's reluctant. 'I just don't want to get in the way. Do Myles and Clara want me there or—'

'*I* want you there. I need you with me.'

He glances away, and for a moment, I really believe he'll refuse. But then he nods and some of the tension melts away. 'I'll be there.' He pulls me close and kisses the top of my head. 'Sorry, I don't know what I was thinking. Of course I'm coming.'

Stonemill is only half an hour from Frome but the journey to my parents' house is painfully slow. My knee jiggles impatiently and it takes all my willpower not to scream for Oscar to drive faster.

I glance at my phone. It's not even seven in the morning but, as it's the start of the school holidays, we're getting trapped behind cars, their parcel shelves crammed with suitcases and body boards.

As we draw closer, I am battered by too many emotions: fear and anxiety, joy and torrid anticipation. I feel nauseous. My chest tightens painfully. It's as though there are rock-laden ropes tied around my lungs and every time I try to breathe in, the rocks pull the ropes tight and expel all the air. Just as my old therapist taught me, I start listing the colours I see, focusing on those rather than the feelings pressing in on me from all sides.

We pull up to Blossom Hill House. My gaze is drawn first to the green of the cherry blossom tree outside my childhood home, then to the creamy limestone bones of the house. I'm surprised the police aren't already here. In the weeks after Olivia disappeared, there was a wall of media presence outside my parents' house. We stand in front of the navy-blue door with the gold-bee knocker. My heart thumps painfully against my ribs. Dad opens the door. He starts talking immediately, I catch flashes of his white teeth as he does, but I can't grasp his words, they dance about me like falling petals. I stare into the rich navy of his pyjamas. The coffee brown of his greying hair. The sea green of his eyes. He steps aside and if it wasn't for the firm, warm press of Oscar's palm on the small of my back, guiding me, I would have stayed rooted to

33

the doorstep. I am ushered into the living room. I take a seat and press my fingers into the tight, reassuring buttons of the mustard chesterfield. I wait. Oscar's knee rests against mine. He's whispering into my ear, low and comforting. I focus on the ochre jug atop the ivory sideboard.

The milky white of my mother's face appears in the doorway. Her grey eyes are watery and round, her strawberry-blonde hair has come loose from her ponytail. She steps aside to reveal the golden glow of my missing sister.

The woman in front of me is slim. She's wearing an oversized red-and-navy checked shirt – too wide across the shoulders and waist to be a woman's – over a pair of black leggings. Her waist-length blonde hair is wild and knotted around her face. I recognise her the way you recognise a family member you only see at weddings and funerals. Vague and distinct. I see the girl I loved in this woman's heart-shaped face and cupid's bow lips. In her high cheekbones and dimples. In her long lashes and brilliant blue eyes. What I don't recognise is that look in them. Wild and too still. Calculating and far away. Fearful and eager.

I can't remember the sound of her voice. It has faded like a bruise I never wanted to lose. One I haven't been able to pinch back into existence. I try to think of something meaningful and profound to say but the words are lost to me, dissolving on my tongue like candyfloss. Gone before they become anything more substantial than spun sugar.

'Caitlin?' says the woman. Says Olivia. Her voice is silvery, self-assured. It makes me think of summer rain. I was expecting her to call me 'Kitty-Cate' – a nickname only she used. Still, there's a thick, hard, rock in my throat. I breathe deeply. 'Caitlin?' she says again, stepping forward.

I stare into her blue eyes. Ones that always made me think of glacial lakes and summer skies, forget-me-nots and bluebell petals. I see in them something familiar, something sisterly, and a sense of calm eases over me. Like balm on a burn.

I nod.

She crosses the room, wrapping long, slim arms around me. She smells of men's cologne. 'I've missed you, Caitlin,' she whispers into my hair. A feeling I can't place ricochets through me. Before I can catch it, she says, 'I've missed you so much.'

I wrap my arms around her. 'I've missed you, too.'

6

Elinor Ledbury

Elinor's brother is the pivot around which her life revolves. He is the centre of her universe. Perhaps even, the entirety of it. She knows little of the world beyond Ledbury Hall. It has been her home for as long as she can remember, and she rarely leaves its sprawling grounds. When it is raining or too cold to be outside, she burrows down in the library. It smells of strong coffee, of leather and learning. Besides her brother's bedroom, it is her favourite room in the manor. There is beauty in the mahogany wood and large, arched windows; in the stone fireplace and book-lined, floor-to-ceiling shelves with their creaking, rolling ladder. There are books everywhere. Crisp, new paperbacks, static clinging to their pages. Old, yellowing tomes that smell of damp and dust. Elinor pays special attention to the romance novels that belonged to her mother. She's read them all, over and over, their pages dog-eared, their spines creased. And even though she and her brother are named after the characters within them, Heath thinks those types of books are better suited to kindling. Yet Elinor finds comfort in the simplicity of the relationships between the fictional lovers because even when it is complicated, it isn't. They glitter and spin out in the wide world. They do not hide.

Now, Heath lies beside her in his bed, wearing only his boxers, one arm slung over Elinor's waist. It's cold, even with the windows closed tight, but the places where his skin touches hers are warm. Though she enjoys the cosiness of these winter days, of reading beside the open fire and huddling together beneath thick, fleecy blankets, of walks with her brother, crunching across icy earth, she is tiring of the cloud-white skies and dark nights. She misses the summer, the vast expanse of blue above and luscious green underfoot. The warm, lazy mornings spent in his big bed, light streaming in through the large windows. Afternoons spent picnicking on the lawn and watching her brother swim in their pond, even though she isn't brave enough to join. Evenings spent swirling inside a bottle of champagne, listening to records and dancing barefoot in the dining hall before falling into bed.

In his sleep, Heath pulls her closer to him. She smiles. She feels wanted. Someone worth reaching for, even as he is lost to dreams. She rolls over, careful not to wake him, so she can gaze into her brother's beautiful, sleeping face. She feels a wash of love for him. Eventually, though, he stirs. His once deep, steady breath shallows as he rises from the depths of unconsciousness. 'What time is it?' he mumbles into her shoulder.

She glances at the bedside clock. 'Noon.'

He groans.

Uncle Robert will be back again tomorrow, a pin at the ready to burst their Monday to Friday bubble of happiness.

'Only one more day of freedom,' he says.

For the most part, they live in Ledbury Hall alone. Uncle Robert works in London, which is too far to drive every day. The manor isn't his to sell and he'd never give up the pharmaceutical company he's spent years building. So, during the week, he lives in his city flat, returning to the Ledburys' only on the weekends. 'At least he'll be gone by Monday morning,' she says. 'Though I wish he didn't come at all.'

'One more year,' he says, propping himself up onto his elbows.

Then, she would be eighteen, too young to claim their birthright, but Heath would be twenty-one, and ownership of his half of Ledbury Hall and their mother's wealth, would legally transfer to him. Until then, it's all entrusted to Uncle Robert. This angers them. Ledbury Hall and the land has been in their mother's family for over a century. As the Ledburys were old money, Elinor's father Nicholas Brent was eager to take his wife's name. Uncle Robert isn't a Ledbury, he's a Brent. Their father's brother. The manor should be all theirs. *Just* theirs. They are counting down the days.

'Unless Uncle Robert does away with us, like he did our parents,' sneers Heath.

Even as a chill rolls through Elinor, she sits up and fixes him with a scornful look. 'Don't say that. He didn't have our parents killed.' This is what she always says. She's said it so many times, she's never stopped to wonder if she believes it. But it soothes her brother. And soothe him she must. She doesn't want to fan the flames of loathing for Uncle Robert. She worries if she does, it will burn out of control. A forest fire whiplashing across arid plains until there is nothing left but scorched black, smoking cinders.

'He was with them. The boating trip was his idea. How is it he survived and they didn't?' he says.

'Because they drowned.' The delivery of her words is as flat as the emotion behind them. She remembers almost nothing of the parents they briefly shared. To her, they are as fictional, perhaps even more so, than the mothers and fathers in the novels she reads. She was only three when they died. Heath was six. He remembers them. Misses them. She does not.

Heath becomes hard and cold, like marble. He gets out of bed. Without the warmth of his skin against hers, she shivers. He pulls on his jeans, his back to her. From his silence and the way in which he snatches his T-shirt from his bedroom floor, she knows he is angry. She should not have let some of her dispassion over their parents' demise bleed into conversation with her brother. How would he react if he knew the dark, ugly truth? That she is glad their parents are gone. She doubts that if they had lived, she and Heath would be as close as they are now. Even though there is a sweet soreness to the reality that her brother is the only person who has ever truly loved her, there is comfort in it too.

'Can you help me with the physics reading?' she asks him, hoping a shift of subject will instigate a shift of mood.

They have always been home-taught. With the nearest school so far away and Uncle Robert residing at Ledbury Hall only part time, he was quick to hire a tutor. Though, she was let go before Elinor's thirteenth birthday. Heath says this is because Uncle Robert didn't want their education to eat into money he considers his, but Uncle Robert claims it is because the Ledburys are bright and didn't need handholding. Now, once a month, work is posted to the house by a remote tutor.

'Can't. I need to go into town,' says Heath.

The panic is immediate. 'Again?'

'We need food. You want to eat, don't you?'

She stands. 'So, take me with you.'

'I can't.'

'Why?' She can feel her bottom lip pushing into a petulant pout. She hates that she is sulking, but it is the second time this week he has left her.

'You'll slow me down.'

'Thanks.'

'You don't like going into town.'

This is true. But what she hates more is being left behind, all alone in this huge house. 'People stare,' she says by way of explanation.

'You're beautiful. People will always stare.'

She takes her silver-blue slip from the chair where it was tossed last night and slides it over her head. Heath watches but doesn't speak. She wonders if leaving again is punishment for the way she coldly talked about their parents. She isn't brave enough to ask. He tells her he will be back before she knows it. 'How long?'

'Don't know.'

He leaves the room. She follows. She tries not to whine. 'How long?'

'Two hours. Maybe three.'

As she walks with him to the hall, she bites down hard on her lip to stop herself from begging him not to go. She doesn't want to think about the seconds and minutes and hours he will be gone, but she does.

At the door, he comes to a stop so abruptly she almost collides with him. He turns to face her, brow furrowed in concern. He smooths his thumb across her jaw and tilts her face up to his. 'Ellie, you are your own person. You need to cope without me sometimes.' He presses a kiss to her forehead. 'Home soon, little sister.'

He goes out into the watery winter sun. Anxiety swilling in her stomach, she watches him jog down the frozen stone steps towards the car. Her breath hangs in a milky-white cloud in front of her and through that cloud, she sees him drive away. And then she is alone. Silence pours in along with the wind. It floods every nook and cranny of Ledbury Hall until she is drowning in it.

Three hours bleed into four, bleed into five. Her uncle is right, she is bright, though her brother is taking her for a fool. Shopping for food doesn't take five hours. She remembers the floral perfume on his skin and wonders again who it belongs to. She decides to find out. After all, just as Heath said, she is her own person which means she can make her own decisions. So, she decides. She pushes her feet into boots and ventures out. For a second, the freezing January air is like a sharp slap, stealing the breath from her lungs. She blinks up at the pearly sky, thick with dense cloud. She is wearing only her silk slip and a thin, cream-coloured cardigan – not enough to keep warm, but she doesn't turn back in case she loses her determination.

She crunches over packed snow, following the long, winding driveway. The frigid breeze whips around her. Her ears are burning with cold and her hands are wrapped around her body, tucked beneath armpits in an attempt to warm them. Finally, she reaches the iron gates. They are high, towering above her two times over. For a moment, her heart sinks at the sight of the padlock. Then she realises it has been placed on the gate but isn't clicked shut. With shaking, winter-bitten fingers, she fumbles with it, and then she is out.

It starts to snow. She trudges along the side of the road on the frozen narrow verge. Cars pass her by and she feels eyes on her. She keeps her head turned away from the traffic and concentrates on putting one foot in front of the other. The snow that settles across her shoulders and in her hair melts to icy damp. Beside her, a car slows. She hears a window being rolled down.

'Need a lift?' asks the driver in a lilting, Irish brogue. She turns to look at him. He has dark hair and an open, friendly face. He can't be much older than her brother. 'Where you headed?'

She keeps walking and his car crawls alongside. 'Town.'

'Sutcliffe?'

She nods.

He pulls over and throws open the passenger side door. 'Get in. I'll take you.'

She hesitates.

'Unless freezing to death is preferable to getting a lift with me,' he says with a roguish glint.

'You're a stranger.'

'So are you.' He smiles. She does not smile back. 'I'm Flynn. Flynn Healy. Now that I'm not a stranger . . .'

She glances down the never-ending expanse of road. She is so cold. The car would be much warmer and she'd get to her brother sooner, too. She makes another decision by herself and slips into the passenger seat. Wordlessly, he shrugs out of his beaten tan jacket and drapes it around her shoulders. She's terribly cold and doesn't protest. It smells of citrus and coffee. He turns the heating on full blast and tilts all the blowers in her direction.

They drive with the radio down low. 'You never told me your name,' says Flynn.

'Elinor.'

'Got a surname there, Elinor?'

'Ledbury.'

She feels his interest. 'As in Ledbury Hall?'

She nods.

'I know you.'

She looks at him as though he is mad. 'No, you don't.'

'I do. I met you years ago at the iron gate to your house. You were maybe six or seven.'

She's shaking her head.

'I did! My bouncy ball slipped through the gap in the railing and you picked it up for me.'

She reaches for the memory but there is only static.

'It was yellow with little green specks.'

Her skin tingles. She still has that ball, it's in a box under her bed. The static clears and a memory blinks to life. A pale, dark-haired boy with eyes the colour of oak leaves, hand outstretched, proffering a ball the colour of sunflowers. 'You let me keep it.'

'That's right. You came to the gate and bounced it back to me but you looked sad so I gave it to you. I left other things for you that summer, just inside the gate. Silly things. A peacock feather. A purple stone in the shape of a heart.'

She remembers finding the feather. She ran around the grounds, running the tip of it along rows of trees in the orchards and along the cobbled wall of the rose garden. She didn't wonder where it had come from. She never found a purple rock, though. 'Why were you at the gate?'

'A dare. I'd just moved to the area with my parents and some local kids said it was a rite of passage. Ledbury Hall was old, the occupants a mystery, there was a rumour that the owners haunted the grounds.'

She looks over sharply. 'My parents, you mean?' But this anger isn't hers, it's Heath's.

He shifts uncomfortably. 'Sorry, I, uh, I didn't think.'

He falls quiet. In the silence, she feels guilty for admonishing him like that. 'If the grounds are haunted by anyone, they're haunted by me and my brother,' she says, a verbal olive branch.

'Heath?'

'You know him?' she asks, surprised.

'He's dating my cousin, Sofia.'

'No he isn't.' The denial is like a reflex, a knee-jerk reaction, but she has smelt the floral perfume.

'He's with her now.'

She's tempted to tell Flynn to take her home but she needs to see Heath's deception for herself. 'Can you take me to him?'

Flynn is eyeing her strangely, but he agrees. 'Sure.'

The town is made up of old, wonky buildings and narrow cobbled streets. They pick their way across the slippery stone paths, past the amber glow of shopfronts until they reach one selling music. She catches a glimpse of Heath in the window. Flynn moves towards the door but, eyes still fixed on her brother, she lays a hand on Flynn's arm to stop him. She doesn't want Heath to know she is watching. Through the window, she sees him leaning across the counter, fingers entwined with a dark-haired girl. She's willowy and wears too much eyeliner. He tilts the girl's face up to his and strokes a thumb across her mouth the same way he has done to Elinor a thousand times. Her world starts to crack and splinter. She feels those splinters whooshing through her veins, slicing as they go.

'Will you take me home?' she whispers to Flynn.

He's confused by her reaction, his gaze darting between her and the scene unfolding within the shop, but he nods.

In the car, Elinor is quiet and stares out the window, betrayal burning hotly in her chest.

'You seem upset.'

'I'm not.'

Silence, then, 'You seem it, though.'

Flynn has been good to her and though she can't give him the entire truth, she can break a piece off. 'He lied to me,' she says simply. 'We don't lie to each other.'

'That's a good rule.'

He drops her back at the gate. She gets out of the car and makes to take off his jacket but he waves a hand. 'That looks like a long walk. Keep it.'

'But . . .'

'Maybe I'll see you in town sometime. Or, I don't know, leave it at the gate when it's stopped snowing and I'll come grab it.'

She smiles her thanks. As he pulls away, she feels a wrench of sadness. She is alone again. She trudges back up to the house and hides the jacket in her wardrobe.

By the time Heath returns, she is in bed, feigning sleep.

7

Caitlin Arden

Mum makes tea. Mine goes cold. For half an hour, our parents merrily chit-chat. I let it slide off me. Rainwater on a rooftop. I can't drag my gaze from Olivia. She sits in the dark green armchair, drinking from one of Mum's Emma Bridgewater mugs. The living room has been redone since Olivia was last here. Everything is different. And in many ways, so is she. She is still confidence and compassion, determination and sugar. But something else, too. Something unfamiliar.

My parents don't seem to notice. Mum is regaling Olivia with a story about planting hydrangeas in the back garden. Dad pipes in. It's all disturbingly normal. As though Olivia has just returned from a short holiday and hasn't been missing for sixteen years. I want to leap from my seat and shake them. I feel trapped in a stage play, where every other member of the cast has been given a script. Meanwhile, I fumble blindly, mutely, through the scene. I glance at Oscar, hoping he will pull a face, confirming to me the absurdity of this bizarre situation. But he is leaning forward, staring at Olivia as though she is a fascinating relic. He's transfixed. Everyone is. She hasn't lost that magic. If anything, it's more effulgent.

Questions swarm inside me like frenzied hornets. Where are the police? Why aren't the media crawling all over our front garden like they did sixteen years ago? Why hasn't anyone asked Olivia where she's been for over a decade? How did she escape? Where is her captor now? If he let her go, why? Why now?

Her eyes keep flicking to mine. A thick cloud of confusion and anger and urgency moves through me. I squeeze the handle of my mug until it might crack in my hand. Unable to take any more of our mother's gardening tips, I break. 'Olivia,' I say too loudly, cutting across Mum. The silence that follows is laden. All eyes swivel my way. And though I don't want the spotlight, I must have answers. 'Where have you been?'

There's a beat of silence.

Her lips part. Then her eyes drop to the mug in her hand. The mood in the room curdles, my question like a puddle of spilt milk left beneath the hot sun. But I need to know. We all need to know. I try again. 'It's just, you've been missing so long and—'

'Caitlin,' Dad bites, like my name is a tough bit of steak he wants to spit back onto his plate. 'Your sister will talk when she's ready. Not before. And not because you demand it.'

My cheeks flush. 'I wasn't demanding anything. I—'

'Caitlin, love,' says Mum, getting to her feet. Her smile is fixed. 'Help me take these mugs into the kitchen, will you?'

It isn't a question and I'm relieved to get away from the swirling, stilted strangeness of the living room. We are barely through the kitchen door when I round on her. 'Why aren't the police here?'

She swallows but doesn't answer. Then she starts loading the dishwasher. I stand close behind her, waiting, my patience tracing-paper thin. 'Mum?'

She sighs, closing the dishwasher with too much force. 'Olivia asked us not to call them.'

'She asked you not to call the police,' I repeat slowly, hoping the absurdity of the sentiment will register with her. It doesn't.

'She asked us not to, so we didn't. She needs more time before the police start interrogating her.'

I stare at her, agog. She makes it sound so simple but it isn't simple, at all. 'Olivia's abductor is still out there. What if she escaped and he wants her back? He could be on his way here right now. Or he'll come tonight.' My heart starts cantering. It will happen all over again. He will come into our house with a knife and take her from us again. Maybe this time he will kill us so that Olivia has no one to

45

return to. I feel hysteria rising, hot and thick. 'Mum,' I say, strangled. 'Mum, he could hurt us, hurt Olivia. We must call the police. We—'

'Stop!' she yelps, as though I've stamped on her foot. She glances at the door, then lowers her voice. 'Olivia is home. She's only *been* home for a few hours. We don't want to overwhelm her. We're going to ease her in and ask her questions later. *That's* what she wants. When she's ready to talk and we've heard what she has to say, we can decide if calling the police is best.'

She turns away from me, subject closed. I chew on my anger and frustration like lemon pips. But then I see her hands tremble as she flicks the kettle on and drops teabags into mugs, and I realise she is just as shaken as I am.

'Mum?' I move closer and lay my hand over hers. Despite the summer heat, she's cold. 'Calling the police *is* for the best. Just think about it, how will you explain Olivia's reappearance to neighbours? Friends? Family?' Even as trepidation whirls, I keep my tone calm and reassuring. 'We need to know what happened to her. We need to find the man who took her. He's dangerous and he's still out there.'

She starts nodding and I'm so relieved that I'm finally breaking through, dragging reality along with me.

'Everything alright?' Dad's voice behind me makes me jump.

Mum steps back quickly. 'Everything's fine. Just bringing out the tea.'

He fixes me with a hard stare. 'Something you want to add, Caitlin?'

Beside me, Mum tenses. Trying to get through to Dad is pointless. Once he's made up his mind, there's no changing it. Attempting to will only end in an argument and with Mum's nerves already a teetering tower of cards, I'm worried a row with Dad will be the ace that makes her tumble. So I bite my tongue, feeling a wall rising between us: my parents on one side, and me shut out on the other. I leave the kitchen.

In the hallway I glance at the living room but don't go in. I can't pretend everything is peachy. I stride towards the front door, but as my fingers clasp the cool brass handle, I stop. If I just walk out, what will Olivia think? Oscar? Do I need to give Dad any more reason to be disappointed in me? I step away and wheel towards the stairs.

As I reach the top, I pause, caught in the memory of Olivia standing where I am now, raising a trembling finger to her lips. The masked man behind her. A knife to her throat. I shut my eyes, trying to block it out. It's as vivid today as it was sixteen years ago.

I push open the door to Olivia's old room. The once blush-pink walls are now Farrow & Ball Cornforth White. It's light and airy, done in tasteful neutrals: greys and creams and shades of olive. Everything is wicker or linen. Anything that once belonged to Olivia: the band posters, her collection of frosted lip glosses and butterfly clips, is stored up in the attic.

'It's so different.'

I whirl towards the voice. Olivia leans against the doorway. We're standing in the exact spots we were sixteen years ago, when she caught me with the gold-bee journal. She drifts into the room and sits on the double bed.

I always imagined if she came home, it would feel like slotting a puzzle piece back into its rightful place. It isn't. It's jarring. I examine her closely, looking for clues as to how she's been living these last sixteen years. If she's bruised and scarred, it's impossible to tell; the baggy men's shirt and leggings cover her completely. What I can see of her skin is sunkissed. She isn't as pale as I'd expect a person who'd been kept indoors for sixteen years would be. So maybe she wasn't confined to a windowless room. But then, if she was allowed outside, what stopped her from coming home sooner? She's very slim. And tall, too. Taller than me. Her hair is almost to her waist. It's thick and wild – leaves tangled in it – but the ends are blunt, as though they've been recently cut. Who's cut her hair? It's only a brush stroke from being restored to its former sunset glory. My gaze is drawn back to the leaves. I picture her running through woodland for her freedom, banging into trees, their branches catching in her hair. She rests her hands on her knees.

'Olivia, where have you been?'

She glances at the window, then rises gracefully and walks towards it. Her room overlooks the lawn. At the end is a gate which leads onto a small field and the miles and miles of forest beyond it. That's where the police said he was hiding. That gate is how he entered our garden.

'Have you missed me?'

The answer tips from my mouth, honest and true, 'Every day.'

She looks over her shoulder and smiles. I smile back. It's a strange, welcome moment. A ray of light breaking through a darkening, turbulent sky. It makes me sad to think of how many of her smiles I've missed.

I move closer, wanting to lay a comforting hand on her arm but I don't because she feels like a stranger. I want to get to know her again. To understand. 'What happened to you, Olivia?'

She turns her face away. Silence stretches between us. I'm about to ask her again when she sweeps past me and scoops a candle from the dresser. 'We've got so much to catch up on.' She inhales before turning it over and reading the label. 'Crème brûlée. God, that's divine. We should go to a restaurant and order crème brûlée. Have you ever had it?'

'Yes, I have but—'

'I can't *wait* to try it. Where shall we go? When?'

'Olivia . . .'

'How about this weekend?'

'No.'

Her smile vanishes, and I feel a pang of guilt that I am not leaning into this game of pretend.

'*Please* stop acting as though everything's fine.'

Her gaze hardens. She sets the candle down. 'Aren't you glad I'm home?'

'Yes. Of course I am.'

'Then can we just enjoy that I'm finally here with you?' She looks at me, her large, blue eyes pleading. It's almost enough for me to fold away my questions, but they will only burn through my back pocket.

'Why won't you let Mum and Dad call the police?'

'What good have they done me so far, Caitlin?' she snaps. 'I was gone sixteen years and they didn't find me. How could they possibly help me now?'

She's angry and I'm relieved, because anger is healthier than feigned, delusional normalcy. At least it's honest. 'They'll track down the man who took you from us and stop him from taking you again.'

She's shaking her head. 'I just want things to be how they used to. I don't want to relive what happened. I just want to be . . . normal.' She meets my eyes. 'Like you.'

Guilt slices into me because I can't go back in time and switch places with her. I can't give her all the years he stole, but I refuse to be as useless now as I was then. 'Olivia, if we call the police, he'll never hurt you again. We—'

'No.' She is steel and defiance. 'I said, no.'

I take a deep breath, gathering patience. 'What happened to you? Who is he?'

She swallows and looks away again. She seems to shrink then. Hiding in his shirt. 'I don't want to talk about him.'

We lapse into fraught silence.

A few months after Olivia disappeared, the police speculated she was a runaway. That the man in the mask and The Boy on the Bus were one and the same. That they'd met. He was older. They'd fallen in love and she'd left with him. That's why no one else, not even Florence, knew anything about The Boy on the Bus. They claimed the kidnap was staged for my benefit. I didn't believe that. Not for one second. Neither did those who knew Olivia. She was loved by our family, she wouldn't leave us, not for anyone. But now, seeing her reluctance to get the authorities involved, makes me wonder whether the police were right. 'Is it the boy?'

Her head snaps up. 'What boy?'

'The Boy on the Bus. The one who gave you the diary.'

She frowns.

'The journal?' I press. 'Green with a gold bee? It vanished the same night you did.'

She stares blankly back at me.

'Don't you remember?' It isn't intended to sound like an accusation but somehow, it does. What I'm accusing her of though, I'm not sure.

Her eyes narrow. 'Maybe you're remembering it wrong.'

The police did this to me over the years, suggested details I'd given were incorrect. Even though they had my statement, they asked me the same questions over and over with all the fruitless determination of a person repeatedly returning to an empty fridge, hoping to open it up and find it full. 'I am *not* remembering it wrong.'

We stare at each other. She knows I'm not going to let this slide. I can't.

'Actually, you're right . . .' she ventures, as though the memory has just popped up like a jack-in-the-box. 'It had a gold bee, right? I think the boy who gave it to me had a crush.'

She's lying. She has no recollection; she's just repeating the information I've already handed her.

She picks at her nails. They are neat. This small detail nettles. That's when I see a flash of pink varnish. Pink varnish . . . what kind of captor lets his victim paint her nails? She catches me looking. 'I think I'd like a minute alone.' When I don't move immediately, she adds, 'Please.'

And I leave, unease crawling across my skin.

8

Caitlin Arden

Downstairs, Mum and Dad are in the kitchen talking in hushed voices. When Dad sees me hovering, he closes the door. Cheeks burning, I join Oscar in the living room. He's frantically typing on his phone, so engrossed, he doesn't notice me at first. He works far too much and is always on his email. As I get nearer, though, I see it isn't the white glow of his email but rather his notes. Sensing me, he locks his phone so the screen goes dark and guiltily pockets it.

'It's OK,' I tell him. 'Just because my life has come to a grinding halt, doesn't mean yours has to as well.'

He blows out a relieved breath but shakes his head. 'Just had to type up some bits for work. I'm all yours.' He gets to his feet and wraps his arms around me, kissing the top of my head. I breathe him in and the feeling of unease starts to melt away. 'How did it go with Olivia?'

'Fine,' I lie.

He pulls back so he can see my face. 'What did she say?'

Before I can answer, I hear the kitchen door open. A moment later, Mum appears in the living room. She frowns. 'Where's Olivia?'

Oscar unwinds himself from me. Dad joins Mum in the doorway. And even though I'm surrounded by my fiancé and my parents, I suddenly feel incredibly alone. 'Upstairs.'

Mum is aghast. 'You left her alone?'

'She's literally just upstairs,' I say, but Mum is already hurrying from the room.

51

Dad shakes his head at me. 'I hope you didn't interrogate Olivia.'

Hurt and frustrated that he'd think this of me, I deadpan, 'Not today. Left my waterboarding gear at home.'

Beside me, Oscar stiffens. Though my father is frequently cold or snide with me, I very rarely rise to it, but with everything going on, I'm struggling to bite my tongue.

Dad starts berating me but I don't hear him. My focus is elsewhere, on a domestic, everyday noise that usually fades into the background. Right now though, it makes the hairs on the back of my neck stand to attention.

'What's wrong?' asks Oscar.

I frown. 'Is that . . . Can you hear the shower?'

'Yeah, I think—'

I race from the room, taking the stairs two at a time just as I did when I was a child. I swing onto the landing. Footsteps follow mine, Dad's or Oscar's, I don't know. Mum is coming out of the bathroom, shutting the door behind her, a bundle of clothes in her arms. My gaze lands on the checked shirt and my stomach flip-flops. 'Is Olivia taking a shower?'

She's bewildered by my question. 'Yes.'

'Oh, my God.' I lunge for the door but she steps in my way.

'What're you doing?' she yelps.

All the frustration and fury of the last few hours pour out of me. 'Are you stupid?'

'Caitlin!' Dad barks at my back.

'Olivia is washing away evidence.'

'Evidence?' breathes Mum, panicked now. She looks to her husband. He moves to stand beside her.

'Yes!' I cry. 'Yes, evidence. The police need to examine her. Take samples. DNA.' But Mum doesn't understand. She isn't thinking clearly. I hold my father's gaze, hoping whatever resentment or blame he places on me won't possibly outweigh logic. 'Dad, please, we have to call the police before we destroy their investigation.'

He knows I'm right. He presses his lips into a thin, hard line as he considers his options.

'Olivia asked us to wait,' says Mum as though she's quoting scripture.

'That doesn't matter,' I tell her. 'For Christ's sake, Olivia is a walking crime scene.'

'She's your sister!' bellows Dad. If he was considering listening to me before, he won't now, not in the face of my bluntness.

'But—'

'Caitlin,' warns Oscar, close to my ear. I glance at him. He gives me a tiny shake of his head, urging me to stop pushing.

And finally, I am done. I can't stay inside this madhouse for a second longer. 'I think it's best I go. Say goodbye to Olivia for me.'

I wait by the car, feeling surreal. Oscar is only a moment or so behind me. I imagine him apologising to my parents for the outburst, promising to return later. We drive in silence. It's only once the limestone buildings give way to green fields that Oscar speaks. 'Your parents are in shock. They've wanted Olivia home for so long and now she is, they don't want to do anything that will make her regret coming back.'

'I know.'

Silence. 'It will get easier, Caitie.'

'They *need* to alert the police. The man that took her is still out there. I mean, did she escape or did he let her go? And if he let her go, why now?'

He shrugs. 'What did she tell you?'

I swallow. I can't admit I upset her so much she practically kicked me out of her old room. 'I asked where she'd been all this time.'

He glances at me. 'And what did she say?'

'It was odd.'

'Odd?'

'She was vague. More interested in talking about crème brûlée than she was in giving me any answers. She wouldn't open up about where she'd been or who he was, or how she got back to the house.'

He's nodding slowly. 'She won't keep quiet forever. She's only been home a few hours.'

'I know but . . .' I trail off, trying to understand this feeling that bug-crawls beneath my skin. 'She couldn't remember much about that night, the last conversation we had. She had no idea what I was talking about when I mentioned the journal, or The Boy on the Bus.'

His head whips in my direction. 'You asked her all those questions?'
'Yes.'

'Why?' For reasons I can't fathom, he's annoyed.

'Because I want to know what happened to my sister.'

He's shaking his head. 'You can't expect to have all the answers immediately. Everyone is adjusting and it's going to take Olivia some time to open up. She's been apart from you and your family for longer than she was with you.'

My breath catches as I fight to stay calm. I don't know *how* it has never occurred to me that my sister has spent more time with her captor than she has with us, her family. Sixteen years. I realise now that the crawling sense of unease was because Olivia doesn't feel like Olivia. She feels like a stranger. Because she is. I knew the girl she was before she was taken, but not the woman she's become since.

I stare out of the window. We were only at Blossom Hill House for an hour. It's still early but it's already too warm. Sweat drips down my back and pools in the crease of my knees. Oscar and I don't speak. I turn his words over in my mind and as I do, I'm hurt that he is siding with my parents. Time isn't on our side. Surely he understands the urgency. The danger my family could be in if we don't act now. I feel that while I am certain grass is green, they are sure it is blood red. Even though I know I am right, I can't bring myself to betray them by taking matters into my own hands. Hands that want to reach into my bag, take out my phone and call the police.

When we pull up outside our house, Oscar stares fixedly through the windshield. I can see him mentally counting to ten before he speaks. He doesn't look at me. 'Don't do something you're going to regret, Caitlin.'

Inside, he makes us both a tea. He's distracted, pulling out his phone as the kettle boils, thumbs flying across the screen. He has an important deadline for work for a project he's excited about. His entire face lights up whenever he talks about it. I don't know much, but what I do know is that it's something he's been working on for a long while. I tell him to go back to work.

'Are you sure?' he asks.

I nod because I don't want to sit around with lukewarm tea, dissecting this bizarre morning. 'The annual gathering at my parents' will obviously be cancelled, but we'll go back to the house this evening.'

'Sure,' he says, voice softer than it was in the car. 'Your parents *will* call the police, Caitie. They just need a bit more time.'

He kisses me and I wait until I hear the click of his study door closing before I grab the car keys and venture out.

9

Caitlin Arden

Florence lives in a spacious, three-double-bedroom, Georgian maisonette in the centre of Bath. Her fiancé, Daniel, gets very upset if anyone dares refer to their property as a flat. Over the years, Florence has dated both men and women. I always imagined she'd end up with someone creative, like her. Someone artsy and bohemian with tattoos and piercings. I pictured them living together in a renovated warehouse, a lofty, exposed-brick affair. But she's happy with Daniel and his wardrobe of dark suits and crisp white shirts, his creativity limited to the occasional patterned tie. Still, he's kind, and he's always gone out of his way to make me feel welcome. He's a hedge-fund manager, though if someone put a gun to my head and made me explain what, exactly, a hedge-fund manager is, I'd tell them to put us both out of our misery and shoot me because I don't have a clue.

Outside, it is hot and loud. A crowd is gathering. Today, the summer carnival opens. Performers, gymnasts and dancers, fire-eaters and contortionists, parade down this street, all the way along to Victoria Park where the funfair awaits. I dither on the pavement below the maisonette, not knowing how to tell Florence that Olivia is back. She'll be incredulous, just as I was, and hopeful, too. There will be questions, so many questions I can't answer. And even though I know my parents will be furious, I have to confide in Florence; because she'll be just as outraged that Olivia's reappearance hasn't been reported, and maybe her conviction will bolster my own, giving me the push I need to ring the police myself.

I press the buzzer. Daniel answers. Though surprised to see me, he's too polite to ask why I've showed up unannounced. Mutely, I step inside and slip out of my trainers. There are golf clubs by the door. It is bizarre to me that when something monumental happens, the world continues to spin. That the same morning my missing, presumed-dead sister, drops back into my life, he's off to spend a pleasant few hours hitting balls with metal sticks that cost more than my monthly mortgage.

As I follow him into the lounge, my heart gallops so hard in my chest, I feel it in my lips. The secret that my sister is back rushes through my veins. Daniel is talking to me but I can't take in any of what he's saying so I nod along, instead. In an attempt to ground myself, I focus on the colours around me. Warm terracotta walls. Olive-green sofa. Beige cushions, fat and welcoming. Gold hardware: candlesticks and drawer handles, wall sconces and trinket dishes. Gold. Just like her hair. My chest tightens and I push my toes into the soft clotted-cream rug underfoot.

Then Florence sweeps into the room, clutching what I assume is another script, brightly coloured sticky notes slid between pages. Her dark brows knit together. 'Did we have plans? Did I know you were coming over?'

I shake my head, words locked in my throat. There is so much inside me, swirling and writhing, I want to expel it from my body on a banshee's howl.

Florence and Daniel exchange a look.

'Go,' says Florence to her fiancé. 'You'll be late if you don't leave now.'

He kisses her cheek but keeps his concerned gaze on me. 'Good to see you, Caitie.'

When he's gone, she says, 'Is everything . . . are you OK?'

The truth is on the tip of my tongue but then I see the angry twist of my father's mouth and the watery-grey eyes of my mother, and I swallow it down.

Florence takes a seat beside me and I breathe in the comforting, familiar scent of her Jo Malone perfume. She bought me a bottle as a graduation present. She's been with me in moments big and small. Moments Olivia couldn't play a part in. These last few years, Florence has been a sister to me. I know I can trust her yet the words stick in my throat.

'What's happened?' she presses gently.

And suddenly, sitting still is impossible. Feeling like a coiled spring, I surge to my feet and start to pace. 'Do you ever think about what it would be like if she came back?'

A beat of silence, then, 'Olivia?'

I nod.

'Of course. All the time.' She gets up and drops the script onto the coffee table. She is all concern and breathless anticipation. 'Caitie, what's happening?'

'I've pictured it. Every day. Sometimes, I bargain with a god I don't even believe in. *Bring my sister back and you can take twenty years off my life. Bring her back and I'll give up everything I own. I'll wander barefoot around the city if I can just have* one *more day with her.*'

I stop pacing and move to the window, turning my face to the sun, though I am cold and can't feel its warmth.

'I'd have done anything to bring Olivia home. But then I'd think about what she's been through. All those years made up of all those seconds and minutes and hours. What's been done to her.' My breath comes harder, faster. 'It's no secret why men take young girls, is it? It's not a mystery. It doesn't take a genius. And when I thought about the damage he'd have done to her, I knew she'd never come back the same, and I wondered . . .' I inhale. Exhale. Feel the words catching in my throat like splinters of glass. 'I wondered if she'd be better off dead.'

The silence falls around us like burning ash. I can't look at Florence. Can't believe I said it out loud. I feel her move behind me. Feel the heat of her body at my back. Close but not touching. I stare down at the stream of people below. The procession has arrived, dancers in vibrant costumes of feathers and sequins. The crowd is thicker now, lining the streets on either side of the road. The music is so loud, but not loud enough to drown out the sound of my rushing pulse. 'I always hoped if she was dead, it was quick,' I say. 'Painless. That she didn't see it coming.' I rest my head against the sun-warmed glass. I imagine pushing my forehead into it until it cracks. I imagine myself falling through air, splitting open like a watermelon on the hot pavement below. 'How can I look into her eyes knowing I'd wished her dead, Florence?'

More silence.

The bright-red shame of my admission soaks into my clothes, stains my skin, seeps beneath my fingernails.

'It's OK,' she tells me, taking my hand in hers. We stand shoulder to shoulder. Her fingers tighten around mine. Reassuring. 'It's going to be OK.' She sounds so certain I almost believe her. 'The anniversary is always difficult . . .'

My tongue is cut from lead. Telling Florence that Olivia is back commits me to calling the police right away. I can't do to her what my parents have done to me. I can't burden Florence with this monumental news and make her promise to silently bear its weight.

I open my mouth, not sure what I'm about to say, when Florence's phone vibrates across the coffee table behind us. She steps away from me and picks it up.

'Who is it?' I ask, worried it's my parents, or Oscar, trying to track me down.

'No one,' she says too quickly.

'Who?' I move towards her to catch a glimpse of the caller ID. 'That's your agent.'

Reluctantly, she nods. The phone continues to vibrate in her hand. 'I was waiting to see if I'm narrating the next Noah Pine book but—'

'Answer it.'

'Caitie—'

I take the phone from her, accept the call, and then hand it back. She gives me a small, grateful smile and mouths, 'I'll be quick,' before disappearing into the hallway.

I go back to staring out the window. What am I doing here?

I should be with Olivia. Maybe, if I go back to the house now, I can convince them to alert the authorities. Surely, once the shock of Olivia's reappearance has worn off, my parents will see sense. They'll call the police so an investigation can be launched and her captor can be found. But what if, in the meantime, he returns for her?

Panic flutters in my chest; I need to leave. I need—

My stomach drops.

On the street below, the crowd shuffles along the pavement slowly, following the tail end of the procession. Everyone's attention is fixed on the performers. Everyone but a figure dressed all in black: jeans and a hooded coat. Too warm for the summer heat. This person is too broad to be a woman. Too tall. He stares directly up at the maisonette. Directly up at me. People surge around him. He's a black hole in a moving sea of colour. The sun splashes across his Venetian mask. One I have seen before. Its long nose and furious, furrowed brow has stalked my nightmares. It isn't black, as I'd thought in the darkness of our landing when he abducted my sister. It's midnight-blue. The deepest, darkest navy.

A rope of fear tightens about my chest until I can't catch my breath. I am ten years old again, paralysed, watching him steal my sister. Watching him ruin my life.

A hand seizes me from behind and I whirl, fists raised to fend off my attacker.

Florence leaps back. 'Caitie!'

Heart cantering, I spin back towards the windows. But he's gone. 'No,' I breathe. 'No.'

He was there. I *saw* him. Then I am running across the lounge and out into the hallway. Florence follows. I don't stop to put on my trainers. I yank open the front door and race barefoot down the stairs. Florence calls after me. I keep running, determined to reach the masked man. I throw open the entry door and tumble out into the blinding sun. It's loud. People are drunk and sunburnt and clumsy. Then I am stumbling down the stone steps and shouldering my way through the crowd. The carnival procession is further up the street now. I jog across the road and stand where he stood, just moments ago. I swivel left and right but there's no sign of him. For all I know, he's whipped off his black, hooded coat and shoved it, along with the mask, into a bag. He could be anyone here.

Florence grabs my arm and spins me to face her. I go up on to my tiptoes and strain to see over her. 'Caitie, what the hell is going on?'

'The man who took Olivia was watching your building,' I say, still searching for that black hole.

'What?'

I shrug out of her grip and start marching along the street, not yet willing to give up. 'I knew he'd come back for her.'

Florence swings into my path. 'Come back for who?'

'Olivia!'

Confusion. Shock. I see it all on her face. I don't have time to explain so I pivot right and jog up someone's front steps to get a better view of the crowd. But I'm not high enough. Beside me is a cast-iron railing. I start to climb it. Florence's fingers clamp around my wrist and she jerks me to her. 'What're you doing? *Please* just tell me what's going on. You're scaring me.'

I stare up into her big, brown eyes and I can't keep the secret a second longer. 'Olivia is back.'

Her face drains of colour. 'What?'

'She turned up at my parents' house in the small hours of the morning.'

She's shaking her head. 'Are you sure?'

'Mum and Dad are refusing to call the police because Olivia won't let them. She won't talk about where she's been or what happened to her or how she got away. She pretends not to remember anything about that night and witters on about crème brûlée.'

'Caitie—'

My mind is still spinning. Cold, clammy panic spreads like a fog through my chest as I have visions of the masked man sliding in through the French doors of my childhood home, a blade clutched in one gloved hand. I imagine him creeping down the hall into my parents' bedroom. I hear their screams. See the blade cut through skin and muscle, lodging into bone. This time, he will make sure Olivia has no one left to return to. My resolve hardens. I take the phone from Florence and I do what I should've done hours ago: I call the police.

10

Elinor Ledbury

Ledbury Hall is full of strangers. Caterers and decorators, barmen and waitstaff. They crawl all over Elinor's home like ants over a picnic, spoiling everything. She stands on the grand landing and watches them scurry to and fro, carrying crates of wine and ostentatious floral arrangements. They are setting up for the party Uncle Robert has paid someone else to organise. The pharmaceutical company he works for has recently merged with another organisation and this is their first social gathering.

'He has no right taking over our home like this.' Heath appears at her side. She does not look at him. Has barely looked at him since she caught him with the dark-haired girl, *Sofia*, in the music shop. Not that he's noticed, he has abandoned Elinor every day this week and lies constantly to her about where he is going. She knows he is with *her* but she can't bring herself to confront him. She's too afraid it will push him further away. That he will go and never come back. 'Ledbury Hall is ours.'

'Not for another year,' she answers coolly, just to hurt him. 'Have you invited anyone?'

'No,' he says as though it should be obvious. 'Have you?'

'Maybe.'

He stiffens and opens his mouth to press her but then Uncle Robert stands in the foyer, bellowing their names. Elinor moves quickly. As always, Heath takes his time.

A light sheen of sweat is slicked across Uncle Robert's skin and

Elinor can't tell whether he is excited for his party or stressed by it. 'I've had new outfits delivered to your rooms for tonight.'

At this, Elinor feels a frisson of excitement. She almost never has new clothes. Most of what she wears is her brother's and everything else in her wardrobe once belonged to her mother. Beside her, though, Heath sneers.

'This party is very important,' insists Uncle Robert. 'I want you both on your best behaviour. It's imperative my colleagues see that we are a happy family.'

'You want us to lie for you, *dear* Uncle?' Heath asks, bored and mocking.

Uncle Robert closes the gap between them and raises one pointed finger. 'I mean it, *boy*. Best. Behaviour.'

Heath's lips curve into a taunting, contemptuous grin. 'But I already promised Elinor I'd be on my worst.'

Uncle Robert's hand clenches into a fist. Heath's eyes burn with challenge; he is spoiling for a fight, but any daggers exchanged between Heath and their uncle usually pass through Elinor first. While their uncle's temper has always petrified her, Heath is immune to it. He took a few beatings from their uncle as a child, but he's older now. Stronger. And Uncle Robert knows it. With some effort, he lowers his fist. Slowly, he turns and strides into his study.

Elinor, angry with her brother for goading him, goes straight up to her bedroom. She makes to shut the door but Heath holds it open with ease. He meets her eye and slinks inside. 'What's wrong?'

She sits on her bed and presses her back against the headboard.

'I don't want people in our house, either,' he says softly.

She chooses not to accept his pearl of camaraderie. She wants him to feel as alone as she does every time he leaves her here to be with Sofia. She ignores him and reaches for her book, but she's so furious with him for his secret relationship, for deliberately and always rubbing their uncle up the wrong way, that the words blur on the page. Heath takes the paperback from her and sits on the edge of her bed. 'How many times have I told you not to read romances?'

'Because you don't believe in love?'

He levels at her a gaze so intense, it makes her breath hitch. 'Because I *do* believe in it. Because the only thing these books will teach you is that happily-ever-afters are as common and as easy to find as dirty pennies.' She tries to get up but he blocks her with his arm. 'It's all sugar-spun lies. Nothing worth having comes easy, Ellie. Nothing.'

It is on the tip of her tongue to ask if she is worth having, but she bites her lip to stop herself because it isn't her he wants. It is the dark-haired girl in the music shop. It is Sofia. 'Leave me alone.'

He raises one brow at her tone, his lips twisting in amusement, as though he has been nipped by a kitten. 'What's wrong?'

'You,' she snaps. 'You always have to bait Uncle Robert. It's one party, Heath, and it's important.'

'Did you stop to wonder *why* it's important? He thinks because he has our money he has power but he clearly needs us. Tonight, sister, the power is ours.'

'I don't want power. I want . . . I want . . .' *I want you to want me*, she thinks, but can't bring herself to say.

His face softens. 'What do you want, Elinor?'

She swallows hard. 'I want you to do as Uncle Robert asks. I want you to be on your best behaviour so we can get through this awful night in one piece.'

His eyes roam her face, searching. She fears he will push for more and that she will give in to him. 'OK,' he says simply. 'As you wish.'

When he leaves, she takes Flynn's jacket from its hiding place under her bed and slips it on. During the long hours in which her brother has abandoned her this last week, she has found herself reaching for it so she can breathe in the coffee and citrus scent of him. For reasons she can't explain, it makes her feel less alone.

11

Caitlin Arden

The noise of so many reporters and journalists and cameramen stationed outside Blossom Hill House is constant. Like the hammering of rain in autumn, or the drone of a fan in summer. How long will they make our lives the nation's business? This story, with my hauntingly beautiful sister at its centre, means a reprieve is far from our reach.

It's been a week since I made that call to the police. Since they arrived at my parents' house and brought everyone in for questioning. Predictably, my father was fuming. Judging by the look on his face now as he sits opposite me in the suffocating heat of their living room, he still is. We are silent, listening to the rise and fall of too many strangers' voices in their front garden. The police are outside, too, keeping them all back. This morning, I was jolted awake by nightmares of reporters pouring into the house like a plague of cockroaches, falling through windows and doors, falling over each other, all the while screeching their questions at glass-breaking pitch. And among them, standing strong and perfectly still, the masked man.

I blink the image away but my father's angry face isn't much of a reprieve. His fingers tighten around the handle of his mug as a particularly loud journalist hurls his questions at the drawn curtains of the living room. Dad stares at me with two hard, green pebbles for eyes.

I shift uncomfortably in my seat, longing for Mum and Olivia to return from the police station. I glance down at my phone, ignoring all the messages from friends who have seen the news – I have a dozen missed calls from Gemma – and check the time. Morning has bled into afternoon, bringing with it a sticky heat. 'They should be back soon,' I offer.

He doesn't respond, just frowns and sips his tea. Sadness swells because, naïvely, it seems, I thought that if Olivia ever returned, our family would go back to how it was before, and the frostiness between my father and me would thaw. It hasn't. In fact, the roads between us are icier and more treacherous than ever.

There's a reason my father withdrew from me after Olivia's abduction. I've never been brave enough to bring it up. Maybe I never will.

I cast around for something to say but I don't have the words to fix what has broken. I can't go back and undo my decision to tell the police, and even if I could, I wouldn't. At least now, with the house surrounded, we are safe. Olivia is safe. Isn't that important to him? 'The masked man won't dare approach now.'

He looks away. This small rejection makes my stomach clench. I don't think he believes I saw anyone outside Florence's building that day. He probably thinks I fabricated the entire thing just so that I could call the police sooner rather than later. For my father, control is paramount, and I took that away from him when I disobeyed his instruction not to involve the authorities. Maybe he is worried that the decision not to act quickly reflects badly on him.

The front door opens. With it, a wave of noise rushes in, the clicking of cameras and roar of excitement. Then the door slams shut and the wave recedes. I imagine cockroaches again, flinging themselves at the wood, splatting against it.

Mum appears in the doorway, looking drained. 'Vultures,' she hisses. 'I wish they'd leave us alone.'

Dad goes to comfort her, shooting me an accusatory look. Guilt colours my cheeks.

Olivia wanders into the living room, frowning down at a pile of leaflets in her hands. God, she is incredibly beautiful. Her face angular and symmetrical, her lashes long and thick and curled. I was right about her hair. All it took was a shower and a comb to restore it to its former silky, golden perfection.

Dad turns to her. 'Hello, darling.' And there is more warmth in those two words to Olivia, than there was in the half an hour I spent with him before she arrived.

She doesn't reply, though, because she glances up and sees me, her face splitting into a wide, white smile. 'You're here.'

She brushes past Mum, ignoring Dad completely. I stand. She flings her arms around me, the brochures she's been holding crumple between us as I hug her slender frame. There's a petty curl of satisfaction that she breezed past Dad and came straight to me. The same, small satisfaction you feel when a cat turns its nose up at every other lap in favour of yours. It is the feeling of being chosen by a wild, coveted creature.

I breathe in the sweetness of her cherry shampoo. Over her shoulder, I see Mum and Dad exchanging a look. She mouths, 'Nothing' to him. Mum told me yesterday that she was hoping on the drive to and from the station today, she'd be able to coax a little more information out of Olivia. At twenty-nine, she's an adult, and the police don't have to share details of the investigation or repeat to us anything Olivia has divulged about her time in captivity. As a result, we know almost nothing. Whenever any of us attempt to talk to her about it, she goes remarkably still, like a silent, bronzed statue. Now that the reality of her daughter's reappearance has settled in, Mum is desperate to know what happened. Dad, on the other hand, craves normality. They were bickering as I left here yesterday: Mum insisted they push for more details while Dad urged her to drop it. But *I* want to know, too. None of us will ever truly understand what life for Olivia has been like these last sixteen years but choosing to be ignorant to it won't benefit anyone.

'Missed you,' she whispers.

'Don't crumple those,' instructs Mum, relieving Olivia of the creased leaflets. 'What's this?' she asks, plucking a small, cream business card from the pile and holding it up.

'New therapist,' answers Olivia in a bored voice, taking it back from her. 'The family-liaison officer gave it to me. Appointments start this week.'

Mum pulls a face. 'Another therapist?'

Olivia sighs. 'Yep. I'm such a headcase, they've given me an entire team of mental-health professionals. Aren't I lucky?'

An awkward, stunned silence creeps over us.

'You're not . . .' there's panic in Mum's eyes, 'a headcase. You just . . . you're . . .'

'Shall we go upstairs?' Olivia whispers to me.

Dad's phone rings. He clears his throat and disappears into the kitchen to take the call. It's probably work. The council are putting quite a bit of pressure on him to return.

'I'll make us some lunch,' announces Mum with forced cheer.

'Not hungry,' says Olivia.

'I can make lasagne. That's still your favourite, isn't it?'

'I'm fine,' Olivia replies flatly. Behind her, Mum looks stung. Olivia either doesn't notice or doesn't care. 'So,' she says, 'where's Oscar?'

'London,' I answer, trying to catch Mum's eye to make sure she's alright, but Olivia shifts to the right, eclipsing her from view.

'Why is he in London?'

'Work meeting.'

She brightens. 'We should go to London soon.'

'What?' Mum's voice is shrill. 'You can't go to London. It's not—'

Olivia grabs my hand and drags me out of the living room, into the hallway and up the stairs. At the top, I glance down. Mum is at the foot, wringing her hands, face pained. My stomach flips guiltily, the way it always does when she's anxious or upset, even when I'm not the cause of it. I'd have taken her up on the lasagne, even if I'd eaten a full roast minutes before she offered, just to please her.

Olivia tugs me into her room. She's started a collage on the wall behind her bed. Images from our childhood, that last holiday to Cyprus, the two of us floating in the pool on pink lilos; her and Florence waiting in line to see the Spice Girls; me and Olivia dressed in matching Christmas jumpers, beaming up at the camera, surrounded by presents. Dad is off to one side, just visible in the frame, holding open a bin bag, ready to scoop up any discarded wrapping.

On the bed is a pile of her diaries. Olivia shrugs, even though I haven't asked a question. 'Dad got them down from the loft for me. I wanted to remember.'

'You could ask,' I say gently. 'If there's anything you want to know or . . .'

She nods.

Then I spot a diary I know well. It's fluffy and purple. And mine. Olivia scoops them up and shoves them back into the moth-eaten cardboard box before sliding them under the bed. I remember how she reacted all those years ago when she caught me with her bee journal. A childish part of me wants to narrow my eyes and calmly hold out my hand, palm up, waiting for her to give it back, just as she did. Would panic and guilt swirl in her stomach too?

'Did you read it?' I ask, imperiously.

'Well, it was in the box.' A nonchalant shrug. 'Mum must've thought it was mine.'

'But you knew it wasn't.'

She blushes guiltily and I get this petulant little thrill at admonishing my big sister. Still, I'm not annoyed. Not really. My journalling lasted only a few weeks before it turned into another sketchbook.

'I was curious. I missed so much of your life. When I left you'd never even kissed a boy and now . . .' She gives a disbelieving shake of her head, her eyes falling on my left hand. 'Now, you're engaged. You grew up and I missed it.'

I feel terrible for teasing her just now. I'm not sure what to say in the face of these sad facts. I run my fingertips over my words like flowers along a garden path, unsure which to pick. But before I can petal-pluck them free, she continues, gaze fixed on the window behind me. 'Everyone's lives just carried on after that night.'

Our lives carried on only in the sense that our hearts continued to beat, but the rhythm was altered, faster somehow, fluttery with panic. 'Every day without you was torture, Olivia,' I say honestly. 'Wondering where you were, if you were ever coming home, if he'd ever let you. I—'

'Your dress is lovely,' she says, cutting me off, artfully dodging the topic of her captor again. She glances down self-consciously at her borrowed outfit. Another from Mum's wardrobe. It's too big, bagging around the chest and drooping beneath the armpits, billowing around her tiny waist.

70

'I could bring you some of my clothes,' I offer. 'They might be a little bit big for you still but . . .'

'Maybe.' She plonks down onto her bed and chews her thumbnail. 'I wish I had my own clothes. Since coming back, I don't even feel like a real person.'

I sit beside her. 'What do you mean?'

'I feel like a doll, dressed in clothes I didn't choose, told where to go, what to eat, *when* to eat it. I'm prodded and poked and pushed by police and therapists and medical examiners. I don't make any decisions for myself.' Her laugh is mirthless. 'Actually, I'm less like a doll and more like a bag of evidence.'

I stare remorsefully at my own hands, remembering how I'd coldly referred to her as a walking crime scene that first day. I glance up, wondering if she heard.

'Mum *smothers* me,' she laments. 'Treats me like a child.'

'She loves you so much. Hovering and making lasagne . . . that's just how she shows it,' I say, rushing to Mum's defence, even though I've felt the suffocating embrace of her care myself. So absolute, it sometimes feels like a hundred thick, woolly blankets being piled on top of you. Comforting at first, until you're lost beneath them, struggling to breathe.

'You're right,' Olivia says contritely. And I feel a stab of regret for making her question how she feels. 'I'm being unreasonable. I'm—'

'Mum *can* be a bit much,' I offer quickly, then bite my lip, shocked I've just stabbed my adoring mother in the back. Then Olivia smiles and something between us crystallises. Something sisterly that eases the unforgiving grip of loneliness.

'She can be, can't she?' Olivia tucks one leg beneath her and leans forward conspiratorially. 'She's everywhere. All the time. I wish you and I could go and do something on our own. Get away from everyone.'

'Me, too.'

She glows. 'Really?'

I nod.

Then she is up, off the bed, pulling the box of diaries out from beneath it. She plucks mine from the top, flips it open and riffles through the pages until she finds whatever it is she's looking for.

71

'What're you doing?' I ask.

Apparently satisfied, she grins at me and slaps the diary shut before tossing it onto the dresser. She leans around the doorframe and hollers for Mum, sounding so much like she did when she was thirteen.

Mum is at the top of the stairs a moment later, eager and hopeful. 'Everything OK?'

Olivia nods. 'Sorry about earlier,' she says in a creamy voice. 'Going to the police station always puts me in a weird mood, I shouldn't have taken it out on you.'

'You don't need to be sorry, darling,' says Mum. 'If there's anything I can do, you know I'm always here.'

Olivia's mouth quirks up in a satisfied little smile. 'I'd love lasagne for dinner if you're still happy to make it?'

'Of course.'

'And Caitie's going to stay for dinner, too.'

Mum glances at me. 'You are?'

'Sure. That'd be great.'

'Perfect. I love it when we're all together. Just like it used to be,' says Olivia, pulling her into a tight hug. Mum's eyes widen in surprise, but then serenity slides across her face and she squeezes her daughter back. 'Caitie was just telling me about this delicious cheesecake from Butterwick Bakery in Bristol. She said it's the best she's ever had.'

She's lying, I haven't once mentioned Butterwick. I can only assume this is the detail she was searching for in my diary just now. Bemused, I watch the scene unfold.

'Gosh,' says Mum. 'Yes, we haven't had a cake from there in a long while.'

'Can we have one tonight? For dessert?'

'Well . . .' she frets. 'The bakery is the other side of Bristol.'

'Is that too far?' asks Olivia, all buttery innocence.

Mum glances at her watch. 'It's an hour's drive. I'd have to leave now to make sure I get there before they close.'

Olivia's bottom lip juts out. The pout of a child model. 'I haven't been hungry all day and then Caitie talked about this insane chocolate-orange cheesecake and now it's all I can think about.'

'Well . . .' Mum looks between the two of us, her resolve faltering beneath her instinct to please her daughter. 'I suppose so.'

Olivia grins. 'Thanks, Mum. You're the best.'

Mum bathes in the compliment, the warmth of it turning her cheeks pink. 'I'll tell your father to make sure he's back from the office in good time. We can make a trip of it, maybe stop for coffee along the way.'

'Actually, can Caitie and I stay here? I don't think I can face pushing through the wall of press again today.'

Mum's disappointment is quickly replaced by concern. 'On your own?'

'I won't be on my own, I'll be with Caitie,' she says, sidling so close to me that her arm brushes mine. 'Besides, there are police outside. We'll be fine, won't we?'

'Yes,' I say, feeling a prickle of trepidation. What is she doing? 'Absolutely.'

Mum dithers, clearly not wanting to leave us here alone. Though we are adults now, she is remembering us as girls. That final night she kissed us goodbye and returned to only one daughter. She bites her lip. 'As long as you're sure?'

And even though I'm anxious about the man in the mask, I remind myself we are surrounded by police. We both nod.

Soon, she is gone and we are alone.

'What was that about?' I ask as we hear the car pull out of the driveway. But Olivia is jogging down the stairs, swinging into the kitchen.

She takes my handbag and thrusts it at me. 'Where did you park?'

'Why?'

'Because, little sister, we're going shopping.'

I open my mouth. Close it again. 'We can't.'

'Of course we can. We'll get to Bath and back before Mum arrives home. She'll never even know we left.'

'But—'

'They can't keep me locked in this house forever. I've basically exchanged one prison for another.'

'Olivia . . .'

'I'm meeting Florence next week and I can't do it in another of Mum's Marks and Spencer's dresses. I won't.' She lifts her chin. 'So either you come with me, or I'm going alone.'

The idea of her venturing out alone makes anxiety swarm low in my stomach. *He* is still out there. After seeing him outside Florence's building, I am sure he has plans to get her back. He's hunting us again. I don't have a choice.

12

Elinor Ledbury

Elinor can hear people arriving downstairs. There are a thousand butterflies beating their wings in the pit of her stomach. She wonders whether she can feign an illness and spend the evening in her room.

Heath taps once at the door before slipping inside. He smiles when he sees her. She's wearing the dress Uncle Robert chose. The thick, velvet fabric clings to her slim frame and the navy complements her eyes. Heath drinks her in, gaze running over the dramatic slit that shows off her long legs. For once, her brother is speechless.

'Well?' she prompts.

'Breathtaking.'

She smiles, even though she is still angry with him for goading their uncle and for continuously leaving her to be with Sofia. Still, she is glad Heath is here tonight. Begrudgingly she says, 'You look good, too.'

The slate-grey suit is an expensive cut and fits him well. Her brother is classically handsome. The kind of face Greek sculptors carved from marble. She meets his eyes in the mirror. Her devious, dashing, deceitful brother who she has loved always. Who she can feel herself forgiving. After all, it is her he is with tonight, not Sofia.

Elinor has never been in a space with so many people. It feels to her as though they are swooshing around her in ever decreasing circles. Getting closer and closer. A sea of diamonds and cologne and unfamiliar faces that swallow her. Panic takes flight in her stomach and she reaches blindly for her brother. He puts a reassuring arm around her waist and squeezes.

Ledbury Hall glitters. In every room, there are strings of golden fairy lights and candles. Tapered candles in brass holders, small, floating candles in water-filled glass bowls, pillar candles in hurricane jars. The air is filled with the sickly-sweet smell of flowers. They sit in crystal bowls and in vases on every available surface. The bar is set up in the library, and in the reception room is a string quartet. She takes a deep breath and closes her eyes but Heath tugs her along. She expected him to liberate a bottle of whisky and for the two of them to escape upstairs as soon as possible, but Heath dives seamlessly from one conversation to the next, slotting into this party as though he were hosting it. A seasoned socialite. He is a beacon of charm; guests are drawn to him. Elinor finds herself squinting under the glare of his charisma. Even Uncle Robert is impressed. He stands, glowing with pride, as Heath discusses the second law of thermodynamics with a reedy gentleman sporting a flamboyant tie. And though, academically speaking, Elinor can contribute to the discussion, she finds the words jam in her throat, sticking to the roof of her mouth like toffee. It is only now that she can see the gaping chasm that lies between her and her brother. He's spent so much more time in the world than she has and it shows. He offers these strangers his straight white smile and wit, while she stands mute and dumb beside him.

She tries hard to tune back into the conversation. Uncle Robert is gone but at least four more people have joined their group in his absence. It reminds Elinor of the Hydra; cut off one head and two more will spring up in its place. She just wants to be alone with her brother.

'The best brownies are at Nom Café in Worcester,' Heath tells his court.

'I've heard of that place,' says a woman wearing a red dress and an attractive smile. 'It's a hidden gem.'

'Brownies,' scoffs the rotund man at her side. 'Oh, Anna, who eats brownies?'

Heath grins. 'Me.'

'You've never taken me there,' says Elinor, surprising herself.

'Well, if my husband doesn't want to eat brownies with me, maybe you and I will have ourselves a road trip,' Anna quips, gaze fixed on Heath. She is at least fifteen years his senior but she is looking at him as though she is a schoolgirl with a crush. Elinor decides she doesn't like this woman.

'Our uncle is looking for us,' says Elinor. Then she hooks her arm through Heath's and the two of them start weaving through the crowd. When they are far enough away, she says, 'Have you really been to a café in Worcester?'

'Yes.'

She stares at him. 'When?'

He shrugs, then takes two glasses from a passing waiter and hands her one. Hers is water, his is wine. She wrinkles her nose.

'You aren't old enough to drink,' he reminds her.

'But we always drink together.'

'Not in public.'

She sips her water, wishing it was a passion fruit martini. Her brother makes the best cocktails. Then, she pushes the topic he is eager to avoid. 'So when did you go to Worcester to eat cake?'

'Not cake,' he corrects. 'Brownies.'

'When?' she asks for a third time.

'A couple weeks ago.'

'You *just happened* to drive there and then *just happened* to stumble across a hidden gem that sells the best brownies in Worcester?' she asks incredulously. He doesn't answer, just gives her a small, enigmatic smile. 'Why didn't you take me?' But then she knows: because he had taken Sofia. Angry with him but not brave enough to admit why, she snaps, 'I thought you didn't even want this party but you're all dimples and charm.'

'Because you asked me to be,' he says. He strokes her long hair. 'You have more power over me than you know.'

Before she can respond, Heath is accosted by Uncle Robert and another of his colleagues. They whisk him away to the bar. Elinor stumbles after them but Uncle Robert shoots her a look. 'Go and be sociable, Elinor,' he commands in a low voice. 'You aren't his faithful pup.'

Humiliation burns across her cheeks. She snatches a glass of wine from another circulating waiter and before he can stop her, she downs it. A forceful, tidal wave of unhappiness washes over her and she goes hunting for more drinks.

Later, she is standing in the corner, trying to melt into the walls but there are always eyes on her. Men she doesn't know who are too old to be looking at her the way they are. She searches for her brother's gaze but never finds it. She distracts herself, tuning into the conversations around her, flicking through them like radio stations.

'I must say, Antony, it *is* an impressive party,' concludes a man with a thick moustache and a heavy, expensive-looking watch.

Antony raises a brow. 'But is it enough to win the board's favour?'

'They want a *family* man in charge of operations to help with their new, *family*-friendly image. I think Robert's proven his case, trotting out the orphans he raised.'

He sips his whisky. 'The board want wealth, too, someone who can invest and rub elbows with the right clientele. Surely that's a point to Johnathan Jones?'

'Look around.' The man with the moustache throws out an arm to encompass Ledbury Hall. 'Robert clearly has considerable wealth.'

'I heard he's merely the trustee of this estate,' Antony says haughtily. 'It's borrowed money.'

'Unless he offs the children.'

The men laugh.

'If he loses his job,' replies Antony darkly, 'he might just off himself.'

'The board did make it clear this merger means there's only *one* Director of Operations position up for the taking.'

'Robert Brent, Johnathan Jones.' Antony shrugs. 'They're both ruthless bastards.'

'But one of them has to go.'

They share a look.

Elinor decides she has heard enough and slinks away. Heath was right, the two of them do have the power this evening. Uncle Robert needs them to be on their best behaviour in order to perpetuate his family-man persona and win the board's favour to keep his job. He's worked for his company for twenty-five years. It's his entire life.

She goes in search of Heath. She isn't sure she wants to share with him what she knows. Although Heath claims she has power over him, she isn't sure he'll be able to resist the opportunity to hurt Uncle Robert, and she'll do almost anything to avoid a confrontation between them. That, and she's enjoying knowing something her brother does not.

She moves through the throng, looking for Heath but he's nowhere to be found. The music and people and the heat of so many bodies are starting to make her pulse quicken. She wonders if he's taken himself upstairs, retreating to his room with a bottle of whisky. Maybe he is waiting for her. But when she pushes open his bedroom door, disappointment sinks like a stone in water. He isn't here. She paces, dreading the thought of going back downstairs alone. Growing hot with panic, she flings open the window. That is when she sees him. Heath standing on the gravel drive, cast in the amber glow of the manor. He is not alone. Sofia is with him. She is wearing a floor-length gown in black silk and lace. She's dressed for the party. Why would her brother invite his secret girlfriend to Ledbury Hall when he's never even mentioned her to Elinor?

The girl folds her arms across her chest and shakes her head at the ground. Even from up here, Elinor can see they are arguing. Heath takes her by the shoulders but she shrugs out of his grip and starts marching away from the house. Heath reaches out and snatches her wrist, spinning her to face him. He kisses her. Sofia doesn't resist. She is clay in his expert hands, moulding to him, being moulded by him. Jealousy is a handful of hard, green pebbles in Elinor's mouth that threaten to break her teeth. She turns away from the window and rejoins the glittering party below.

13

Caitlin Arden

Blossom Hill House is detached and there are only two other houses on our little street. The back garden gate opens up onto a shared, narrow lane which we cross to reach the small field owned by our neighbours, Ray and Eileen Butler. It's private, but the Butlers have always let our family use it. When we were children, it was immaculate: the lawn beautifully maintained, with big, wooden flowerbeds bustling with fruit and vegetables. Now they're older, it's fallen into disarray. The grass reaches mid-shin, the beds are barren, and the shed in the corner is falling apart, green paint split and curling.

I am led by Olivia, my hand in hers, as she strides across the field. The sun beats down relentlessly, so hot it is turning my skin pink. Sweat beads on my top lip and collects in the hollow of my neck, gathering behind my knees.

We stand on the edge of the woods. They are dark and dense, wild and pitted. We got lost in them once when we were very young and I haven't ventured into them since. The trees crowd together, their branches thick and their canopy so impenetrable, even on the sunniest days, they block out the light, making the woods difficult to navigate. 'Olivia, I have no idea how to reach the streets this way.'

Her lips curl into a smile. 'I do.' But I'm unconvinced. Sensing my hesitation, she closes the gap between us. I stare up into those eyes. Glacial lakes and summer skies, forget-me-nots and bluebell petals. 'Don't you trust me, Caitie?'

* * *

The woods are as dark as I remember. The little light that breaks through is golden and glitters in the silk of Olivia's hair. Bark bites my bare arms as we squeeze between trunks. Small, low hanging branches scrape across my cheeks. At least it's cooler here. I breathe in the damp, earthy smell. There is only the sound of our own breathing and the snapping of twigs underfoot. We feel a million miles away from the house, even though we only left twenty minutes ago. Out here, who would hear us scream? Dread needles my skin as I think of the masked man. The police said that as he entered through the French doors at the back of the house, he must've come through the woods and across the field. For the first time, it occurs to me that this must be the same path he took with Olivia the night he snatched her. I picture her stumbling alongside him, his fingers bruising, the pinch of the blade against her throat. I imagine the sharp stones and twigs piercing her bare feet, the sound of her pulse roaring in her ears, the blackness of these woods wrapping around her like a blindfold. I have wound myself up so much, I feel him behind me, close. I whip around, heart galloping. There is nothing but trees and dirt and something small and wild scurrying in the bracken.

I start talking to distract myself. '*How* do you know your way through the woods so well?'

'Florence and I used to meet here, sometimes. We'd collect flowers and leaves to make perfumes or, after one too many watches of *The Craft*, potions, too. Usually a love potion. Florence was always falling in love. There was Jacob and Lawrence, Jessica and Eve. You're never lost if you can find landmarks. Look,' she says and speeds up until we make it to a small clearing. There's a tiny, rotting shed. It's in a much worse state than the Butlers'. It's half finished, one wall missing completely, as though it was abandoned in a hurry. The sunken roof is covered in a thick layer of moss. The remaining wooden panels are splintered and weatherworn. Vines creep up the sides. A rusted can of red paint is deserted by the door. Olivia smiles at me, all confidence and triumph. 'The shed means we aren't far.'

And she is right. Soon, we are breaking free of the woods and emerging onto the street. 'Right,' she says and gives me a dazzling smile. 'Where's your car?'

Bath is bustling with tourists. Lugging cameras, rucksacks, shopping bags, and expectation, they amble too slowly along the crowded high street, stopping every few paces to take a photograph of another beautiful building. I was concerned that Olivia might find being around so many people overwhelming, but she is fizzing with excitement.

While the press of people brings more heat, the anonymity is welcome. I worried Olivia would be recognised instantly – her face is everywhere, on the news, on websites and blogs, on social media and in the papers – but as soon as we arrived, I nipped into a supermarket and bought her a large sunhat and dark glasses. People, mostly men, still notice her, but not because she is that missing Arden girl, because she is beautiful. The kind of beauty you spot across the street, that lingers in your memory even after you've passed by.

In the first shop, she grabs armfuls of silk and linen and lace. Everything looks good on her tall, slim frame. Out of Mum's clothes and into ones she's chosen herself, she's confident, happier. At the till, I scramble for my debit card, trying not to blanch at the hefty bill, when Olivia smoothly plucks one from her shoulder bag and hands it over. Myles Gregory Arden is embossed on the front. *How* does Olivia have our father's credit card? She taps in the pin and the transaction is complete. Soon, we are out on the street, carrying three glossy bags with thick rope handles. Immediately, I miss the air conditioning. Heat rises from the pavement, sticky and thick.

'I was going to pay,' I tell her.

She grins. 'No need.'

'I can't believe he gave you his credit card,' I say, struggling to imagine Dad, sensible and financially minded, simply handing it to her and telling her to go wild.

'It's not as though I've cost him a penny in the last sixteen years, is it?' She teasingly arches one brow. 'Jealous?'

'No,' I lie, because I can't bring myself to admit I am. It's not that I want or even need money from my parents, it's that even if I did, he'd never have given me his card.

'I'm starving,' announces Olivia, as we weave in and out of people on the busy street. 'Shopping is ravenous work.'

With Mum still on her cheesecake mission, we have time to stop for lunch before heading home.

'How about Thai?' she asks. 'Or Italian? I never say no to pizza.'

I grin, knowing exactly where I'm going to take her.

The restaurant is the kind Oscar and I reserve for extra special occasions. It has high ceilings, marble tables, highbacked chairs and glossy dark-wood floors. Usually, you have to book a few weeks in advance, but the manager is a parent at my school and ushers us through.

'This place is so fancy,' whispers Olivia. 'Do you come here all the time?'

I shake my head. 'They have incredible desserts.'

'They have incredible everything,' she says, looking around. The last time she'd have sat in a restaurant was that final summer we spent together. I cast my mind back, trying to remember. It would have been nothing more thrilling than a McDonald's or, at a push, Pizza Express. I'm glad I could do this for her, take her somewhere lovely she's never been to before.

Olivia orders a passion fruit martini, but because I'm driving I stick to water, pouring it from the heavy glass decanter. It's only as she sips her cocktail that I wonder if it's her first taste of alcohol. I watch for her reaction but she drinks it as easily as though it is juice.

Our sharing platter arrives. Strong cheese, cold meats, fresh bread. It's only as I'm tearing into the most expensive sourdough I've ever bought that I realise this is akin to the meal we shared in the wild meadow before she was taken. I've spent years believing, really believing, I would never see her again. That she was never coming back. I'm grateful to have been proven wrong. This is the first day in over a decade that I haven't been dragged under by roiling waves of loneliness. Sitting opposite my sister, I feel a contentment that is smooth, and shiny and polished.

'I can't believe how grown up you are,' she tells me, swirling bread in olive oil. 'Mum said you're a teacher.'

I nod. 'Primary school.'

'What's it like?'

I avoid her keen, interested gaze in favour of spreading butter onto sourdough and carefully layering it with Brie. 'There isn't much to tell,' I remark lightly. 'You know the saying, those who can't do, teach.'

She sets the bread down. 'Teaching doesn't make you happy.'

It is a statement, not a question, but I answer it anyway. 'No, it does . . .' Oh, but it doesn't. During term-time, Sunday feels like a type of purgatory, dread gnawing at my gut. Then the sweet, fierce relief on that last day of every term, knowing that besides a few hours of prep work, I have a reprieve for at least a few weeks.

'You're lying,' she says simply. Boldly.

She's right. I'm not sure why I wasn't honest with her. I suppose, over the years, I've become accustomed to saying or doing things I think will make others happy. Especially our parents. I have spent years shrinking myself to make room for their wants, their plans, their idea of who I should be. But Olivia isn't Mum. She isn't Dad. She's my sister. I don't want to deceive her. 'Teaching isn't what I wanted to do with my life.'

'Then why did you?'

'For Mum. She and Gran were teachers, remember?'

'But Mum isn't anymore.'

'No, but only because it was difficult for her to be around so many girls your age after you were taken.' I shrug. 'Even so, she'd still have taken it personally if one of us didn't follow in the family footsteps.'

'And with me gone, there was only you.' There's an apology in her voice that sends guilt ricocheting through me. I should not be complaining. Olivia had her entire life stolen. All her choices stripped away. Of the two of us, I got the best deal. 'So what did you want to do with your life?'

I take a sip of water and shake my head. 'It doesn't matter.'

'I want to know. If I didn't, I wouldn't ask. And it's all worked out, hasn't it? I'm back now.' She takes my hand in hers. 'I want to know you, Caitie. I want to know my sister.'

And she is so sincere, I have no choice but to be honest. More honest than I dare be with anyone else. 'I want to travel, to paint, to see the whole world.'

She stiffens, her expression darkening. She whips her hand from mine and busies herself refilling our water glasses.

'What's wrong?'

'Nothing.'

'Nothing?'

She sets the decanter down hard enough that the people on the next table glance over. 'I just came home and you're telling me you want to leave.'

'No, Olivia. That's not . . . I'm not going anywhere.'

Her eyes search my face. After a moment, she seems to relax a little.

'We could even travel together,' I say, thinking out loud. 'We could dance to street music in New Orleans, swim with turtles in Bali, explore the Louvre in Paris.'

She isn't excited as I'd expected, but rather, sceptical, dour even. 'Just the two of us?'

I nod.

'What about Oscar?'

I shake my head. 'He did all his travelling in his gap year. He'd like to do more, but he's an only child, it would be difficult for his parents if he vanished for months on end. He's thoughtful like that.'

'OK,' she says lightly, but her gaze is glass-sharp. 'But really, he's only thinking of his family. Not about you. Not about what you want.'

'Well, I mean . . .' I trail off, surprised by her take on my fiancé.

'He knows you want to travel but he's put his family first, is that right?'

My laughter is thin. 'I guess if you look at it that way.'

'Is there another way to look at it?'

I open my mouth. Close it again. I'm floundering because there's truth in her perspective. Once, a year or so ago, high on the success of Wanderlust Illustrations and desperate to travel further afield, I threw caution to the wind and asked Oscar if he would at least consider a few months of travelling. He turned me down, insisting the mortgage and our parents were insurmountable obstacles, that it would be irresponsible and selfish to take off. Still, I fumble for the words to defend him now. 'His parents need him.' I stuff a grape into my mouth.

'Are they old?' She cocks her head to one side. 'Ill? Financially tied to him?'

I bite down on the grape. It bursts in my mouth. Bitter. 'No, nothing like that, just . . .' I think of his parents. Of how they coddle him. Smother him, even. Talk to me about him as though he is their prize stallion, out on loan for the sole purpose of breeding. They insist on cooking us Sunday lunch every week, even during the summer months, and we can't ever turn the invitation down without being reminded that they contributed to the deposit for our house. Nothing from them comes without strings. And, over the Yorkshire puddings and roast potatoes, his mother will say things to me like, 'Oscar would make a wonderful father. It would be a frightful shame if he never got the chance.' As though I am the only reason they don't have a brood of doting grandchildren at their feet. The truth is, Oscar isn't interested in children. He backs away from babies as though they are car bombs, going as far as to change tables in a restaurant if we're seated too close to a toddler. Of course, he won't admit any of this to his parents because he doesn't want to let them down. I'm sure when push comes to shove, that just like me with mine, he will do whatever it takes to appease them, even though his heart won't be in it. Maybe this should bother me more than it does but, at this stage in my life, babies and bedtime routines rarely cross my mind.

'Just what?' she prompts.

'Just that Oscar is close to his family. They wouldn't be happy if he disappeared, even for a few months.'

'Would you struggle to be away from Mum and Dad?'

'I don't know. I like to think if I'm doing something I love with someone I love, I'd manage.' I shrug, playing down my smacking disappointment. 'But, you know, people deal with things differently, don't they?'

On the table next to us is a couple, laughing loudly. They haven't stopped holding hands. Olivia notices them, too, her eyes falling on their wedding bands. From the way they can't stop touching each other, I imagine they are newlyweds. So different from those silent couples who, after so many years, have run out of things to say. 'Why haven't you married Oscar yet?'

I almost choke on my water. 'What?'

'Oh, come on, Caitie. Why?'

I meet her gaze. It's penetrating. Intense. As though she can read my thoughts as easily as words on a page. 'It felt wrong to have a big wedding and get married without you.'

She is silent, her expression unreadable. 'I understand,' she says carefully, in the same soothing tone a therapist might use with a particularly tricky patient. 'That makes sense. The thing is, I'm here now. So, will you get married soon?'

I stop and give this question the thought it deserves. I always told myself the only reason I wasn't rushing down the aisle is because Olivia was missing. This wasn't a lie. At the time, I believed what I was saying. But Olivia is back and I still don't have an overwhelming desire to start a wedding board on Pinterest or pour hours into choosing the perfect invitations. It's not because I don't love Oscar. I do. I really do. And not in the way some of my friends talk about, where their relationship is akin to an old, bobbled jumper they keep because it's comfortable. Finding it easier to cling to something well-worn than to go out and find something new, even if it might fit better. Oscar still excites me. He's exactly what I want. Yet somehow, marrying him feels like closing the door on my dreams of travel because married people have roots, they are one tree, not two. They are stationary which makes them strong. 'I don't think I'm ready for marriage.'

She lifts one slender shoulder in a half-shrug. 'Maybe he just isn't the right one.'

'He is,' I insist, feeling the truth of it.

'I think I could find you the perfect husband.' She grins at me, popping the last grape into her mouth.

The waitress comes and clears away our empty plates. Olivia's entire face lights up. 'Can we order dessert?'

I am gripped by the kind of anticipation you feel when you know you have the perfect present and can't wait to see it opened. Right on cue, the waitress returns with the dessert I secretly ordered when we arrived. She sets it down in front of us.

Olivia's smile is wide. 'Caitie, is this what I think it is?'

I nod. 'Your wish . . .'

She eagerly picks up her spoon and says, 'I can't believe you've done this for me.'

'It's just crème brûlée.'

'No.' Her eyes glisten. 'No. It's so much more than that. You're the only one who really listens to me. I thought about you every day. Every. Day.' There's a fierceness to her expression. A rawness. 'We'll never be apart again,' she tells me earnestly. 'I promise.'

And I believe her.

I motion for her to do the honours. She pushes her spoon down until the top of the crème brûlée snaps. We grin at one another and tuck in. After only a couple of spoonfuls, I remember why I never order crème brûlée. 'Is it everything you dreamed it would be?' I ask.

She bites her lip, laughter in her blue eyes. 'It tastes like congealed custard and burnt sugar.'

'It *is* congealed custard and burnt sugar.'

We give up on the crème brûlée and order chocolate fondant instead. It's rich and thick and dark. I pay the bill with a flourish. If you'd told me a month ago that I'd be enjoying lunch with my sister in a beautiful restaurant in Bath, I'd have thought you delusional.

Outside, the air is still and hot. I am desperate to slide into the air-conditioned Fiat. We start walking to the car park when Olivia pulls me into another shop. 'We need to get back,' I tell her, but stop protesting as a cool blast from a fan soothes my baking skin.

It takes me a moment to realise we are in a bridal boutique. The carpet is white, the walls are white, the dresses are white, even the art hanging on the walls is in varying shades of white. In fact, there is so much white that if I squint, I can pretend we are standing on the planes of a snowy Alaskan landscape.

'Why are we here?' I whisper sharply.

Olivia's answering grin is all mischief.

A tall woman with dark curly hair and too much perfume greets us.

I'm turning to go when Olivia places a hand on my arm. 'My sister is getting married. We'd *love* to have a browse.'

'Olivia . . .'

She turns to me with large, imploring eyes. 'Please.'

Saying no to her is like kicking a puppy – unthinkable. I check the time. 'Twenty minutes,' I warn.

She beams.

Champagne flutes are pressed into our hands, and a tray of luxurious chocolate truffles and little cakes is brought out.

We riffle through tulle and lace, silk and chiffon, velvet and satin. Some are beautiful, some are hideous. I pluck a feathered monstrosity from the rail and Olivia's eyes widen in horror.

I'm still browsing, trying and failing to imagine myself walking down the aisle in any of them, when I notice Olivia and the sales assistant carrying dresses into a changing room. Alarm bells ring. I cross the room and whisper to Olivia, 'What're you doing?'

'You've got to try at least one.'

'No, I really don't.'

'Caitie,' she says with a cocktail of authority and desperation. 'I've missed so much of your life. *Huge* events. The last time I saw you, you'd only just taken the stabilisers off your bike and now you can drive.' She takes my hands in hers. 'You're getting married and I want to be involved. Please try on a dress for me?'

And how can I deny her that? What kind of person, what kind of *sister*, would I be if I let my own irrational unease at the idea of marriage, stop her from feeling welcome in my life?

Despite myself, as I slip into the first dress, my heart starts to race in anticipation. I've never seen myself in a wedding gown before. I'm nervous, wanting to look every inch the beautiful bride, even if I have no intention of becoming one in the immediate future. I am sorely disappointed. As I step out of the changing room, I already know it isn't right.

Olivia waits with a second glass of bubbles on the velvet chaise. When she sees me, she bites her lip to stop herself from laughing.

'It's terrible,' I say.

'It isn't that bad.'

I pluck at the puffy skirt. It's huge. So big, I could confidently house a family of orphans beneath all this too-shiny satin.

She wrinkles her nose. 'What are those loo roll cover ups called?'

I glare. 'Toilet Dollies – the kind Nan had in the bathroom?'

'Yes! *That's* what you look like.'

'Christ, I'm done.'

Olivia, laughing now, surges to her feet. 'One more. Please.'

While I wait, I decide I hate wedding dresses and vow to marry Oscar in my comfiest loungewear set. Start as you mean to go on. It's not as though he's going to come home every day to find me doing the washing up in £3,000 of Mulberry silk, is it?

Olivia pulls back the changing-room curtain and slides inside, holding up a slip of ivory. I reach for it, but she whips it away, hiding it behind her back.

'Close your eyes,' she tells me.

I open my mouth to protest.

'Close them,' she instructs, firmer this time.

Wanting to get back to the car sooner rather than later, I do as she says. She helps me dress. Her hands on my skin are soft, soothing even. She is behind me, close. I breathe in her sweet floral perfume. I let her lead me from the changing room. The heavy curtain brushes my shoulder as we pass through it. She turns me and I imagine I am facing the floor-length mirror.

'Ready?' she whispers.

Heart fluttering in my chest, I open my eyes, stare at my reflection and suck in a breath. 'Olivia . . .' I hear my own astonished voice. 'It's gorgeous.'

The fit is perfect – Cinderella-and-her-glass-slipper perfect. It has a sweeping V-neckline and sheer, fluttery angel sleeves. Dainty, embroidered leaves and vines wind down the bodice and across the waist. I turn in the mirror and gape at the jaw-dropping low back. Tiny, perfect buttons run all the way down to a small train, embroidered with more leaves and twisting vines. It's romantic and striking and absolutely right.

Olivia steps up behind me. In the mirror, our eyes lock, hers glisten beneath the softly glowing spotlights. It's only now, as both of our reflections stare back, side by side, that I realise our eyes are almost the exact same shade of blue. Olivia is the kind of beautiful found only in the pages of a fairy tale or written into legend. The kind that inspires princes to slay dragons or that launches a thousand ships. As a child, my sister's beauty didn't bother me, but maybe, if we'd grown up together, as a teenager and maybe even as an adult, it would have. But this dress has woven a type of magic, because for the first time in my life, I feel comfortable stepping out of Olivia's shadow, and instead of fearing the burning sun, I let it warm me.

'You're perfect, Caitie,' she whispers. 'He'll be speechless.'

I change back into my clothes which feel painfully dull compared to the ivory gown I've unexpectedly fallen in love with. When I emerge, hooking my bag over my shoulder, I see Olivia is transfixed by another dress. This one is silk and off-the-shoulder with a cowl neckline. It's elegant and classic. Gorgeous. Olivia's fingertips hover over it. She hasn't heard me. Doesn't realise I am standing only a couple of feet away. Her expression – one of pained longing – makes me feel as though I am intruding.

'Just like mine,' she whispers.

'*What?*'

She jumps and swings round to face me.

I take a step towards her. 'What did you just say?'

We stare at one another, her words swirling around us.

Just like mine.

Is she . . . Is Olivia married? My gaze instinctively drops to her left hand, as though a wedding band will suddenly appear. But there is no ring. No mark on her skin from years of wear. Nothing.

Then she is turning away from me, walking fast. She pushes out of the door and onto the street. The assistant looks up from where she is sliding gowns back onto hangers. I race past her, chasing after my sister. The fierce heat of late afternoon needles my skin. Up ahead, I catch a glimpse of Olivia seconds before she is eclipsed by a crowd who spill out of a pub, pints sloshing onto the pavement. I stumble around them, heart machine-gun fast in my chest. I call her name. She doesn't stop. Doesn't even slow. I break into a run and almost immediately slam into another wall of people. Tourists stepping off the bus. I ping-pong between them but when I break free, I see *him*. Across the street, marching along the pavement on the opposite side of the road is a tall, broad figure I instinctively recognise. He's dressed all in black, hood pulled up to conceal his face. Among the stream of pedestrians wearing shorts and T-shirts, his oversized, dark clothes in heavy fabrics stand out. His head is at an angle. He is watching my sister. Keeping pace with her. She is oblivious. An unwitting gazelle being stalked by a predator. Behind him, the weir roars as loudly as the blood in my veins.

I sprint for her, bellowing her name, shouldering past meandering window shoppers, ignoring their muttered curses as I do.

'Olivia!' I shout.

She falters long enough that I close the gap between us. My fingers curling around her wrist, pulling her to a stop. She is terrified. Shaking. Has she seen him, too? I whip around but the man in black, the man I know to be her abductor, is gone. I stare disbelievingly into the crowds of shoppers, fear still snaking through me. 'Let's go home.'

14

Elinor Ledbury

Elinor takes another glass of wine from the bar and drinks it quickly. It is warm and bitter. When she's sure she isn't being watched, she leans over and helps herself to an open bottle of vodka and a water glass. She pours the alcohol into it and wanders through the party, taking much larger swigs than she should.

Anna, the attractive woman in red who Heath was talking to earlier, appears at Elinor's side. 'They're very beautiful,' she says, nodding towards the two box frames mounted on the wall. In each one is a butterfly: a monarch and a blue leaf. There used to be three, but when Elinor was only nine years old, she knocked one off the wall with a ball Uncle Robert had explicitly told her not to throw in the house. She was terrified, standing in front of the shattered glass and broken frame, the dark jezebel butterfly lying crumpled in the middle of it all. Those frames were some of the only personal belongings Uncle Robert kept at Ledbury Hall. Heath found her and wiped the tears from her cheeks with the pad of his thumb before he set about cleaning up the mess she'd created. But Uncle Robert returned home before Heath could finish.

'Who did this?' he asked calmly, reasonably, but the children saw his hand balling into a fist at his side. Heard the light, dangerous lilt in his voice.

Elinor started to stammer through an explanation when her brother stepped forward. 'It was me,' he said. 'I was playing with the ball. I'm sorry. I—'

Uncle Robert backhanded him. An angry, red mark blossomed across Heath's cheek. He lifted his chin and levelled a steely glare at their uncle. One that looked too adult on a twelve-year-old's face. Uncle Robert wanted Heath to cower and when he didn't, he hit him again. This time, with his fist. Heath fell to his knees, cradling his face, and burst into a storm of tears.

Elinor is pulled from her memories when Anna says, 'Your uncle is very proud of you.'

'He is?' she asks, not bothering to censor the disbelief from her voice.

'Oh, quite. Robert's always boasting about his beautiful, intelligent niece and nephew. He told us that at eight years old, you learned piano? That he taught you himself when he took his sabbatical?'

'Yes.' Elinor's voice sounds flat and very far away.

The autumn their uncle declared the Ledburys were to learn piano was the worst of Elinor's life. They were made to sit for seven hours a day, six days a week, doing *only* piano. When they made a mistake, he would slap the backs of their hands with a wooden ruler until their skin split. Even then, Heath was taking care of her, going over the sheet music with her after Uncle Robert retired for the night. *That* is how their dear uncle taught them piano.

'Well, it's lovely he's taken such an avid interest in your studies. He's setting you up nicely for the future. What do you want to be when you're older?'

Elinor looks back at the two remaining butterflies, beautiful and dead, trapped in this house forever. She thinks of her brother whose hands once tidied shattered glass and right now, are exploring another woman's body, just metres away from where she stands. She knocks back the last of her vodka. It burns on the way down. She answers: 'Loved.'

The party moves around her like a merry-go-round. In the dining room, she sways in the corner, breathing in the too-sweet, cloying stench of vanilla-scented candles. She wants to get away from the people and the music. She is desperate for fresh air, but outside in the garden is the billowing, heated gazebo that houses yet more merry strangers. She won't flee to the front of the manor. Not with Heath and Sofia on the gravel drive.

Everything around her seems to spin away. The air grows thicker, making it difficult to breathe. She puts an arm out to steady herself. Somebody takes it, gripping her elbow. She looks up into the impossibly beautiful face of her brother.

'You're going to catch fire,' he says and moves a tall, thin candle away from her.

'Oops,' she says.

'Oops, indeed.' Heath's lips press together. 'Are you drunk?'

She doesn't feel the need to lie. 'Yep. Are you?'

'Jesus, Elinor.' His eyes flick around the room. 'What were you thinking?'

She stares at his lips and thinks of them devastating the mouth of that other girl. Betrayal burns through her like the vodka. And something else. Something cold and sharp and deeply sad: the feeling of being unloved by the person who knows her best in this world. 'Where have you been?' she slurs.

'Here.'

'No,' she whimpers. 'You were outside. With *her*.'

His eyes widen slightly. Before he can respond, they are accosted by a man with ruddy cheeks and greying hair.

'You must be Elinor and Heath,' he says. 'Brent's children?'

'Niece and nephew,' corrects Heath smoothly.

'That's right. Charles Vine. I'm on the board.' He offers his hand to Heath but his gaze wanders to Elinor. 'I didn't realise you were so grown up. Heath, you're how old?'

'Twenty.'

'Wonderful,' he says absently, eyes still on Elinor. He takes her hand, too. 'And you, my love?'

'Seventeen.'

'Really?' He blinks. His gaze drops to her chest. He blinks again and relinquishes her hand. Charles clears his throat. 'You should meet my youngest son one day. I think you'll have a lot in common.'

'Why?' she drawls. 'Does he have tits, too?'

Charles pales and stumbles a response Elinor doesn't catch. Heath apologises and then sweeps her into a corner until she is nestled between another table of burning candles and the heavy floor-length curtains. Tears well in her eyes.

'Water,' he snaps and wheels away from her, but she panics. She doesn't want him to leave her again. She lurches forward. The room whirls and she trips, knocking into the table. It topples and hits the ground in an almighty crash. Hot wax flicks up across her arm and she yelps in pain. She is on the ground. Heath kneels beside her. She's vaguely aware of a crowd gathering.

Then a shriek rents the air, loud enough to make Elinor's ears ring. The room erupts into panic.

Heath drags Elinor to her feet. She glances over her shoulder and sees the flames licking up the curtains. Heath shoves her away from the fire. The crowd surges out of the dining room and into the hall. From a nearby table, Heath snatches a bucket of ice that has all but melted and sloshes it across the curtains, higher up than the snaking flames. At first she thinks he's missed but then she realises by wetting the fabric, he has stopped the fire's ascent. The flames spit and hiss. Elinor spins, searching for another bucket of water. She reaches for a vase of flowers but she's clumsy and too drunk. The vase topples. Heath scoops it up and throws the water onto the flames. The two of them stand and watch as they die out. The curtains are blackened and smoking.

Then Elinor is on her knees, emptying her stomach onto the floor. She stares at the puddle of alcohol and acid soaking into the expensive, patterned rug. Heath's polished shoes appear, dangerously close to the pool of vomit. He crouches and takes off his suit jacket. He uses it to dab at her mouth. There is so much sadness inside her. She wonders if she sticks her fingers down her throat, that she can empty herself of that feeling, too.

He puts an arm around her and lifts her to her feet. A wave of nausea roils and she closes her eyes against it, resting her head on his warm shoulder.

She hears a man's voice. 'The fire brigade is on their way.'

Uncle Robert's clipped tone penetrates her drunken stupor. 'It's all under control. No need for that.' Then she is breathing in cigar smoke and cologne. Uncle Robert is close. 'What the hell happened?'

His voice, a quiet hiss, reminds her of the flames. 'What's wrong with her?'

She doesn't open her eyes. She turns her face into her brother's chest and nuzzles into him. Then she is being guided out into the hallway and up the stairs. She stumbles. 'Give her to me,' Robert demands, yanking her away from Heath. Her eyes fly open as she is ripped from her brother. There is a bright burst of pain where Uncle Robert's fingers dig into her arm. He starts dragging her up the stairs, out of view of the guests gathered on the front lawn in the freezing cold.

At the top of the stairs, Uncle Robert pushes her against a wall. 'You've ruined everything.' He is fuming, his rage burning hotter than the blaze that destroyed their curtains. 'How dare you embarrass me like this? In front of my colleagues? The board?' His grip tightens and she presses her lips together to stop herself from crying out. 'Do you have any idea what's at stake?' He shakes her. A whimper leaks from her mouth. 'Where did you get the drink?'

'It's a party. There's alcohol everywhere,' Heath says. Then he tacks on a lie, 'I let her have a glass or two of wine.'

Uncle Robert rounds on Heath. 'You got your seventeen-year-old sister so drunk she almost burned down the house,' he sneers. 'Mummy and Daddy would be proud.'

Heath takes a menacing step towards their uncle. A thin layer of ice forms beneath Elinor's skin. She shrugs out of Uncle Robert's grip, but she's unsteady on her feet, and flings her arms out to her brother like a child. He pulls her to him and holds her against his chest. 'I'll put her to bed.'

'Drown her in the pond for all I care,' barks Uncle Robert.

Her legs are lifted off the floor. She is carried past her uncle but his voice follows them down the hall, venomous and grave, 'I'll deal with you later, *boy*.'

15

Caitlin Arden

The traffic on the way back to Blossom Hill House is horrendous. Somewhere, there has been a terrible accident. We are diverted again and again. I glance at the clock. Mum will be home soon. We'll never beat her back to the house.

Earlier, I let myself get so swept up in the excitement of a shopping trip with my sister, I didn't think through the basics. Like, how to explain away bags of new clothes. But then, if Dad didn't want her to have new things, why give her his credit card? I suppose they'd intended to escort her. It would have been a meticulously planned trip, not a spur of the moment race across the neighbouring field and a twenty-minute stumble through the woods. They'll be furious we went without telling them. Which is ridiculous. We aren't two naughty children disobeying curfew. We are grown women. Old enough to drink and drive and have a mortgage. Still, that childish terror of disappointing my parents weighs heavily on me. And, if I'm being fair to them, this situation is difficult to navigate – because though Olivia *is* an adult, she's vulnerable too. Vulnerable to the media, vulnerable to her masked abductor, vulnerable to any stranger who may have recognised her. Maybe, though, if I can get back before Mum, and return Olivia safely, there will be less for our parents to be angry about.

I think about the man all in black. It was him. I'm sure it was. I glance at Olivia. She stares determinedly out of the window. Did she see him? And what about her wedding-dress comment?

Just like mine.

Is my sister married to her abductor?

My phone starts vibrating fiercely in the bag I've slung on the backseat. I don't need to see the caller ID to know it's Mum. I start groping for it, but Olivia, rising from her silent reverie, says, 'Don't answer. You're driving. Isn't it illegal to take a call when you're driving?'

She's right, but my heart still stutters anxiously in my chest. 'If I don't pick up, she'll lose her mind.'

Olivia rolls her eyes and twists to retrieve my phone. Then she holds down the side button until the screen goes dark.

'You turned it off?' I ask, astonished. I don't think I've ever turned off my phone when Mum calls, too afraid it will send her into a tailspin. Too afraid of Dad's wrath for ignoring her. Too guilty for the part I played in the vanishing of their eldest.

'You're welcome,' she deadpans, slipping my phone back into the bag and dropping it into the footwell.

There isn't time to trek through the woods and race across the fields, so I tell Olivia I'll park on the drive. But, just around the corner from the house, I pull over. This is my last opportunity to talk to her before we are surrounded by the media and then by our parents.

She's frowning, sitting up straighter in her seat.

I take a deep breath and dive right in. 'Are you married?'

She is stricken, as though my question is a knife across her palm. 'You can't tell anyone.'

My head is spinning – with confusion, with questions, with the sickening feeling that the police were right, and my sister chose to run away with her secret boyfriend. Which would mean the abduction was staged so I'd have a story to feed to our parents and anyone else who wondered about her. Is the person she married The Boy on the Bus? He gave her that diary. Maybe it detailed their relationship. Maybe that's why they took it when they fled.

'It isn't what you think,' she tells me. 'That marriage wasn't . . . *legal*. It isn't registered or anything. It was just me and him and . . . and . . .'

I push my question out through shock-numbed lips. 'That night . . . did you go with him willingly?'

'No,' she says firmly. 'I would never have left you like that. I didn't ever want to leave you.'

So whoever he was, he *did* abduct her, but that doesn't necessarily mean he was a stranger. 'Did you know him?'

'No.'

'But you married him?'

'He wanted to do things properly. He wanted us to be married first.'

'First?' I ask.

Her cheeks colour.

Realisation crawls beneath my skin like a thousand skittering cockroaches. 'How old?'

She swallows. 'Sixteen.'

Bile rises, thick and fast, but I try to keep my expression blank. I don't want her to confuse my disgust with this man for disgust with her.

She picks at the skin around her nails until it peels and bleeds. 'I was never meant to tell you about the wedding. That was one of the conditions. That's the rule. I promised not to tell. He's going to be furious . . . He . . .' She covers her face with her hands and digs her fingers into her skin until her knuckles turn white. Her breath is coming too hard, too fast, like the panting of a wounded animal.

I unbuckle my seatbelt and twist so I can face her. I shift as close as possible, the gearstick digging into my thigh. 'Olivia,' I say, forcing a note of calm into my voice. 'Olivia, look at me.'

She does. I take her hand and press her palm against my chest, right above my heart. 'Focus on my breathing,' I tell her. 'Copy it.'

I breathe slowly and deeply. In and out. My therapist did this with me whenever I had a panic attack during a particularly difficult session. I still remember the debilitating fear, the tight coiling of every muscle, the mantle of control I thought I had over my own body slipping completely out of reach as my thoughts came as fast as my panting breaths. After a couple of minutes, Olivia's chest rises and falls in time with mine. I keep hold of her hand but gently lower it.

'I'm sorry,' she whispers.

'You never need to apologise.'

Her long, dark eyelashes are wet with tears. 'Can you keep it a secret?'

My pulse kicks. Being told a secret is like being asked to take care of someone's baby: it's a burden, but there's satisfaction in being trusted with something so treasured. 'I won't tell our parents as long as you promise you're confiding in the police. They have a much better chance of catching him if they have all the information. You do want him to go to prison, don't you?'

She nods. 'I've told them all of it. More than I'm comfortable with, honestly. The reason I keep details private from everyone else is because I don't want to be pitied. I don't want to be defined by the abduction, because it's all they'll see when they look at me.'

I understand why she feels that way. I've spent the last sixteen years trying not to *only* be the sister of that missing Arden girl. I don't even use my real name at work so I agree to keep it a secret from Mum and Dad.

She gives me a small, relieved smile. 'I missed you, Caitie.'

'Missed you more.'

'Impossible.'

I'm relieved that the crowd outside Blossom Hill House is much smaller. I suppose some of the journalists have left to cover the accident nearby. We get out of the car and rush for the front door. Reporters swarm around us. We are met with a symphony of clicking cameras and bellowed questions. They don't even look human. They are bodies with Canons for heads. I keep one arm around my sister, tucking her close as we are swallowed up by them. Surrounded, all we can do is shuffle forward. I am shouting for them to *please* move but my voice is swept beneath the cacophony. Then there's a break in the crowd as a police officer starts shoving desperate, groping reporters aside. There are hands on us. Guiding us. And finally, we are spat into the house and the door is slammed shut.

Immediately, Mum is there, wrenching Olivia from me and enveloping her. With palpable relief, Dad watches his wife take hold of their daughter. Then his gaze swings my way and the relief swiftly bleeds into fury. Always fury. 'What were you thinking?'

'Olivia needed some new clothes. We've only been gone a few hours.'

'Without telling us? Without telling *them*?' He throws a hand out towards the police officer who hovers awkwardly on the fringes of this melodrama. Someone should offer him a seat and a bucket of popcorn.

I glance at Olivia. She looks worried. I can't tell whether it's because I could renege on my promise or because I could tell our parents the excursion was her idea. 'I'm sorry,' I say to Dad. Beside me, Mum is gripping Olivia's hand, examining her face as though she is an auctioneer, checking a priceless piece for damage. 'She's fine,' I assure her. 'We're both fine.'

'How could you be so irresponsible?' spits my father.

Olivia opens her mouth to defend me, but I cut her off quickly. 'I wasn't thinking,' I offer in a small voice. My sister's brow creases and I shoot her a look to keep quiet. He has decided I am the troublemaker. He's angry with me because he wants to be. Let him. What difference does it make now? He's spent the last sixteen years being angry at me. One more day won't hurt. 'I insisted on a shopping trip. We went through the woods so we wouldn't be seen. I thought we could get back before anyone noticed.'

'Well, people noticed,' he barks, thrusting his phone at me.

I take it. There is an online news article littered with photographs of us at lunch, browsing shops. I didn't even notice anyone taking them. I feel violated. Never in my life have I been followed and photographed by strangers.

'You claim to have seen her abductor lurking around Florence's building, yet you thought it was safe to traipse through the woods alone? The same woods he dragged her through the night she was taken?' He blows out a furious breath. 'I'm not sure you even saw him at all.'

'I did,' I insist indignantly. For a moment, I consider telling him about the man dressed in black. The one I am sure was following Olivia in Bath. But it will only thrust me deeper into the scalding pan of my father's rage.

'Honestly, Caitlin.' He sighs deeply, as though I am the human equivalent to a migraine. 'This isn't the right way to go about getting attention.'

There's a pang of pain, like he's just pressed the burning end of a fat cigar into my skin.

Mum looks away from Olivia long enough to register my hurt. She scowls at her husband. 'Myles, that isn't fair.'

'She's been acting up ever since we got Olivia back, you said so yourself.'

Her face drains of colour but she doesn't deny it.

Betrayal spreads inside me like a dark moss. I've become used to my father's contempt, but I never expected it from my mother. Growing up, my father made sure there wasn't so much as a millimetre of space for me to put a foot wrong. I had to be the perfect daughter because he believed I'd robbed them of the one they had. I never wanted to add to their worries. So, while my friends went to parties and kissed boys and drank cheap vodka and broke curfew, I stayed at home. While they applied for their dream courses at dream universities, I took a degree I knew would please my mother at a university that was close by. And while friends travelled around Europe, enjoying their gap year, I applied for jobs in the local area. Even as I folded pieces of myself away, shrank myself and my ambitions until I fitted into the box they had built, my father viewed my efforts through a lens of disappointment. It was never enough. *I* was never enough. And I did it all so they could stand here and tell me I am attention-seeking and difficult, because for the first time in my life, I have disobeyed them.

Olivia opens her mouth again but I shake my head. It isn't worth the breath. She doesn't know that our father blames me for her abduction.

A month after she was taken, I overheard our parents talking.

'We have a list of emergency numbers pinned to the fridge!' snapped Dad. 'How could Caitlin be so *fucking* stupid? So *selfish*?'

I was devastated he thought that of me.

'She's only ten years old, Myles,' said Mum, soft and placating. 'She was terrified.'

'So was Olivia. *She* was terrified. She . . .' He started sobbing. Great, gut-wrenching sobs. Because of me. Our poised, confident, unshakable father was coming undone because I had been stupid and selfish. And in that moment, I was sure the masked man had taken the wrong daughter. I wished he'd snatched me from our house instead. I think my father wished it, too.

The things I overheard that night have acted as a poison, slowly killing our relationship until we are left staring at the bones of what we had.

That memory and the fresh sting of my mother's betrayal tips me over the edge. The walls of this house seem to close around me. I swallow my anger and my hurt, then turn on my heel and stalk out of the house.

No one comes after me.

16

Caitlin Arden

Six days after the confrontation with my parents, I still haven't been back to Blossom Hill House. Though I did have a courier drop off my old mobile phone for Olivia. She calls me every night. Mum and Dad weren't happy about it. They want to wrap her in cotton wool and shield her from the whole world, but she isn't a teenager anymore, and for her to have even a slim chance at a normal life, she needs to be exposed to regular, everyday things like mobile phones and restaurant dinners and shopping trips. In the future, she might want a career, or a house, a husband or a child, or maybe she won't. Maybe she'll want to travel and see the world. And our parents have to let her. I won't allow them to curtail her ambitions the way I've allowed them to do to mine.

I've tried not to mope too much, but Dad's words, his claims that I am attention-seeking and difficult, have stuck inside me like hot needles. Oscar is meeting a client, and the quiet leaves too much time to dwell. It's an effort but I push all thoughts of my parents aside, like sweeping loose pieces of paper from a crowded desk. With a cup of fresh mint tea, I go upstairs to the tiny box room I converted into my workspace. The far wall is panelled and painted ivy leaf green. Against it is the mango-wood desk I bought at a market, complete with a vintage, wicker chair. There is artwork: prints and pressed flowers, small original watercolours and framed embroidery. Opposite the door is a lockable cupboard where I keep projects in progress for Wanderlust Illustrations, alongside tattered exercise books and terribly dull files filled with seating plans and lesson outlines. I put the standing fan on – it's so hot in Somerset, I'm sure I could fry an egg on the windowsill – and sit at my desk, intent on tackling some of my school workload for the looming September start. After only half an hour, though, I am almost bored to tears, and the call of Wanderlust Illustrations is too much. I get out my phone and log onto the website.

Since Olivia's return, I've neglected my page and online shop. There is a backlog of orders, so I spend a couple of hours forwarding them to my printer in Bristol. They ship them too, taking ten per cent of every order. Any money I make from Wanderlust goes into a savings account. There's a decent chunk in there now. I'm not sure what exactly I'm saving for. In the back of my mind it was a travel fund. But if the likelihood of me abandoning my fiancé, my job and my family to backpack around Europe was low *before* Olivia returned, now, it is non-existent.

There are dozens of comments on my last post, all asking where I've gone. There's even some speculation that I'm closing my business. I don't respond. Instead, I go through my phone gallery, find a photograph of my latest piece that I hadn't yet uploaded, and do so. Within minutes, there is a flurry of responses, all of them positive. I smile, joy dousing the burn of my father's words.

I hear Oscar's key in the door and a couple of minutes later, he is in my office, tugging me from my chair and pressing his lips against mine. When he pulls back, his dark eyes are playful. 'Go pack a bag, I'm taking you away.'

St Ives is gorgeous. It's all quaint ice-cream parlours and bakeries, seafront art galleries and winding cobbled streets. I spend an hour in the St Ives Bookseller and come out with a bagful of paperbacks. We check into the most beautiful cottage before going for a walk around the town, ducking in and out of bookshops and art galleries and boutiques. We share a newspaper bouquet of salty chips and sit on a bench overlooking the beach. A breeze rolls across the sea and for the first time in weeks, I don't feel like I'm breathing in the arid air of an open oven. We people watch. I spot a man with a mullet throwing a ball for a bouncy Labrador.

'Cute dog,' says Oscar.

'Very,' I agree, helping myself to another chip. 'But too big.'

He pulls a face. 'You prefer a chihuahua?'

'Too small.'

'Greyhound?'

'Too bony.'

He laughs. 'What're you? The Goldilocks of the canine world?'

I grin. 'Cocker spaniels are juuuuust right.'

'We could get a cocker spaniel.'

'Really?'

'Sure. I work from home most days; you have the school holidays.'

'Shouldn't we start small? Get a goldfish or a hamster or something?'

'Why?'

I shrug. 'Dogs are a huge commitment.'

'And we're committed.' He pauses. 'Aren't we?'

'Of course we are.'

'Maybe we just get a pet mayfly. Easy to manage, only lives for twenty-four hours. Can you commit to that?'

'Absolutely, we'll name him Egbert.'

Oscar laughs but it doesn't reach his eyes. I would love to bring a dog into our home but I imagined that home being filled with trinkets from our travels. A dog, much like a marriage, is something I thought I'd tick off my list after I'd seen more of the world. Painted it. Experienced it. But I made a promise to Olivia that I wouldn't go. In a way, the second I accepted Oscar's proposal, I made the same promise to him, too. Hopping on a plane and disappearing for months isn't an option. I'd have to leave my job and without an income, how would I cover my half of our mortgage? It would be selfish to expect Oscar to pick up the bill. Then there's the strain of being so far apart . . .

'So, you really want a dog?' I ask again, trying to unwind my fingers from the string that tethers me to my travelling fantasies. I need to let it go, watch it soar into the sky like a lost balloon.

'I really want you and I to build something long-lasting. I want us to get married. Get a dog.' He looks out over the beach. 'We could get married here, on the seafront. We could do it this autumn.'

That's soon. Very soon. Will I be able to prise my fingers from that string in just two months? 'What's the rush?' I ask.

'We've been engaged for almost three years, Caitie,' he deadpans.

Guilty, I glance away.

'I want to marry you. The sooner the better. Marriage is important,' he says. 'It lends us more credibility.'

'With who? For what? I don't think the dog will care whether or not we're married,' I offer, trying to lighten the mood. I wonder if his parents are putting pressure on him. They don't think I'm good enough for their precious son. I don't take it personally, though, they haven't liked a single one of Oscar's previous partners. But maybe he's hoping the little comments will stop once we're married.

He dips his head to catch my gaze. He is all frown lines and solemnity. 'You do want to marry me?'

'You know I do. I wouldn't have said yes if I didn't.' And it's true. I've never loved anyone the way I love Oscar.

'It's just, I thought you were hesitant because the day would be difficult without Olivia. But now . . .' He shrugs. 'Things are different. She's back.'

'She is,' I concede, choosing my words carefully so as not to hurt him. 'But she's only been back a few weeks. Can we let her settle in first? Let the media attention die down a little?'

He stares at me, chewing on this request as though it is a lump of gristle, but he swallows it down. Then he sighs, resigned. 'Sure. You're right. I'm sorry. I don't know what I was thinking. Stupid idea.'

I take his hands. Hands that know my body almost as well as I do. Hands that held me as I opened up about my sister. Hands that taught me how to play Billy Joel on guitar. 'Not stupid,' I say. 'Never stupid.' Some of the tension eases out of him and I relax, too. 'Let's set a date. This time next year maybe?'

Disappointment flickers across his face. 'Yeah. Next year.'

We fall quiet and go back to watching the man with his Labrador. 'The dog is beautiful,' I admit. 'Same can't be said for the owner's mullet.'

He arches a brow. 'Not a fan?'

'Mullets are *the* most effective form of contraception.'

'You don't think I'd suit one?'

'*No one* suits them. They belong in the eighties.'

'That guy is actually from the eighties.'

I frown. 'He's younger than we are.'

'He's a time traveller,' Oscar declares with a playful smile.

I lean into it, glad the tension is dispelled, like shaking sand off a beach towel. 'Delorean or Tardis?'

'Magic armbands. Slip them on and—' he throws his hands up, fingers splayed '—poof! He's here to stoke a mullet revolution. He's the founder of MAS.'

'MAS?'

'Mullet Appreciation Society.'

I grin, enjoying this whimsical side of my fiancé. I point out a few more people and Oscar concocts wild, hilarious tales about them, too. I'm still laughing when he gets to his feet, picks up the remnants of our chips and puts them in the bin. He takes my hand and we start walking along the seafront.

'You're good at that game,' I tell him. 'Making up stories about people. I didn't realise you were so creative.'

'I'm a web designer,' he says with mock-outrage.

'I know but that's *computer* creative. It's different.'

He shrugs. 'I used to love writing. I joined the creative-writing society at university.'

'I didn't know that.'

He shrugs. 'Dropped it after second year.'

'Why?'

'My degree amped up. Dad wasn't keen on me splitting my focus. Granddad owned the farm shop before him, always intending to pass it to Dad and so he felt his path in life was set. I think he felt trapped. He wanted more for me. Encouraged me to get into computing because he knew it would be lucrative. Typically, there are more job opportunities in technology than in writing.'

'That's how my parents felt about a degree in English Literature versus one in Art.'

Wanting to please your parents is one of those universal instincts, like opening your mouth to apply mascara.

On the beach below, a group of teenagers throw a frisbee. There is a cooler of beers and the remnants of a barbecue. Two girls break away to cartwheel across the sand. They shriek and giggle when one of them tumbles and lands on her back. I don't think I was ever that carefree. I never flirtatiously stole a boy's hat and put it on just so he would chase me. Never snuck out. Never stole vodka from my parents' house and passed it back and forth with a friend. My mother's anxiety and my father's austerity anchored me to the house.

'You OK?' asks Oscar, giving my hand a little squeeze.

'Yeah, I just   I was never like them.'

His gaze swings towards the teenagers. 'Drunk?'

My smile is wan. 'Happy-go-lucky. Rebellious. I had to be perfectly behaved to make my parents' lives easier. It was exhausting.'

'You feel like you missed out?'

'It was small things. Parties and sleepovers made Mum anxious. And bigger things, too. Like where I studied and chose to live after graduation. I stayed close because it was important to her. I'm aware of my privilege. I grew up in a beautiful house. I went to a good school. My parents loved me. Provided for me. But I always felt like I was dragging a weight behind me.' I stop myself from saying more because if I picture that weight, it is her. It is Olivia. I grew up tethered to the rotting corpse of my presumed-dead sister. Lugging her around school, her wide, unseeing eyes staring up at me from the classroom floor as we learned Pythagoras' theorem. Lugging her cold, stiff body up the stairs to my room at night where she would lie beside my bed, grey and decomposing. She'd still be there in the morning, greeting me with her milky stare. Lugging her down to breakfast where I would slowly and mechanically eat cereal as she mouldered on the tile beneath my chair.

'But Olivia is home,' he says, pulling me from the reverie. 'You can let that weight go. You can *do* anything, *be* anything. You've done well to keep up with your art, Caitie. Maybe one day, you can just focus on Wanderlust Illustrations and give up teaching altogether.'

'It would mean a pay cut, at least for a while.'

'Doesn't matter. We'll manage. I'll make sure of it.'

'My parents wouldn't approve of me leaving my career.'

'Sometimes, the only person worth satisfying is yourself. It's your life, you've got to live it for you.'

And there is my silver lining; just because I have to let go of my desire to travel the world, it doesn't mean I have to let go of my ambitions to make a career out of being an artist. Oscar is so supportive. I'm lucky to be with someone who whisks me away to beautiful seaside towns and on a sandy beach encourages me to build a life I love. There's a fullness in my throat. It is pure, uncomplicated affection. I kiss him. It is deep and lusty and exactly right. His hands run beneath my T-shirt and up my bare back. 'Let's go back to the cottage,' I whisper against his mouth.

He gently untangles himself from me. 'I've actually got something to show you first. Walk with me?'

He stands and leads me down to the beach. I slip my sandals off my feet. The sound of the waves rushing to the shore is soothing. The breeze lifts my hair, making it dance around my face. We pass the giddy teenagers but I hardly notice them, my focus on Oscar. He's humming with anticipation. We make it to a flight of stone steps that are carved into the cliff face. We walk around the corner, the velvet sea to our right. We come to a ledge, the man-made path sprawling out into jagged rocks and smooth boulders. The setting sun is a line of fire splitting sea and sky. He squeezes my hand, gaze fixed ahead. I follow it. That is when I see a wooden easel with the blank canvas. Beyond it, a postcard-perfect view of the Cornish sea.

'You did this?' I say.

He grins, then tugs me over to the easel. He shrugs out of his rucksack and opens it to reveal art supplies. Acrylic paints, new brushes, chalk.

'You're so damn talented, Caitie. You haven't drawn in weeks. Go ahead.'

Love for him bubbles up. I kiss him and wonder how I got so lucky. 'I can't believe you did this – thank you.' I take the tubes of paint and turn towards the easel.

And for the first time in my life, that barrelling wave of loneliness falls softly, like rain. Fine, inconsequential rain. I won't drown, not now. In fact, it won't even leave me damp. I have my sister back. I have Oscar, always. The only thing more valuable than being loved is being known by someone. Truly known. And he knows me so well. I'd never have given myself a gift like this, during a time so turbulent for my family, but I *need* it and Oscar knew.

Later, with my painting drying by the door, Oscar runs me a bath and pours two glasses of wine. But I'm not interested in wine. I want him. Still, I strip and lower myself into the warm water. When he sees me, gaze drifting over my wet, naked body, his fingers tighten around the stems of the glasses. He sets them down and without taking his eyes from mine, he strips too.

Before he climbs in, he pauses for just a moment, grinning and shaking his head as though he can't believe his luck.

I straddle him. We kiss. The paint washes off my skin and runs rainbow streams into the bath water, turning it peony pink and indigo, violet and cornflower blue. My desire for him burns like a fever. We have sex. Or we *try* to have sex, but the tub isn't as big as I thought. My knees bang against the sides and the taps dig into my ribs. We slip and slide and laugh it off. We move to the shower where he presses me up against the cool tiled wall and I gasp into his wet shoulder.

The next morning, we have breakfast at Beach Café Bar. We sit outside, nursing cups of coffee as we wait for our food to arrive. It's stifling today, but the sea breeze offers intermittent relief. Oscar is scrolling through his phone when he whispers, 'Jesus Christ.'

Thinking it is another difficult client, I don't take my eyes off my own phone as I ask, 'What's wrong?'

'Caitie, have you seen this?'

The trepidation in his tone makes my stomach swirl nervously. I take the phone from him and my insides twist. It is an article about Olivia. Some two-bit journalist exhuming the long-buried theory that Olivia was never kidnapped and instead was a lovesick teen who ran away with an older boyfriend. I skim the article, knowing it is trash, but anger sours on my tongue as I see the photographs. They are of me and Olivia in the bridal boutique. From the angle and clarity, it's obvious they were taken by the sales assistant. She didn't let on that she recognised my sister. It's such an invasion of privacy. Photographs taken without our consent, as though we are animals in a safari. This article will be another dagger for my father to fling at me when the urge strikes. Boiling over, I thrust the phone back at Oscar. Then I am struck by a sickening thought. I snatch the phone back from him. I scroll and scroll and scroll. I read every word carefully this time, heart hammering. I'm relieved, so relieved, the shop assistant didn't overhear Olivia's comment about the wedding dress. The press would've had a field day with that.

'Are you OK?' Oscar asks.

I nod and hand him the phone.

He leans forward and lowers his voice. 'What's going on?'

I've kept Olivia's marriage revelation a secret for a week. It has squirmed beneath my skin like a parasite. I look at Oscar and know I can trust him. He's my fiancé and one day he'll be my husband. He'll keep Olivia's secret. So I open up to him. Tell him about the man I've seen twice now. Tell him what I know. Everything Olivia told me. And it feels good to flush the secret out.

His mouth hangs open, a tunnel of disbelief. 'Married?'

'Not legally. Apparently. I can't stop thinking about it.'

His brows rise so high, they almost disappear into his hairline. He clasps his hands at the nape of his neck, making his biceps strain against the cotton of his T-shirt, and leans back in his chair. 'Christ,' he breathes. 'This is huge. Marrying a sixteen-year-old girl? Simon is sick in the head.'

I still, cup halfway to lips. 'Simon?'

His face drains of colour. Flustered, his eyes flit around my face. 'Who's Simon?' I demand again.

He opens his mouth. Closes it. 'Don't be angry.'

Foreboding edges beneath the gaps of me. 'Tell me.'

He blows out a breath. 'My cousin, Rachel, her husband works for the police. I bumped into him. We talked. He assumed I knew far more than I did and he told me things he shouldn't. He was mortified. As soon as he realised his mistake, he made me promise not to say anything to you or anyone else.' He thrusts his fingers back through his sandy hair. 'This is serious. He could lose his job, Caitie.'

My breaths are coming faster. 'What did he tell you?'

He shakes his head. 'I promised.'

I put my mug down so hard, coffee sloshes over the side. The woman on the table next to ours glances up. 'She's *my* sister.'

He scrubs his hand over his face. He doesn't want to tell me anything, but what choice does he have? 'Olivia called her captor Simon, but he never gave her his surname. She was kept in a tiny rural house in the woods. She doesn't know where but, based on the information she gave the police, they're focusing their efforts on the Forest of Dean.' He holds up his hands as though in surrender. 'That's it. That's all I know.'

A waiter arrives with our food. I wait until he leaves. 'She hasn't told me any of this.'

'She told the police. *That's* the main thing. Caitie, you can't tell Olivia or your parents what you know.'

I'm nodding, even though I am desperate to talk to my sister about it. How did I manage to unburden myself of one secret in exchange for half a dozen more? Oscar picks up his knife and fork and starts slicing into bacon and maple-drenched waffles. My stomach rebels at the sight. I watch him, this man I was so sure only minutes ago I could trust. Yet, he has kept all this from me with startling ease.

Feeling my eyes on him, he looks up. 'What is it?'

'You lied to me.'

'I didn't lie. I didn't tell you, sure, but I didn't lie.'

'You're seriously going to argue semantics?'

He softens. 'You're right. Look, I wanted to tell you but I didn't think it was a good idea to pile all this information on you only to insist you keep it from your family. I was trying to protect you.'

I scoff. 'I didn't ask for your protection, Oscar.'

'You're right, I'm sorry. But there was so much more to it. I didn't want a man to lose his job, his income, because of an honest mistake. I'm sorry I kept it from you. I really am. But my hands were tied. You do understand that, don't you?'

Accepting the reasons behind his deceit feels a lot like swallowing stones. He lays his hand on mine and I resist the urge to snatch it away. 'Sure.' My smile is forced. 'I won't repeat anything.'

Satisfied, Oscar tucks into his breakfast. But I am too distracted to eat.

Simon.

A perfectly mundane name. It isn't villainous or menacing. Simon, the man behind the mask who held a knife to my sister's throat. Who stole her and ruined my family. Simon, who married a child and locked her away in a cabin, deep in the woods. Simon, who put himself inside a young, terrified girl. Simon who isn't made of smoke and malice but of blood and bone. I imagine myself coming face to face with him, with this ordinary man and calling him by his ordinary name, right before I sink a knife into his chest. I imagine it slicing through flesh and sinew, lodging into bone. Not much different from carving a beef joint. I pick up my butter knife. It glints in the sunlight. I turn it over in my hands and I know, if it comes to it, I could do it. I could kill my sister's captor.

17

Caitlin Arden

The following Tuesday, I am tasked with picking Olivia up from her therapy appointment in Bath. She sends me a message, telling me to meet her at a coffee shop down the road from her therapist's office. I haven't seen her since our spontaneous shopping trip or since Oscar told me about Simon. Though I'm desperate to tell her what I know, to ask her the many questions this revelation has dredged up, I don't want to push her into talking to me before she's ready. Yet, keeping it all to myself feels like a betrayal. As though I am a peeping Tom, peering through the curtains, looking in on something private.

I walk down the high street. On either side of me, the cream buildings glow in the sunlight. People spill onto the pavements outside pubs and drink cider poured over pint glasses of ice. They are noisy and brash and on the wrong side of tipsy. It's the first day of August and heat pulses through the city. Doors and windows are flung open but there's no breeze. I'm exhausted and wilting by the time I reach the coffee shop.

I almost don't recognise Olivia. She's dressed in one of the outfits she bought during our shopping spree. She looks different. Confident. You'd never guess she'd spent more than a decade of her life locked in a cabin in the woods. She's wearing a long, rust-coloured skirt and a cream crop top that shows a sliver of toned, tanned midriff, paired with dark sunglasses and white trainers. Her hair is in a low, tousled ponytail. If I wore my hair like that, I'd look like Gaston from *Beauty and the Beast*. Everything about her is effortlessly chic.

When she sees me, her face splits into a smile. We hug. 'You look incredible,' I tell her.

She pulls back and dips a little curtsey. 'Why, thank you. So do you.'

I glance down at another of my floral summer dresses, damp with sweat after my brisk walk from the car – she's just being polite – next to hers, my outfit is obvious and boring. 'Thanks.'

I'm about to suggest we head for the car when a man rounds the corner, calling my sister's name. He is tall, broad, dark-haired, dressed in a crisp, white shirt and navy trousers. His long legs eat up the distance quickly. He reaches us, his smile white and wide, and holds out a black, leather shoulder bag with a gold clasp. 'You forgot this,' he tells Olivia.

She takes it from him. 'That was silly of me. Thank you.'

My eyes dart between them. 'And you are?'

He turns to me, taken aback by the whipcrack of my tone. His eyes are olive green, framed with long black lashes, the kind I can only hope to mimic after four coats of expensive mascara. 'Doctor Gideon Temple,' he says in an Irish lilt. He offers me his hand and I take it. It is so much larger than my own, and somehow, his skin is softer, too.

'You must be the therapist,' I say, realisation dawning.

When he smiles, he is all dimples. 'I like to think there's a little more to me than my vocation but, yes, I'm the therapist.' His stubble is a shade darker than the coffee curls of his hair, and beneath it is a square Hollywood jaw and a cleft chin. He's older, late thirties maybe, but the kind of attractive that commands attention. 'You must be the sister?'

I smile. 'Yes. I'm the sister.'

'Well, *sister*, it's nice to finally meet you.'

'Caitie.'

'Caitie,' he says my name slowly, as though it is a single square of dark chocolate melting on his tongue. He releases my hand but my palm still tingles from the contact.

'I talk about you a lot,' offers Olivia.

'All good things, I hope?'

'Great things,' he confirms.

I stare up at him, but the eye contact is so intense, it's like standing too close to an open fire.

'Doctor Temple actually wanted to speak to you, Caitie,' says Olivia.

'You did?' I ask him.

He glances uncertainly at her. 'Well . . .'

'I'll go grab a drink while you two talk,' she says. 'Anyone want anything?'

We both shake our heads. She ducks inside the coffee shop.

'You wanted me?' I prompt. He smiles and as my words ricochet, my cheeks redden. 'You wanted to speak to me?'

'Yes, I was going to set up a meeting with you in my office, not ambush you on the street without warning.' He looks apologetic. 'Olivia was . . . eager for us to have a conversation.'

'Impatient,' I correct.

He grins knowingly. 'And then she just *happened* to leave her bag behind and here we are. She's resourceful.'

'Manipulative,' I offer. It isn't the first time Olivia has played ringmaster, having us all jump through her hoops. She so deftly tricked our mother into driving miles away so the two of us could sneak out.

'You're very astute.'

'And you're very diplomatic.'

The air is thick with heat and voices and something else. Something that crackles and hisses between us. His eyes are beautiful. They aren't olive like I thought. They're lighter than that, clear, like glass, jade-green.

Then he clears his throat, and the tension spits and sparks before dispersing altogether. 'Let's find a time for you to come to my office so we can talk about Olivia. Next week, perhaps?'

My stomach drops. A week? I can't wait that long. I am *desperate* to hear what it is Olivia wants him to discuss with me. 'Can we talk now?'

He glances up and down the near-empty pavement.

'*Please*,' I say.

He's reluctant. I suppose it isn't usual for therapists to conduct confidential conversations on the street but there isn't anyone around to overhear us. Then shaking his head as though he can't believe he's giving in to me, he tugs me into an alcove and says, 'How do you think Olivia is coping?'

I take a moment to consider my answer. Wanting to say something insightful and intelligent. To impress him. *Why* do I want to impress him? But, drawing a blank, I plump for honesty instead. 'She's resilient. She seems to be assimilating quickly, far quicker than I ever thought possible. Looking at her today, you'd never know what she's been through. She seems just like any other beautiful twenty-something in the city.' I leave my words to hang in the space between us, and carefully watch him to catch his reaction. I'm not sure why, but I want to know if he agrees that my sister is beautiful. He keeps his expression carefully blank, waiting patiently for me to continue. He is a man who is comfortable in gulfs of silence. 'But she avoids discussing *him*, her life at his hands, it's as though a shutter slams down. She won't talk to anyone but the police.' He inclines his head, but the minute change in his expression tells me I'm wrong. Of course I am. 'I suppose it isn't *just* the police she tells her secrets to. She obviously talks to you as well.'

'It's my job. Sometimes it's easier to burden a stranger than it is those closest to you.'

It's odd to think this man knows more about my sister's life than I do. I imagine them together in his office of dark wood and dark walls as she cuts herself open and it all comes pouring out. She bleeds all over his office, the horrors of these last years swilling in her veins and settling in drips and puddles on the solid oak floor. She bleeds on him and bleeds on him, and, as he dresses her wounds, trying to heal them with his PhD and his ability to sit comfortably in gulfs of silence, of other people's pain and misery and thorny secrets, he falls in love with her. Just as everyone does. Just as the nation has. He knows the intimate corners of her in a way I don't. So I ask, 'How do *you* think she's coping?'

'She isn't sleeping. She has night terrors. She's . . .' he pauses, just for a moment, considering his next words carefully, 'she's struggling with your parents.'

'She finds Mum suffocating.'

'She told you.'

'She's my sister.' There's a snap in my voice. I'm being defensive and I hate it. She isn't a rope in a game of tug of war. This isn't a competition. 'Aren't you breaking patient confidentiality?'

'Olivia wants me to share some of what we've discussed.'

'*Some?*'

He nods. His dark brows draw together in a frown. I feel him assessing me. I've always prided myself on having the shiniest, most precious pieces of who Olivia is. But that's of the girl she was before, not the woman she is now. This man, this total stranger, has more of her than I do.

'These types of cases are highly specialised,' he says. 'Nuanced. But it isn't uncommon for the person who's been away to struggle slotting back into their old life. Feelings of disorientation, anger and loneliness are all normal.'

My gaze snaps to his. 'Loneliness?' I ask. 'Olivia is lonely?'

The thought of my sister being *lonely* fills me with horror. I know loneliness, the taste and smell and shape of it. The clawing desperation to slough it off like dead skin. Loneliness is the most harrowing kind of poverty.

'She is,' he says.

My heart flutters urgently in my chest. 'What can I do?'

He shifts his weight, looking a little uncomfortable. 'Olivia feels it would be easier for her to adjust if you moved back into the family home. Temporarily, of course.'

Silence. Move back to Blossom Hill House. Leave Oscar to live with my mother – worse, my *father*. The loneliest I've ever felt were the years I spent in that house after Olivia was taken. Each evening during supper, my father would laugh and smile with my mother, but barely make eye contact with me. If ever it were just the two of us in a room, if only for a few minutes, he'd busy himself on his phone or with a book. The occasions, though rare, when Mum would visit her sister in Worcester, Dad would hand me a wedge of twenty-pound notes and send me off to Florence's house for the weekend. He was never cruel, at least, not outwardly, or in a way that was noticeable to others, but I felt the razor blades that laced the space between us; one wrong move would illicit a thousand bloody cuts. When I escaped to university, local though it was, living on campus gave me room to breathe. I don't want to go back to Blossom Hill House. I can't. 'I'll have to discuss it with my fiancé,' I hedge.

There's a flicker of disappointment on Gideon's face, but it's fleeting, like headlights in the distance, and then it's gone. 'Of course.'

I glance down at his left hand. His ringless finger. When I look up, I catch him staring at the solitaire diamond on mine.

As though embarrassed he's been caught looking, he lifts his chin and says, 'How're you dealing with it all?'

'Fine.'

More silence. He waits. I force myself to stay quiet. To stay still so as not to belie how uncomfortable silence makes me. His mouth quirks, just a little. He knows. 'Well, if you ever need to talk, just get in touch.'

Olivia emerges from the coffee shop carrying two iced drinks. Smiling, she hands one to me. I look between her and Gideon and think they'd make a striking couple. More at home on a red carpet than a busy street.

We say goodbye to Gideon and then we leave. As we near the end of the street, I glance back and try to ignore the swirl of satisfaction when I see he is watching me go.

18

Elinor Ledbury

It has been over a week since the party. Uncle Robert had left early the next morning, before either Heath or Elinor had risen. She had breathed a sigh of relief, remembering their uncle's threat to deal with Heath later. Yet, their uncle did not return to Ledbury Hall the following weekend.

'Good riddance,' said Heath. 'Maybe he'll finally leave us alone.'

But Elinor worried. Every Sunday Uncle Robert left them a pile of cash. This is how they paid for food and other essentials. What would they do without that money? Everything that belonged to them was his.

'I'll take care of it,' said Heath. And he did, coming home the next day with bags of fresh fruit and vegetables, meat from the butcher's in town. Though Elinor is grateful, she eats almost all her meals alone, if she has the appetite to eat at all. Heath is out every day, disappearing for hours at a time. Neither of them have mentioned Sofia since the night of the fire. Elinor still feels guilty for the trouble she caused, so she doesn't complain when he leaves early and comes home late, that floral perfume clinging to his skin.

It is early morning. Heath is already gone and the house is clean so she curls up in the library with a book. She has barely read a chapter, when the buzzer in the hallway rings out, making her jump. She can count on one hand the number of times people have rung that buzzer. She goes to the intercom, pressing the button to speak to whoever is at the gate. 'Hello?'

'Elinor?' comes an Irish lilt. 'Still got my jacket?'

'Flynn?'

'How many other Irishmen's jackets have you collected?'

She grins. 'I'll come to you. Give me five minutes?'

She runs upstairs, takes his tan jacket from beneath her bed and strokes the sheepskin lining. She's reluctant to return it even though she knows she must. With a sigh, she takes a thicker jumper from her drawer and pulls it on. The February air is so cold, you could snap it in two. At the front door, she laces her leather boots, pulls on a hat and scarf and starts off down the driveway. She is carrying Flynn's coat but it's so cold, even in her jumper, that she slips it on.

A cocktail of nerves and excitement makes her heart beat a little faster. She walks quickly down the driveway. He waits for her at the gate, hands shoved in jean pockets to keep warm. He's wearing a chunky-knit sweater the colour of custard-cream biscuits, his dark, glossy hair peeking out from beneath his rust-coloured woollen hat. When he sees her, he beams.

She smiles back, even though she is more nervous now than excited.

'How've you been?' he asks.

'Disgraced,' she answers honestly. She isn't sure why she is being so candid. Maybe it is loneliness that loosens her tongue. Maybe it is just a relief to hear another person's voice. Maybe, she thinks, being near another person will stop her fading quickly into nothing, like a handprint on cold glass.

He frowns. 'That doesn't sound good.'

'It isn't.'

'I was thinking about going to the Rawcliffe ice rink if you want to join? You could come along, tell me all about it.' When she hesitates, he adds, 'I'll even let you keep hold of my jacket a while longer.'

She glances back at the manor, unsure, but then she imagines her afternoon crawling along in silence as she drifts around that old, huge house all alone, and the thought is so unbearable that she turns to Flynn and nods.

The ice rink is the temporary kind, set up for a month in winter. Flynn pays for their entry and they sit on a wooden bench, lacing up their rented skates. It's a Thursday afternoon and not very busy. Only a handful of skaters stumble or glide effortlessly across the ice. There are strings of fairy lights zigzagging high above the rink, glowing against the milk-white sky.

They totter across the rubber floor and onto the ice. 'You skated before?' he asks.

She nods. Six years in a row, Heath has broken them into the York ice rink afterhours so they had the entire place to themselves. Each night, they would skate for hours, returning home as the sun rose. Not this winter, though. Not since he spends so much of his time with Sofia.

Flynn lays a hand on Elinor's elbow. 'You can hold onto the side if—'

She flashes him a smile and then takes off, blades cutting easily through the ice. She is poise and speed. Light and powerful. The music is loud and throbbing, the lights above are twinkling. She spins and skates backwards, searching for Flynn. He is watching her in open-mouthed awe. She smiles, a card player about to reveal a Royal Flush, and checks her shoulder to makes sure she has enough space. She skates into the centre, lifts a leg in an arabesque and spins. Faster and faster, ignoring the tremble in her legs.

Flynn is wide-eyed and bemused. She throws her head back and laughs, high on adrenaline. No one but Heath has ever seen her on the ice. The handful of skaters have moved to the sides of the rink. She's a little self-conscious now and thinks about skating back to Flynn but the way he watches her, as though she is a mystical creature, gives her a thrill which is so much better than the consuming loneliness she has been swallowed by, trapped inside of, for weeks. So she chases that thrill, sweeping in more powerful circles. Her heart thuds in anticipation and her thighs burn as she soars across the rink. She feels all eyes on her. Can hear the sharp inhalation of the crowd as she leaps. She is weightless. A paper aeroplane, a snowflake on the wind, a drifting feather. Her skate lands cleanly, and she is met with applause.

Her legs shake and her ankle feels as though it's made of marshmallow. Though Elinor isn't accustomed to being the centre of attention, she feels like a daisy unfurling in the sun.

She makes her way back to Flynn. 'If I'd known you were so awful at skating, I'd never have brought you,' he deadpans.

She laughs and the two of them start doing laps together. She tells him she used to come with her brother but omits that they break in. 'So, it's just you, your uncle and Heath?' he asks.

'That's right.'

'You're close?'

'To my brother.'

'But he didn't tell you about Sofia?'

'No.' She tries to keep the irritation from her voice. 'He didn't.'

'I've only met him a few times but he doesn't give much away, not even to my cousin.'

'Why would he?' she says in a pin-sharp voice.

'Because they're together . . .' he answers, as though she is being deliberately belligerent, which she supposes she is.

'I don't know anything about her.'

'What do you want to know?'

'Nothing,' she says. *Everything*, she thinks. 'So, do you have any siblings?'

'Two brothers. I'm the youngest.'

'Did you grow up in Ireland?'

'Until I was five. Moved here when my mother got a job as a headteacher.'

'And your father, is he still around?'

He nods. 'Mum and Dad are happily married. They celebrate their twenty-ninth wedding anniversary next month.'

She wonders what it would be like to have parents. A solid, complete family unit. She wishes she could try it. If only for a short while. Just to know. 'I bet you have a golden retriever, too.'

He laughs. 'We do actually. Her name's Honey.'

Her uncle has forbidden a dog. He's allergic. Heath has promised her she can have one as soon as they have full possession of the estate. She'd like one with a lolling tongue and velvet ears. A companion that will sit with her while she reads, that will walk with her around the grounds. A dog that won't leave the second it catches the scent of a bitch on heat. 'Do you work?' she asks Flynn.

'I'm a student.'

She smiles. 'Of the world?'

'Of the University of York.'

'Impressive. What're you studying?'

'What do you think I'm studying?'

She shrugs. 'I have no idea.'

'Guess.'

She recalls the travel guide of South Africa in his car, shoved in the driver's side compartment. 'Geography?'

His mouth quirks up. 'Nope. Try again.'

'Geology.'

'Geology?' He snorts. 'Where'd that come from?'

'You claimed to have left me a purple rock.'

'Claimed?' He lifts a hand to his chest in feigned outrage. 'I did.'

'I never found it.'

'Did you try?'

She grins.

'Right,' he says. 'One last guess.'

'Art?'

He looks surprised, then he smiles. 'You only get onto university art courses if you promise to cut off an ear.'

'Van Gogh would be proud.'

Flynn comes to a stop at the side of the rink and bends to adjust his skate. 'Why art?'

'The paint on your hands. I saw it when you were driving.'

'Paint . . .' He stands and looks at his nails. 'Shit,' he mumbles and scrapes at the remnants of black around his cuticles. 'It's nail varnish,' he tells her. 'I, ugh, thought I'd got it all off.'

'Decided black isn't your colour?'

'My dad hates when I wear it. Says it's for women.'

'I don't think the varnish will discriminate.'

'Neither do I.' Flynn picks at his nail. 'It isn't so much my dad that minds, but my grandfather. He's a barrister. Very serious. Very traditional.'

'Maybe he's just jealous,' she says. 'Offer to paint his nails, too.'

Flynn grins at her. 'Any other guesses?'

She shakes her head.

'How about I tell you over a hot chocolate? There's a place not far from here.'

They choose a little table for two in front of the window. Elinor feels like she is in a fishbowl or a zoo. The little village coffee shop boasts dark-wood furniture, exposed redbrick and latte artwork on the walls. At the centre is a large, squishy orange sofa and two plush armchairs around a low table. Though the coffee shop isn't crowded, it isn't empty, either. There are mothers bouncing babies on their knees, small groups of friends talking loudly, a couple who hold hands across a nearby table, talking quietly. The way the man looks at her, with so much love, makes Elinor's chest ache.

She thinks about Heath and Sofia, together somewhere right now. He doesn't know Elinor is out in the world, not just without him, but *with* someone else. She is aware that people who see her don't even know Heath exists. Sometimes she feels their very existences are woven so tightly together, that if one were to perish, the other would, too. But, in this coffee shop, she isn't just Heath Ledbury's sister. She could be anyone. Flynn could be her boyfriend or her boss or even her brother. It's a thrilling, freeing thought. Just for a moment, she is untethered, floating away from her life with Heath, and being swept into another. One of coffee shop dates and uncomplicated kisses.

Flynn is ordering their drinks. She takes the time to study him. He's handsome with his crooked smile and wide, inviting mouth, but what Elinor finds most alluring about him is the way he feels like a shiny new penny. Or a hot-air balloon. Or virgin snow. He is unmarred by tragedy or loss. There's a buoyancy to him that she hopes is contagious, because the more time she spends out in the world, the more obvious that gap between her and everyone else becomes.

Flynn returns to the table carrying two ginormous hot chocolates, loaded with lashings of thick, whipped cream and fluffy marshmallows and even a chocolate flake. Elinor covers her mouth with her hands in delight, then lowers them to take the drink, and beams up at him.

'You have the prettiest smile,' he says.

The compliment colours her cheeks and she looks away.

He clears his throat and sits down. 'Medical.'

'What?' She blinks, sure she has missed something.

'My degree.'

She nods. 'You want to be a doctor?'

'I'm interested in the mental-health side of the profession. You know, a psychiatrist or something.'

'You want to put people in straitjackets and padded rooms?' she teases.

'I want to help people. It sounds like a load of tripe but—'

'No, it doesn't.'

They make eye contact and something electric passes between them. His eyes travel slowly down to her lips and her skin warms in response, as though she is basking beneath the sun. It's a feeling that excites and terrifies her.

'I'm doing a placement year in South Africa,' he says quickly. He studies her face which she keeps carefully blank despite the swirling disappointment.

'Hence the travel guide.'

He nods. 'Not until September, though.'

She smiles, relieved he isn't going to abandon her anytime soon.

They sip their hot chocolate. She licks cream from her top lip and he follows the movement with his eyes. 'What about you?' he asks. 'What do you want to do?'

Truthfully, she hasn't ever given it much thought, assuming her future is already written. She and Heath have spoken endlessly about finally receiving their inheritance, but never mapped out what their days would look like afterwards. Until now, she didn't imagine days turning into weeks, into months, into years, into decades. 'I don't know.'

'I suppose with a house that grand you probably don't have to work.'

'True.'

'Won't you get bored, though? Don't you want a purpose?'

Her eyes narrow in consternation. 'I have purpose.'

Embarrassed and remorseful, he looks down. 'Of course. I didn't mean . . . Sorry.'

She sips her drink but it scalds her tongue. When Heath turned eighteen, Uncle Robert bombarded him with stacks of university brochures. He flipped through them lazily and discarded them quickly, deciding he would rather wait for his inheritance than go away to study. Elinor didn't argue. But she did read every page of those brochures as though they were storybooks, imagining herself on a leafy campus on the outskirts of a new city, sitting with a group of friends and poring over heavy textbooks, a melee of coloured highlighters at the centre of their group. A life that felt more fantasy to her than anything Tolkien could ever write. 'How are you supposed to know what you want to do?' she asks in a small voice.

'I guess you think about what you enjoy doing and you chase it.'

'Reading,' she tells him after a moment. 'I like to read.'

'English Literature, then?'

'Probably. I play piano, too.' She frowns and corrects herself. '*Played* piano.'

'What happened?'

She's self-taught, using the books in the library and listening to her parents' old cassettes. One weekend, Uncle Robert heard her playing. He became obsessed. Every weekend thereafter, he'd lock the two of them in the reception room for hours, making her play the same pieces over and over until her fingertips bruised. He'd watch her, a glass of Scotch in hand. The more he drank, the more demanding and less patient he became. It came to a roaring crescendo when, in fury, he slammed the fallboard down. If she hadn't whipped her fingers away, he'd have broken them.

'Why did you stop playing?' Flynn presses.

She shrugs. 'My uncle sucked the joy out of it.' He is quiet, waiting for her to go on. She is remembering another of her uncle's cruel lectures. 'Your father coasted through life on his dashing good looks and all the other hereditary gifts the pair of you see in the mirror,' he'd sneered. 'Just like you and your wicked brother, he squandered his intellect and his talent, too. Beauty fades, brilliance breeds legacy. Remember that.' Elinor sighs. 'My uncle thinks if you're good at something, you should be great at it. Flawless, even.'

'He sounds like a difficult man to please.'

'Painfully so.'

'And you're feeling disgraced because of him?'

'Because of me,' she says. 'I got drunk at his work party and accidently set fire to the curtains.'

She holds still, not wanting to miss Flynn's reaction, wondering if he'll turn away from her in disgust and leave her here to find her own way home. He doesn't. He cocks his head to one side, eyes glittering playfully, and says, 'Sounds like a regular Tuesday to me.'

It starts to get dark. Flynn drives her home. At the gate, she makes to take off his jacket but he holds up a hand. 'Keep it,' he tells her. 'It looks better on you.'

Her smile is jubilant. She's enjoyed spending the day with him. An unexpected, perfect adventure. Riding on the wave of excitement, she leans forward and presses her mouth to his. It's brief; she pulls away quickly and when she does, she sees the heat in Flynn's eyes. He leans forward, wanting her to kiss him again. She feels desirable, powerful, even. She hasn't felt either in a long while. She opens the gate but he gently catches her wrist. 'Can I see you again?' he asks. 'Tomorrow?'

'Monday,' she says.

When he's driven off, she slips through the gate and decides to spend some time looking for that purple stone before it gets too dark. It takes only a few minutes of brushing a light covering of snow from stones before she discovers it. She can't believe she found it. She slips it carefully into her pocket before making her way to Ledbury Hall, feeling like an untethered kite. The manor comes into view but so too does her uncle's car as it tears down the driveway towards her. She stumbles back. The car slows and her uncle's thin lips spread into a sardonic twist, his eyes meet hers, taking on a malevolent glitter. Then he speeds up again, towards the gate.

She looks back at the house. Dread whispers through her when she sees Heath's car parked outside. She runs, remembering her uncle's threat. *I'll deal with you later, boy.* The front door is wide open. She calls her brother's name.

Silence.

The kind that settles in a graveyard.

'Heath!' she shrieks again, racing from room to room, searching for him.

He doesn't answer. He doesn't answer because he can't. She finds him lying on the kitchen floor in a pool of blood. A lead pipe discarded beside him.

19

Caitlin Arden

I collect Florence from the train station. Her hair is a short curtain of inky silk, falling halfway between jaw and collarbone. Her lips, which are usually painted red, are rosy and glossed. Her pale blue dress is full length and tiered with billowing sleeves and an open back. The material is linen. Expensive.

'Gorgeous dress,' I tell her as she slides into the passenger seat.

She bites her lip. 'It's not too much?'

I pull out of the train station car park. 'I don't think so.'

'I'm so nervous. *Why* am I so nervous?'

'Because you haven't seen her in sixteen years. But it'll be fine. Promise.'

She gives a nervous little laugh. 'And we're sure it's Olivia?'

I glance away from the road to see if she's serious. 'Of course we're sure.'

'Just checking. I mean, it's a shock, isn't it? I never thought I'd see her again.' She exhales loudly, as though trying to dispel her tension. This is new. Florence is certainty and strong coffee. Ambition and whimsy. 'Anyway, I'm sorry we've had to rearrange this a couple of times. Olivia wasn't too upset?'

I shake my head. 'No. She's looking forward to seeing you. She understands you had to work. Speaking of, how was London?'

'Busy, dirty, congested.' She launches into a rant about the horrors of underground commutes. I only half listen as I weave us between hissing buses and determined joggers who run out in front of me.

'But I'm glad I went,' she says. 'This new Noah Pine book is set to be another bestseller. I can't believe I was chosen to do the audiobook. It isn't even out yet and I'm already being asked to narrate books for other authors.'

'That's great. Your mum must be thrilled.'

Florence glows. 'Naturally.'

I feel a twinge of envy that she grew up with a parent who supported her dreams. Even when those dreams consisted of being a Broadway actress. Susan didn't push her daughter into teaching or some soulless tech job because it paid well. Florence loves her mother, but I don't think she can ever truly appreciate how lucky she is to have a parent who encourages her to pick whatever path she wants in life and happily holds her hand as she walks down it, no matter whether it leads to a dead end or a pot of gold.

'So much has changed in such a short space of time,' she says.

'Yep. You got your first big narrating break . . . I got reunited with my long-lost sister.'

'Can you believe it was just three weeks ago we met in that bar and debated whether I should be Odell-Fox or Fox-Odell?'

I shake my head and join the clug of cars snail-crawling across Bath and its torturous one-way system.

'Missed you,' she says.

'Missed you, too.'

'Really?'

'Yes,' I say, checking my rear-view mirror. 'Why would you even question that?'

In my peripheral, she shrugs one slender shoulder. 'Olivia is back.'

'And?'

'And I assumed there wouldn't be as much room for me in your life. Rightly so, obviously.'

'There's nothing obvious about it. You're as much as a sister to me as she is. You always will be. Olivia coming back doesn't change that.'

'Sure?'

'Yes! You're one of *the* most important people in my life, Florence. I mean, Jesus, I've known you since I was seven. It's been nineteen years. If our friendship was a person, she'd be old enough to drink. She'd be standing in line for a club and she wouldn't even need a fake I.D.'

Florence throws her head back and laughs.

I go on. 'She's old enough to vote. To drive. To pilot a plane. She can legally buy scissors and have sex.'

'I hope she doesn't get the latter two confused.'

I grin.

'So . . .' she says. 'What you're telling me is that our friendship is old enough to legally suck a dick?'

'Yep.'

We're both laughing now. Love for her fizzes up. Florence is family in every way that matters. In every way but blood.

'It's just, I don't have a sister,' she says with so much of her soul bared to me, 'but with you in my life, I feel like I do.'

We're in standstill traffic. I put the handbrake on and twist in my seat so I'm facing her because I need her to see how sincere I am. 'And that's *never* going to change.'

At the house, I send Florence out into the garden with an icy pitcher of Pimm's before heading upstairs to find Olivia. When we arrived, Mum told us she was decompressing in her bedroom after a particularly taxing trip to the police station this morning. I'm expecting to find her curled up on her bed, exhausted and raw, instead, she is fastening the last wooden button of her ivory dress. It's billowing and romantic with a tie waist and balloon sleeves. It's jarring, how beautiful she is, she is more beautiful every time I see her – her dark lashes, angular face, her long, luscious gold hair, and the confident way in which she holds herself. I assumed if she ever returned, she'd be a hollowed-out shell, timid and awkward, unsure of the world around her. She isn't. Gideon talked about the night terrors and anxiety, about how she is struggling and lonely, but, looking at her now, you wouldn't know.

I feel her thinness as we hug, the gaps between her body and her dress scrunches as we collide. I breathe her in; blackberries and night jasmine. 'I've really missed you,' she whispers into my shoulder.

'You, too,' I say as we break away.

'I've got another appointment with Gideon this week. Mum and Dad are going back to work so would you mind picking me up again?'

'Of course.'

I perch on Olivia's bed. At her dressing table, she spins the jewellery stand. The necklace she chooses is one I recognise. It's an emerald on a dainty, gold rope chain. Mum adored that necklace; Grandad Aubrey gave it to Nana on their first wedding anniversary. I've begged Mum for that necklace a thousand times and she's always quipped, 'It's yours when I'm dead.'

'Everything OK?' asks Olivia.

I'm frowning. I feel the deep lines of disapproval carved into my brow. 'Yes, all good,' I say, trying to smile through the gnawing jealousy. I know it is wrong to feel this way because it's likely Olivia saw the necklace and, like me, fell in love with it. After everything Olivia's been through, how could Mum deny her the emerald?

'Are you sure because—'

'Gideon seemed great,' I say, cutting her off in a bid to change the subject.

'Oh, yes, he really listens.'

'Isn't that what therapists are supposed to do?'

'Well, yes, but some do it better than others. There are three I deal with on a regular basis, and he's the only one who seems to care more about how I feel and what I want, and less about squeezing me for juicy, morbid details. I come out of those other appointments feeling like a squeezed-out lemon.'

I'm nodding. 'He's nothing like the therapist I used to see.'

'How so?'

I think of the dowdy, red-faced woman who smelt of mothballs and was forever pushing a pair of cheap glasses up her crooked nose. I swallow. 'Just, you know, he seems young.'

She pulls a face. 'He's in his late thirties.'

I redden. 'Well, age aside, I'm glad he's helping.'

She takes a brush from the drawer and works it through her hair. 'Do you think he's easy to talk to?'

I nod.

'And what did you talk about?' she asks.

'When?'

'Outside the coffee shop.' Her voice is light and easy, as though she isn't that interested in my answer, but the tension that squares her shoulders betrays her. 'You were talking for quite a while.'

She wants to know if Gideon floated the idea of me moving back to Blossom Hill House. Naïvely, I hoped this notion would melt and disappear completely, like ice cubes in water.

'He asked me if I'd consider staying here for a while.' I clear my throat, dreading the news I know I must deliver. 'But I can't do it. I can't move back in with Mum and Dad.'

She stills, hairbrush in hand. 'Why?'

'I have a fiancé, a home of my own.'

'But it's just a few weeks,' she reasons. 'Until you go back to school. Won't Oscar let you?'

In truth, I haven't even brought it up with him because I don't *want* to live with my family again. 'He isn't like that. He wouldn't stop me from doing anything.'

'Except travelling.'

'Olivia,' I scold, stung.

'Then what? Why won't you move home for a while?'

'Because Blossom Hill House isn't my home. Not anymore. I can't just abandon my entire life.'

Her expression sours. 'Of course. I mean, what kind of functioning adult is single and jobless and lives at home with their parents?' She slaps the brush down onto the dresser.

I push to my feet. 'That's not what I meant. I'm sorry I haven't seen you a lot recently. I've avoided coming here since my fight with Dad but I'll make more of an effort. I'll come round every day.'

The longest, coldest silence.

Olivia bristles with disappointment and anger. 'Do whatever you need to do, Caitlin.'

Caitlin. She never calls me Caitlin.

She smooths down her dress. 'Is Florence here?'

I nod.

'Great.'

She turns and heads for the door.

'I'll grab some glasses and we can—'

She spins on her heel. Lifts her chin. Determined. Stony. 'Actually, I think I'd prefer to spend some time with her alone. It's probably easier to reconnect with your childhood best friend when your little sister isn't hanging around.'

She turns and leaves without looking back.

I go after her but Mum catches me at the bottom of the stairs. 'Can I have a quick word?'

I look past her. I can't see Olivia, but I hear her grabbing glasses from the kitchen cupboard.

'Whose idea was it to take Dad's credit card the day you and your sister went shopping?'

I'm distracted, eager to catch up with Olivia before she goes out into the garden. 'Dad gave it to her.'

'You didn't take it from his office?'

I hear the French doors opening.

'Did you?' she presses.

I drag my gaze away from the kitchen door and see that Mum is anxiously twisting her wedding band around her finger. 'Did I what?'

She sucks air between her teeth, irritated. 'Take your father's credit card?'

'No. I just told you he gave it to Olivia.'

She turns her face away.

'Didn't he?' I ask.

A beat of silence. 'Yes, that's right.' She smiles. 'Aren't you joining the girls in the garden?'

Girls. As though they are still thirteen years old. I nod and walk quickly down the hall and into the kitchen, stopping at the French doors. Olivia and Florence stand in the splash of sunshine, drinking each other in. Florence lifts a shaking hand to her mouth. Then they collide. They are a tangle of hair and breath and sweet, disbelieving laughter. They cling to one another. And I see it. I see the moment they slot perfectly back into one another's lives. The last sixteen years of separation dissolves between them. Florence pulls back, still clutching Olivia's hands as though she is terrified that if she lets go, even for a second, she will vanish, a mirage

137

melting beneath the too-hot sun. Then they are hugging again. Tightly. So tightly.

I sit in the cool kitchen for half an hour before I venture outside to join them with a fresh pitcher. After all, the plan was for the three of us to spend time together. The sliced fruit and ice clink against the jug as I cross the garden. They don't even look up as I approach. They laugh, heads bent close. I hover beside the table until Olivia's gaze flicks up to mine, her smile white and wide. But it is a smile that was never intended for me. It's left over from the brilliance of Florence's company and I am dining out on the crumbs of their shared joke.

She sobers quickly, her smile wilting in the afternoon heat. 'Everything OK?' she asks in the same tone you'd spit, 'What the fuck are you doing here?'

'Everything's fine,' I answer, gripping the handle of the jug so hard my hand starts to ache. The air around us grows rigor-mortis stiff with awkwardness. I have slipped back in time, I am the clingy, irritating little sister, desperate to hang out with Olivia and her cool friend. But it's different now. It *should* be different now. Florence is *my* friend. She's been my friend, and only my friend, for the last sixteen years.

'Thanks,' says Olivia, gaze falling on the jug in my hands.

'Oh, sure.' I set the cocktail mix down on the table as though I'm a waitress.

They smile at me. They are waiting for me to go. Rejection needles my skin and I turn to go. But then Florence catches my wrist and says, 'I'll come find you before I leave.'

'You don't need me to drive you home?'

'Daniel's going to come get me.'

'Great.' I take in the two of them, wishing they'd ask me to stay. 'I'll . . . leave you to it.'

As I make my way back up the garden path, their easy conversation resumes.

In the kitchen I am alone.

Mum asks for my help bringing boxes down from the attic. They're full of photo albums and old family videos. I assume they're for Olivia. I'm just stacking the last dusty box on the landing when

I hear the two of them come in through the French doors. They are giggly. I move to the stairs so I can talk to Florence before she goes. I'm not even halfway down when I see Florence kiss Olivia's cheek before disappearing out the front door.

She didn't say goodbye. She forgot to say goodbye to me. I stand there, staring at the spot Florence had been just seconds ago, feeling like a jumper that's become too itchy and too tight, shoved in a drawer, and forgotten.

Olivia turns around, sees me dithering. My heart beats faster, wondering what she'll say, but she barely glances at me as she climbs the stairs. She moves by without so much as brushing my shoulder.

A moment later, her bedroom door slams shut.

20

Caitlin Arden

It's been four days since Olivia and Florence reunited, and while I've received nothing but radio silence from my sister, I've had one quick, *Sorry, I'm so busy. Catch up soon!* message from my best friend. Yet, Mum told me on the phone last night that Florence had been at the house all day with Olivia. And I am a child again, sitting outside my big sister's bedroom door, desperate to be included. I try to keep busy, but Oscar is working more than usual, and even creating new prints for Wanderlust isn't enough to expel me from my pity party.

Worried I haven't been out or seen anyone in days, when Oscar left for a meeting in London this morning, he told me to give Gemma a call. The thing is, I feel really flat and grey, and I know I'm not much company. If I could make amends with Olivia, I might feel better but when I told her I wasn't moving back into Blossom Hill House, I hurt her. Unless I agree to do what she wants, I can't make it right. Maybe I should've just said yes, but how long would I have to stay until she was happy for me to leave?

I sit on the sofa and click mindlessly through my socials. I scroll and scroll and scroll. I ignore my messages. Since Olivia's return, they are mostly from people I haven't spoken to in years who try to disguise their morbid curiosity with concern. I feel a thud of disappointment that I haven't had more contact from Florence. Since the abduction, I've felt a shade darker than everyone else around me, as though witnessing it left a visible stain somewhere that matters, somewhere that means I am not carefree enough to be fun or easy-going. But that never mattered with Florence because she knew about Olivia, *knew* Olivia, and so she understood without me ever having to explain.

I click on the profiles of my university friends. Evie has posted a handful of photographs of her six-month-old son. Her feed used to be filled with images of Maple, her little blonde cocker spaniel, or her bouldering adventures, weekends away with her husband, weekends away with friends, brunches and birthday celebrations, cocktail snaps and the road trip she and her cousin took around America last summer. Now, there are only photographs of her son lying down. Lying on a colourful mat. Lying in his crib. Lying in someone's arms. At six months old, he has less than a handful of expressions, yet there are so many images of him that Evie's feed looks like a game of spot the difference . . . minus the differences. It's as though her entire personality exited via her vagina along with the baby, and she's had the afterbirth made into edible tablets. Even her profile photo is of her child.

I remember at the baby shower, Florence gave Evie a gift basket along with a card that read, 'Sorry you're leaving' which everyone found hilarious. Still, it was pretty spot on because since he was born, Evie's shed all her child-free friends and replaced them with other mothers.

'She's on the other side of the wall now,' said Florence after Evie cancelled lunch with us for the third time. 'So glad I spent seventy quid on the breast pump she wanted and suffered through five rounds of Labour or Porn.'

I click on my last conversation with Evie. My last four messages have gone unanswered. I fire off another, asking how she and the baby are doing.

Then I am browsing Gemma's page. She's posted a photo of her on a hike with a caption about relishing the school holidays. As I look at her warm, friendly smile, I struggle to understand why Florence didn't take to Gemma the way everyone else does.

'Isn't Gemma a little bit clingy?' she'd asked after meeting her at my engagement party. 'I heard her asking you to go to that Katherine Ryan gig but we said we'd see her next time she was in Bath. Do you want to book tickets or should I?'

But with Florence distracted by Olivia, I need to put more time into others. I call Gemma. She answers on the fifth ring. 'Wow . . . Caitie. Are you OK?'

'Yeah, I'm fine, I just wondered if you were around to grab lunch or go for a walk?'

'Today?'

'Yes, if you're free?'

Silence.

'I'm actually seeing Sarah this afternoon,' she says, as though I should know who she's talking about.

'Sarah?'

'Newbury.'

I sit up.

'You know her, don't you?' she asks.

I'm glad we're on the phone so she can't see my face. 'Yes, of course I know Sarah. I introduced the two of you at my engagement party a couple of years ago.'

'That's right! Sarah and I were literally talking about this yesterday. Neither of us could remember what the occasion was. Engagement party, that makes sense.'

'What're the two of you doing?' I ask politely even as this conversation leaves a sour taste on my tongue.

'Shopping for her hen weekend next month.'

Silence.

I can practically hear her realise her mistake. I am not invited to Sarah's hen weekend. Sarah, who I've known since secondary school. Sarah, who I coached through her break-up with Wesley after she spent a year self-medicating with casual sex and tequila. I knew she and Gemma had hung out a couple of times after they met, but I had no idea they were friends. Good friends. Better friends than we are.

'You can come along if you like?' suggests Gemma, trying to rescue the situation. 'I'll ask Sarah if she minds and then—'

'No,' I say because I don't want a pity invite. 'That's fine. We can see each other another time.'

'Sure.'

'Lunch next week?'

A beat of silence. Then, 'Can I check my diary and get back to you?'

Her reluctance is palpable. OK, so I could have, *should* have, put more time into my friendship with Gemma, but I've never been unkind to her. We've never had a fight or even a disagreement so why is she being so cold? 'Is everything . . . are you OK?' I ask.

More silence pours down the line. 'Caitie,' she says, wearily. 'Why didn't I know you have a sister?'

I feel my heart pounding with panic as I open my mouth but nothing comes out.

'It's just, I had no idea,' she says quietly. 'You never told me.'

'Not a lot of people know . . .' I stumble into silence. I want to tell her about the pool of loneliness I always have one toe dipped into, that it sometimes surges up and drags me down into the twisting dark. A loneliness that floods my eyes and ears and mouth. I want to tell her it started the night Olivia was taken. That I'm afraid there is something wrong with me, *seriously* wrong with me, and if I let people through the door of me, they will smell the damp and the rot and they will run, and then the loneliness will never let me come up for air. But I don't. I can't. Fear is like duct tape over my mouth. So I only manage, 'It's never been easy to talk about.'

'Yeah.' She sighs. 'I suppose it's the sort of thing you only trust really close friends with.' She falls quiet too. *Say something*, I think, *say anything*. 'Look, I've got to go. Sarah will kill me if I'm late.'

When she rings off, I sit in a thick, depressing silence.

Soon though, my phone is vibrating with an incoming call. It's Olivia. At first, she doesn't speak. There is only the rush of traffic and the frantic pant of her breath.

Sensing something is wrong, I surge to my feet. 'Olivia?' Still she doesn't talk but I can feel her fear hissing down the line. Then I am in the hallway, sliding on my sandals and grabbing my car keys. 'Where are you? I'll come and get you.'

'I don't know,' she gasps. 'I got on a bus and then I started walking. I'm lost. I'm—' She is sobbing so hard; I can't understand her.

'Drop me a pin so I can find you.'

'I don't know what that is.'

Of course she doesn't. 'OK, just, tell me what you see.'

Realising she's in Bradford-on-Avon, I tell her to wait for me at the park by the canal.

Twenty minutes later, I see Olivia by the bridge, leaning against the wall that overlooks the water. She's wearing an oversized cropped T-shirt and shorts with trainers, their laces loose. I imagine her shoving her feet into them before fleeing the house. As soon as I reach her, I pull her into my arms. She clings to me. There are a couple of leaves in her hair, which tells me she left the house via the woods and past the abandoned shack. Her breaths are frantic and too shallow. I tell her to inhale through her nose and slowly out through her mouth, but she is sobbing so hard, she can't do it. I smooth her sweaty hair back from her face and hold it in my hands. People nearby are slowing as they pass, gazes fixed on us. I ignore them.

'OK,' I soothe. 'Focus on things around you and, out loud, start naming them and the colours you see.'

She's still crying, her face red and tear-stained and sticky.

'We'll do it together,' I say. 'I'll start.' I look around. 'Navy bench.' I wait. Through tears, she manages to look completely bewildered. I do another one. 'Yellow slide.'

She follows my gaze to the children's play area across the park. 'Gr-green grass.'

'That's it!' I'm nodding, giving her my most encouraging primary-school teacher smile. 'That's it – great!' It's my turn again. 'Blush-pink roses.'

Slowly, I lower my hands from her face but she takes hold of them. Hers are clammy.

'Red,' she breathes. 'Red swing set.'

'Grey-stone bridge.'

Her fingers tighten around mine. She shakes her head. She's slipping again, eyes filling with tears. I cast around desperately. 'Aureolin sunflowers.'

She frowns. 'What?'

'Aureolin sunflowers,' I repeat.

'*Aureolin*.' She smiles. 'That's not a colour.'

'It *is*. It's the colour of those sunflowers.'

'Aureolin.' She laughs.

'Why're you laughing?'

'You couldn't pick something normal?'

'Like what?'

She laughs even harder. 'Like yellow!'

'I said yellow earlier. Yellow slide. *Stop* laughing. It's a colour. A normal colour.'

'Aureolin,' she sings-songs. 'Aureolin, aureolin, *aureolin*.'

I start laughing, too, because the more she says it, the more ridiculous it sounds. 'It's warmer than yellow. Happier. Sunshiny.'

'Sunshiny *aureolin*,' she manages between peals of laughter.

Then we are both gone, laughing so hard our shoulders shake. Passers-by stare, which makes us laugh even more. And though I don't yet know what caused Olivia's panic attack, I bathe in the warm glow of knowing that when my sister needed someone, she called me. That, at least to her, I matter.

She tells me she had a really difficult interview at the station and when she came back to the house, Mum was all over her. That she is angry everyone's lives have moved forward while she is stuck in the past, still being treated like a child by her parents. She wonders, almost to herself, if she'll ever have a normal life. We talk for almost an hour, walking around the park in the baking heat.

We make our way onto the high street in search of drinks.

'Here?' asks Olivia, nodding towards a café with flower baskets hanging outside.

'Sure.'

'Can I wait outside? I can't do crowds right now.'

I grab two bottles of water from the fridge and carry them to the counter.

Then I stop, shock rooting me to the spot.

In the corner, at the back of the café, is Oscar. He isn't in London. And he isn't alone. He is, in fact, having lunch with another woman. She's slim and tanned with blonde hair and the kind of long legs men fantasise having wrapped around their waist. I stare at the two of them. The woman says something I can't hear but it must be hilarious because Oscar laughs so hard the corners of his eyes wrinkle.

145

'Hello?' calls the cashier in a voice that tells me it isn't the first time she's tried to get my attention. I stumble forward. As she scans the drinks, my focus is trained on my fiancé enjoying a secret get-together with a woman I don't know. Between them is a slice of chocolate cake. One dessert. Two spoons. Oscar is leaning forward, his hand just millimetres from hers. I've seen enough. Once I've paid, I leave.

Olivia and I head to the car park.

With shaking hands, I take my phone from my bag and check the calendar I share with Oscar. He's supposed to be in Southbank, meeting a new client called Sam.

I send him a message.

How's London? Meetings going well? Is Sam a good guy?

I wait nervously for a reply. He'll correct me. He'll tell me there was a change of plan and, funny story, he's actually in Bradford-on-Avon and yes, Sam's great, but she isn't as pretty as I am or as funny or as fuckable either.

My phone vibrates.

You know London, overcrowded and underwhelming. Meetings are going great! He really knows his stuff. Don't forget we have dinner with my mum tonight. Dad's away so it's just the three of us.

I reread his message a dozen times. *He* really knows his stuff, not *she*, *he*. And London . . . Oscar is still claiming to be in London. Is he having an affair? The thought fills me with such enormous grief that a strangled noise is ripped from me.

Olivia's head snaps up. She has drained the water bottle. 'You OK?'

I nod and swallow and nod again. Then I push the contempt and betrayal to the bottom of myself. 'Let's go.'

21

Caitlin Arden

Oscar tells me his train is delayed and he'll meet me at his parents' house for dinner. Since Olivia's return, I have deigned to miss four Sunday roasts with the Fairviews. This is our make-up dinner and I promised I'd be there. If I don't go, Oscar will know something is wrong and then he'll have time to concoct a story. Another, more well-woven lie. Catching him off-guard is the best way to get the truth.

I put a lot more effort into getting ready than usual. I step into the shower and wash my hair with volumising shampoo. I use my intense conditioning mask and sit on the shower floor while it sinks in. I shave my legs with Oscar's razor because it is a fact that men's razors are better and less expensive than the ones sold to women. I exfoliate and moisturise. Then I step into a new, expensive, sage-green summer dress. I take time doing my make-up even though it will mean I am late. As I buff light-reflecting concealer into my skin, I pretend all this effort is for me, an act of self-love, and not a desperate attempt to appear more attractive to my cheating fiancé than the woman he was secretly sharing chocolate cake with today. I curl my lashes and stroke bronzer across my cheeks. I do it all with a glass of wine in hand. It disappears quickly so I pour myself another. Once that's gone, I book an Uber.

If he is having an affair, I'll leave him. I'll have to, but the thought of no Oscar makes the wine turn over in my empty stomach. Oscar is funny, ambitious. He pays attention to every small detail of who I am. But he is most definitely a liar and most probably a cheat. I try to imagine myself having an affair. Feeling the weight of another man on top of me. The rush of new hands across my body. When I look up into this other man's face, it is one I know, jade-green eyes and dimples, coffee curls and stubble. An Irish burr in my ear as he thrusts into me.

In the hallway, outside Oscar's study, I wait for the Uber. I've never riffled through his things before. I've never snuck his phone and scrolled through it, either. I've never needed to. But now . . . I think of the blonde woman he was with. Determined not to be taken for an idiot, I slip inside his office. I feel awkward and ridiculous and guilty as I start moving things around on his desk. His laptop isn't here. So I pull open his drawers and shove my hands right to the back, fingers groping. I find only stationery and half-used notepads. No women's underwear or pack of condoms or anything else that would suggest he's been unfaithful. I'm about to close the drawer when I see a little silver tin. I pick it up. It's round with little roses carved into the lid.

Inside is a blonde lock of hair tied with dark green ribbon.

My insides clench, thinking of the blonde woman he was with today.

I'm welcomed at the front door by Helen. She has the same sandy hair and dark eyes as her son. As always, she's wearing a jumpsuit. I swear she has one in every colour known to man. I kiss her cheek and try not to think about the fact she has to get fully naked whenever she needs to pee.

Oscar is in the kitchen. I hover by the door for a moment, trying to get myself together before I follow Helen inside. I do not want Oscar to sense my mood. I don't want to talk to him about what I know until we are home.

I breathe in and breathe out.

Then I go inside.

I smile.

There is fancy French wine I can't pronounce and a cheeseboard of fancy French cheeses that will no doubt pair perfectly with the fancy French wine. Oscar turns to me and I'm swept into a memory of when we met, across a cheeseboard at the farm shop. He was tanned and lean and the smile he gave me sent shivers down my spine. Some people wait their whole lives to be smiled at like that. Does he smile at her like that, too?

He sweeps me into a kiss. I imagine him kissing that blonde woman the way he is kissing me now. I feel sick, but I give Helen and Oscar my dimples and my charm.

We eat. We talk. Or, *they* talk and I listen, providing head nods whenever is appropriate, but beneath it all, I am angry and getting angrier. I should be focusing on Olivia, not my relationship. Not this dinner. How could he be so selfish and dishonest? I try to give the man I love the benefit of the doubt, because maybe he isn't having an affair, but then, why lie? All those late nights. All the times he's swept his phone out of reach when I've entered a room or slapped his laptop shut. The new, mysterious project he's constantly working on.

I pick up my wine glass and drain what's left in it. I reach over for the new bottle and pour more in.

'Any further along with the wedding plans?' asks Helen, pulling me into the conversation. The engagement is the only thing she ever wants to discuss with me. Whenever I change the subject, she is disappointed, as though my betrothal to her son should be the single most defining characteristic of my personality.

I drag my heels. 'Nope.'

'Oh, well, that's a shame.' She sips her wine. 'A terrible shame. The two of you really ought to get a move on,' she's saying as though we are misbehaving schoolchildren. 'You don't want to be one of those couples who goes through life only ever being engaged. You do want your children to have the same surname as you, don't you, Caitie?'

I glare. 'Why wouldn't my children have my name?'

Silence. Helen shifts uncomfortably in her seat. She isn't used to me challenging her. I've long suspected that in the Fairviews' eyes, I am a cheap, spare part, an interchangeable accessory to Oscar's life, and they've deemed me adequate only because I am easy. But I am tired of being *easy*. Easy for my parents, picking the path I know they want me to tread. Easy for *his* parents, organising my weekends around them and keeping my mouth closed whenever they make outdated, offensive comments. Easy for him, folding away my own ambitions and storing them under the stairs like a collapsible ironing board to make more room for him and what he wants. Being easy is exhausting. 'Why wouldn't *my* children have *my* name?' I ask again.

I feel Oscar's gaze burning into the side of my skull.

'Well,' says Helen. 'Mothers give their children their father's name.'

'Why?'

'It's just the done thing.'

I open my mouth to tell her that if I'm the one battling morning sickness, sore tits and heartburn, going through the trauma of labour and having to be sewn back together afterwards, I would *not* crown my baby with the father's name simply because *it is the done thing*. To tell her that other than sperm, a man contributes nothing to the growth and birth of a child. To tell her that if it comes out of my body, it's getting *my* fucking name. But Oscar starts talking instead.

'We've actually decided a date for the wedding,' he says, with extra spoonfuls of enthusiasm. 'We'll be getting married next summer.'

Helen grabs this shiny distraction with both hands. 'That's marvellous!' She beams at her son. 'Oh, this *is* exciting. Maybe I won't be the last of my friends to have grandchildren, after all. A year isn't very far away though, Caitie, you really do need to organise yourself.'

I reach clumsily for my wine and see it is almost empty. 'I've been a little distracted by the whole long-lost sister thing.'

Silence.

Oscar clears his throat and moves to take the wine bottle away, but my fingers curl around it first. He's looking at me like I shouldn't be the way I'm being. I think I'm fine, personally. I'm not drunk. Or I am, a little, but that is a perfectly allowed thing to be.

Helen sets her own glass on the table and gives me a sympathetic head tilt. Still, I see the sliver of glee in her eyes, the excitement at sinking her teeth into a juicy piece of gossip. 'And how is she?'

'Mum . . .' says Oscar, shaking his head.

'You said I couldn't bring Olivia up unless Caitie did. Well, Caitie brought her up.'

'Olivia is struggling, actually. I had to help her fight off a panic attack today,' I tell her. 'But she doesn't like to talk about what happened. To be honest, if you want any information about my sister, just ask Oscar. He knows more than I do.'

He stiffens.

She frowns. 'What do you mean?'

'Rachel's husband works for the police. He told Oscar things he shouldn't have. Things my parents weren't even aware of.' Dropping him in it is petty and I'm not proud, especially since I promised I wouldn't tell anyone what I know, and maybe I'll regret it when I'm sober, but, for now, I enjoy seeing him squirm.

'Your cousin Rachel?' Helen asks him.

He stuffs garlic bread into his mouth and nods.

'But I thought Tim worked at that estate agent's in Midsomer Norton?'

My skin prickles. Slowly, I turn to Oscar. He avoids my eye. Was this another of his lies? If Rachel's husband didn't give Oscar that information, who did? And how does he know so much about my sister?

'He changed jobs last year,' he tells her.

'I saw Tim last month and he never mentioned it,' she says. 'But I suppose he and Rachel have had their hands full recently. That reminds me, Caitie, sweetheart, did you send them a gift?'

I tear my attention away from my fiancé. 'Who?'

'Rachel and Tim.'

'Why would I . . .'

'Rachel's had the baby.'

Why is it, as a woman, when you gain a partner, you also gain a pile of admin too? Remembering important dates and organising the corresponding gifts and cards for *his* family. Somehow, women become their partner's unofficial, unpaid PAs.

'Didn't you tell Caitie that Rachel and Tim had the baby? I told you to let her know.' Helen admonishes him in that half-hearted way mothers scold their sons because it's almost impossible for them to ever be truly angry with their perfect baby boys.

'I forgot. Work's been really hectic.'

I round on him. 'Yes, you're working a lot on that *exciting* new project lately and you've been in London *all* day, snowed under with back-to-back meetings, haven't you?'

His cheeks redden. 'Yeah.'

'All day,' I say again. 'In London?'

He frowns at me, trying to figure me out. I stare at him, seething, confused, desperate to know why he's lying. Helen, oblivious to the tension, thrusts her phone at us. Oscar takes it. 'Baby Violet,' she says. 'Isn't she gorgeous?'

'Oh, yeah, beautiful,' he enthuses.

I scoff.

I feel their eyes on me. I shake my head at Oscar. 'Why are you pretending to care? You *hate* babies.'

He splutters. 'No I don't.'

'You said babies cry a lot for people who don't pay rent or know what inflation is. You said *all* babies look like the wrinkly nut sacks they come from.'

'Oscar!' scolds his mother with more ferocity now. 'You didn't say that, did you?'

'No. No. I didn't.' He glares at me and I glare right back. He lies so easily. So easily. He lowers his voice. 'What's gotten into you?'

'You,' I say. 'Stop *lying*. Just stop it.' I fling my arm out and the jug topples and cracks. Water spills across the table.

Oscar apologises to his mother and I make a clumsy attempt to clean up the mess. After all, it's not the jug's fault my fiancé is a deceitful tosser.

'I'm going to take her home,' says Oscar to his mother, as though I am a toddler overdue a nap. I stand in the hallway now as the walls sway around me. The two of them talk quietly in the kitchen, probably about me and the state I'm in.

Then Oscar and I are outside, his arm around me as he steers me down the street. If I look over my shoulder, I know I'll see his mother standing on the driveway, watching fretfully on and telling herself she was right to have reservations about me. She'll convince herself it's because I haven't donned a wedding dress already, and I was behaving erratically tonight, but really it's because if mothers are honest with themselves, they don't think anyone is good enough for their sons.

Dusk has almost fallen but the heat from the day lingers. Once we round the corner, out of sight, Oscar tugs me to a halt. 'What the hell, Caitie?'

I shrug out of his grip. 'What were you doing today? Really?'

'Working.'

'In London?'

I see it click into place. He knows I know. He backtracks. 'Mostly. I came back to Somerset early afternoon.'

'And went to Bradford-on-Avon.'

'So what? You're stalking me now?' He gives me this incredulous little laugh that sets my teeth on edge.

'No. I was there with my sister. I saw you sharing dessert with another woman.'

'So you just *happened* to be in Bradford-on-Avon in the *exact* café where I was having lunch? You expect me to believe that?' he says, irritation hacking out like a cough. 'I can't believe you're following me. That isn't normal, Caitie.'

'How are you twisting this around? I saw you. With her.'

He steps close to me. Crowding me. He's angry, really angry. 'Stop playing games and just *fucking* ask me.'

I swallow thickly. This is new territory for us. Oscar and I don't fight. We bicker. We bicker about how he never uses the many coasters littered around the house and how I always leave my wet towels on the bed, but we do not fight. I lift my chin and meet his dark eyes. 'Are you having an affair?'

His mouth opens, as though he can't believe I asked him the question he was pushing for me to ask. 'You're insane! I am *not* having an affair.'

And he is so sincere, so convincing, it would be easy to believe him. To apologise for how awful I've been this evening and to spend the next week making amends but still, he has lied and been evasive. If he isn't having an affair, I am sure there is something he is hiding from me. 'So who is she? And why did you lie about being in London?'

'I DIDN'T LIE!' he bellows. Then he spins away from me, a ball of frustration. I stare at his back, watching the frantic rise and fall of his shoulders as he tries to rein himself in. I glance up and down the street to see if anyone heard him and has come outside to investigate. They haven't. Oscar turns and faces me again. 'I didn't lie. I just didn't give you a play-by-play of every hour of my day. I *was* in London this morning. I *was* in back-to-back meetings all day.'

'And who is she?'

'Someone I'm working with.'

'In your messages, you referred to her as "he".'

He throws his hands up. 'An honest mistake.'

'What's her name?'

'Samantha.'

Which makes sense since the name in Oscar's calendar was Sam. I start to believe him, and regret creeps in. Still, I have to be sure. 'What company does she work for?'

He pauses. Just a beat. Then, 'Adaline Fray Interiors.' I see the lie. Like some small animal scurrying past in the dark. 'I'm designing their new website. Sam is their head of marketing. It was a business meeting.'

I'm nodding, even though I *know* I'm being deceived. 'And this is the new project you've been so excited about?'

'They were recently featured in *Vogue*. It's a big deal. A big client.' He shakes his head, disappointment coming off him in waves. 'You really embarrassed me tonight. You embarrassed us both. How much have you had to drink?'

Shame colours my cheeks. I've had more than I should, more than I normally would. The wine sloshes through me along with the mortification. His version of events, his explanations, all make sense. Yet, I have this niggling feeling he's not being totally transparent. 'And what about the blonde lock of hair I found in your desk?'

He goes ridged. 'You went into my study?'

I swallow thickly. 'Whose hair is it?'

Fury comes off him like steam. 'Mine.'

'Yours,' I repeat, disbelieving.

'Yes. From my first haircut as a child. Mum gave it to me for my eighteenth birthday.'

I search his face for the lie. 'I just . . . I thought . . .'

'What? That me and my supposed mistress were exchanging locks of hair?' He closes his eyes. Pinches the bridge of his nose as though staving off a headache. 'Honestly, Caitie, it might do you some good to book in with your sister's therapist.' There's a flash of pain, like he's just tipped scalding tea onto my lap. 'I take it you had a few glasses before you came to Mum's?'

I nod solemnly.

'So you left the car at home?'

Another solemn nod.

He sighs. 'Fine. The train it is.'

Then he pivots and starts walking away. I watch him go. He doesn't turn to see whether I'm following. He becomes smaller and smaller before disappearing around another corner. He's gone. But I don't feel I'm alone. There are eyes on me. I look back in the direction of Helen's house and there, at the end of the street, a figure dressed in black watches. A figure with a nose too long to be natural. I feel a clench of something visceral and dark. I swing my gaze around in search of Oscar but he is out of sight. When I look back towards the end of the street, the masked man is gone.

22

Elinor Ledbury

Elinor calls an ambulance for her brother. There is an agonising wait but she sobs with relief as the flashing blue lights speed towards the manor. The paramedics ask her what happened. She and Heath made a pact years before to keep their uncle's temper quiet in case social services got involved and split them up, so she lies, telling the police and medical professionals that she has no idea who assaulted him.

At the hospital, after hours spent alone and terrified, her nails bitten and raw, she is told that although her brother has a gash to the back of his head, bruised ribs and a treasure trove of marks and cuts, he'll be OK. Uncle Robert has never attacked either of them this savagely before. And it is all Elinor's fault. She paces the glossy, white corridors of the ward, regret pounding through her like a second heartbeat. She loathes the unfamiliar, clinical smell of antiseptic and bleach. The sound of doctors and nurses rushing back and forth. The soles of their shoes squeaking on the vinyl. The beeping of so many machines.

It is impossible to get warm, even though she is still wearing Flynn's jacket. Only, there are bloodstains on the cuffs now. She shoves her hands into its pockets and that is when she finds the folded-up scrap of paper with a phone number and a note: *If you ever need ice-skating lessons. Flynn x*

She smiles a thin, watery smile. Then she goes in search of a phone.

He is with her in under an hour. She makes him promise not to ask if she's OK and bans him from talking about what happened – she doesn't want to think about it and doesn't want to have to lie to him, either. She longs for the simplicity of their afternoon spent on the ice and then tucked away in a coffee shop.

Elinor leads him to the little room that splinters off the main waiting area where she's spent most of the evening. She'd been drawn to the brightly coloured plastic chairs and the meadow mural painted across the back wall. It's only when Flynn points out they are in the children's entertainment area that she notices the half-empty box of toys squirrelled away in one corner. She blushes but makes no move to join the depressing, drab section reserved for adults. Besides, there are no children here. Just her and Flynn. He offers her a weak tea from the vending machine which she takes in her trembling hands but can't bring herself to drink.

'I, uh, haven't told Sofia about Heath. I figured you wouldn't want too many people around.'

She nods, relieved. She hadn't even thought about Sofia. 'Heath will call her when he can.'

'What about your uncle? He must be beside himself. Is he on his way back from London?'

She blanches. 'Yes,' she fibs. 'I found your purple stone,' she adds by way of distraction.

His face lights up. 'No way.'

She nods, a small smile playing about her lips.

'Fate,' he concludes. 'It was fate.'

She considers reminding him that stones don't move or blow away in the wind so, as long as he put it where he said he did, it would've been there another decade from now, but she doesn't for fear of spoiling this romance he is conjuring.

'I haven't read this in years,' he says, getting up and retrieving a hardback from the tiny bookshelf opposite.

'What is it?'

'*Rapunzel*.'

When she doesn't react, he says, "'Rapunzel, Rapunzel, let down your hair.'"

'I've never read it.'

He turns it over in his hands. 'You look like her.'

She takes it from him and flips through the pages. 'And so . . . is Ledbury Hall my prison tower?'

He arches a brow. 'Does that make Heath, or your uncle, the wicked enchantress?'

She swallows hard and looks away.

He clears his throat. 'Next you'll be telling me you've never seen a Disney film.'

'A Disney film?'

He gawps at her.

She shifts uncomfortably, feeling as though she is failing a test. '*Cinderella, The Little Mermaid, Pocahontas*?'

She shrugs. She doesn't like being reminded that she was brought up in a different world to everyone else. Before Flynn, it never bothered her, but with Heath leaving her alone more and more, Elinor feels like a flower reaching for the sun, trying to thrive out in the wild, but the differences Flynn points out make her feel less like a flower and more like an unwelcome weed.

Flynn grins. 'Don't worry, we can fix this.'

Anger flares like a struck match. 'I'm not a situation to be fixed.'

He reddens. 'I didn't mean . . .'

She sighs, guilt layering on top of guilt. She is tense, but Flynn isn't to blame. 'I'm sorry, I'm just . . . I feel terrible. What happened to Heath is my fault.'

'It wasn't. You couldn't have stopped someone breaking in and hurting your brother without getting hurt yourself, and nobody would've wanted that. Elinor, you're a good person, a good sister. Calling the ambulance probably saved his life.'

She starts to cry. He crouches in front of her, taking her face in his hands. His hands are so warm and she is still so cold. 'Elinor—' She kisses him. He kisses her back. Her arms wind around his neck and his hands move down to her waist. She doesn't think of girls trapped in towers or bloodied brothers or lead pipes. She thinks only of Flynn's mouth on hers. He tastes of tea and mint and glittering possibility.

23

Caitlin Arden

I told the police about the masked man, but they were sceptical and basically won't do anything to chase it up because I'd been drinking and Oscar didn't see anyone. It caused *another* row between the two of us.

'Maybe you're claiming to have seen him to distract from our fight,' he'd snapped at me after the police left.

'You think I'm *lying* about seeing my sister's abductor to smooth over the cracks in this relationship?'

'Seriously, Caitie, go and speak to someone because your dad is right: this isn't the way to go about getting attention.'

I moved out of our house three days after that dinner with his mother, and now I'm living in Blossom Hill House, back in my childhood bedroom, just as Olivia wanted. It looks nothing like it used to. The walls are an olive green and there is a huge cream rug over the hardwood floor. The bedding and curtains are all in soft whites and pale greys. A large White Company candle sits on the chest of drawers, filling the room with a sweet, floral smell.

Last night, I ducked into Olivia's room to say goodnight and found her thumbing through a copy of *Rapunzel*. It brought me right back to when we were little. Living with my parents makes me feel like a child: being called down for dinner, having Mum barge into my room without knocking, dealing with Dad's disapproval if I dare check my phone at the dining table. It's all a bit much. And even though things between Oscar and me are fraught, I find myself longing to be at home with him. He was shocked when I said I was leaving but he didn't fight it. But then, apart from our trip to St Ives, we've hardly seen each other these last few weeks. He's constantly working and I'm always at Blossom Hill House. We've never ever fought like this before, and I'm honestly grateful I have so much going on because it leaves me very little room to dwell on my relationship. And maybe some intentional time apart will be good for us. Maybe he'll miss me so much, he'll forgive me for accusing him of being unfaithful. I wince, the memory ricocheting back. Then I sweep it aside and assure myself things will eventually be OK.

Now, I am sitting at the dining table in the kitchen, sorting old photographs into piles to give to Olivia. Mum and Dad are back at work. The house is quiet. The swarm of paparazzi has all but gone, their attention grabbed by the grisly murder of a CEO's husband a few miles away. Lately, there are only ever one, or maybe two, reporters outside at any one time and always a police officer. The family-liaison officer assured us we'll be looked after while the investigation is ongoing. I suppose they can't promise they'll stay until Simon is caught, given his incarceration isn't guaranteed.

Olivia is going out with Florence. Again. I haven't been invited. Again. I mean, I have to be OK with it, don't I? They have sixteen years to catch up on. Besides, this afternoon, I've got my first appointment with Gideon, Olivia's therapist, so even if they'd bothered to ask me, I couldn't have gone. I breathe through the wave of jealousy. I'm still Florence's best friend. I'm still her maid of honour. And Olivia is still my sister. That means something. It means more.

With Oscar and me separated, and Olivia and Florence occupied, I have an opportunity to spend more time with Evie and Gemma. I realise now, hopefully not too late, that if friends are like flowers, I have watered and pruned and nurtured my relationship with Florence and let others wilt.

Olivia bounces into the kitchen in a short, silk dress, an oversized pair of sunglasses on her head and the emerald pendant around her neck. It still hurts that Mum just handed it to her after she'd promised it to me.

Olivia pulls two ice-cold water bottles from the fridge and sets one down for me. 'That house is pretty,' she says, leaning over to see the photograph in my hands.

It's of Uncle Donald's holiday home, Hathaway Cottage, in Castle Combe. It's like something from a postcard with its thatched roof, honey-brown stone walls and A-frame doorway flanked by hanging baskets. Inside is all wooden beams and flagstone floors and cosy rugs.

'Where is that?' asks Olivia.

I stare up at her, confused by her question. We joined Uncle Donald, Auntie Carol and our cousins Edward and Josie there every Easter, but I can see from the genuine interest on her face that she has no memory of it. 'It's Hathaway Cottage,' I answer slowly, waiting for her to laugh and reveal she's just winding me up, because of course she remembers it.

But she shrugs and makes her way over to the kitchen island. I stare after her, shocked she can't remember. *How* does she not remember?

'We spent weeks there every single year since we were born,' I tell her back incredulously.

She stills. Then takes a shiny red apple from the fruit bowl. She does not turn around. Does not meet my gaze. My bewildered, baffled, bulging gaze.

I get that feeling again, the crawling sense of unease I felt the day she turned up here, remnants of pink polish on her nails. The unease I shoved aside because my sister was *finally* home. My heart beats frantically beneath my ribs. Silence pulls taut between us, so tight I could reach out and pluck it like a violin string. Then, she spins on her heel and gives me her smile and her charm. 'Looking forward to seeing Gideon today? He's honestly brilliant.'

I nod dumbly. Beneath the swift change of subject and her nonchalance, I see something. Something wild and too still. Something coiled. My mind races. I need to choose my next words very carefully. 'I suppose it's been *years* since we were last at the cottage. A really long time, actually.'

She shrugs again, as though this entire conversation is boring, yet I see she is watching me, taking note of my response in the same way I am taking note of hers. She throws her apple up into the air and catches it one-handed.

'Uncle Donald and Auntie Carol have been thinking about selling Hathaway for a few years now,' I continue lightly, as though this is throwaway gossip. 'But Edmund got really upset about it.'

I wait, my breath locked in my chest. Will she notice my deliberate mistake – Edmund for Edward? Having no memory of the cottage could maybe be overlooked. After all, it's just bricks and mortar. But surely, *surely*, she will remember our cousin. She grew up with him. Their birthdays are only a week apart. If she corrects me, I have no reason to worry. But if she doesn't . . .

Please, I think, *please correct me.*

'Poor Edmund,' she says, nodding sympathetically. And I cannot believe . . . cannot believe my bear trap has snapped its jaws around her. She hasn't realised. In fact, she visibly relaxes even as my entire body stiffens. She blunders on, 'But I'm sure his parents won't sell if he asks them not to, right?' Her white teeth sink into the apple's flesh. Then her phone vibrates in her bag. 'That'll be Florence, I'd better go.' She presses a quick kiss to my cheek before bouncing out of the room and down the hall. A moment later, I hear the front door open and close.

The room tilts.

And doubt bleeds in properly for the first time.

Is that woman really my sister? And if she isn't, who is she and what does she want?

24

Caitlin Arden

Am I seriously considering that the woman sleeping in my parents' house isn't the real Olivia? The thought is absurd and I reject it almost immediately, but it rears its head over and over, and I find myself playing a version of Whac-A-Mole as I shower and dress. Eventually, I sit on my bed and take a minute to go over any evidence I have to suggest this woman isn't my sister. My thoughts are a jumbled tangle of necklaces shoved at the bottom of a bag, so I take out my phone and type up a list in an attempt to unpick them. I turn the brightness of the screen down until it's practically grey because I'm getting a headache. I start typing.

1. *She couldn't remember the gold-bee journal or The Boy on the Bus.*

This was the first red flag. I remember the night she was taken as though it's a scene from a movie I can stop and rewind. Surely it's the same for her? When she denied knowing anything about The Boy on the Bus and the journal he gave to her, I wondered whether she was trying to protect him. That perhaps he *was* her boyfriend and they did stage the abduction so they could run away together. That maybe, in the years that followed, that relationship turned sour so she came back. But now, I'm wondering if the reason she doesn't remember is simple: it never happened to her. After all, the public weren't made aware of the journal. It's a detail known only to a handful of people.

2. Her appearance when she arrived at the house.

Her hair had been recently cut; she had fewer split ends than I did. Even her tan was better than mine. And then there were her nails, short and neat with the remnants of pink polish. Maybe this isn't evidence of anything but I imagined a kidnap victim to be more unkempt or neglected. Olivia looked as though she'd not long stepped out of a salon.

3. She never reminisces about our childhood.

She tells me all the time that she missed me, but we never talk about our lives before she was taken. She reads her old diaries, and mine, as though they are novels. Maybe for her that's exactly what they are. Stories about someone else's life, and she's devouring them like champagne truffles because all research is useful research, especially when you're playing a character.

4. She doesn't remember Hathaway Cottage or our cousin Edward.

This is the most compelling piece of evidence I have. There's no way Olivia would forget. It's more than likely that my sister wrote about the cottage and our cousins in her diaries, but if this woman isn't Olivia, she's got at least five years of someone else's life to digest, remember and recite, which means gaps in her knowledge are likely. Gaps like holiday cottages and cousins.

Still, is this enough evidence to prove she isn't my sister? Am I certain that's even the case? Have I lost my mind for even *considering* she might be an imposter? And if she is, why am I the only one who spotted it? Surely the police did a DNA test to verify her claim . . . But if they didn't, and she's lying about who she is, why? What does she want? She let slip she'd been married. I believe that to be true.

She was mortified when she told me and no one is that good of an actress. So, if she isn't Olivia, maybe she's running from an abusive husband. Maybe that's who I've been seeing in the mask. But why run to a family she doesn't know? Perhaps the man she's running from is so awful, assuming someone else's identity is the only way she could escape.

I scrub my hands over my face, more confused than ever. I've already been accused of being attention-seeking and difficult; I can't voice my suspicion to anyone until I have solid proof. *If* there even is any. The thing is, she looks exactly how I imagine Olivia would look at twenty-nine. And she *feels* like a sister. That must count for something . . . mustn't it? Or maybe I've been so lonely and so guilt-ridden and so desperate to have her back, I've convinced myself she's Olivia because that is easier than accepting she's never coming back.

I save the notes to my phone, mind still sifting through it all, panning for the truth the same way others pan for gold.

By the time I arrive at Gideon's office, I'm composed. I sit on the expensive two-seater sofa while he sits in the highbacked armchair opposite. If it weren't for the notebook in his hands, you'd have no idea this was a therapy session. I was right about the dark furniture, I look around now at the mahogany desk and mahogany shelves and the mahogany cabinet in the corner. His office is cosy, all plush sofas and a large soft rug and floor-to-ceiling bookcases. Behind his desk is a gallery wall of his many awards and qualifications.

'Tell me about your week,' he says smoothly.

He leans back in his chair and the buttons of his white shirt strain against his broad chest. He is distractingly attractive. Maybe Oscar wouldn't have been so eager for me to attend these sessions if he was aware my therapist wouldn't look out of place on the front cover of a fitness magazine.

'I moved into Blossom Hill House.'

His brows quirk ever so slightly, as though he is surprised, yet approving, of this revelation. 'And how's that going?'

'I've only been there a couple of nights but I think Mum is enjoying having me home.'

'And your father?'

He's found a bruise and presses his thumb into it. I shrug, wanting to move on. But Gideon presses harder. 'You don't think he's enjoying having you home?'

Dad has barely spoken two words to me. I catch him looking at me as though I'm a stray that's wandered in off the street. It would be easy to lie to Gideon, but easy isn't always right, and something about him, about his wisdom and his confidence, about his strength and insight, makes me want to rub up against his attention like a cat that is invited. I decide to be honest.

'I don't think my father likes me very much.'

This pearl of truth spills from my mouth and rolls across the hardwood floor. He picks it up and examines it. 'What is it you believe he doesn't like?'

'He blames me for Olivia's abduction.' I tell him about the argument I overheard between my parents after she was taken.

'Do *you* believe what happened to Olivia was your responsibility?'

'I mean, I didn't hold the knife to her throat and walk her out into the woods, but I didn't get the police when I should have, either.'

He is supposed to remain neutral, but he lowers his notebook and his face creases with compassion. 'You were only a child.'

I shake his sympathy off like a horse refusing a saddle. 'But I knew to call the police in an emergency and I didn't.'

'Did you want your sister to disappear?'

'No.' This truth is absolute. It's no secret that even before Olivia was taken, she was the star of the show. I didn't mind. I was happy to be the supporting actress. When she disappeared though, like an understudy who hadn't learned her lines, I wasn't prepared. Despite my efforts, I never quite performed as well as she did, and my father knew it.

'So why didn't you call the police?' Gideon asks, without accusation.

'Terror.' I'm remembering it now, the kind of fear that turns your bones to cement.

'So you didn't make a conscious choice not to call for help?'

'No.'

'And so how can you or your father hold you responsible?'

'Conscious decision or not, my lack of action gave the masked man the chance to get away with her.'

'I disagree. Even if you'd called the police right away, there's no guarantee they would've found her, Caitie.'

I dig my nails into my palms to stop myself from crying. Tears don't change the past. I am not that same terrified little girl anymore. Gideon is leaning closer. I get the feeling he wants to reach out and touch me. 'Either way, my father thinks it's my fault and he hates me for it.'

He scrawls in his notebook. 'Have you ever discussed this with him?'

I shake my head.

'Why?'

I swallow. Then I take a magnifying glass and hover it over my reasons, over the thick frost that coats my relationship with my father. 'I'm worried the blame he places on me isn't the sole reason he doesn't like me.'

This piques Gideon's interest. 'Go on.'

'I worry that he's the only person who can really see me. I've tried to live my life in a way I knew would please my parents but . . . I . . .' The words are on the tip of my tongue like beads of poison. I spit them out. 'I *resent* them. I resent my parents, even though it isn't their fault. They didn't force me to live a certain way, but I knew if I did what I wanted to, they'd be disappointed. And with Olivia gone, I owed them a perfect daughter. But I'm not perfect, I'm not Olivia, and my father can see it's all an act. He can see who I am at my core and *that's* the person he doesn't like.'

'And who is that person?'

'She's someone who wants to travel the world and paint it. She doesn't care about owning a home or having a steady income, at least, not right now. She's not sure she ever wants to get married or have children. She doesn't want roots.'

'Why?'

'Roots keep you anchored to one place and leave you vulnerable, because once they're chopped away, you're felled.' I laugh self-consciously through my tears. 'Sorry, I'm not making sense.'

He gets up and takes a tissue box from his desk. He crouches and hands me one. He doesn't go back to his armchair. I breathe him in, sea salt and sage, lemongrass and clean skin. 'The person you described isn't dislikeable.'

If I lean my forehead down, it will touch his. His skin would be warm. This is so intimate. I can feel the heat coming off his body. I want to curl up in it. 'But I can't be her,' I tell him. 'It's too late. If I went travelling now, I'd be abandoning the life I've built with Oscar.'

'Are you happy, Caitie?'

This question takes me by surprise, because how often does someone look you in the eye and ask if you're happy? How often do you ask yourself that same question?

I look past him, out the window. It's so quiet here in this tucked-away side street. The kind of quiet that forces you to listen to your own thoughts. 'Sometimes, I wonder if I'm even capable of real happiness.' Admitting this makes me feel as though I'm betraying Oscar because he does make me happy and I love him so much that the thought of being without him snatches the air from my lungs. But am I as happy as I could be? Gideon waits. He wants more. I plunge deeper into the weeds of myself and find what he's waiting for. 'I have all these brilliant things – a house, a career, a family, a fiancé, my . . .' I was going to say 'sister' but now I am riddled with doubt so I clamp my mouth shut around the word. 'I have all these things yet my happiness feels dull, like an echo.'

'Is it possible the reason you don't ever feel truly happy is because you don't allow yourself access to the things you really want?'

It's true. I feel how true it is. I lie back and bathe in it, letting it lap against my skin like cool water on a blistering day. 'Maybe real happiness is living the life you want, the way you want, without worrying about other people's expectations.'

He grins and I know I've just found a pot of gold. 'You just have to be braver.'

As our eyes meet, I feel that crackling, zinging tension again.

He clears his throat and goes back to his armchair. Even though I shouldn't, I miss the closeness immediately. 'You haven't talked very much about Olivia. How has it been having her back? Living with her again?'

At the mention of her, my pulse kicks. 'Great.'

He's watching me carefully. 'Nothing you'd like to add?'

'That's it.'

Silence. I feel my cheeks heat under his scrutiny. 'Is there something you want to discuss?'

I shake my head and reach for the glass of water on the side table.

'Caitie.' He holds my name in his mouth as though it is something precious. Those jade eyes stare right into the depths of me. 'I'm here to listen. You, right now, are my sole priority. As long as we're in this room, you have my undivided attention but that's only useful if you seize it.'

I lick my lips. 'You're going to think I'm mad. You'll have me sectioned.'

'You seem perfectly sane to me.'

'Is that a professional assessment or a personal one?'

His mouth quirks up into a grin. 'Both.'

I relax a little. I *need* to tell someone about my suspicion. I need to know if I could be right. 'Olivia . . . she . . .' I fight to find the words. I'm looking for a spoonful of sugar to make them more palatable, but there aren't enough granules in Guatemala to sweeten my doubt. 'I'm not sure that the woman who came back is really my sister.'

Silence.

My skin prickles. He's perfectly still and working very hard not to give away what he's thinking. 'I don't understand.'

I am too hot. Far too hot. I get up. I start pacing. 'She claims to be Olivia Arden, but is she? Was a DNA test ever done to verify her claim? Is that something the police do?'

'I'm sure if they had any concerns regarding her identity they'd have notified your family.'

'But she's an adult. Can they force her to give up her DNA? I just . . . I'm not sure if she's telling the truth.' My heart beats so hard, I feel it in my fingertips.

'Why?'

'Little things at first, and now bigger ones, too. It just doesn't add up. I made a list on my phone. Can I . . .'

'Of course.'

I retrieve it from my bag and read it out to him. Somehow, we have both ended up sitting on the same sofa. He listens intently, and when I'm done he says, 'Have you raised this concern with anyone else?'

'No. I can't. I'm not even sure this is evidence of anything.'

'If she is Olivia, and everything she's said happened to her is true, she's suffered a terrible trauma. We don't yet know the extent of physical duress she experienced. If she's suffered a head injury at any point, her long-term memory could be impacted. Not remembering places or people, even ones that are otherwise significant, could be a result of that.'

I stare down at the phone in my hands and feel ridiculous because that had never occurred to me.

'You aren't insane, Caitie,' he assures me. 'If you have a gut feeling, you should explore it. Get to the bottom of it. Even if you don't find anything that supports your theory, you may at least come away with a better understanding of why you felt the way you did.'

I nod. We lapse into silence. He may not have known Olivia *before* that abduction but as a trained therapist, he should be able to read people quite well. 'Do you think she's really Olivia?'

'If I had any substantiated concerns, I'd flag it with the relevant professionals,' he tactfully rebuffs me.

'But if she was dangerous, would you know? From your sessions I mean.'

His smile is wry. 'If all it took to detect a dangerous individual was a few conversations, the world would be a much safer place. At the moment, you're the best person to answer your own questions.' He shifts. He's so close, his knee presses against mine. 'Don't be afraid to play the main character in your own life. Don't be a person that things just happen to because it's easier than being a person who makes things happen.'

25

Caitlin Arden

Olivia's voice rises and falls above me as I stand in the hallway of Blossom Hill House. Silently, I close the front door and move to the foot of the stairs. I can't make out the words, but I hear the urgency, the sharp snap of her tone. I creep up each step, avoiding the creaky ones as I go. She's in her room, the door part-way open.

'What am I supposed to do now?' she says.

A pause.

'But she *knows* something. She—'

Silence. A different kind of silence. Not a pause in conversation as she listens to whoever is on the other end of the phone. The kind of silence that makes the tiny hairs on the back of my neck rise.

My insides twist as the door swings open. Our eyes meet. Her surprise at seeing me quickly hardens to anger. She slams the door shut and I skitter back down the stairs. I'm pacing the kitchen, wondering how I can explain my eavesdropping, when I see a mobile on the kitchen island. I pick it up. It's Olivia's. The one I gave to her. So then, whose phone was she using just now?

'What're you doing?' I jump at the sound of Olivia's voice and pivot towards her. She's standing so close; we are almost nose to nose. 'That's mine,' she says and holds out her hand, palm up, just as she did with the gold-bee journal all those years ago. Back then, she was determination and sugar. Now, she is steel and ice. A stranger.

Panic and that sickening feeling of being caught swirls in my stomach as I relinquish the phone. 'Who were you talking to?'

'When?'

'Just now, you were on the phone.'

'I wasn't.'

'I heard you.'

Her smile is cold. 'I wasn't on the phone. How could I be when it was down here?'

'My question exactly.'

Deciding the conversation is over, she turns away from me and opens the kitchen drawer.

But I refuse to be dismissed. 'Only drug dealers have two phones, Olivia.'

She turns, brandishing a knife as long as my forearm. A cold, clammy bolt of fear shoots through me as I realise I am alone with her. 'Well, I wouldn't know anything about that.' Then she takes a large bar of dark chocolate from the fridge and chops it into smaller pieces. The sound of the knife hitting the wooden board jangles my nerves. She tips the chocolate into a bowl, leaving the knife on the side. It feels like a threat. She slinks towards me and simpers with feigned concern. 'You seem really tense, Caitie. You should go for a lie down.' Then she pops a square of chocolate onto her tongue and smiles like she has won.

She is a completely different person to the one she was this morning. Like a switch has been flipped. An actor changing roles, swinging from damsel to villain.

As she walks away, I hear Gideon telling me to be braver. To be a person that makes things happen. 'Our cousin's name is Edward. Not Edmund,' I tell her. I want her to know I'm onto her. That she hasn't won because the game isn't over.

She pauses, the hand that was reaching for the door suspended in mid-air. Slowly, she turns, and though she appears composed, I can tell I've ruffled her perfect feathers. She closes the distance between us. Her gaze travels leisurely over my face. Her eyes narrow. 'If you have something to say, little *sister*, just come out and say it.'

It is a dare. My heart races in response, breaths coming hard and fast. But I can't. The words stick to the roof of my mouth. Not because I'm afraid or because I think I might be right, but because I am desperate to be wrong.

Her smile is all satisfaction and triumph. 'Didn't think so.'

I go to bed early but can't sleep. I toss and turn and remember Olivia reading me *The Princess and the Pea* when we were children, only the pea that bruises my back now is the hardening certainty that she isn't who she claims to be. While the girl I split a crème brûlée with, who pealed with laughter repeating 'aureolin' in the park, felt like my sister, the woman downstairs who lied and smirked, did not. All the sisterly moments that came before the confrontation in the kitchen were an act. How far is she willing to go to keep it up? And what will she do to me if she thinks I could expose her? Is this a scam? If so, what's the goal? Money, fame, revenge? But revenge for what? And who was she on the phone to earlier? I must find her second mobile. Maybe she was talking to the masked man. It's possible they're working together. But to what end? And how do I play this game if I don't know the rules?

I could go to the police with my suspicions, but once that inevitably gets back to my parents, they'll be devastated. They think they have their little girl back. If I try to come between them now, I won't be believed. I need irrefutable proof. I need that phone.

I'm not sure what wakes me, but I am ripped from a dream I can't remember. The only feeling worse than waking up alone in the dark is sensing that you aren't alone at all. I lie still, blinking into the blackness of my bedroom. My phone is on the nightstand but I am too afraid to reach for it. There's the steady rhythm of someone else's breath in this room. I *feel* them in here with me. In my peripheral, a figure emerges. Heart in my throat, I whip my head towards it.

'Olivia?' I breathe.

Eyes adjusting to the gloom, I make out her waist-length hair and lithe limbs. She drifts closer. A silent ghost. She looms over me. A crush of fear presses down, squeezing the breath out of my body and holding me in place. She could have a knife. She could plunge it into my flesh and bone and I will bleed to death in this bed. I open my mouth to beg for my life but only a whistle of air escapes. Then she steps back. Moves towards my bedroom door and leaves without a word. When I'm sure she's gone, I push myself onto my elbows and stare after her; my heart still pounds. The house is silent now. It wasn't a dream. It wasn't . . . Was it?

I climb out of bed and turn down the hall towards her room. The door is ajar and through the gap I see her sleeping soundly. Am I *losing* my mind?

Crawling back to bed isn't an option, I know I won't sleep. So I go downstairs to make a tea. I'm quiet and don't turn on any lights in case I wake my parents, though the kettle sounds like a small rocket taking off. There's enough moonlight streaming in through the window that I find the teabags and mugs with ease. By the time I'm filling it with boiling water, I've convinced myself I dreamt Olivia in my room.

I'm halfway out of the kitchen, tea in hand, when I hear *scratch*, *scratch*, *scratch*, behind me. I stop. Dread starts in the pit of my stomach and slowly replaces my blood pint for pint.

It comes again, louder this time.

Scratch, scratch, scratch.

I need to turn around. I know I need to turn around. There is someone behind me and I need to turn around. I take a breath. And slowly, I pivot. The shock is immediate. There, pressed up against the kitchen window, is the man in the Venetian mask. Closer to me now than he has been in sixteen years. The long, curved nose and furious, furrowed brow makes that old terror yawn open inside me; it rushes up and out of my mouth on a scream. I leap back and tea sloshes over the rim of my mug, splashing across my hand. I scream again, this time in blistering pain. I drop the mug and it shatters. More scalding tea is thrown across my bare feet and up my legs. Above me comes the thunder of frantic footfalls. A moment later, my mother tumbles into the kitchen. 'What is it? I heard a scream. Are you OK? What happened?'

The light is flicked on and I am momentarily blind. Dad pushes into the kitchen, Olivia at his heels. All three pairs of eyes, wide with panic, are fixed on me.

Mum spots the smashed mug and my red, raw hands. 'Caitie!' She grabs them for a better look. I yelp. 'Cold water. Now.'

Terror still writhing beneath my skin like a living thing, I look towards the window. Towards the masked man. But he's gone.

'What were you doing making tea in the bloody dark?' Dad barks at me as Mum ushers me to the sink.

I pull back, rearing like a defiant horse. 'No,' I burble. 'No.' Mum reaches for me again. 'Stop! Listen, the masked man was here. At the window.'

'What?' says Olivia, backing away. 'He's . . .' she splutters. 'He's here?'

Dad rips open the French door as Mum yells for him to stay inside. He barrels outside, barefoot and unarmed. Ignoring the blistering, tight skin across my burned feet, I sprint in the opposite direction, towards the police officer still stationed in a car outside the front of the house. The second he sees me stumbling up the path, he bolts into action. Soon I am back in the kitchen waiting with shredded nerves as he and my father search the garden. Olivia has shut herself upstairs in the bathroom where Mum tries unsuccessfully to soothe her. If Olivia *isn't* Olivia, she deserves a fucking Emmy, but I don't have time to dwell on that before Dad and the police officer return.

'There's no one there,' says Dad, the unmistakable snap of accusation clear. And when he looks at me, I see it in his eyes too: *liar*.

26

Elinor Ledbury

Uncle Robert hasn't returned to Ledbury Hall in the three weeks since he viciously beat Heath. For the first fortnight, Heath stayed at home with Elinor while she took care of him, cooking his meals, making sure he took his medication, reading to him. They shared a bed every night and it felt good to have her brother back, even if he was worse for wear. He suffered nightmares, ones that left the sheets damp with sweat. She apologises again and again for the part she played in what Uncle Robert did. She relayed to her brother the conversation she overheard at the party, explaining why it was so important. Heath didn't say much but she could see him turning the information over in his head.

Last night, in bed, he tucked her against his chest and whispered, 'I've missed this.'

'Me, too,' she said into the dark.

After a moment, he said, 'He's a coward.' He was, of course, talking about Uncle Robert. 'The way he snuck up behind me. I won't let it happen again, Ellie. Next time I set eyes on him, I'll kill him.'

'You can't kill him,' she said. 'I'm not convinced we'd get away with it.'

'Ye of little faith.' He smoothed her hair across the pillow. 'Where were you that evening? When I came home, you were gone.'

She swallowed, glad he couldn't see her face. 'Walking the grounds.' The lie tasted like blackened ash on her tongue. 'And where had *you* been all day?'

He kissed her shoulder. 'Running errands.'

Well, at least now we're both lying, she thought, and took his hand in hers.

In the morning, when she woke, she was alone. She knew Heath was with Sofia now, so she didn't feel guilty that she'd spent the past week with Flynn. They'd walked hand in hand around the frozen lakes, visited the cinema where he kissed the salted popcorn from her mouth, whiled away an afternoon in a bookshop. Flynn treated her to as many paperbacks as she could carry. She waited for him to sneer as she browsed the romance section. He didn't. They took them back to Ledbury Hall and read them in front of the fire, her legs in his lap.

She'd given him a tour of the grounds and was surprised by how much she enjoyed it, assuming that sharing Ledbury Hall with anyone except Heath would feel like letting a stranger riffle through her underwear drawer. It wasn't like that with Flynn. He'd marvelled at the turrets and lead lattice windows, the handsome red brick and the intricate carved arch that made up the porch, whistling long and low on the stone steps leading into the house. 'You can tell someone is wealthy if their front door is twice as tall as they are.'

She stuck out her tongue and tugged him inside. He was curious but respectful, not touching anything unless she gave it to him. The manor is filled with first edition books, embroidered pillows, ivory chess sets, carnival masks, taxidermy animals mounted on plaques. Everywhere, there are beautiful things collected by her parents on their worldly travels. Flynn's favourite was the marble bust of Aphrodite.

'Heavy,' he said, handing it back to her.

'She's the Greek goddess of love.'

He kissed her then.

She led him up to the roof. From there, you can see across the grounds for miles and miles, and in every direction. She pointed out the rose garden and the pond that was almost the size of a lake, with its stone lovers.

'Do you swim in it?' he asked.

She didn't want to admit she was too terrified to try so she said,

'One night, we should bring some blankets up here, some candles, watch the sun set.'

He grinned. 'Definitely.'

They kissed again, right there on the roof.

Now, they are in her bedroom, on her bed. Flynn is on top of her, kissing her neck. She runs her hand under his jumper, dragging her nails across his warm skin. He moans, covering her mouth with his. Then he pulls back. 'I've been thinking,' he tells her. 'Come to South Africa with me.'

She laughs it off. 'I can't. I don't even have a passport and I'm not likely to get a ticket on goodwill.'

But he is serious. He goes on, 'I get that your uncle controls your money but there's so much stuff in this house you could sell. I can tell you're lonely here, Elinor.' He brushes her hair away from her face. 'You don't have to be lonely anymore. Not with me.'

She feels as though she is standing on the precipice of something great, and if she were to jump she'd be safe because she'd leap with his hand firmly around hers. She reaches up and kisses him again. He starts unbuttoning her dress. Beneath the music is their excited panting breath. She does not hear her brother climbing the stairs. Does not hear him standing outside her door. She only notices him when he kicks it open in a brilliant burst of noise. Elinor and Flynn spring apart.

Heath moves fast. He grabs Flynn by the jumper and swings him off the bed, slamming him so hard into the wall, Elinor is worried he might go through it.

She stumbles to her feet. 'Heath!'

'What the fuck are you doing with my little sister?' he growls.

'Get off me!' Flynn shouts. 'Get off!'

'Heath, stop!' she begs. 'Let him go.'

Flynn throws a punch but Heath ducks and then pivots still holding double fistfuls of Flynn's jumper. He rams Flynn into the adjacent wall. He brings his face close to Flynn's. 'She's fifteen fucking years old.'

Flynn pales, gaze darting to Elinor's. He looks as though he might be sick. She frantically shakes her head, refuting her brother's lie.

179

'I think the police would be really interested to know I caught you undressing a fifteen-year-old in my house, don't you?' Heath sneers.

'That isn't—' she starts, but at a look from her brother, so acidic it makes her skin burn, she closes her mouth.

Heath lets Flynn go.

Flynn, shaken, pushes his fingers back through his hair and stares at her with abject disgust and slapping disappointment. Elinor feels as though each of her bones is breaking. She wants to go to him, to tell him her brother is lying, but she is rooted to the spot, pinned there by Heath's fury.

'Leave,' he barks at Flynn.

Without another word, Flynn goes, almost tripping over his bare feet on the way out. Heath is stony and silent. Neither he nor Elinor move until they hear the front door slam closed. Then, unbelievably, Heath begins to laugh. 'Jesus, Ellie, *that's* your type? Flynn Healy? He's like a fucking golden retriever.' He walks past her and thumps casually down onto her bed, resting his arms behind his head. He appraises her. 'Little sister, sort out your dress.'

With trembling hands, she buttons it. 'What is wrong with you?'

'Did you expect me to stand at the foot of the bed and film it? Or would you prefer I joined in?'

'Don't be glib,' she snaps. 'You lied to him.'

His faux joviality evaporates and he springs to his feet. 'No, *you* lied to him. What did you promise him? A future? A house? A bounding pup and a couple of kids? You aren't meant for him.' His eyes are like two knife points piercing her skin. 'Did you fuck him?'

She lifts her chin. 'Did you fuck Sofia?'

He stills, caught off guard, then says, 'Flynn told you.'

'No. I *saw* you.' She can't stop the tears welling. She shakes her head, refusing to let them fall. 'I was worried, I went to town to find you and I saw the two of you together.'

He's surprised. 'You went into town alone?'

'Yes! Weeks ago because I'm not . . . Rapunzel, Heath. Ledbury isn't a . . . a . . . prison tower and you aren't my keeper.'

His lips twitch. 'Rapunzel?'

'Fuck you.' She makes to leave but he grabs her arm.

'It isn't what you think.'

'Isn't it?' She glowers at him and wonders what her life would have been like if she'd had a sister instead of a brother. In this moment, she wishes she did.

'Sofia doesn't mean anything to me.'

'You invited her to our home the night of the party.'

He's shaking his head. 'She just turned up. I sent her away. I'm only with her because she's useful.'

She shrugs him off. 'I bet she is.'

He sighs. 'She got me a job at the music shop.'

'A job?' She frowns. 'Why do you need a job?'

'Because we have no money. No way out. Robert has everything.'

'But when you turn twenty-one . . .'

'*If* I turn twenty-one. He tried to kill me.'

'No, he—'

'We're more useful to him dead than alive, because with us out of the way, the money, the estate, all of it goes to him. So I got a job. *That's* where I go every day. I've been saving my wages.'

'Why?'

'Because you're the most important thing in the world, Ellie. The only important thing. I thought if I could get enough together for us to leave, you'd be safe.'

Her stomach churns. 'Leave our home?'

'Just until I'm old enough to come back and claim the inheritance. Or, at least, my half of it.'

She knows the reason Heath hid this from her is to protect her. To stop her worrying. He is forever protecting her. She wants to insist that Uncle Robert doesn't want them dead, but she can't because after the lead-pipe incident she believes Heath to be right.

He sighs. 'Not that I'll be welcome back to the shop once Flynn tells Sofia what happened.'

Guilt coats her skin like a sheen of sweat. 'Look, Uncle Robert doesn't need the Ledbury fortune. He has money because he has his fancy career.'

'Does he? After the stunt you pulled, I don't think that's likely. They'll give his position to his colleague.'

'Johnathan Jones.'

'Yes. The one who doesn't have a pyromaniac for a niece.'

She covers her face with her hands. 'I'm sorry.'

Gently, he tugs her hands away and holds them in his. 'I don't need you to be sorry. I need you to do better.' He pulls her to him, holding her against his chest. She breathes in his familiar scent. 'Don't worry about Robert. If he ever touches you, I'll kill him.'

27

Caitlin Arden

Any hope I had of being vindicated dissolves the following evening when the police reveal they've found no evidence of the masked man's presence. The security camera covers the back door but not the window. Forensics weren't able to lift a shoe print from the garden, either. They say this could be because it's mostly paved and the earth is bone dry. No fingerprints were found on the gate or the glass but he most likely wore gloves. What they don't say, but do leave in the silences to be discovered and unwrapped, is that maybe he was never here at all and I am either delusional or lying.

Dad turns on me the second the police leave, all simmering rage and resentment. 'What is wrong with you?'

'I saw him,' I insist, but he looks at me as though I am a hysterical child, claiming Bigfoot is living under her bed. 'You don't believe me.'

'Caitie, love, he isn't saying he doesn't believe you,' assuages Mum, trying to build bridges out of sand.

'Do you?' I ask him with so much hope because I want so desperately to be believed. I want my father to pull me into his arms and whisper soothing things into my hair like he did the night Olivia was taken. 'Do you believe me?'

'No one else has laid eyes on him. No one. How do you explain that?'

'I was the only one down here! If *you'd* been in the kitchen, or Mum, then—'

'Why would he risk coming to this house just to stand outside the window on the slim possibility you'd wander into the kitchen?'

I hadn't stopped to consider why he was here. Seeing him had been such a terrible shock, it has eclipsed everything else. Dad is right. It was a risk – with the police so close by the masked man could've been caught – and to what end? Just to scare me? That doesn't seem likely. I shake my head. 'I don't know.'

'He was never there, Caitlin.'

'So you think I'm lying?'

He takes a step closer. I sometimes forget how tall my father is. He's at his tallest right now, towering over me in the hallway. 'I think you were the centre of our attention for a very long time and now you aren't.'

The acid that drips from his mouth hurts more than the scalding tea.

Mum starts scrabbling around in the sand again, even as the tsunami looms. She lays a hand on my father's shoulder. 'Myles, let's talk about this tomorrow when everyone is less fraught.'

She looks imploringly to me. It would be better for everyone if I back down, apologise, lean into his narrative that I am an attention-seeking liar, refusing to share my parents with my sister. I open my mouth, the apology on the tip of my tongue, but then I hear Gideon telling me to be braver.

'No, let's talk about it now,' I insist, fixing my gaze on my father. 'What attention did I ever get from you growing up? You were *always* working. I've seen more of you in the last three weeks than I have in the last sixteen years.' My laughter is hollow. 'I've wasted so much of my life trying to win your pride and for what? So I could stand here while you accuse me of being an attention-seeking brat?'

'He didn't say that,' Mum argues.

'He didn't have to.' I look to my father, expecting more bullets, more insults, more anger. Instead he seems defeated. Seems to shrink. I wait for the wave of triumph that doesn't come. His melancholy is somehow worse than his hatred.

'You gave us all a fright last night, Caitie,' Mum tells me, picking up the gun my father has apparently dropped.

'*I* gave you a shock? What about the psycho who broke into our garden?'

'Caitlin,' she breathes, wary and irritated. 'There was no sign of him.'

'What about the woods behind the house? The old shed, did they check that?' I ask, remembering Olivia used that shed as a landmark to find the road.

'What shed?' asks Mum.

'The one in the woods.'

She frowns. 'A homeless man illegally built that ten years ago. I thought the council tore it down. It's dangerous, Caitie, no one is hiding in there.'

Dread pulses through me. Ten years . . . the shed is only ten years old. If that's true, how did Olivia know about it when she went missing sixteen years ago? Over half a decade before it even existed?

'Mum,' says Olivia from her place at the foot of the stairs. 'This isn't Caitie's fault.'

'Don't.' I round on her because she is an insidious imposter and if it wasn't for her meddling in our lives, I wouldn't be in the middle of a row with both my parents. 'Don't you dare defend me. You don't even know me.'

'Caitlin!' berates Mum.

'How did you know about that shed?' I spit at her.

'What're you talking about?'

Of course she's feigning ignorance. I try again. 'Why were you in my room last night?'

She wrinkles her nose. 'I wasn't.'

'You were. I woke up and you were standing over my bed.'

The three of them share a look, as though I'm a pyromaniac waving around a can of petrol and a box of matches. 'Caitie, that wasn't me. I didn't go into your room. I would never.'

'You're *lying*.'

Her eyes are so wide with sham innocence, her baby-doll lashes almost touch her perfect brows. 'I'm not lying but I am worried about you.'

She reaches out and rests a patronising hand on my shoulder. I slap it away. The sound echoes, bouncing off the walls. Olivia's bottom lip wobbles expertly. My parents are horrified. And it's too much. All too much. I go upstairs and pack a bag.

* * *

Staying another night in Blossom Hill House, where the atmosphere is so thick, I could slice it up and serve it on sourdough, isn't an option. No one said a word as I left, my overnight bag slung over one shoulder. Now, I sit in the car outside my house. Mum hasn't even sent one of her worrisome 'Are you home yet, sweetie?' messages. In fact, since Olivia came back, they've stopped altogether. I never thought I'd miss them.

I left a voicemail for Oscar earlier, explaining I was coming home, at least for tonight, but he must be locked away in his study again with his headphones on because he hasn't replied.

As I let myself in, I see his study light is on. I hear him moving around, but when I call out to him, he doesn't reply. Sighing, I take my bag upstairs and change into the silk pyjamas Oscar always compliments. Back in my own home, breathing in the familiar scent of our house, I'm finally able to relax, tension flowing out of me like melted snow.

A loud bang from downstairs makes me jump. Leaning out of the bedroom door, I shout down to Oscar. 'Everything alright?'

I wait. Silence greets me.

'Oscar?' I yell.

My phone vibrates in my hand. I stare down at the caller ID, confused. Oscar is phoning me. *Why* is Oscar phoning me when we're in the same house? Then I realise with his headphones on, he isn't even aware I'm back. I roll my eyes and answer the call as I make my way downstairs to see him.

'I'm home,' I tell him by way of greeting.

'Sorry, just picked up your voicemail.' Oscar is somewhere loud and busy. 'I'll be back soon.'

Outside of his office now, I freeze. The door is part-way open, the light glows softly beyond it. I hold my breath to listen. Inside, someone is riffling about. Someone who isn't Oscar.

'Caitie? You still there? Can you hear me?'

I squeeze the phone, terror pulsing through me. 'You . . . you aren't home?'

'No.'

My insides clench.

Fear snakes through me.

I glance down at the little key in the lock.

My hand whips forward, but before I can turn it, the door is flung open. I see the mask a second before I am tossed aside. I hit the ground so hard, all the air whooshes out of me. My phone cracks against the skirting board, out of reach. Chest burning, I gasp into the wood. I cannot breathe. I feel him standing over me and I throw myself onto my back. He is swathed in black: black boots and black jeans, black gloves and a black hoodie. He is built like a barn door. I open my mouth to scream but he lunges, snatching my wrist and hauling me up. I am slammed against the wall, pinned there by the hardness of his body. He brings his face close to mine and I stare up into black holes where his eyes should be. Another scream rushes like bile, but his gloved hand comes down over my mouth. I kick and flail. He secures me easily. Still holding me in place, he stomps. Once. Twice. Three times. Breathless, I see the shattered screen of my phone at our feet. My only hope of calling for help now lies in pieces.

'Please,' I whisper into his hand, but my plea is muffled by the leather. The smell of it clings to the back of my throat and makes me think of stretched, bloodied skin. He's going to kill me. I am going to die in this hallway. I scream again. He moves fast, grabbing me by the throat, cutting off my cry for help. For several terrifying seconds, I can't breathe. He swings me to the side and throws me backwards with frightening ease. I tumble into Oscar's office and land in a bruised, panting heap.

The masked man slams the door shut. I hear the key turning in the lock on the other side. But I'm not trapped. I scramble to my feet, stagger to the window and unlock it. I throw it open and look down. Thank God his office is on the ground floor. I climb up onto the window ledge and jump.

28

Caitlin Arden

When Oscar heard me scream on the phone, he called the police. They found me racing down the street. They searched the house and found no sign that the masked man had ever been there. No forced entry, no fingerprints, nothing. Both the front and back doors were locked and when I made my escape out the window, I had to unlock it first.

'He must have a key,' I tell Oscar and the police because this is the only explanation.

I am met with puzzled, disbelieving silence.

'And how would he have gotten that?' asks one of the police officers in a voice I imagine she doesn't think is patronising.

Olivia, I think, 'I don't know,' I say.

'That theory doesn't stand,' interjects Oscar. 'Not unless you've been handing our keys out to strangers?'

'Of course not.'

'You say he locked you in the office so you went out the window?' asks the officer, ignoring the rising tension between me and my fiancé.

I nod.

She exchanges a look with her colleague. 'The thing is, Miss Arden, the door to the office isn't locked.'

I stare at her, dumbfounded. I *know* he locked me in. I heard the unmistakable click of the key turning.

Oscar sighs.

I start picking at the skin around my nails, wishing they'd all stop looking at me as though I'm a circus freak. Still, I can't blame them for not believing me. Nothing has been taken from the house. Our laptops and TV, my jewellery and any cash we had, were left untouched. On the phone, Oscar heard my petrified scream, but the masked man was silent throughout the assault. The only evidence that he was ever in the house is the ruffled state of Oscar's office, my broken phone and the bruises up my arms, like smudges of ink. But these are things I could've done myself. The police humour me, at least, taking my statement. Oscar holds my hand throughout, but it's weak and feels perfunctory. There's no warmth in his touch, no reassurance or safety. The police tell me I'd likely interrupted a thief mid-ransack, though neither of them can explain the locked doors and lack of forced entry.

After they leave, Oscar sits down on the sofa with his head in his hands.

Tentatively, I take a seat beside him. I want to touch him, to lay a hand on his shoulder, but there's an awkwardness between us. I can sense he doesn't want to be touched. At least, not by me.

'Caitie,' he says into his hands. 'Are you sure you saw someone?'

'I didn't just see someone, Oscar, I was attacked,' I say, struggling to hide my irritation.

He groans into his palms. Finally, he looks up and regards me with the same weariness as a parent with a misbehaving child. 'He attacked you, but you're largely unharmed, don't you think that's odd? Why break in, stand in my office, then lock you inside and leave?'

He has a point. I know he does, but it *did* happen. It did. I can still feel his gloved hand covering my mouth, can still smell the leather and feel the hardness of his body pinning me against the wall. Oscar should've been here. Why wasn't he home? 'Where were you tonight?'

'Drinks with friends.'

'What friends?'

He stands up. 'You don't think it was me, do you?'

'No, of course not. I just . . . What friends?'

'Why does it matter?'

I don't like that while I am sitting, he is standing, so I get up, too. At this, Oscar scowls. Then he walks past me, out into the hallway.

I follow him into the kitchen. Given what I've been through, I don't know why I care so much about who he was with and where, but I do. I ask him again.

He angrily boils the kettle and yanks two mugs from the cupboard. I stare at his back. I *long* for the man who set up an easel on a cliff in St Ives, who had sex with me in a rainbow bath, who whispered into my naked back that I am beautiful, that I am his entire world. But that Oscar is gone. The one who yanks open the fridge and slams the milk onto the side feels like a stranger.

'Who?' I press.

'Steven and Tim,' he snaps.

'I thought Steven was on holiday?'

He wheels on me. 'What're you suggesting?'

The kettle is bubbling but we ignore it. We look at one another. It clicks itself off.

'Nothing. I'm . . .' What *am* I suggesting? That he's working with the masked man? That *he* handed out our key? That he picked up my voicemail sooner than he admitted and he told the masked man I'd be home alone? Maybe. What I know for sure is that Oscar has been hiding something from me for a while now. 'What aren't you telling me?'

He looks at me as though I am his greatest, smacking disappointment. 'Why are you sidestepping into *another* fight?'

He doesn't even wait for my answer, just goes back to making tea. He is only making the one cup. I slink off to bed alone.

I spend the few days holed up in my room. I don't shower or dress and everything I eat tastes like plastic buttons. Oscar has been sleeping in our spare room down the hall. I don't ask why and he doesn't offer an explanation.

I think he must've called my parents and told them about the break-in that he isn't even sure happened, because they're at my house, treating me as though I am a mirror to be handled with care. First one to cause a crack gets seven years' bad luck.

Dad comes to my room. He stands in the doorway, looking at me with pity and concern which I'm not sure is any better than simmering hatred and disappointment. We lock eyes. He wants to say something. I see him shuffling through his words like cards in a deck, looking for the perfect hand. Before he finds it though, Mum calls him downstairs. He lingers for just a moment and then he's gone, taking whatever he wanted to tell me with him.

Mum is cleaning, doing all the chores I've failed to do. I lie in bed and stare up at the ceiling, listening to the spray of polish and a few minutes later, the continuous drone of the hoover. I yearn for those easy Sunday mornings with Oscar, when the two of us would put on music and tidy the house. We'd sing along, loudly and badly. Then, between the chorus and the verse, he'd pull me to him, a duster still in hand, and tell me he loved me.

The irony is not lost on me that the life I am missing now is the same life that, just days ago, I was complaining about to Gideon. Now, though, alone in my room and wondering if I'm losing my mind, I fall in love with Oscar, with our life together, all over again, as though it is a forgotten dress, rediscovered at the back of my wardrobe, fashionable once more.

Since the break-in, I've been stuck in a loop of fear and uncertainty. I fear the masked man and the memories that come to me in searing flashes. I fear that I have lost my fiancé and pushed away my family and friends. I fear that I am slowly going insane. My mind like one of those timelapses of a rotting apple left out in the sun to decay. Maybe everyone is right and I'm delusional? Maybe the masked man was never here – not outside the kitchen window at Blossom Hill House and not in Oscar's study? Maybe that woman *is* my sister and, on some subconscious level, just as my father suggested, I am struggling with her rejoining our family, and so I'm finding reasons to reject her. That sounds more plausible than being stalked by a man in a Venetian mask who no one else can see.

Loneliness spreads inside me like a swell of ink. I examine the backs of my hands and swear my veins are darker. I feel desperately alone. The kind of loneliness that is a physical ache, as real to me as the masked man's hand squeezing my throat. There was a brief reprieve from the loneliness when I believed my sister had returned, but now that I'm doubting it's her, I am lonelier than ever.

I sit up. The covers are damp with sweat and my hair sticks to my head in greasy clumps. I can't stay in bed forever, questioning my sanity. How can I expect anyone to believe I am a stable, functioning adult if I hide away in a bed-nest?

Because it is my only option, I finally shower.

I close my eyes beneath the hot spray of water and imagine the last few weeks of my life, the fear and the uncertainty, the suspicion and the loneliness, washing off me like dirt and disappearing down the drain along with the shampoo suds.

It feels good to wear real clothes. I smooth my hands over my lilac summer dress and pull my freshly washed hair into a high ponytail. It's too hot to wear it down. My stained, sweaty pyjamas lie at my feet like a costume for a tragic, mentally disturbed hermit. Out of them, I convince myself I am free of that role. I gather them up, strip the bed and bundle it all into the washing basket on the landing.

Then I hear voices down the hall, behind the closed door of the spare bedroom. I hear Olivia laugh. Hear the low, flirtatious burr of Oscar's voice. One I've felt whispered against my own naked back. I pad quietly towards them. My heart becomes a hummingbird in my chest as I reach the door handle. I can't make out what they're saying but the tone is clear. Affectionate. Teasing. Their laughter comes again. Part of me wants to turn and walk away, pretend I don't know that my sister and fiancé are squirrelled away together in a bedroom, but another part of me, the part that stares at road-traffic accidents or picks at a scab, wants to know. So I open the door.

I see them a second before they spring apart, her hand on his arm, their heads bent close together as they sit knee-pressed-against-knee on the edge of the bed. I stand in the doorway, feeling I have interrupted something intimate. Oscar leaps up, eyes wide and guilty. Olivia rises slowly, a small, private smile on her lips.

'Caitie, you're up,' he says with too much cheer. 'We were just going to come in and see you. Thought I'd give Olivia a tour. Do you want something to eat or drink? I think your mum is making lunch, or I could run down to the deli? Shall I do that? Get your favourite?'

I am barely listening, my focus fixed on Olivia. *Who are you?* I think. *What do you want? Why are you trying to take away my sanity, my best friend, my family and now my fiancé, too*? Oscar steps into my line of sight, eclipsing her from view. He puts an arm around me and starts guiding me out of the room, rubbing circles on my back as though he's escorting his dementia-addled grandmother. I shrug him off, finally finding my voice. 'Great idea, go to the deli, save Mum making lunch for everyone.'

'Do you want to lie down and I can bring it to your room when I'm back?' he offers. Usually, this would be a trademark thoughtful gesture from Oscar. Right now, it feels like he's trying to get me as far away from Olivia and what I saw as possible.

'Do I look like I need to lie down?' I ask sweetly.

He takes in my clean, brushed hair and my clean, ironed dress. I am together. I am composed. 'No, you seem . . .' He trails off, struggling for the word.

Past his shoulder, I see Olivia watching with a small smirk as though this is a mildly entertaining drama she's stumbled across whilst flicking through the channels. I will ask Oscar why he was alone in a bedroom with my sister, the door shut, later. In private.

'I'll be fine. You can go,' I tell Oscar in the same voice I use to dismiss misbehaving children in my classroom.

He glances at Olivia who, bored now I've put an end to the tension-fuelled interaction with my fiancé, has moved over to the chest of drawers where she picks up a stray red lipstick.

He places an awkward, chaste kiss on my cheek before he leaves.

Olivia applies my lipstick, painting her rosebud lips a deep scarlet. 'You know,' she says, admiring her reflection in the mirror above the drawers. 'I finally understand what you see in Oscar. He's adorable.' She looks at me over her shoulder, that infuriating, private smile still in place. 'So . . . attentive.'

'Stay away from him.'

She pouts. 'But aren't sisters supposed to share?'

'What're you doing in my house?'

'That's not very kind, Caitie.'

'Kitty-Cate,' I correct her.

She cocks her head. 'I'm sorry?'

'Kitty-Cate.'

'In English please.'

'That's the nickname *you* gave me, don't you remember?'

She shrugs and slides me another sly smile. 'Sure.'

I close the distance between us, so close I'm breathing in her blackberry-and-night-jasmine perfume. I take the lipstick from her and place it back on the drawer. 'Didn't you read about it in *her* diaries?'

She raises an eyebrow. This is the first time I have been brave enough, bold enough, to land an arrow of suspicion so close to the mark. 'Say it,' she dares me. She's enjoying this, the thrill of the chase, as though we are predator and prey. 'Go on, little *sister.*'

I lift my chin. My heart quickens. The adrenaline that hits my bloodstream, as potent as a shot of tequila, emboldens me and finally, I say it. 'I'm not your little sister.'

She looks surprised, then impressed. She didn't really think I'd say it out loud. She doesn't rush to defend or deny. And I feel a kick of victory as I realise I have fired my first arrow, straight and true. She isn't flustered or concerned. From the way her face has lit up, it's as though she's been waiting for this – eagerly waiting for this the way a child waits for Christmas. I don't understand what game she is playing and why she has chosen to play it only with me. 'Who are you?'

She moves past me, grinning. 'What's that old cliché? That's for me to know and for you to etcetera, etcetera . . .'

29

Caitlin Arden

After Olivia and my parents left, I confronted Oscar. He stuck to his story, claiming the reason they were alone in the bedroom is because he was giving her a tour of the house. I didn't believe him. I told him as much. He called me paranoid. Insisted I go back to my therapist.

Oscar left for Birmingham last night, right after our argument. I'm glad for the space, to be free of the tense atmosphere that has sloped into our home these last few days. Still, I'm getting cabin fever. I can't bear the thought of another day stretching out before me in the tedium of freshly hoovered carpets and daytime TV and lunch for one, all the while, loneliness trailing after me, a wraith with hooked talons and blackened teeth and icy breath. So I go for a walk in the park and leave it behind.

It's sweltering, but I keep to the shade of the tree-lined path. There's a bandstand in the far corner that has been decorated with balloons and bunting and banners for a child's birthday party. Mothers cluster together, bouncing babies on hips whilst keeping one eye on the children who are old enough to race around the park and hit each other with sticks. A queue of people wilts beneath the sun outside the little café that serves ice cream and cool bottles of lemonade. A group of twenty-somethings enjoy a picnic of shop-bought sandwiches, crisps and rosé. And weaving in and out of them all is a medley of dogs, tongues lolling and tails wagging. I let the balmy, summer magic sink into my skin like sunscreen.

Soon though, the questions I promised myself I wouldn't think about during my walk, start sprouting, leaning towards me as thorny wildflowers lean towards light. I am *sure* this woman isn't my sister, she all but admitted it in my spare room two days ago, but she's convinced everyone else, and on top of it all, she *looks* like Olivia. Those eyes. Glacial lakes and summer skies, forget-me-nots and bluebell petals. How is that possible? I wonder again if Olivia and the masked man are working together. If this woman *isn't* Olivia, then the masked man can't be my sister's abductor. So who is he and what does he want?

Appearing at the kitchen window and vanishing, breaking into my house and disappearing, it all feels like a game. One in which I'm the only outside player. But why me? Why go out of their way to make me look like a liar? It's so personal. So vengeful. I don't know of anyone who hates me with such vigour. I mean, statistically, most women are harmed by a partner, and even though things between Oscar and me are sandpaper-rough, we do love each other. He's been working on a secret project for weeks . . . Am *I* the secret project? He and Olivia were cosy together in our spare bedroom, despite his claims they weren't. Is it possible they're having an affair and either one or both of them is trying to drive me away? Drive me mad?

Olivia isn't concerned that I suspect she isn't my sister. She doesn't think I'll be believed because she's aware I have no solid evidence. Though a DNA test would prove me right. But how do I go about it? Can the police force someone to hand over their DNA? Surely they wouldn't even consider it unless they were the ones to suspect she isn't who she claims to be. At the moment, I seem to be the only person questioning her integrity. My reputation with the police is trash. I've seen the masked man on one too many occasions without a shred of evidence, and because of that they think I'm unreliable and unstable.

I consider, only briefly, approaching my parents, but know that's a dead end. I can't prove she isn't their daughter. It's my word against hers. She'll deny not recognising Hathaway Cottage, deny not remembering our cousin is Edward, deny knowing about the shed in the woods, deny our intense, strange conversations that always leave me with more questions than answers. My parents have had sixteen years of wishes and prayers granted: their daughter, safe and alive. If I'm right about this woman being an imposter, I will be whipping Olivia out from beneath them once again. Will they ever forgive me? In this case, is ignorance truly bliss? Or is the woman sleeping feet away from them each night dangerous?

I'm on my third lap of the park when I see Gideon jogging towards me. His long-legged, powerful strides quickly eat up the space between us. As he draws near, I lift my hand in greeting. He slows to a stop, removing his earbuds.

He's wearing shorts and a thin, navy T-shirt, damp with sweat. He has the thick, muscular thighs of a rugby player. When I pictured him out of his office, it was always with a glass of red wine and a steak, not a protein shake and an egg-white omelette. 'You're a runner,' I say. 'I had no idea.'

He smiles. 'Warned you I wasn't just a therapist.'

'It's so weird to see you out of a suit.'

'Tweed and blazers aren't typical jogging attire.'

'Bit sweaty?'

'Bit restrictive.'

Damp, his hair is even curlier, but the sides remain artfully swept back. 'What're you doing in Frome?'

'Park run at the show field.'

'You finished the park run and then decided to come here and keep on jogging? Has anyone ever told you you're a glutton for punishment?'

His grin widens. 'Been running a few years now.' He shrugs. 'Clears the head.'

'So that's what I'm doing wrong, I should be sprinting around here, not walking.'

I immediately regret my hiccup of honesty because he takes me in, paying closer attention than before, and I'm suddenly too aware of the shadows under my eyes. 'You needed to clear your head?'

'Something like that,' I say, trying to downplay my woes. 'I'm fine.'

He doesn't buy it. 'How's your week been?'

'Is this an impromptu session? Are you billing me for this conversation?' I laugh to lighten the mood but it's brittle, even to my own ears.

'No, not at all, just, you look . . .'

'What?'

'Lonely.' Though it isn't his intention, the word stings, as if he's slapped me hard across the face with it.

I swallow and attempt to brush it off. 'I suppose that happens when you're walking alone.'

He lifts his hand, just a little, then stops himself. I get the feeling he wants to touch me. To comfort me. To smooth away the loneliness. 'Are you OK?'

'Not really,' I admit. 'I think I'm losing my mind.'

I can't look at him as I say it, so I stare out across the park to the bandstand where children sit cross-legged, engrossed by a clown making balloon animals.

'Why?'

I tell him about the break-in, about the lack of proof and that everyone thinks I'm either lying or delusional.

'But you aren't hurt?' he asks, not with scepticism, but with genuine concern.

I shake my head. 'He would've done me a favour if he'd broken my arm or something. At least then I'd have evidence he was in my house.' I still don't understand why he left me largely uninjured. He was strong enough that if he wanted to, he could've killed me, even without a weapon. He was so tall and broad and . . . My gaze slides to Gideon. Gideon who commands the build of someone who could move a grand piano or carry a chest of drawers up the stairs.

'What?' he asks, sensing my dawning consternation.

I shake my head. Reminding myself that just because he and the masked man have a similar build, it doesn't mean they're the same person. Until just a few weeks ago, he didn't even know me. He has no reason to terrorise and attack me. If I let it, paranoia will overwhelm me.

We step aside to let a couple pass. They stroll hand in hand. The man pulls her to him. They kiss, right there in the middle of the path. It's such an easy, simple display of affection. When was the last time I was kissed like that? When I glance up, I see Gideon is watching them, too.

'Do you have a wife?' I ask because while he is in possession of so many sad, intimate details about me, I know almost nothing of him. And I find myself wondering. I chase that desire to delve to the bottom of someone else's life; a brief reprieve from constantly kicking just to tread the waters of my own. He considers me a moment before he answers, those jade-green eyes roaming my face. I think we're both wondering why I want to know.

'Yes. But we're separated.'

I wait for a sign that I have dug my nails into a still-healing wound, when he doesn't so much as flinch at my question, I ask another. 'What happened?'

He raises an eyebrow at my boldness. I worry he'll shut this conversation down because we aren't friends. We are therapist and patient. Standing in a park discussing his home life with me probably goes against whatever code of conduct he subscribes to, but I sense he doesn't want our conversation to end either.

'She was my whole world but I was only a part of hers. She started to get restless, unhappy, she wanted more than I could give her.' He shrugs. 'I had to let her go.'

'I'm sorry.'

'She deserves to be happy. I didn't want to hold her back.'

If I'm honest, I think Oscar and I have been holding one another back for a while. Him reluctant to travel, and me, reluctant to walk down the aisle. Until recently, though, I don't think either of us considered letting the other one go. My stomach clenches, just at the thought. 'Do you think you'll get back together?'

His smile is wry. 'She told me I should meet someone else.'

I wince. 'Right.'

I try to picture his wife. I imagine she is lean, the type of woman who rises early to do yoga and has the body to prove it. In my mind, she is whip-smart and capable, a doctor or therapist, like him. She's ambitious, always striving for the next big goal, never stopping to appreciate or be still with the things she already has. Maybe that is why she left him.

'And how're things with Olivia?' he asks.

My pulse kicks at the mention of her. I tell him about the phone call I overheard and the conversation we had where she all but admitted she isn't my sister. He listens patiently and without judgment. Still, I worry what he thinks of me. 'Am I a total headcase?'

'No.'

'You don't think it's all in my mind?'

'I don't.' He says this as though it is fact. The sky is blue, fire is hot, I trust what you are telling me.

It's a relief to be believed. For the first time in days, I am breathing easier. 'Why do you believe me when no one else does?'

He comes a little closer. Close enough that I am breathing in sea salt and sage, lemon and sweat. 'Because when I look at you, I don't see a liar.'

I tilt my face up to his. 'And what do you see?' I don't know why I ask it, but immediately there's an atmosphere. Sticky and dark. It wasn't intended to be flirtatious, or at least, that's what I tell myself. 'Thank you for believing me,' I add quickly, before he can lean into, or away from, the crackling tension.

I think I see a flash of disappointment but it's gone before I'm sure. 'I don't think you have any reason to lie to me,' he determines. We start walking together, side by side which, in some ways, is better because the intensity of his gaze can't burn me, but I find myself missing the heat of it on my skin. 'So you think if you get hold of whatever phone Olivia was using, you could prove she isn't your sister?'

I nod. 'But she's always in the house which makes it impossible to search.'

'That does sound like a challenge.' He's quiet a moment, I can feel him thinking. 'Will you be dropping Olivia off at her session with me next Tuesday?'

'No, I—'

'She needs to be at my office for 9 a.m.' He keeps his gaze fixed ahead. He's talking faster than usual. 'The session is about an hour and a half.'

He's helping me, letting me know exactly when she'll be away from Blossom Hill House so I can go through her things without getting caught. I feel a rush of fondness for him. 'Next Tuesday?'

'Next Tuesday.'

We share a knowing look. For the first time in weeks, a piece of the loneliness breaks off and falls away, and I can feel the sun on my face. We've walked all the way back to where we met. In the farthest corner of the park, the children at the birthday party shriek with laughter. I look over.

A rock hits the bottom of my stomach. Beyond the bandstand, I catch a glimpse of a chillingly familiar profile: his long, hooked nose, hood pulled up. He's exiting the park, disappearing out of view. I glance around to see if anyone else noticed, but all the children are wearing silly hats and animal masks, delighting at the juggling clown. Even some of the parents have donned masks. If anyone saw my stalker, they'd assume he was a performer or guest at the party.

'What's wrong?' asks Gideon.

'By the gate, I thought I saw that masked man leaving, I—'

Gideon sprints towards the exit.

I follow, dodging between dog walkers and parents with prams and children with sticky ice-cream fingers.

We make it to the black, cast-iron gates. This close to the party on the bandstand, I can hear the tinkling circus music coming from a speaker set up behind the clown's bag of tricks.

Gideon steps out onto the street, head swinging left and right. Walking up the hill towards us is a couple with two bouncy cocker spaniels. Across the road, nestled between the row of big, beautiful Georgian houses with big, beautiful bay windows, is a paved alleyway that leads to the allotments.

'We won't find him if he's headed in there,' I say.

Gideon looks tempted to try, and I feel a wave of affection for him. 'It's fine,' I say.

'It isn't fine, Caitie. It isn't fine to be stalked by a nutjob in a mask. It isn't fine that he broke into your house. It isn't fine that he put his hands on you. Nothing about this is fine.' He is burning with indignation, with an urgency of someone who truly cares.

'Is this a professional assessment or a personal one?' I ask, just as I did during that first session in his Bath office.

I expect him to answer 'both' with an impish grin, just as he did before, but he turns to me, chest heaving from the rush of adrenaline and the sprint to make it to the gate. That jade-green gaze is fixed unwaveringly on me, the heat of it making me breathless. 'Personal.' It is an intimate burr, one that makes me wonder what his stubble would feel like on the inside of my thighs.

It would be easy to lean into him, to go up onto my tiptoes and kiss my therapist. I could chase away the loneliness with sex, become a creature made up only of desire. But, no matter how cold things between Oscar and me become, I could never cheat.

'I should get back,' I say.

He doesn't want me to leave.

'Oscar will wonder where I am,' I say, even though Oscar isn't even home and I have no reason to leave.

'Sure,' he says, voice thick with disappointment.

And then I walk away before I change my mind.

30

Elinor Ledbury

Heath finds a gun hidden in a cupboard in Uncle Robert's study.

'Is that even legal?' asks Elinor. She is on her knees, surrounded by dusty files and loose pieces of paper.

'It's a hunting rifle,' he tells her, lifting it to look through the crosshairs.

'Do you even know how to shoot?'

'No.' His smile is lazy. 'But I'll learn.'

Elinor eyes the weapon, unease winding through her. Robert has been away from Ledbury Hall for six weeks, not returning since the attack, so Heath has seized the opportunity to go through every drawer, every cabinet and every box in search of paperwork relating to the estate. If they can find a legal loophole or even another relative who can take over as trustee, they won't have to leave their home. Though slogging through the files is laborious, Elinor's glad of the distraction, it has stopped her from dwelling on the dull throb of losing Flynn.

'In fact,' Heath tells her, slipping the rifle's strap over his head. 'I'm going to go and practise now.'

'You're going to shoot that on our land?' She is disbelieving, anxiety fluttering beneath her breast. 'What if someone hears?'

He arches a brow. 'Yes, who do you think will report me first – the deer or the badgers?'

'Ha ha,' she deadpans. 'What about the gardener?'

Mr Morris and his team are the only staff Uncle Robert has kept on at Ledbury Hall. Heath frowns. 'He let them all go,' he tells her. 'Haven't you noticed? They've not been for weeks.'

She presses her lips together, trying to understand what this means. What will happen to them if Uncle Robert never comes back? Once, after he'd found out the Ledburys had been sneaking his whisky, he didn't pay the electricity bill and they were cut off for a week. Luckily, it was in the summer, so they didn't freeze to death inside the echoing manor.

Heath sighs, holding out his hand to lift her to her feet. 'I'm going to take care of you.' As he speaks, his fingers slide up her bare arms to rest on her shoulders. He presses his forehead against hers so she can count the little green flecks in his eyes. She wants to ask him if he misses Sofia the way she misses Flynn, but she can't because they promised not to talk about the Healys again.

Heath broke up with Sofia. She didn't take it well, calling the housephone over and over until he ripped it from its socket. At least he is with Elinor now and has been all week. They have cooked together, and he has taught her Claude Debussy's 'Clair de Lune' on piano, they have walked the grounds, stopping at the little lake to gaze upon the statue of the two entwined lovers at its centre. Then Heath took Elinor in his arms, much in the same way, and whispered against her throat, 'I will love you. Always.'

'Fine,' she says now. 'But be careful. A bullet is very different to a lead pipe, and you're not a cat.'

'One life,' he says. 'Got it.'

He kisses her forehead and then he is gone.

31

Caitlin Arden

I surprise Florence by beating her to the restaurant.

'You're never early,' she tells me, removing her sunglasses.

'Well done, Caitie, you're on time, Caitie, I'm so proud of you, Caitie,' I say in mock imitation.

She smiles.

I won't admit I'm early because, for the first time in our friendship, I was nervous to see her. It's been so long since we spent time alone together. I've told myself it's because she's planning a wedding, but that isn't why. Pre-Olivia, we talked almost daily. Post-Olivia, I'm lucky to speak to her once a fortnight. If Florence's attention is a banquet, Olivia has arrived at the feast and devoured it all, leaving me only with crusts and gristly pieces of meat. For weeks, I have been starving, wondering when I'll get my next meal. Now, I plan to savour every bite.

I settle into a morning spent with one of my favourite people. The restaurant is packed. Waitstaff weave expertly between tables, carrying plates of poached eggs and smashed avocado on toast. There's a lively, optimistic energy about the patrons that is unique to Saturdays, when the slog of a grey Monday morning feels farthest away.

Our drinks arrive. Florence raises hers and we clink glasses. 'Brunch without a mimosa is just a sad, late breakfast,' she announces.

I shake my head. 'The only sad thing about this brunch is your gluten-free sourdough.'

'It's for the wedding – I'm trying to avoid a skin flare-up.'

'It's for people who want their food to taste like disappointment.'

She grins and I realise just how much I've missed her. 'How're the wedding arrangements going? Do you need any help?' My offer is sincere. I'm lonely with nothing much to do. At least, nothing I *want* to do. This week, I should be in handover meetings with the current Year 4 teacher, but even the thought of talking through grade projections and SEN plans and learning objectives bores me to tears. And when I'm not avoiding work, I'm obsessing over Olivia and the masked man. Occasionally, my thoughts stray guiltily to Gideon. Those jade-green eyes, and broad shoulders, his delicious Irish burr. A day spent printing wedding menus would be a welcome distraction.

'Actually, we're pretty much done with the wedding.'

'Really? What about all the little things like cutting ribbon for the chairs or prepping the favours?'

'All done.'

'I'm impressed. I can *just* about organise a trip to the bathroom each morning to brush my teeth.'

'I've had help.'

'You have?'

She nods. 'Olivia.'

A vivid, uncomfortable silence descends upon us. I wade through hurt and confusion and slow burning indignation. I try to tamp down thoughts of *I'm* her maid of honour. *I'm* her best friend. *I'm* supposed to be the one sitting on her living room floor divvying confetti into rolled up newspaper cones. 'If you'd told me you needed help, I'd have been there. I've offered a hundred times.'

She winces. 'I know, I know, I didn't plan for her to come over and do it all with me but the college talk ended early so—'

'College talk?'

'Yeah . . . Olivia's joining Bath College in September, didn't she tell you?'

My mouth falls open. 'To study what?'

'Art.'

'*Art?*' It bursts from me, an accusation. 'Are you fucking kidding?'

Florence pulls a face. A very involuntary face. Her lips press together and she gives the slightest hint of a head shake. 'She's a grown adult, if she wants to take a foundation art course, she can.' She regards me then. 'I know you wanted to go to university to study art, Caitie, but you didn't.'

I grit my teeth. 'Yes, because after my sister was abducted I didn't want to add to my parents' upset,' I say tightly. I am trying very hard to contain my frustration, reminding myself Florence doesn't know that Olivia *isn't* Olivia. That she is, in fact, a manipulative imposter.

'Well, they aren't upset about Olivia studying it. They're happy for her,' she says pointedly.

I sip my drink.

'Maybe she's taking the course so the two of you can bond,' she offers.

This isn't about bonding, Olivia is toying with me, trying to wind me up until I lash out, but why? She's got my parents and my best friend wrapped around her little finger and, by the looks of how comfortable she was alone in a bedroom with my fiancé, she has Oscar in her snare, too. And now she wants to study art. I can't believe I told her my dream of being an artist, of painting the world and travelling around it. Telling her was a big deal, or maybe we both just acted like it was. I relished reprising my role of little sister and she relished stepping into her new one – The Returned Arden Girl. But that's all it was, theatre. And not even good theatre, at that. I need to tell Florence. But I've barely opened my mouth when she beats me to it. 'Look, I have something to say.'

'OK.'

'Olivia is going to play at the wedding.'

I frown. 'Play what?'

'Piano.'

That doesn't make any sense. 'Olivia can't *play* piano.'

'She can. I heard her. She hopped on a community piano in Bath and she was brilliant. She's performing Claude Debussy's 'Clair de Lune' during the drinks reception after the ceremony. It's her wedding gift to us.'

This is wrong. So wrong. My sister can't play piano. Our grandmother used to have one but the most we learnt was 'Mary Had a Little Lamb'. Before I can push my point though, Florence says, 'And I decided to ask Olivia to be joint maid of honour.'

I almost drop my drink. 'What?'

Our food arrives. The waitress, sensing the tension, sets our plates down and leaves quickly.

'It just felt right,' she says. 'It's a difficult situation because Olivia and I always used to talk about our wedding days. We agreed to be each other's maid of honour years ago.'

The truth is, if Olivia had never disappeared, Florence and I probably wouldn't be friends. It would have been Olivia holding Florence's hair back at her graduation party as she puked green-glitter vodka shots. It would have been Olivia who lugged a million boxes up the stairs to her first apartment. It would have been Olivia who sat with her on the floor of her bathroom, squeezing her hand, waiting to find out if that broken condom had condemned her to a life of snotty noses and Peppa Pig, then celebrated with a very expensive bottle of champagne when it was one line instead of two. It would have been Olivia who painstakingly organised a hen weekend away in the Cotswolds, which felt less like corralling women she only vaguely knew and more like herding cats.

The knowledge that it should have been her and never me, smarts.

'I mean, this is OK, isn't it?' she questions. But we both know that if she really cared about my opinion, she'd have asked *before* she went to Olivia.

'Sure,' I say because this is her wedding and everyone knows what the bride wants, the bride unquestioningly gets. She keeps talking and I keep smiling. What I feel though is a thud of despair. The shame of not being enough. Of being sidelined once more as the understudy, because the star of the show has returned. She's telling me how fun it will be having two maids of honour. How it will be less stressful for me. How I'll appreciate the help on the day. She's dressing this up as a neatly wrapped gift for me. But it's one I never asked for and don't want. Still, it would be churlish to reject it, so I make my smile even wider until it feels clownish on my face.

'I'm really pleased you don't mind,' she says. 'I've been stressing about telling you.'

'No need to stress,' I say. We smile at each other. It's strained and awkward because we both know I'm not OK with it and that she wouldn't be, either.

Olivia, or rather, the woman impersonating her, is a brood parasite, a cuckoo intent on pushing me out of the nest so she can get fat and happy on my life. I stab at the bacon on my plate, at the still sizzling fat, and decide I'm not hungry. We lapse into uncomfortable silence. I listen to the women on the table beside us plan a minibreak to Slovenia. My fingers itch to book a plane ticket to literally anywhere. To run from Olivia and the masked man and Florence, too. All of them.

'Are you OK?' she asks. 'You look . . . Are you sleeping?'

I think about the layers of brightening concealer I used to hide the dark circles under my eyes. Apparently, I needn't have bothered. 'I'm sleeping,' I lie. 'But it's been trickier since the break-in.' This, at least, is true. Sometimes, just as I'm about to drift off, I feel his gloved hand close around my throat, can taste the leather, and I jolt awake.

She nods. 'Olivia mentioned it.'

I feel a pang of annoyance imagining the tales Olivia has spun. 'And what did she tell you?'

She looks uncomfortable as she carefully chooses her words, trying to sand down the serrated edges of whatever Olivia has told her before she repeats it. 'That you thought there was someone in the house but the police couldn't find anything.'

'I didn't *think* there was someone in the house. I know there was. I was attacked.'

Her eyes widen, in disbelief or shock, I'm not sure. '*Attacked?*'

'He pinned me against a wall and locked me in Oscar's office, didn't Olivia mention that bit?'

She doesn't meet my eye as she slices into poached eggs and kale. 'But he didn't hurt you? Didn't take anything?'

Her scepticism needles. 'No, he didn't.' I still can't explain why or what he wants, but I need her to know I'm telling the truth. 'He's been following me.'

She sets her knife and fork down. 'Following you?'

'Yes, I saw him a couple of days ago when I was in the park with—' I cut myself off, not wanting to tell her about Gideon because I know she won't understand.

'With?'

'My . . .' I hesitate, not sure what to call him, 'therapist.'

She raises an eyebrow. 'Why were you in a park with your therapist?'

'We bumped into one another and it's really beside the point.'

'Did your therapist see this masked stalker?'

'No.'

Silence.

She picks up her cutlery. 'OK.'

Under the table, I dig my nails into my palms. She doesn't believe a word I'm saying. I am a child trying to convince an adult she's seen Father Christmas. Maybe if she knew Olivia isn't really Olivia, she'd understand. I think carefully about how to broach the subject, like easing yourself slowly into a scalding bath. 'Do you think Olivia is . . . like she used to be . . . before?'

She blinks, surprised by the swift change in topic. 'Remarkably so. I was prepared for this rabid, broken wildling the day you picked me up to meet her, but she's . . .' she shrugs, 'Olivia.'

'Olivia . . . in what way?'

She thinks a moment. 'Fun, but not frivolous. Kind, but not a wallflower. Confident, but not cocky. She was just the same at primary school.' She sips her drink thoughtfully. 'I met her on my very first day, did you know that? I joined halfway through Year 4 and I didn't have a uniform. Half an hour in, this mean-faced girl comes up to me and tells me my buttercup-yellow dungarees are babyish.'

I wince, knowing at that age, this was a verbal bitch-slap of the highest order.

'Then Olivia with her perfect, swishy ponytail, strides up to me and announces to the room that my dungarees are cool.' She grins at the memory. 'The next day was mufti day and almost everyone was wearing them, even the mean-faced girl.' She tucks an inky strand of hair behind her ear. 'I never felt alone at school, with her hand in mine, skipping around the playground. Then later, hanging out in our form room, sharing one pair of headphones, listening to Placebo on repeat. It's rare to meet someone who holds so much power over others but chooses to use it to lift people up, instead of taking them down.'

She remembers Olivia just as I did. As a kind of nicotine electricity. Someone other people craved to be around. But I am certain that the girl who was snatched from Blossom Hill House and the woman who returned to it sixteen years later, are not the same. 'Did you and Olivia talk about that?'

'What do you mean?'

'You've spent a lot of time together since she came back, do you reminisce? Does she remember the same things you do?'

'I don't know. She . . . We talk about lots of things. Mostly, we've talked about Daniel and the wedding. Why?'

I bite my lip, unsure. But then, Gideon believed me, didn't he? And he doesn't even know me, not really. If he has faith in my theory, in me, Florence should, too. 'She couldn't remember Hathaway Cottage or our cousin Edward.'

Her gaze narrows. 'Right . . .'

'She knew about this old shed on the land behind our house even though it was built *after* she was taken.'

'Caitie . . .'

'She has a secret second phone and I caught her talking to someone about me. She—'

'Stop,' she implores, holding up a hand as though halting traffic. 'Just don't.' She sets her cutlery down again, angry this time. 'Look, do not say what you're going to say.'

'Florence—'

'Listen to me, Caitie. She *is* Olivia. Everyone knows she is. The police – everyone. You're going to make yourself seem completely mad and paranoid if you claim otherwise. If your parents find out you're smearing their daughter, you're going to alienate yourself from them entirely.' She fixes me with a look that is both stern and disapproving. 'They're so happy to have her back and you should be, too.'

'It *isn't* her.'

She closes her eyes, as though wishing me away. 'Why would someone pretend to be Olivia?'

'Fame, money, attention.'

'What fame, Caitie? She's refused every single interview, and all the money that comes with them.'

'I think she stole my father's credit card the day we went shopping,' I say, remembering how Mum had questioned me as Florence and Olivia reunited in the garden. I'd been distracted and hadn't paid Mum much attention at the time.

'You think she's impersonating your sister for a few dresses and bags?' She shakes her head.

'I know it *sounds* wild, but—'

'It does.' She sighs as though I am a wayward child.

'A DNA test would prove me right.'

She stares at me as though I've just announced I can't count to ten. 'They *did* a DNA test . . .'

My world starts to tilt off its access. I grip the table. 'What?'

'They did a test,' she repeats.

'How do you know?'

'Clara told my mum.'

'No,' I whisper. 'They couldn't—'

'The results were inconclusive due to some fault with the sample and when the police asked for another test a week later, Olivia said she'd been poked and prodded enough, and your parents backed her.'

'So, she did something to the test on purpose.' I lick my dry lips. 'She still might not be my sister.'

'Of course she's your sister. Can you hear yourself, Caitie?' Our gazes lock. She's staring at me as though I've grown a second head. 'Your parents backed her because they know their own daughter.' She snatches up her already empty glass and drains it without noticing there's nothing left. 'You're tired. You're just over-tired and you're struggling to manage this enormous change. Oscar and Olivia said the same.'

My face burns with indignation. 'You're all talking about me?'

'Yes, because we all care.'

I laugh, harsh and dry. 'But *none* of you care enough to listen to what I have to say.'

'We are listening, Caitie, and that's why we're worried. A fake sister? Stalking? A masked assailant no one else has seen?'

My phone starts vibrating across the table. We both ignore it.

'Why does that sound so insane? My sister was literally abducted by a masked assailant.'

She pulls a face.

'What?' I ask.

'Olivia doesn't remember a mask. She said the police asked about the mask during her first interview and she told them she never saw one.'

I stare at her, mouth agog. The woman falsely claiming to be my sister has been undermining me from the very beginning. 'He was masked,' I insist.

'Not according to her.'

'Well *her* version of events doesn't count because she isn't who she claims to be!' I spit with more volume and venom than intended.

The women at the table beside us fall quiet.

'Caitie,' Florence says in a placating tone. 'Are you sure you want to be my maid of honour? It's a lot of responsibility and I need the day to be as stress-free as possible. I don't want to load any more onto your plate.'

I stare at her, wounded, sorrowful tears of rejection stinging my eyes.

This time, it is Florence's phone that rings. She looks relieved as she answers it, glad for the brief reprieve. 'Erm . . . yes, I'm with her now.' She glances at me. 'I'll pass you over.'

She hands me her phone.

'They've found him.' It's Mum, her voice is shaky, thick with emotion.

'Who?'

'Briggs.'

Florence leans forward, listening, a crease between her brows. 'Who is Briggs—'

'Simon Briggs. The man who took Olivia.'

Florence claps a hand over her mouth.

'The police found him,' says Mum.

I loosen with relief. We're safe. We're all going to be safe. And now they have him, the truth will come out. He'll admit Olivia isn't my sister. He'd confess to stalking me and the police will make him tell them why.

'He's at the police station right now?'

'No,' she says. 'The morgue.'

I go from hot to cold and back again.

'He's dead, Caitie. Has been dead for weeks. It's finally over.'

32

Caitlin Arden

We rush to my parents' house. Oscar arrives seconds after Florence and I do. I didn't call him but I suspect Mum did, looking for me. There's no time for us to speak before we are ushered into the living room to listen to the police. Olivia, having already been spoken to, goes upstairs to her room with Florence.

I've seen so many officers these last few weeks that they all blur into a mass of black uniforms and earnest expressions, but I'm familiar with Lead Detective Inspector Grimshaw. He's in his late fifties with iron-grey hair, wide rectangular eyebrows, and a crooked nose. He tells us that although Olivia didn't know her captor's surname, they were able to locate Simon's property based on the description she provided. Apparently, the house was exactly how she said it would be, right down to the locks on the bedroom she was kept in.

'Twenty-three years ago, Simon Briggs was Deputy Headteacher at an all girls' school in Northamptonshire. A colleague caught him at a local bar indulging in . . .' he clears his throat, 'inappropriate behaviour with a former student. He resigned, lost his fiancée and turned to alcohol shortly after. Within a year, he'd sold his house and moved away,' he tells us. 'Records show he purchased a piece of rural woodland in Gloucestershire.'

'That's where he kept her?' asks Mum.

He nods. 'At the time of his death, Simon Briggs was a fifty-nine-year-old hermit. A doomsday prepper. We found a larder stocked with enough supplies to last several years. He lived without

215

a television or mobile phone but he was well read. Lots of—' he shifts his weight '—interesting books.'

It's difficult to untangle what happens next: what Grimshaw relays and what I concoct. It's as though he's handed me a paint by numbers. His words make up the picture, but I colour in the detail.

I imagine Briggs's house. It's small and rickety. He fills it with dog-eared paperbacks: a library of agricultural manuals, conspiracy theories, erotic fiction. Glad to be rid of the floral prints his fiancée hung on the walls of their townhouse, he replaces them with crude, graphic sketches of naked women. They're all young with long hair and doe eyes.

'How did he die?' asks Dad, eager to skip the origin story and get to the scene where the villain is gruesomely felled.

'We found a vial of thallium and a near-finished bottle of whisky beside the body,' answers Grimshaw.

Dad frowns. 'Thallium?'

'A type of metal. Poison. A frightfully painful way to die.'

'Go on,' says Dad. He wants to hear how Briggs suffered. I can tell by the feverish glimmer in his eyes that he hopes it was excruciating. He isn't disappointed.

'Symptoms include nausea, vomiting, fever. Some people complain of a burning sensation in the soles of their feet and the palms of their hands. Eventually, it causes paralysis, sweeping through the body, shutting down organs in its wake until suffocation.'

There's a stunned silence as we digest this. I see Briggs in his living room, agonising convulsions forcing him into the foetal position. He pushes his face into the worn, musty rug and screams until his lungs burn.

'He killed himself?' asks Mum, aghast.

'It seems that way,' answers Grimshaw. 'Thallium is tasteless, mixed with whisky it would've gone down easy enough.'

'How can you be sure it was suicide?' It's the first time I've spoken. Several pairs of eyes find me.

'There was a letter.'

'But why poison?' I press.

'We found a shotgun on the premises but the barrel would've

been too long, preventing him from shooting himself. As a recluse without access to the internet, he used what he had.'

'And why would he have thallium?' I ask.

'It's sometimes used to poison rats. Briggs had a well-stocked larder to protect.'

Something gnaws at the edge of my belief. 'Why not slit his own wrists or hang himself?'

Oscar and my parents, horrified by my direct, morbid questions, exchange looks, but Grimshaw regards me with interest. 'All good questions. It's possible he didn't intend to die. Thallium can take several days to end a life. One might consider he hoped, if he were found and saved, a judge would be more lenient on a reclusive, alcoholic who was so overcome with remorse, he tried to take his own life.'

I suppose there isn't a lot of sympathy for a sadistic, sexual predator. Still, I can't imagine anyone *choosing* to die so painfully, so slowly. 'Do you know when he died?' I ask. It's been a truly hot summer, how long has Briggs been baking in his house and his own sticky fluids?

Mum shoots me a look which I ignore. I need to know if Briggs is the masked man.

'We'll have more information after the autopsy, but it appears he died only a handful of days after Olivia was returned.'

This means he's been dead for weeks. I don't understand. My last sighting of the masked man was just a couple of days ago in the park with Gideon. If Olivia's captor has been dead this entire time, who has been stalking me and why? Could there be more than one abductor? Is it possible that the masked man and Briggs were working together? But then, how is the woman claiming to be Olivia involved? Maybe she's the student Briggs was having an affair with? If so, where is my real sister? And why is her imposter targeting me?

I swallow. I don't look at Mum or Dad as I ask, 'Is it possible Briggs was murdered?'

Grimshaw's gaze narrows and holds mine. 'It's a possibility,' he says slowly. 'But that would mean our only suspect is Olivia.'

My parents are glaring at me. I feel their gazes burning into my skin like lit cigarette ends.

'Nope,' Mum shrills, eyes wild, as though afraid a SWAT team might burst through the windows and take her daughter away in handcuffs. 'That's not possible. You found a note.'

'That's right. His former workplace provided us with a handwriting sample which matched the note signed by Briggs.'

If Briggs was working with someone else, surely there'd be evidence of that at his house. I ask if they found any sign of a third party, prints, DNA.

'Just Briggs and Olivia,' confirms Grimshaw. His thick, rectangular brows are knitting together. Whilst he's intrigued by my questions, my parents are agitated by them. I want to request Olivia undertakes another DNA test because I'm *sure* she isn't my sister, but I can't ask without hurting my family. Florence was right, they'd struggle to forgive me.

Oscar drives us home. We don't speak. He's angry with me again and I don't know why. We go inside and he hasn't even taken off his shoes before he snaps at me. 'What were you getting at back there? All those questions about murder and going through the house with a fine-tooth comb for third-party DNA.'

'The police *should* be going through the house with a fine-tooth comb,' I say archly. 'According to Olivia, it's a crime scene.'

He pulls a face. 'According to Olivia? What's that supposed to mean?'

We are standing less than a metre apart, gazes locked, but I've never felt further away from him. A gulf has opened between us these last few weeks. 'Oscar, why did you talk to Florence and Olivia about me?'

He splutters, 'Because your best friend and your sister are concerned for you.'

'She isn't my sister.' I'm not entirely sure why I've chosen this moment to tell him but then I remember how Gideon reacted when I admitted the same thing to him. He didn't treat me as though I'm hysterical. He listened with an open mind. He believed me. I realise I'm testing Oscar because I want my fiancé to believe me too.

He doesn't. He looks at me as though I'm frothing at the mouth. '*What?*'

'She isn't my sister.'

'You don't really believe that.'

I lift my chin. 'I do.'

'Of course she's your sister.'

And there it is, I am dismissed, my feelings crushed beneath the sole of his foot as easily as a crumbling autumn leaf. 'How do you know? Other than your *liaison* in our spare room and a few sly group chats about me, you don't know her.'

He shakes his head, angrily kicks off his shoes and moves past me to the living room. I hate when he does this, ends a discussion by walking away, allowing the issue to fester like a bacteria-ridden wound, and leaving me to trail after him, regretful, repentant, using my words like antiseptic and gauze. And though I follow him now, I promise myself I won't apologise. Not this time.

He's sitting on the sofa, scrolling through his phone.

'You don't know her,' I say again.

He sighs loudly and drags his gaze up to mine. 'I know that girl is Olivia Arden and not some . . . I don't know . . . evil doppelgänger.'

'She isn't a girl, she's a woman. A manipulative stranger.'

'Caitie, this is ridiculous.'

'You haven't even asked *why* I think she's an imposter.'

He thrusts his fingers back through his sandy hair. 'Fine.'

'Fine?'

He looks to the ceiling as though he can't believe he's entertaining my madness. 'Yep. Go ahead.'

I stiffen, tempted to back out of the conversation now. But how can I expect him to believe me if I never explain why I feel the way I do? So I list off all the oddities. At first, he's sceptical but that scepticism soon evolves into panic. He's up on his feet, pacing back and forth, eyes wild. 'Who else have you told?'

There's a nervous, fluttery energy in the room that makes my heart race. 'Why does it matter?'

'Who else, Caitie?' he snaps.

'Do you believe me?' I ask. 'Do you believe it isn't really Olivia?'

'Who else?' he bellows.

I shrink away from him, fear pulsing through me. When I don't answer, he strides forward, desperate and infuriated. Before I can think, I'm turning towards the door, an instinct urging me to flee. He's faster, though, his palm comes down on my right and slams it shut. I stare at the oak of the closed door and become all too aware that if he wanted to, he could hurt me. This is an uncomfortable reality that women in the company of men must face. Men can hurt us if they really want to.

Maybe he wants to.

'Who else have you told?' he asks with barely contained hostility.

'Florence.' I don't admit to telling Gideon. The same instinct that told me to run, tells me to keep Gideon a secret.

'Stop digging. Just be happy your sister is back.'

'She isn't—'

'You're intent on ruining everything,' he barks with such malice, a dart of terror shoots through me.

'Ruining what?'

The silence roars loudly in my ears.

'I'm going out.'

His hand slips down to the handle and yanks the door open. I have to leap back to stop it from hitting me in the face.

A moment later, the front door slams shut.

I stand in our living room, feeling shaky and sick. What the hell was that about? Where did all that anger come from?

I wonder again what he's hiding from me. For weeks, I've had the feeling he's been telling lies. I think about the woman – Sam – I caught him with in the café. Where did he say she worked? Adaline Fray Interiors? The moment I suspected Oscar wasn't being truthful, I should've called the company to verify his story but I didn't want to believe my fiancé would deceive me. Now, though, afraid of his temper, I must act. I go into the hall and retrieve my phone from my bag. After a quick Google search, I find the number and call it.

'Good afternoon, you're through to Adaline Fray Interiors, how can I help?'

'Is this Sam?'

'Unfortunately not, I'm Mel, Ada's PA,' she tells me. 'Can I help?'

'I'm looking for Sam. Sorry, I don't have a surname. She works in your marketing department?'

A pause. 'We don't have anyone here by that name.'

My stomach drops. 'Are you sure?'

'It's a small team.'

I apologise for the confusion and hang up. 'He lied,' I say out loud to no one. I'm gripping the phone so hard, my hand hurts. And if he lied about Sam, what else is he lying about? All this deception started after Olivia returned. It *must* have something to do with her. I turn towards his office. I never wondered before *why* the masked stranger was in that specific room. There must be a reason. Maybe he was looking for something. If he didn't find it, perhaps I can. But, when I try the handle, I realise the door is locked. Oscar never locks it. I glance down, the little key is gone.

33

Elinor Ledbury

Heath spends at least two hours a day shooting the gun on their land. He offers to show Elinor but just the feel of it in her hands makes her skin crawl. She doesn't trust herself not to accidentally shoot herself. Or her brother. So, he goes out alone. When he is gone, she thinks of Flynn. They never loved each other the way she and Heath do, but maybe, in time, they could have. Flynn hasn't tried to contact her, not once. She still has his jacket, the bouncy ball, and the purple stone, too. When she looks at them, she grieves what could've been. She thinks of the romance novels her mother loved – all those lovers spinning, wild and free and content out in the wide world – and jealousy snaps at her heels, momentarily eclipsing the grief. She rests her head on her knees and waits for the pain to pass. It does, ebbing away into the silence of the house, and she is once again struck by the rightness of things now that Heath is home.

She hears a door opening downstairs, her brother returning from his shooting, and makes her way to him. As her foot hits the bottom step, she is greeted only by silence. She stands still in the foyer and listens. Nothing. Maybe she was mistaken, but as she turns towards the dining hall, she stops, the hairs on the back of her neck lifting. She is sure she heard movement coming from the study, but trepidation has sealed her mouth so she does not call out for Heath. She moves towards the noise, a moth drawn helplessly to flame. Though she knows the study door was closed when she went upstairs, it is now ajar. Slowly, she pushes it open, already knowing it is not her brother inside. She stares at the back of her uncle's dark head. Sensing her presence, he turns, and she knows he is drunk. She can tell by his pink cheeks and unfocused, bloodshot eyes. He must've driven all the way from London to Ledbury Hall in his intoxicated state. His skin is sallow and he's grown an unruly beard. He looks ten years older and somehow, smaller, than he did the last time she saw him. He turns back and pours himself a drink.

'Want one?'

'You need to get out of here,' she warns him.

He chuckles mirthlessly. 'Out of my own house?'

She worries what Heath will do if he comes back and finds Uncle Robert here. Her heart hums in her chest. 'You hurt my brother.'

'Survived, did he?' He slurs his disappointment, then downs his drink before pouring himself another.

She checks her shoulder, looking down the hallway, knowing Heath is due back any second. 'Please, just go back to London.'

'Can't.' He stumbles across the room and slumps into his armchair.

'Why not?'

He takes a swig. 'Sold my flat.'

'Why?'

'Lost my job.' He raises his glass. 'Thanks to you and your wretched brother.'

Her stomach churns like a washing machine full of bricks. She moves further into the room to stand before him. 'I'm sorry.'

He looks up at her sharply. 'Goody.'

She swallows and clasps her hands tightly, keeping her gaze low. 'Please, Uncle Robert. If Heath—'

He slams his glass onto the side table, sloshing amber liquid over the rim and making her jump. 'He's just like his father – an arrogant, lazy, entitled, sneering little *fuck*. My brother relied on his film-star good looks, too.' He snorts. 'And look where that got him!'

She has rarely, if ever, heard Uncle Robert talk about her father. When her uncle moved into Ledbury Hall, he removed all the family photographs and burnt them in the garden. That, she thinks, is the day Heath decided he hated Uncle Robert. Her brother had got down on his hands and knees, risking burns to try and save some of the pictures. Uncle Robert had just turned and walked back into the house, leaving the two of them to watch their memories, the only images of their parents, burn to cinders.

'My parents were so proud of their golden boy,' he spits. 'It didn't matter to them that *I* was the academic one. That *I* went to university. That *I* secured a position at one of the top pharmaceutical companies in the world, while their first born did nothing but marry rich and reproduce. They didn't care about *my* achievements, *my* education, *my* career. None of that mattered once he married your mother.' Uncle Robert hauls himself up and stumbles back to the bar cart. 'And do you know the worst part?' He sways a little. Elinor can smell the alcohol on him. 'The worst part is it should've been *me* with Alison.'

And there it is. Elinor always suspected he'd had a thing for her mother. She'd seen a photograph of her in his wallet, years after he burned the others.

'A parcel for Ledbury Hall had wound up at my parents' address by mistake. My mother asked me to drive it over but when I went to do so, it was gone. And guess who'd taken it?'

'My father.'

'BINGO!' he shouts. 'Somebody give this girl a prize!' His laughter is hollow. 'That's right, *Nicholas* fancied himself a trip to Ledbury Hall. The second he set eyes on this manor, Alison was his. She was too good for him, your mother. Endlessly kind. Always spoke highly of me. She quickly put an end to Nicholas's belittling comments. My "little job", that's what he used to call it. Got our parents referring to it as such. The only thing I'd ever been proud of was my career and my brother was determined to ruin it, but Alison stood up to him.' Elinor has always thought of her uncle as being cold and unfeeling, hard like granite, but when he talks about her mother, he becomes warm and inviting, like maple syrup poured over pancakes. 'I'd have loved her for who she was, not for her money. Not the lifestyle. Not like your father did.'

Elinor feels as though she is his priest and this is his confession, so she stays quiet, hoping once he is done telling this story, she can usher him out of the house before Heath returns. 'It was my brother's idea to go out on that yacht, even though he didn't know how to sail. All to impress our parents.' Uncle Robert finishes his drink. 'They died that day, too.'

Elinor is shocked. She knew her grandparents were dead but she never knew how they'd passed. She thinks drowning is the worst, most terrifying, way to die. 'I'm sorry,' she whispers but he doesn't seem to hear.

'Truth is, people like you, people like your brother, always win.'

She frowns.

'*Pretty* people,' he clarifies. 'It's a privilege to look like you.' He reaches for another bottle but knocks it over. It lands on the rug with a dull thud. 'I tried my best. Tried to teach the pair of you to use your brains, your minds, as well as your . . .' he eyes her, 'your *beauty*. Because beauty fades, Elinor, but your brother refuses to learn, refuses to fall in line, just like Nicholas.'

Elinor looks to the door again, sure her brother will burst through it. She crosses the room and lays a hand on her uncle's arm. 'Please leave before Heath comes back,' she begs. 'Call a taxi and—'

He starts to sob. He leans on the bar cart, shoulders shuddering. 'All I had was my career. But it's gone. All gone.'

Elinor has never seen him cry. She feels a pull of pity for him and lays a comforting hand on his back. He meets her eyes and for the first time she sees a fatherly love in the way he looks at her. 'Your career is something to be proud of,' she tells him. 'Your company was lucky to have you.'

His face is tear-stained. He straightens but sways. He smiles at her with genuine affection. 'You sound like your mother,' he says fondly. His gaze roams over her face. 'You look just like her, too. You have her eyes. She was the most beautiful . . .' He reaches out and strokes her hair.

Out of the corner of her eye, she spots Heath's shadow, cast in a square of sunlight. Uncle Robert sees it, too. Panicking, he jerks away but his fingers tangle in her hair and she yells out, startled.

Heath lifts the gun. There is a click.

Uncle Robert's eyes widen. 'Now, Heath ju—'

There is an explosion of noise. Of fire. Elinor feels warmth spatter across her face. Uncle Robert is flung backwards. He hits the ground, his chest split open like a pomegranate.

34

Caitlin Arden

I let myself in to Blossom Hill House. It's Tuesday. Olivia is at her appointment with Gideon and my parents are at work. I stand alone in the hallway. Even though this is my childhood home, I feel like an intruder. The fear of getting caught makes my heart race. I start to remove my trainers, then stop. If someone comes home and notices them by the door they'll know I'm here and the entire point of this visit is to get in and out undetected.

In Olivia's bedroom, I get to work, looking for that mobile phone. It's possible she keeps it with her, but I'm hoping she doesn't. Maybe I'll uncover another kind of evidence – a hidden passport or driver's licence, anything that might tell me who she really is. I'm surprised when I open her wardrobe. She has so many expensive, beautiful clothes. She's clearly been helping herself to my father's credit card on more than that one occasion. I riffle through drawers and under the bed. I find the box of diaries and flip through them, angry all over again that she read my sister's innermost thoughts and used them to manipulate everyone into believing her tale. I slide them back under the bed and though I keep looking, I don't uncover anything incriminating.

With every passing, fruitless minute, my frustration grows. The phone isn't here. Something inside me cracks and I have to bite my tongue to stop myself from screaming. My best friend and fiancé don't believe me. I *need* some evidence. The truth is, without that phone, I have no way to prove she isn't my sister. Knowing the police won't do another DNA test without doubting her claim, I wonder if *I* could do my own test. Now I'm alone in her room, surrounded by things she has touched and used, I'm convinced this is a possibility. I take out my phone and google home DNA kits. I skim a few sites and quickly realise as long as I have her hair or, even better, saliva, and send it off alongside my own, I can prove we aren't related. Hope washes through me like sunlight. I rush downstairs and grab a couple of Ziploc bags from the kitchen drawer.

Back in her bedroom, I take as much hair from her brush as I can and carefully place it inside. Then I go to the bathroom and take the head off her electric toothbrush. As Mum and Dad have an en suite and Olivia is the only one to use the main bathroom, I'm confident this toothbrush is hers. I take a new, identical head from the cupboard to replace it, hoping she won't notice. With shaking hands, I try to slip my prize into the bag but in my haste, I drop it. I bend to pick it up and as I do, I notice something stuck to the underside of the basin. Not stuck . . . taped. I peel it from the porcelain and stand to examine it. It's a small white case that fits into the palm of my hand. I pop it open. Inside, a pair of forget-me-not blue irises stare up at me, bobbing in a clear solution.

I am catapulted back to that first reunion with Olivia in my parents' living room. I'd been hesitant but when my eyes found hers, ones that had always made me think of glacial lakes and summer skies, forget-me-nots and bluebell petals, I was convinced. In my mind, that detail had cemented her as my sister. But it was all pretend. Another deception.

This is further confirmation that she's an imposter. I wait for the surge of triumph that I've found evidence but it doesn't come. Instead, a chasm of grief opens, threatening to send me tumbling into the dark because my sister is still gone and I am still alone. Anger creeps in and I grab at it with both hands because it is better to be angry than it is to be heartbroken. I snap the case closed. I have to tell my parents but then . . . what if they don't want to believe that I found the lenses in their bathroom? Olivia could claim they aren't hers. I stare down at the little plastic case, confidence dwindling because the proof I think I've found can be easily explained away. I'll have to wait until I get the results of the DNA test. Even if they remain sceptical then, it might push them to do their own. I put the case back and leave.

Half an hour later, I pull up outside my house but I don't go inside straight away. Recently, our home has felt like a museum filled with relics of a long-since extinct relationship. I imagine tourists walking through our house. This is how they lived, this is what they ate, this is how they loved. Since our fight three days ago, Oscar and I have barely spoken. On Monday morning, he left before I woke. There was a note on the kitchen counter explaining he was heading to Oxford to visit his cousin. He's due home tonight and my stomach twists at the thought. When he returns, I am going to confront him about Sam and demand he tell me the truth.

I stay inside the car a while longer, shuffling through my many questions as though they are tarot cards that might reveal some elusive truth. Olivia – the imposter – is connected to Simon Briggs because her fingerprints and DNA were found in his house. It's possible he was murdered and the note was faked to make it look like suicide. But, as Grimshaw pointed out, that would make Olivia his murderer. But why murder Briggs? And why run to *my* family, pretending to be my missing sister? And what of my masked stalker? Is it possible he *is* the man who took my sister? But why reappear now and why follow *me*?

I want to believe my real sister is out there somewhere, alive and fighting to stay that way. But that truth, the same one I felt as a child the night she was taken, in each beat of my heart, in every breath, even in the bright red of my blood, remains: my sister is never coming home. She is gone.

With the air conditioning turned off, the relentless August heat is baking me inside the car. I get out. Unfortunately, the cloudless blue sky doesn't herald rain. When I push open the front gate, I stop, because standing outside my door is Gemma. Her dark hair has been cut since I last saw her. That night at the bar with Florence, pre-Olivia's return, feels as though it happened years ago.

'Gemma,' I say.

She jumps at the sound of my voice, spinning towards me. 'You're here.'

I nod. 'Everything OK?'

She glances at the front door and then past me towards the gate. 'Yeah, everything's fine.'

In the silence that follows, I try to find an inoffensive way to ask *why* she's here. I'm glad to see her but I didn't expect to, not after our phone call three weeks ago.

'I was going to phone ahead first but I didn't know what to say,' she explains. 'I thought it would be easier to just stop by.'

'Are you OK?'

She nods. 'I just . . .' She picks at her chipped lemon nail polish. 'I've been feeling guilty for being so cold with you. I was hurt when I saw on the news that you had a sister. I thought we were good friends but to not know such a huge, important thing . . .'

'We are good friends, Gem.' I think again about how I've poured so much more time and effort into my relationship with Florence at the expense of everyone else, and I regret it. But Florence knew me before that night. And our shared grief at losing Olivia meant she understood in a way I'd learned no one else would.

'Why didn't you tell me?' she asks.

I hesitate, but then I hear Gideon's voice again, telling me to be braver. So I explain to Gemma that confiding in anyone about Olivia always raised questions I'd rather avoid. Judgment-laced ones that echoed my father. Like *why* didn't I call the police right away? And I feared being rejected by others the same way I'd been rejected by him.

Gemma listens and finally, she nods. 'I can see why that would stop you from opening up. But look, Caitie, the people who matter are the ones who won't rush to judge.' Her brow creases with sincerity. 'I don't think any less of you.'

I give her a small smile, and wish I'd trusted her before. 'Oscar's out. Do you want to come in for a coffee and a proper catch up?'

She glances past me. 'I can't.'

I laugh. 'Worried the Nescafé will lead to harder stuff like lattes and mochas?'

She smiles but there's a sadness to it. 'Actually, the other reason I wanted to see you is to say goodbye. Tomorrow, I'm catching a flight. I'm going travelling for a few months.'

'What about school?' I ask, because most schools start back next week.

'I quit.' At my expression, she laughs. 'It's fine. It wasn't even a permanent position. I was just supply teaching. And I only did my PGCE because I had no idea what I wanted to do with my life. If I'm honest, teaching makes me miserable. I have no ambition to work my way up until I'm the queen of the tiniest, most underfunded castle in the country. So I'm going to travel, gain some life experience and regroup.'

I think about all the times I've sat in my classroom, feeling as though I could scream so violently, so loudly, I could crack open my life and then crawl out of it like a discarded snakeskin. I've never admitted to anyone how unhappy I am, especially in my job, because it feels like a betrayal of my parents and the life they wanted for me. Now, I find myself once again wishing I'd confided in Gemma sooner. 'What about your mortgage? Finding a job when you come back?' I ask because these are the questions that stop me from buying a plane ticket myself.

'I'm renting my flat out and, as for a job, I can worry about that later, you know? My friend Cleo owns an aerial fitness studio and she needs a hand. I mean, I'm not even thirty, there's still time to change track. If I've got another forty years of working, I want to make sure that whatever career I choose, it's one that will make me happy.'

I'm nodding, agreeing with it all. I'm not surprised she's decided to travel. One of the first conversations we ever had, in the staff room of our first placement, was about all the places we wanted to visit. I'm happy for her, of course I am, but I'm envious, too. 'Why now?'

'I broke up with Lisa.' She holds up a hand, halting the condolence that was on the tip of my tongue. 'No, don't worry, it was my decision. She wanted us to buy a place together but I'm not ready for that. There are things I need to do first.'

She's brave. Braver than me. 'I'm going to miss you.'

'Well, if you want to fly out and join me for a few days in the half term, that'd be great.'

Go with her, whispers my wanderlust, *quit your job too and go*. God I want to. I glance up at the house and know I can't. I have Oscar. My parents. Ones that could be in danger from the masked stranger or the insidious imposter.

'Is Oscar working in an office now?' asks Gemma.

'No, he's still remote but he's forever travelling to meet clients. He's in Oxford today visiting his cousin.'

She frowns. 'Today?'

'Yes. Why?'

She presses her lips together. 'It's just, I saw him in Bath this morning. A couple of hours ago.'

My skin prickles. 'Where?'

'I was stuck in traffic in Oldfield Park and he was walking along Moorland. He had a bag with him, maybe he was on his way to the station?'

'No. He isn't due back until this evening. Was he alone?'

She opens her mouth. Closes it again. 'I really don't want to cause any trouble.'

'You won't,' I reassure her, trying to keep my tone calm and even.

'I recognised her from the news.'

'What do you mean?'

At her earnest expression, I feel a thud of dread. 'He was with your sister.'

As soon as Gemma's gone, I pull out my phone to call Oscar, but stop when I see half a dozen missed calls from a private number. My mobile has been on silent since this morning. I was worried if someone returned to Blossom Hill House during my search, my phone might ring and give me away. Just then, the private number calls again.

'It's me,' says Gideon as soon as I answer. 'I've been trying to warn you. Olivia didn't turn up to her appointment. If you're at the house, you need to get out now.'

'It's OK, I've already left.'

Relieved, he sighs, and I feel a rush of affection for him. 'Did you get what you need?'

'No. The phone wasn't there but I found some contact lenses. Whoever this woman is, she's been using them to trick everyone.'

'You need to go to the police.'

'With lenses she'll claim aren't hers? What will the police do? Pin her down and peel them off her eyeballs? They don't even suspect she's lying. No one does. But, I had another idea.' I tell him about the toothbrush and the hair and the DNA kit I've ordered.

'You should've done this weeks ago.'

'I know, I didn't even think. Apparently the police did one but it was inconclusive. I googled how this can happen and as they let her take the sample herself, she could've deliberately not swabbed properly or even added a drop of soap, bleach, perfume. All of it would interfere with a result.'

I hear the rustling of fabric and he switches ears. 'Just be careful. She could be dangerous. As soon as you get your result back, tell the police. I've got to go, my next client is here.'

We ring off and I let myself into my house. On the hallway floor is an A4 manila envelope addressed to me. I pick it up. It's heavy, almost three inches thick. There isn't a postage stamp which means it must've been hand delivered. I glance back at the door, wondering if it was left by Gemma. As I walk towards the kitchen, I tear open the envelope. I stare down at the first page, at the typed black letters, and my stomach twists.

I flip through the stack. I read and read and read. I cannot believe what I am reading. Once the shock has subsided and reality sets in, so too does the rage and betrayal and the unbearable breaking of my heart because between trembling fingers, I am holding Oscar's secret project.

35

Caitlin Arden

I wait for Oscar to return. I sit in the kitchen at the dining table we chose together. I remember how I'd run a hand over the wooden backs of the chairs in the showroom and pictured the dinner parties we'd host as a couple, our home bustling with the laughter and quick-witted conversation of our friends. Alone in the silence, my head bustling with fury and loss, I feel like an idiot.

In the hours since receiving the parcel, I've read almost every page, barely resisting the urge to tear each one to shreds. By the time I hear Oscar's key in the front door, the sun is hanging low in the sky. He's whistling as he enters our home. It's the song that played in the bar on our first date. He's oblivious as he takes off his shoes and comes down the hallway to the kitchen. I can smell the takeaway. He's surprised me with my favourite from Yum Yum Thai in Bath.

'Hey, gorgeous,' he says, coming around the table and placing a kiss on my unfeeling cheek. I press my palms into the oak to stop myself from churlishly wiping it away. He is all bounce and brilliance as he moves to the counter and starts unpacking the dinner, only I know we won't eat.

'Where have you been?' I ask his back.

'Didn't you get my note? I've been in Oxford.'

'*When* did you get back to Somerset?'

And finally, he stills. He turns to me. Our eyes meet. Whatever he sees in my expression makes him put down the takeaway. 'This morning,' he admits.

'What've you done all day?'

He scratches the back of his neck. He's considering a lie but, certain I know something, though how much, he isn't sure, he decides to skirt around the truth instead. 'In meetings.'

'Meetings?' My voice drips with cold disbelief.

Silence.

Tension creeps into his shoulders. He is caught. He just doesn't realise exactly how caught he is. He hasn't noticed the wad of papers lying neatly on the table in front of me. 'It isn't what you think.'

I lean forward. 'And what do I think?'

He throws his hands up. 'I don't know – an affair?'

I scoff because an affair would've been better. That, maybe, I could forgive.

'You were with Olivia.'

Surprise flits across his face, quickly followed by anger. 'Are you following me now?'

He's trying to rile me, to deflect, but I remain calm. 'No.'

He eyes me, unable to figure me out. Frustrated I didn't take the bait and barrel into another argument, he tries again to steer the conversation into a direction he can control. 'Following your fiancé isn't normal, Caitie.'

'You were with Olivia,' I say again because I refuse to be derailed.

He starts to pace. He's desperate to sweep his rendezvous under the rug to avoid admitting his deceptions, but the rug is so lumpy now, one wrong step would mean a nasty tumble. A broken neck. There's no room left under that rug. And as he meets my eye again, he knows he's out of options. 'Yes.'

'Does Olivia know?' I ask.

He stops. He frowns. 'About what?'

I wait. I give this impending revelation the silence it deserves. Or maybe I'm just clinging on to the last few seconds of our life as a couple because as soon as I reveal my hand, there is no going back. There is no us. I lay my palm on the stack of papers and slowly slide them across the table towards him.

'What's this?' he asks.

I don't answer. He steps forward and picks up the first sheet. His mouth forms a perfect circle of horror. Slowly, his gaze rises to meet mine. 'How did you get this?'

'It doesn't matter how I got it, Oscar.'

The wild, darting panic in his eyes reminds me of a rat desperately scrabbling to free itself from a trap.

A cloying, treacle-thick silence has enveloped us. 'A book, Oscar. You wrote a *fucking* book about my sister's abduction.'

I snatch the manuscript from the table and flip through the pages, through conversations had as we strolled hand in hand around a sunny park or on grey Tuesday afternoons in the sanctuary of our home. My innermost private thoughts, my deepest insecurities, my darkest secrets. All of them stolen and penned, sold to be read by the rest of the world without my consent. I slap it back down.

Oscar stares at the wall behind my head. 'You weren't meant to find out like this.'

'And how was I meant to find out?' I snap. 'At the book launch party or when the hardback appeared in Waterstones?'

He closes his eyes. 'Keeping it from you has been so hard.'

'And here I am without my violin.'

He ignores the snakebite. 'I've wanted to tell you since the day we met.'

The ground beneath my reality shifts as a knot of foreboding tightens in the pit of my stomach. 'You've been writing this book since we *met*?' I'm shaking my head because that doesn't make sense. 'But you didn't even know about Olivia when we met. You—' I stop, remembering the free tickets to the cheese-and-wine night at his parents' farm shop, emailed to me in a competition I hadn't entered. He'd told me it was fate. But it wasn't. It was design. *His* design. 'That's why you started dating me – research?'

'Caitie . . .'

'Is that all I ever was to you?'

I see the answer in his face before he even opens his mouth. 'Yes, I knew who you were before we met. I found your email address online. I didn't think you'd come.'

I blink up at the ceiling. Something inside me shatters. The broken shards sweep through my bloodstream, shredding and tearing.

'Caitie,' his voice cracks. 'I didn't mean to fall in love with you that summer but I did, and I don't regret a second of our lives together.'

He comes around the table but I push to my feet and stumble away from him, grabbing the kitchen counter for support. 'In St Ives you talked about how marriage lends us more credibility. You didn't mean as a couple, you meant for yourself as an author.'

He presses his lips together. I'm right. Anger boils through me. 'Did your publisher help you pick out my *fucking* ring?'

'I proposed to you because I want to marry you.'

'And pushing for the wedding sooner rather than later had nothing to do with the launch of your book?'

He hesitates, just a beat, but it's enough. 'No,' he lies.

I grip the counter until my knuckles turn white. I breathe deeply, swallowing my rage. It burns like acid. 'Does your cousin's husband really work for the police?'

His cheeks colour. 'No. I have a contact at the station.'

And once Oscar slipped up by giving me Simon's name, he had to think up a story that would explain it all away. I glower at him. Lies upon lies upon lies. 'And the woman you met with – Sam – who is she?'

He sighs. Shakes his head.

'Who is she?' I press.

'My editor.'

I nod. 'From Harriers?' I catch his surprise. 'Saw their name on the inside page. Congratulations,' I deadpan. 'They're the biggest publishing house in the country, aren't they?'

'Caitie . . .'

'Did you ever stop to think about my parents? They've been so good to you, Oscar.'

'I know, but we can explain to them that—'

'*We?*' My laughter is bitter. 'Explain what? That you used me. Betrayed me. Betrayed my entire family.'

'It's not like that.'

I push away from the counter. I yell, 'IT'S EXACTLY LIKE THAT.'

He's shaking his head. His blatant, arrogant denial of the truth enrages me.

'My parents never wanted to be in the media. They refused television deals, book deals, all of it. The only press they ever did was to raise awareness. You *know* this. I told you all of this. You really believe they'd be OK with you selling our family's story, our trauma, to the highest bidder?'

'I knew if you could forgive me, they could, too.'

And in this moment, I feel my ribs cracking, the broken bone piercing my heart because he doesn't realise what's happening. He is like a Labrador being led, oblivious, into the veterinary room and placed on a steel gurney. A dog that has bitten you, drawn blood, who stares up at you now with a soft, trusting gaze and soft, lolling mouth, tail wagging hopefully. And all the while, just inches away, a needle waits. I can't forgive him. I can't. This is the end. It has to be. But first, I have questions I need answering. I swallow thickly. 'Does Olivia know about the book?'

He nods. 'Harriers were keen to get her on board for a follow-up book, but she doesn't want to contribute.'

'Wow,' I say with mock cheer. 'It hasn't even hit the shelves yet and they already want a sequel.' I rub my hands over my face. I'm getting a headache but still, the revelations keep on coming. 'This is why you were so angry when I told you I think Olivia is an imposter. It would damage your *credibility*, the follow-up you want her to be a part of, if it turned out she isn't who she claims to be.'

'It *is* Olivia,' he insists. 'I met with her today to talk. It's definitely her. I'm certain.'

'How would you know? Until a few weeks ago, you'd never even met her.'

He pushes his fingers back through his hair and turns away from me.

Trepidation maggot-crawls across my skin. 'What? What is it?'

He can't look at me. 'I knew her before I knew you.'

'What do you mean?'

He swallows and then lifts the lid of Pandora's box. 'I'm The Boy on the Bus.'

The room tilts. 'No.'

'I don't want to hurt you, Caitie.'

Emotion closes my throat. 'Too late.'

'I spent a few weeks in Stonemill with my grandparents the summer Olivia went missing. I met her on the bus. We talked. I had a schoolboy crush. I gave her the gold-bee journal.'

I realise now the extent in which I have been living my sister's life. Maybe, if she hadn't been taken, they'd have fallen in love. Maybe she'd have documented their romance in that first journal, just like he told her to do. Maybe he'd have gifted her one every year they were together. Maybe they'd have bought a house and she'd be wearing the ring I am wearing now. The one that has never truly felt like it belongs to me. I am certain if she hadn't been abducted, Oscar and I would never have happened. The truth is, she was his prize and I was just the consolation. The tears come. The room blurs beneath them. He comes to me. He takes me in his hands and I let him. Hands that have loved me. That have stroked my hair back from my face a thousand times. Hands that have built flat-pack furniture, that have twirled me around our kitchen, that have run along the inside of my thighs. Hands that I know the weight and shape and breadth of as well as my own.

'When Olivia returned, my editor wanted more chapters. That's why I've been so stressed. Snapping at you. Shutting myself away. I'm not proud of how I've treated you. You can't see it now, but it will be worth it. I did all of this for us,' he assures me. 'You want to go travelling? Great, we can go, Caitie. We have the money. Harriers are paying me a lot of money. Paying *us* a lot of money. We can travel for a year if we want and still afford the mortgage. You can quit your job, you can paint, focus on Wanderlust Illustrations if that's what you really want.'

He presses his forehead against mine. His breath is warm on my face but despite the summer heat, my skin is cold.

He is offering me everything I've ever dreamed of. But at what cost? I'll never trust him again. I'll never know if we're together because he loves me or because he loves what I can do for his career. 'What I want is for you to pull the book. Tell Harriers you aren't interested.'

He stills. His hands drop from my shoulders. He is silent. I feel my heart beating in my lips. I stare at his chest, too afraid to look him in the eye. But I must. I force myself to search his face and allow myself to hope. But he takes that hope, a springtime flower, and crushes it in his fist. 'I can't.'

My chest burns. Tightens and burns. I can't catch my breath. He doesn't love me enough to fix the damage he has done. He doesn't love me enough to even try.

'I can't,' he says again, almost to himself. 'I just . . . can't.' The words are strangled. I think this is a battle he's fought within himself for a long time. And before I'd even asked the question, he knew the answer, he just hoped it was one he'd never have to voice. 'I know I've made mistakes in this relationship,' he says. 'I lied. I lied from day one. But I do love you. I love you even though you've made mistakes, too, Caitie. You wanted to travel more than you wanted to marry me. *That's* why you wouldn't commit to a date.'

Maybe, I think, but maybe some part of me knew he couldn't be trusted. Sensed that he was lying. Always lying. And whenever he was caught, he went out of his way to make me question my sanity. That isn't love. Or, it isn't a love I want. I feel the words falling out of my mouth before I realise I've even said them. 'Oscar? I think this is it. We can't do this anymore.'

I can't believe I've said it. I'm in as much shock as he is. He takes my hand in his again. Being held by him used to make me feel safe. But it doesn't. Not anymore.

Then he lets go.

'You want us to break up?' he asks.

I nod.

He looks to the ceiling. His chest rises and falls, then rises again. 'OK.'

I feel a clench of disappointment that he isn't fighting for us. I blink away the tears and wonder if he ever wanted a future with me or if he just convinced himself he did to feel better about using me. Now he's got what he needs from me, from us, he's at peace with it being done. He's standing on the precipice of a life he's always wanted as a published author. A life his parents denied him. Now, though, he can go to them with a success story. From what he's said about the money, he can leave the IT career he never wanted and remain financially stable. And all it cost him was me. He was OK with that and I have to be, too.

I breathe in the betrayal and violation and the anger and the grief, and then I breathe it out. I let it go. It will find me again in quiet moments for months and maybe even years to come. For now, though, I expel it into the air and ask him to pack a bag.

I sit at the dining table and listen to the sound of him leaving. Drawers opening and closing. A suitcase being dragged from beneath the spare bed. Toiletries being collected from the bathroom. He appears in the kitchen doorway, red-eyed and tired.

He lifts a hand. 'Bye, Caitie.'

For a moment, the reality that I will shortly be alone, truly alone, terrifies me, and I open my mouth to beg him to stay. But then I think of the words he has written, *my* words, ones that feel as though they've been ripped from my mouth like teeth without anaesthetic, and I know he has to leave.

I raise my chin. 'Goodbye, Oscar.'

And then he is gone and I am alone.

36

Elinor Ledbury

Neither of them can think clearly with Uncle Robert lying on the floor, a soup of entrails spilling across the rug, so they wrap him up in it. It is ruined now, anyway. Blood-soaked.

They work in silence, speaking only when they must.

'His hand . . .'

'I know. Grab his leg.'

'Got it.'

They lug him into the woods on their land. Heath offers to dig the hole alone but Elinor snatches a shovel from the shed and gets to work alongside him. The earth is frozen. They dig for hours in the dark and the cold. When it is done, their clothes stained with blood and dirt, Heath reaches out to Elinor but she slaps his hand away, collapsing to her knees and vomiting onto the frozen leaves beside the grave. Vaguely, Elinor wonders what Flynn would think if he could see her now, wiping sick from her mouth with a hand that is crusted with her murdered uncle's blood.

After burning the clothes they were wearing, they go inside and shower. Elinor scrubs her skin until it is pink. As the sun rises, filling Ledbury Hall slowly, frothing upward like champagne, they tumble into Elinor's big bed and fall asleep holding each other.

In the morning, she wakes with her heart in her mouth. She is alone. She goes in search of Heath and finds him in the study. He is sitting in Uncle Robert's chair, a drink in his hand. It is the same glass their uncle was using moments before he died. It is chipped where it hit the ground and there's a speck of red on the rim. Heath has the darkest, plum-coloured circles under his eyes. Elinor doesn't think he has slept for more than a few minutes, if at all.

She crouches in front of him. The air is still and stale. She breathes in the smell of bleach and she is sure, beneath it, the metallic tang of blood. 'What do we do if people ask questions about Uncle Robert?' she queries softly.

He gulps his whisky. 'No one will ask questions. He didn't have anyone but us.'

She licks her dry lips. 'Will his company come looking for him?'

'*Former* company. You said they fired him.'

'They did. That's what he told me.'

'Then, no.'

Silence.

She can tell he wants to be left alone but she doesn't think sitting by himself staring at the spot where their uncle died is good for him. 'I know you didn't mean to . . .' she swallows '. . . do what you did. You thought he was hurting me. It was an accident. You didn't mean to kill him, Heath.'

He fixes her with a hard, blank stare. 'Yes,' he says, 'I did.'

He tips back the last of his drink, gets up, and leaves the room.

Elinor has nightmares. She dreams of girls trapped in tall towers and men falling from them, their chests ripping open like pomegranates. She struggles to eat. To do anything at all. She worries constantly, fearing she and Heath will get caught. That the both of them will be hauled from their home and locked away.

As days turn to weeks, Heath is rarely without a glass of wine and he is quick to anger. His rageful fits almost always end in something being broken, a tumbler, a frame, even a door. She starts to feel as though she is living in a house with a rabid dog; one wrong move and she'll get bitten. She realises, with a deep, severing sadness, that for the first time in her life, her brother is not her safe place.

Time and time again, she replays the last few moments she shared with Uncle Robert. She'd felt sorry for him. She'd wanted to comfort him. She'd hoped it was the start of a more meaningful connection with him. That things would be different. Better. And then Heath shot him as though he were nothing more consequential than a rabbit. Uncle Robert was cruel to the Ledburys, but did he deserve to be murdered? It is no secret that Heath bore the brunt of their uncle's brutality, but by killing him, Heath has condemned them both to a life of uncertainty and fear, always looking over their shoulders. As far as Elinor can tell, they've exchanged one fearful existence for another. Resentment towards her brother grows within her like black mould. Because of him, she knows the smell of human blood. Because of him, she knows the ache of muscles after hours spent digging a grave. Because of him, she can't look herself in the mirror. But she swallows her anger because Heath is all she has left.

More than anything, she wishes she could slip into another family and become someone else entirely.

37

Caitlin Arden

It's been three days since Oscar left. He's staying in a hotel in Bath. We agreed not to tell people we're separated until I work out how to break the news of his book to my parents. It's publishing in October, just in time to sweep up those Christmas sales. My insides feel like a wrung-out dishcloth at the thought of seeing it in bookshops, supermarkets, the airport. I think of my father, how he's always connected more with Oscar than he has with me. I wonder if *I'll* get the blame for Oscar's deceit. After all, I'm the reason he was able to get so close to the family.

My parents were proud when I bought this house. I'm sure they won't be pleased when the time comes to sell it. I'll be glad to, though. It no longer feels like a home. Hasn't for weeks. I wonder where I'll end up. Whether I'll have to house share or whether I'll be able to afford a place of my own. There is so much change ahead, so much uncertainty. That's the thing with break-ups, you aren't just mourning the person you loved but the life you planned together. All of it, gone, lost on the wind.

The house is so quiet. A constant reminder that I'm alone. The loneliness used to feel like a wave that threatened to close over my head and drown me, but since Oscar left, it has shifted into something wilder. Something clawing and feral. But I push it down. Push it away. There's no time to wallow because tomorrow is Florence's wedding. In just a few minutes, I'll be on my way to the venue to spend the night there before the big day. It was Florence's idea. Her way to negate any chance of me arriving late to the morning preparations which, for a fastidious timekeeper like Florence, is a cardinal sin. There's a tight schedule for hair and make-up and pre-wedding photographs, and I've *promised* I'll arrive promptly. Sleeping in the same building means there's no excuse.

I'm carrying my overnight bag out to the car when I see a Post-it note lying beneath the console table in the hallway. I pick it up.

You needed to know. See you soon.

I don't recognise the handwriting. I read it a few times, trying to figure out where it's come from or what it's in relation to. Then I realise . . . the manuscript. I can see myself now, walking down the hallway towards the kitchen, tearing open the manila envelope. I didn't even check for a note. But this is it, isn't it? It must've fallen out.

I haven't given much thought to who was responsible for delivering the book. I didn't really care. All that mattered was that the last five years of my life has been built on lies and manipulation. So who is the anonymous sender? And how did they have a copy of Oscar's book? Gemma was hovering outside my house that day – is it possible the real reason she was here unannounced was to deliver the manuscript? But *why*? How would she have become embroiled in all this? Surely the only people who know about the book are those working in publishing or . . . what about Florence? She's an audiobook narrator for Harriers. It was only a few weeks ago she was narrating Noah Pine's next bestseller. It's plausible she had access to their other upcoming projects. But she's my best friend . . . Or she *was* until recently, surely she'd have told me herself?

Then there's Olivia. Oscar had confided in her about the book and, from the start, she didn't take to him, suggesting she'd be able to find me a better match, a perfect husband. I'd put that conversation down to sisterly concern but, if she isn't my sister, then why does she care who I'm in a relationship with?

At the time the masked man broke into our house, we assumed he hadn't taken anything, but what if he had? He'd been riffling through Oscar's study. What if *this* is what he took – the manuscript? Oscar's laptop was in there, all it would have taken to copy over his files is an easily concealable USB. Or perhaps he swiped a physical copy. The more I think about it, the more certain I am that he's responsible. I can't go to the police; they didn't believe anyone broke into the house, so I can't imagine they'll do anything about a stray Post-it note.

See you soon.

Fear shivers through me as this threat sinks in.

Not a threat, I realise, a promise.

Forty minutes later, I arrive at Fawsley Hall. It's a beautiful country-house hotel. A stone building with arch windows and exposed beams. Florence and Daniel are having supper with their parents in a private room. It's only me and a handful of other wedding guests who are staying at the venue tonight. It's almost 7 p.m. and I haven't eaten all day. Everything I put in my mouth tastes like a handful of lint. I decide once I've checked in, I'll order room service. As I approach reception with my bag, I remember how Oscar and I had planned to enjoy the spa and have dinner in the restaurant together to make the most of it. I sent Florence a message this morning to apologise for Oscar's absence and explain he's terribly unwell with flu. I didn't want to lie, but how could I burden her with the truth the night before she walks down the aisle? Everyone knows the unwritten rule of not bothering the bride in the run-up to the big day.

Maybe, once she's back from her honeymoon and I have the results from the home DNA test kit to prove Olivia isn't Olivia, I'll explain everything to her. Until then, I will smile and nod and apologise and lie.

The receptionist hands me my room key. Two of them. I forgot to inform the hotel that Oscar won't be joining me. I'm about to hand one back when I feel someone standing close behind me. I whip around and the keys slip from my hand. Standing too close in a blush-pink floor-length dress is Olivia. She's holding a hardback book, and beyond her, is a library with plush sofas and floor-to-ceiling shelves lined with novels. On one of the dark-wood coffee tables is the teacup she's abandoned. I bend to scoop up the room keys and hotel pamphlet I dropped but she beats me to it. I glare at her butter-wouldn't-melt smile and snatch them from her, stuffing them quickly into my handbag.

'Just checking in?' she asks.

'No, I'm juggling cats, actually.'

She chooses to ignore the sarcasm. 'No Oscar?'

I stare at her, silent.

'That's a shame,' she coos. 'Is he ill?'

Her eyes glitter. She knows he isn't unwell. I lift my chin. 'You decided not to tell my parents about his book, then?'

She smirks. 'I prefer not to get my hands dirty.'

Hatred for this imposter bleeds across my cheeks. I grip the handle of my overnight bag, forcing down the urge to tackle her.

'Oh,' she says, 'and Florence asked me to remind you *not* to be late to the suite tomorrow. It's an 8 a.m. start in Room 22.'

My hackles rise because this woman, this stranger, has wreaked havoc on my life, breaking off pieces and popping them in her mouth until I'm left with nothing more substantial than crumbs. It may be childish but I hate that *she* is passing on messages to me from *my* best friend.

'So don't be late, OK?' she says, all condescension and fake, saccharine smiles.

I look into her eyes, scanning for signs she is wearing contacts. They are exactly how I remember my sister's. But this woman's gaze is cool, devoid of her love and warmth. I get a longing for her that is so fierce, it is a physical ache in my chest. 'Do you know my sister?' Unbidden, the question falls from my lips, my voice sad and small, and it surprises us both. 'My real sister, I mean? I miss her. I miss her so much, is she—'

The foyer fills with the noise of suitcase wheels on hardwood floors and the loud, shrill conversation of the group of women who wield them. I glance in their direction and, recognising a couple of them, realise they're here for the wedding, too. Suddenly, there are fingers digging into my upper arms, yanking me close. Olivia's breath is against my ear. From afar, it looks as though she's pulling me into an affectionate embrace but she's gripping me so tightly, I'll bruise.

'He's watching you,' she whispers, frantic, fearful. 'Run, Caitie, run, run.'

'Olivia?' shrieks a woman excitedly.

She lets me go and steps back. As she does, I see terror flashing across her face, like lightning across a darkening sky, and then it is gone, quickly replaced by a smile, like a beam of sunlight, as she turns to the group of women. I recognise the redhead in the navy dress. It's Laura, Natalie's mother, the one who recognised me on that last day of term. 'Olivia,' she says again. 'Oh, my gosh, I can't believe it.'

I stand on the edges of their reunion. The women envelop Olivia, all of them falling over themselves to talk to her. She's once again the queen bee. The others buzz around her, desperate to win court. Then she is swept away into the library. I stare after her, heart cantering.

He's watching you. Run, Caitie, run, run.

Fear spreads through me like a cold, dark fog.

I stumble away, my chest tight, and go up to my room to drop off my bag. I change quickly, then return to the library, planning to wait to catch Olivia once she's done with her impromptu reunion. But, by the time I get there, she and the group of women are gone. I walk the grounds of the hotel, in and out of different rooms, until a member of staff intercepts.

'Can I help?' asks the tall, wiry employee on reception. The woman who checked me in is gone, too.

'I'm looking for my . . . sister,' I say, the word catching in my throat. 'Olivia Arden. Do you know what room she's staying in?'

'I'm sorry,' he says smoothly. 'I can't divulge guest information. Is there anything else I can do?'

'I just really need to see my sister, actually.'

His smile is tight but professional. 'I apologise but due to GDPR, I'm not at liberty to provide you with those details.' He looks pointedly at the phone in my hand. 'Have you tried calling your sister to find out where she is?'

'No . . . I'll do that now.' I step aside and start scrolling for her number.

'Excuse me,' he says. 'We don't allow mobile-phone use in this area.' He nods politely towards a discreet little sign on the wall.

I try not to roll my eyes as I turn and hurry outside. It's still filthy hot and arid. The call goes to voicemail, three times. Frustrated,

I return to reception where I'm met with the strained smile of the wiry receptionist.

'Look,' I implore. 'I can't get hold of my sister. I'm here for the Odell-Fox wedding tomorrow and I really, really need to see her. We're the maids of honour and we have a . . .' I cast around, 'wedding-related emergency.'

'I'm sorry to hear that,' he says in a tone that tells me he is not sorry at all. 'But I'm afraid I can't help.'

I stare at his pencil-thin moustache and decide he's one of those people who accepts carpets in the bathroom and thinks ham sandwiches are exciting.

'Do you need me to have someone show you to your room?' he asks, which is receptionist for 'please get the fuck away from my desk.'

I go back to my room before he calls security and has me escorted out of the hotel. I toy with the idea of knocking on each door until I find her, but this place is vast and someone will most definitely report the mad woman going from room to room like the bloody Gestapo.

No. I'll go to Florence's room early and wait outside for Olivia to arrive so I can question her before we're caught up in the melee of matching dressing gowns, prosecco, and hairspray. I plug my phone in and set my alarm for 6 a.m.

But sleep doesn't find me. I lie awake in bed, staring up at the ceiling. I can't stop thinking about the warning Olivia had frantically, fearfully whispered.

He's watching you. Run, Caitie, run, run.

Feeling like a coiled spring, I get out of bed and go to the window. I imagine the masked man standing on the patio below, staring up at my room. Taking a breath, I rip open the curtains. It's dark now. The lawn stretches out in a muted shade of grey, the pond is a gaping, open mouth, and the moon hangs in the sky, a single watchful eye. But there is no masked man. No one lurking. I crawl back into bed, but still I cannot sleep. I close my eyes and imagine my mind is a building full of rooms. There is one caretaker whose job it is to go into each one and turn off the light. I tell myself that when the building goes dark, I'll be able to sleep. Only the building keeps expanding, with room after room being added. The caretaker starts racing down corridors, lights flickering on in every new addition. Agitated, I flip onto my side, away from the little light at the top of my phone that tells me it's charging.

Questions zip-zap around my head like flies. I try to catch them as they whizz past. Who is the woman impersonating my sister? Why has she chosen now to warn me? Did she kill Briggs? Is she working *for* or *against* the masked man? Why is my family being targeted? Does she know my real sister? Is that how she is so able to convince everyone else she isn't lying? Were they held captive together? If so, where is my sister now? And how can I save her?

I jolt awake. I'm breathing hard, the last threads of a nightmare being pulled from my mind. I press my palm against my chest and feel the frenzied beat of my heart. The room is dark, but through the small gap in the heavy curtains sunlight streams in. My mouth feels like it's full of sand and my head pounds. I don't think I got more than a couple of hours' sleep. Still, my alarm hasn't sounded so maybe I can force myself to get a little more rest. I reach for my phone and frown when it doesn't immediately blink to life. It's off. But how? I didn't turn it off before bed. I know I didn't. I hold down the button to turn it on and wait. When the time flashes up on the screen, my stomach drops to my ankles.

'Shit.' I scramble from the bed. I'm late. *Really* late. I should've been in Florence's room half an hour ago. After the world's speediest shower, I dress and race to Room 22. I knock and knock and—

The door is flung open. A confused, bare-chested man answers. This clearly isn't the correct room. I apologise and stumble back down the hall. I go to reception and almost swear out loud when I see the receptionist I had the delight of dealing with yesterday and, unfortunately for me, he's still treating being unhelpful like it's an Olympic sport. It takes fifteen minutes and a conversation with a different, far more accommodating member of staff to give me the correct room number.

Room 17, not 22, as Olivia claimed.

I knock on the door. A middle-aged woman with wide hips and glossy, dark hair answers. She's frowning. 'You must be Caitie,' she says reproachfully. 'I'm Cheryl, the hair stylist.'

I look past her into the large, bright space with exposed beams and huge king-sized bed. Beneath the music, is the rise and fall of conversation. Morning preparations are well under way. I don't want to go in there. It feels like stepping into shark-infested waters but I can't hover in the hallway all day so I sidle in, red-faced and mortified. Florence is dressed in an ivory robe, her back to me, talking to Olivia and a woman brandishing lipliner who I assume is the make-up artist. Off to one side is Florence's mother, Susan, and Florence's Aunt May. A slim, attractive woman dressed in black, wielding an expensive-looking camera, snaps candid shots of the bride and her maid of honour. Slowly, all eyes turn my way and I get the sickening feeling of having been recently discussed by a group of women.

Florence fixes me with a withering glare. Beside her, Olivia's mouth quirks into a faint, self-satisfied smile. Ignoring her, I meet Florence's steely gaze with an earnest, pleading one of my own. 'I am so—'

'Your robe is on the bed,' says Florence coldly.

The other women exchange an uncomfortable look.

Nodding, I pick up the robe and force myself to walk, not run, towards the bathroom. I change and splash my face with cold water.

I can't believe I was late. If my phone hadn't been switched off, if I hadn't been given the wrong room number . . . I am certain Olivia somehow entered my room in the early hours and turned it off. Maybe she swiped the second key card from me when I dropped them in the foyer. I never did give Oscar's back, and I didn't check to see if I had them both.

This morning, all the traces of the fear I saw in Olivia yesterday are gone. Did she only make those strange, ominous comments to ensure I had a sleepless night? She has set up hurdle after hurdle and I've stumbled at every single one, just as she hoped I would. Rage burns like a fire in my chest. I hate her. I really hate her. *Why* is she trying to ruin my life? Trying to drive wedges between me and the people I love until there are insurmountable chasms and I am left all alone on a lump of arid rock. I remind myself that today isn't about me, it is about Florence, and even though I think Olivia engineered this situation, I was still late to my best friend's wedding celebrations when I promised I wouldn't be. Feeling sick with nerves and battling to extinguish the rage, I leave the bathroom.

Naturally, as the bride, Florence isn't alone for a single second so I can't get close enough to her to explain or apologise. Instead, I am as helpful and upbeat as possible. I become a waitress, a cleaner and a launderer. Organising and tidying the room to ensure it's a perfect backdrop for the candid bridal-prep photographs; making drinks for everyone – I even manage to hold onto my smile when Olivia asks me to remake her coffee. I steam our dresses, my shoulders aching as I erase every single crease from the sage-green silk. Between tasks, I duck into photographs and try not to notice that whilst Florence slings an affectionate arm around Olivia's waist, she leaves a two-inch gap between me and her. The morning passes by in a flurry of champagne and photographs, curling tongs, and mascara wands.

Soon, Florence is in her dress. It has a square neckline, and pearl straps with an asymmetric hem to show off the very expensive shoes she's bought but has yet to put on. Her dark Parisian bob is styled in tousled waves with a simple pearl headband. Her lips, as always, are painted in her signature scarlet. Right now, she is off to one side, being briefed by her wedding planner, Zara.

'Can I get one of the bridesmaids and the maid of honour?' asks the photographer.

I open my mouth to correct her, to tell her we're *both* maids of honour, but then I close it again because it doesn't really matter. Still, Olivia's smile is too smug to be charming. We're asked to pose in front of the large, bay window. We're in our dresses now, hair and make-up done. Olivia is perfect with her thick, waist-length waves tumbling down her back in a glossy cascade. She is all long lashes and long legs and tiny waist. She curls a slim arm around me and I hold myself still even though I want to slap this stranger's touch away.

We smile at the camera.

'Now look at each other.'

Reluctantly, I turn my face to hers. She's painfully beautiful. Her skin smooth and dewy. It's no wonder she's beguiled the entire nation with her tragic story because, of course, ugly lies never fall from the lips of pretty girls.

The camera snaps away.

'Smile,' instructs the photographer.

And, right on queue, Olivia graces me with her most brilliant smile while my own feels strained and clownish.

'The shoes are going on!' squeals Florence. We turn to see her lifting a pair of very expensive bright yellow designer heels from a box. The photographer goes wild.

Florence perches daintily on a chair to slip them on.

Olivia squeezes my waist to get my attention. 'Are they . . .' she whispers to me, 'aureolin?'

I am spun back to that day in the park as we stood beside the sunflowers, laughing so hard the corners of our eyes wrinkled. I smile at the memory and Olivia does too, her face splitting into a grin.

'Aureolin,' she whispers again as laughter takes hold.

Click. Click. Click.

My head whips around. The photographer is snapping a million photographs of me and Olivia. Me and the stranger. Me and the imposter. The laughter that blossomed in my chest withers and I pull away from her and her silly games. Olivia looks hurt by the rejection. Genuinely pained. I stare at her, baffled. She is forever a pendulum, swinging from catty smiles and taunting remarks to laughter and sisterly affection. Sensing the tension, the photographer spins away from us.

The ceremony is close now. I stand beside the window and watch the guests milling around in the courtyard below. I catch a glimpse of my parents – Mum in a lavender fascinator and Dad in a matching tie.

'Not long now,' says Florence, appearing at my side. 'You look lovely.'

I lift a hand to the simple half-up style she chose. 'That's entirely down to you. Remember Emma's wedding?'

She pulls a face. 'Oh, God, yes. Insisting your bridesmaids wear their hair in a low ponytail is an act of aggression.'

We smile at each other, the ice finally thawing.

Knowing we don't have much time, and keen to clear the air, I seize the opportunity, 'I really am mortified. I'm so sorry, Florence. My phone was somehow turned off and I was given the wrong room number and—'

'It's fine,' she says, cutting me off kindly. 'I was livid earlier but . . .' She sighs. 'It's done now, isn't it? You're here, that's the main thing. Just . . . can you promise no more surprises? I want this wedding to run as smoothly as possible from here on out.'

I nod. 'Absolutely. I promise.'

She pulls me into a hug. I breathe in the familiar scent of her Jo Malone Fig and Lotus Flower perfume and hear the click of a camera as the photographer snaps away. Over Florence's shoulder, Olivia watches us. The humour and affection from earlier are gone. Now, her cool blue eyes meet mine and a slow, malicious grin slides across her face.

38

Caitlin Arden

We are gathered in the hallway that connects to the ceremony room. I can hear the excited hum of people, eagerly awaiting the arrival of the bride. I am fizzing with anticipation and nerves. I mustn't trip. Florence will murder me if I end up sprawled on the aisle floor. I've already inflicted enough drama and stress.

Florence's hands are shaking, which surprises me as she's been so calm all morning, but then, having spent most of her life on a stage, she's a performer. I think it's only now that the weight of this moment is hitting her. She looks to me, teeth pressing down hard on her bottom lip, and I feel a pang of overwhelming joy that I'm the one she's turned to.

I move past Olivia to stand beside my best friend. 'Deep breaths,' I tell her. 'Remember: it's you and Daniel.'

Some of the tension eases from her shoulders. She nods. 'Me and Daniel.'

We smile at each other and I feel a wave of love for her.

The string quartet starts up, playing 'She Burns' by Foy Vance.

Then it's my turn to walk down the candle-lined aisle. We were given strict instructions by the wedding planner to keep our heads up, shoulders back, flowers low, smile wide and to walk slow. The room is stunning with its vaulted ceiling and enormous window overlooking the rose garden from which a golden light streams in, making everything glow. I spot my parents. Mum dabs at her eyes and I know she is wishing it were me in the big white dress. It's going to break her heart when she finds out about the break-up. My father is smiling so widely at me, a genuine, heartfelt grin, that I smile back. I'm still bathing in the warmth of his affection as I take my place at the front. Then comes Olivia, gliding smoothly towards me. She is gorgeous. Demure. Glowing. I see now, in this moment, why some women deliberately choose their unattractive friends to be bridesmaids because it is Olivia who steals the show. I glance around, note the hungry, heated looks the men give her and the longing, envious ones the women do.

The music swells and right on queue, Florence enters. She grins and clutches her sunflower and rose bouquet to her chest. This is it; for the rest of her life, at the end of every terrible day, she'll have Daniel to go home to, and she'll never again have to worry about waking up alone. I feel a twinge of envy which is quickly swallowed by a rush of happiness because she is so very deserving of this.

When she reaches the altar and Daniel admires her in all his I-can't-believe-how-lucky-I-am glory, I get a sudden flash of Oscar's face the day I said yes to his proposal. He'd organised a private art lesson, which I thought was odd since he hadn't even mastered a stick figure. The teacher instructed us to paint a moment of happiness in our relationship. When the hour was up, Oscar turned his easel around with a flourish and I gasped, faced with the most beautiful watercolour – it obviously wasn't his handiwork. I recognised it instantly as an original piece by my favourite artist. It was of me and Oscar in that very room, him on bended knee proffering a ring box, me with my hands covering my mouth in delighted surprise. He'd had that painting commissioned especially. It still hangs in our bedroom. I feel a wrench at the reality of its future – gathering dust in an attic.

As planned, Florence hands her bouquet to me. It's heavier than it looks and I'm careful not to drop it. The registrar instructs us to take our seats. Olivia and I sit on the two lone chairs reserved for us on the first row. Cleverly, Florence has had a cluster of brass and glass lanterns put in place of the missing chairs so our row doesn't look empty.

Susan takes centre stage. 'My daughter asked me to read a piece from *Captain Corelli's Mandolin*,' she says, every bit the performer Florence is.

I adore this reading. It's one Oscar and I talked about for our wedding. Tears roll down my cheeks as she talks about love being a temporary madness. God, the way Florence and Daniel look at each other. They're so in love. I'm glad my best friend's heart is in the hands of such a good, trustworthy man.

I jump as Olivia touches my knee. Then, through the silk, her fingers pinch my skin. My gaze snaps up to hers to ask what the hell she's doing, but the venom in her eyes makes the words catch in my throat. She leans close. I feel her breath on my neck. She whispers, 'If you keep digging, we'll bury you next to your *fucking* sister.'

Ice sloshes through my veins. 'What?' I whisper.

She loosens her grip and turns her attention to the bride and groom, as though nothing has happened but I can still feel the hot points in which her fingers burrowed into my skin. If I pull back my dress, there will be a set of angry red marks that are sure to turn into ugly purple bruises.

Did she really just tell me my sister is dead? A tight band of panic winds around my chest, squeezing the breath from me. 'What did you say?' I hiss.

She doesn't even flicker, pretending as though she hasn't heard.

The band tightens. I imagine my sister's cold, bloodied body rotting in an unmarked grave. I see the maggots and worms that eat at her flesh. She'll be nothing but bones now. The room is spinning away from me. My blood vibrates in my chest. 'What did you say?' I stare at her profile. Then I am up on my feet. I am screaming, 'FUCKING ANSWER ME!'

Hundreds of pairs of eyes swivel my way.

A horrified silence fills the room. It's the kind of silence that follows a devastation. A tsunami, an earthquake, an act of terrorism. The kind of silence that can be seen from space. But it isn't enough to stop me. I am a bull and she is my flaming red flag. 'You killed her,' I shriek. 'Where is she? Where's my sister?'

Olivia slowly rises, hands raised as though fending off an attack from a rabid animal. Her eyes dart around the room in an act of confusion. Of fear. 'I don't know what you're talking about,' she says, her voice the perfect mix of incredulity and fright, but loud enough that even those at the back will hear. A small, rational voice inside me breaks through the swell of fury, warning me to stop, warning me that I am feeding into her plot. But that voice is banished beneath a louder, more insistent one that demands answers.

'You just told me you murdered my sister.' Tears of anger and frustration and devastation come. 'Where is she? Where the fuck is she?'

'What? I didn't say anything. I didn't—'

Before I can register what I'm doing, my hand shoots out. The force of the slap is enough to make her stumble to the side. My palm tingles. Burns. Slowly, she turns her face to mine and I see the livid red of her cheek. It isn't enough. I let the rage swallow me whole. I lunge for her. We hit the ground. We roll. My hands are in her hair, pulling, pulling, pulling. Someone is screaming; a wild, wretched sound. Vaguely, I realise it's me.

Hands go under my arms and I am being lifted. The room whizzes past as I'm swung away from her.

'Get her out of here!' someone shrieks. 'GET HER OUT!'

Half feral, my head whips towards the voice. Florence. She has scooped her bouquet from the floor. Most of the flowers are in pieces, petals scattered across the wood. The broken neck of a sunflower hangs limply, tragically. It's this detail that sobers me. The rage drains away. The fury and pain drain away. What's left is shame. Bright red, burning shame. I'm queasy with it, sickened by what Florence must think of me. She is crying. She is furious and she is crying. I hear a door shutting. I have slammed it shut on our friendship for ever.

Olivia stumbles towards Florence, who gathers her up, pulling her close. I wait for the anger, the resentment, to surge again. It doesn't. Because this is my fault. Even if Olivia dangled the bait, I didn't need to snap at it with hungry, hasty jaws. I stand there, as limp as the broken neck of the sunflower. There are hands on me. Pulling me away. I let them.

Soon I am outside, and despite the baking heat I am shivering. My father has my wrist in a vice grip. Mum is stumbling after us, pale with shock. My father isn't pale. He is scarlet with outrage. He drags me to the car park. I try to yank myself free but he is towing me towards their car. I pull and pull. He lets me go so suddenly, I stagger back and crash into Mum.

'What the hell is wrong with you?' he explodes, spittle flying from his lips.

'That woman told me Olivia is dead. Told me she buried her.'

Mum has moved to stand beside her husband. They are confused, looking at me as though I'm in a straitjacket. 'Olivia's not dead, she's in there,' cries Mum, flinging her arm out in the direction of Fawsley Hall. 'You just attacked her. *Why* did you attack her?'

'Because she told me if I didn't stop digging she'd bury me just like she did Olivia.'

Silence. Tight, bewildered silence.

I rush to fill it. 'The woman who turned up on your doorstep claiming to be Olivia *isn't* Olivia. She's a vile, murderous imposter.' I start rambling about Edward and the shed in the woods, the contact lenses, and the secret phone.

'She's lost it.' Dad is talking to Mum as though I'm not here. 'She needs help, Clara.'

'I'm not crazy!' I yell. But oh, I do sound it, don't I? I try to lower my voice, to talk evenly, calmly. 'It's all true. All of it.'

Mum looks scared. Really scared. 'Caitie, love, she *is* your sister.'

'No. No she isn't. I've sent off for a home DNA kit. I'll prove she isn't who she claims to be. I'm sorry, Mum, but Olivia – the *real* Olivia is . . . is . . .' I start sobbing. My entire body is wracked with sobs. They seem to emerge from some untapped well of grief. 'She's dead.'

Tears stream down Mum's face.

Seeing this, Dad steps forward and stands between me and his wife. 'Stop it,' he barks as though I'm one of his incompetent employees. 'Just stop it.'

'I'm sorry, Dad. It's my fault Olivia went missing. You're right, I was *stupid* not to call the police that night. I froze. I was terrified. It isn't an excuse and I've hated myself every day for it.'

His face falls. He takes a step towards me, reaching out to touch me. Then he catches himself. Clears his throat. 'No one has ever said—'

'*You* said. Years ago to Mum. I heard you. That's why you hate me. That's why you've barely looked at me for the last sixteen years. I thought getting the career and the house and the fiancé would make it up to you. I thought if I could be perfect, I'd be enough.' My laughter is bitter and harsh and full of self-loathing. 'But you were right not to forgive me. To blame me. It *was* my fault and now she's dead, she's dead. Olivia is dead!' I start crying again, hopelessly, helplessly, because the reality is sinking into me like a blade: my sister is never coming back.

Dad's eyes brim with unshed tears. 'Caitie,' he says softly, in a tone I hadn't realised I'd desperately been missing. 'It wasn't your fault. I—'

'Listen to me,' Mum cuts Dad off, eyes boring into mine. She is irate and impatient. 'We know she's our daughter because a DNA test confirmed she is.'

I blink at her, sure I've heard her wrong. 'But it was inconclusive. Florence told me.'

'We did another one through the police,' she says.

'That's not possible. No. You would've said so.'

'If I'd known you doubted her identity, of course I would have. But I knew, the second she came home, she was my daughter. We thought you did, too.'

I'm shaking my head. 'Maybe she knew Olivia. Maybe she kept some of her DNA and—'

'STOP IT!' Mum shouts. She takes several steadying breaths. 'The test was done in a clinic by a professional. We were there. You're really frightening me, Caitie.' She glances at Dad who is pale and quiet. 'Frightening us both.'

I hear footsteps approaching. I glance over my shoulder. My blood runs cold. Olivia. Her lip is bleeding, her hair is wild, her eyes are red. She takes a tentative step towards me but I back away. I don't understand. I don't understand any of it. If this is Olivia, *why* has she done so many things to make me think she isn't? Some were small, could be explained away, like forgetting about the bee journal. Some were big and blatant, like the conversation in my spare room, goading me to find out who she really is. But why? *Why?* I didn't imagine it, did I? We stare at one another. I wait for the flash of smugness but I am met only with sorrow. All three of them watch me with the same pitying, woeful expressions. Then, behind Olivia, I see Florence and her family spilling out of the hotel.

Florence.

I destroyed her wedding. I attacked my sister. I ruined my life.

Was it just this morning that my biggest worry was arriving late to have my hair done? Nervous laughter rises up from the pit of me and burbles out of my mouth. I lift a hand to stifle the hysteria but it doesn't help.

I laugh even harder. It becomes this wild, uncontrollable creature. I bend to its will, fold over double, stomach muscles seized. My face is wet. I taste salt on my lips. I'm no longer laughing, I realise. The giddy beast is cowed now, shrinking until it is solemn and sodden, and rolling out of my mouth in animal cries.

Everyone stares. I feel their awkwardness, their shock, their anger, even their fear. No one knows what to do, how to handle me. I am a broken, unfixable mess.

And it's all too much. I turn and I run.

39

Elinor Ledbury

Elinor is playing piano in the reception room when Heath storms in, holding Flynn's jacket in one hand and the box of trinkets in the other. He slams the box down on top of the piano but doesn't relinquish the jacket. She gets to her feet and tries to take it from him but he steps easily out of reach. He is so much bigger than her, so much stronger. There's no way she'll get it back unless he willingly hands it over.

'It's mine,' she says. 'Why do you have it?'

'Yours?' He is furious, the snap of accusation in his voice is like the crack of a belt.

Her heart beats too fast in her chest. She doesn't want to answer his question so she fires at him one of her own. 'What were you even doing under my bed?'

'Looking for your skates.'

This snatches some of the wind from her sails. She frowns. 'Why?'

'We haven't skated this year. I was going to break us into the rink.'

'Or we could go during the day like normal people,' she snaps.

He stills. His eyes burn into her. 'Normal? Is that what you want to be? *Ordinary.*' He says this as though it is a fate worse than death. 'You want to live in a terraced house, working a nine-to-five job, counting pennies, and cooking meat and two veg every night for your normal, *ordinary,* husband?' He closes the gap between them, walking her backwards until she is caught between him and the piano. 'Boring conversation and even more boring, *ordinary* sex from now until you die?' He lifts her chin so she is forced to stare up into his eyes. He brings his mouth close to hers. 'Is that really what you want?'

Her heart is racing. *Is* that what she wants? Heath has the power to make everything feel thrilling and even a little dangerous. It used to be one of the things she loved best about her brother, his wild unpredictability, the way he rejected the smallness and staleness of things. But that was before he had blood on his hands. *Their* hands. Her stomach ties in a thousand knots.

'And who would you have that little life with?' he taunts. 'Flynn? It's his jacket, isn't it?'

'I could have loved him,' she says boldly, defiantly. She has never dared talk to her brother this way but she is angry with him for what he did.

His face falls. She has hurt him. Betrayed him. She regrets it immediately. She opens her mouth, desperate to fix it, but he turns and stalks from the room, Flynn's jacket still in hand. She follows. 'What're you doing?'

'Getting rid of it.'

She grabs his arm. 'Don't.'

He wheels on her, the hurt has burned away, leaving only rage. This close to him, she can see his bloodshot eyes and knows he has been drinking. 'If Flynn's so brilliant, where is he now? He left you. People leave. I stayed.' He shakes his head as though she is too naïve for words. 'Be honest with yourself, Elinor, all you were to him was a good fuck.'

Humiliation bleeds across her face. She fires her words at him like poison-laced daggers. 'At least he isn't a murderer.'

He slaps her hard enough to make her stumble.

He stares at the hot, reddening mark on the side of her face. 'That was your fault,' he seethes. His fists clench, making his veins rope his forearms. He prowls towards her. Afraid he will hit her again, she turns and flees from her brother.

She has been walking for forty minutes when someone pulls over on the side of the road. Her heart surges because she is sure it is Flynn. A wave of wanting him hits her so viscerally, her chest aches and her eyes water. She spins towards the car. It is not Flynn. It is a middle-aged woman with a round, friendly face and a pale, greying bob.

'You're not dressed for this weather, love,' she says. Elinor looks down at her thin cotton blouse and jeans. No coat. It's March and still cold enough to snow, but the shock of being hit by the person she loves most in this world has numbed her to the whip of the frigid wind. 'I can give you a lift,' says the woman kindly. 'Where are you going?'

She bites her bottom lip. Where *is* she going? She thinks of Flynn. 'Town.'

Elinor slides into the car. The woman tells Elinor her name is Trish. They drive in silence for a long while. Eventually, Trish asks, 'You don't have parents who could drive you?'

Elinor stares out the window. 'They're dead.'

'I'm sorry.'

'I don't really remember them.'

'You live alone?'

'Me and my brother.'

They aren't too far from town now. The bare trees give way to rows of houses.

'Did your brother do that to your face?' she asks.

Elinor swallows hard. She wishes, more than anything, that she could spend one day, just one, with the brother she had before he started working at the music shop. Things were never uncomplicated, but they were easier. There was no Sofia, no Flynn, no corpse decaying in the frostbitten ground behind their house. 'He loves me.'

'The thing is,' her voice is soft, motherly. 'You can love something so much that you hold onto it too tightly and crush it to death.'

40

Caitlin Arden

Once I've grabbed my overnight bag, I leave the hotel as quickly as possible. I drive home, even though I know I shouldn't, not in the state I'm in. My tears blur the road and my entire body trembles, adrenaline still swilling in my veins. I all but abandon the car outside my house before going inside. It is deathly quiet. I trudge upstairs to my room and curl up on the bed. But, the moment I close my eyes, the last few hours ricochet back.

Fucking answer me! You killed her. Fucking answer me! You killed her.

It took less than ten minutes to ruin my entire life.

I'm too numb to cry. I have done something that can't be undone. I've said things that can't be unsaid. I have proved myself to be deranged in front of hundreds of people. In front of Laura, a parent from my school. Could I lose my job on top of everything else? My best friend, my fiancé, my dignity, maybe even my parents.

Florence's pained, heartbroken face flashes behind my closed eyelids. God, the way she looked at me. As though I'm an unhinged stranger. I blink, trying to dispel it, but the image is seared into my brain. I think of all the money she and Daniel poured into that wedding, all the time and effort and planning. All of it ruined. Because of me.

The longer I lie here, the longer I dwell. I get up and cast around the room for a distraction when my gaze lands on the painting above the headboard. Me and Oscar alone in that art room, him down on one knee. I loved telling my friends the story of how he proposed.

I'd even felt a little smug because it was thoughtful and romantic and tailored especially for me. I enjoyed how people swooned when they heard it. Everyone loves a good proposal story. But it was all pretend. A means to an end. I don't know why, at my lowest point, I'm revisiting this break-up, deciding now is the perfect time to dig in and inspect the gaping wound Oscar has left in my heart. I'm punishing myself, I think, but this act of self-flagellation, doesn't undo anything. I turn from the painting and start marching around the house. I go from room to room but in each one I see Oscar's absence. The dirty clothes he left in the wash bin, his spare phone charger still plugged in beside the bed, the gold watch his father gave him for his thirtieth birthday lying forgotten by the bathroom sink.

I am so alone. I consider calling Gemma and telling her everything, but she's thousands of miles away and I don't want to burden her in the first few days of her trip. Still, I need to talk to someone. Before I can stop myself, I am calling the only person I have left.

'Caitie, are you OK?' His familiar Irish brogue is like cooling balm on sunburn.

'No.'

I hear the rustle of material and imagine Gideon sitting up. 'What's happened?'

'Can you meet me?'

I don't bother to change out of my dress, but I do slip my feet into the brand-new white Converse I bought for the wedding reception. I drive the twenty minutes to Bath and start walking towards our rendezvous point at the park. As I get closer, though, a fluttery panic takes flight in my chest as I replay the day's events. I'm surprised no one called the police after the assault. God, what if they *have* called the police? I feel sick. There's no way I'll ever make this up to Florence. You get *one* wedding day. One. I am light-headed and uneasy on my feet. I try to remember the last time I ate. I was too agitated last night and there was no time this morning. Guilt and regret and devastation churn in my empty stomach. The park is just across the street. I think I see Gideon waiting at the cast-iron gate but a rush of dizziness takes hold and my vision cartwheels.

I stumble into the road.

Tyres squeal. I whip towards the sound.

Then Gideon slams into me. His hands, strong and firm, are on me, driving me back onto the pavement. We crash into a front garden fence. As the car that almost hit me pulls away, the driver leans out the window to yell.

I could've been killed. If Gideon hadn't shoved me aside, that car would've smashed into me. I hear bones snapping against speeding metal. I see myself rolling over the bonnet and feel the cobweb-splintering of glass beneath me before I am flung onto the tarmac with bone-breaking force.

Gideon stares down at me, chest heaving, his face creased with concern. His hands are still on me. I'm pressed between him and the fence but I'm shaking so hard I'm sure without the support my knees would buckle.

'Are you OK?' he pants.

I force the violent images away and nod even as my heart beats so fast it makes my head spin.

His eyes roam my face. 'I don't think you are. Do you need to see a doctor? Go to hospital?'

I shake my head. I've caused more than enough drama.

He frowns. 'I can drive you home?'

'My car's here.'

'You can't drive. Not yet.' His brow creases. He glances up and down the empty street. 'My house isn't far.'

I hesitate, not sure it's right to seek refuge in my therapist's house. Still, I feel safe with Gideon in a way I haven't felt safe in a long time. I reach for words but they're lost to me, dissipating like bonfire smoke as I try to grasp them. His hands cup my face and I feel like a horse blinkered by its owner but in a way that is comforting. Then I let him lead me down residential streets and across a small field. We arrive at a back gate. Gideon takes out a key and opens it. He ushers me through the garden. It's pretty, with a pond and decking. We slip in through the bifold doors. I imagine we've entered the house through the back because he doesn't want anyone to see him bringing home a patient. This must be a risk for him. Can he get in trouble with some sort of medical board if we're caught?

He asks if I want hot tea or a cold water. I spot the wine rack. 'Red please.'

He takes two glasses from the cabinet. 'Have you eaten today?'

'No,' I admit.

'You should eat.' Nodding at my dress, he says, 'I can wash that for you.'

I glance down at the dirty, crumpled gown. 'I don't have anything else to wear.'

He comes around the kitchen island. 'You can borrow something of mine.'

There's an intimacy in wearing another person's clothes. Material that has brushed their skin, lain against it, now lying against yours. I nod.

'There's a chance I can be persuaded to make us something for dinner while we wait for your dress to dry.'

And despite this awful, ugly day, I smile.

He shows me to the bathroom and hands me a bundle of clean clothes. Once he's gone, I take off the dress. As Florence's only maid of honour at the time, I had free rein in choosing it. I tried on a hundred of them and when I slipped into this one, we both knew it was perfect. Afterwards, giddy and triumphant, we celebrated with fruity, expensive cocktails. What will I do with the dress now? Post it back to her? Give it to a charity shop? Keep it as a reminder of one of the worst days of my life?

The jogging bottoms Gideon's given me are far too big and keep sliding past my hips, so I abandon them in favour of the black boxers and long grey T-shirt that falls mid-thigh. They smell of him, of sea salt and sage, lemongrass and fabric softener.

When I open the bathroom door I'm greeted by music that rises through the floor. I dither self-consciously at the top of the stairs. Am I really about to have dinner with my therapist, in his house, wearing nothing but his T-shirt and boxers? I should leave, but what do I have to go back to? A ready meal for one with nothing but silence for company. The loneliness is suffocating and being around Gideon makes me feel as though I can breathe again.

Taking a moment to calm myself, I look around the large landing.

His house is tasteful; all bare woods, autumnal tones and William Morris prints. A far cry from the black furniture and chrome fixtures of a typical bachelor pad. Then I see the console table drawer is partway open. Inside are a few pieces of loose paper which I ignore in favour of the downturned photograph in a gold frame. I carefully slide it free. It's of a young, attractive brunette in a lace and silk wedding dress. She's posing on the steps of a church and smiling demurely into the camera. Gideon's wife. I don't stop to analyse why seeing she is dark-haired like me and not fair-haired like Olivia makes excitement trill through me. I slip the frame back in the drawer and go downstairs.

Surprise flashes across his face when he notes my bare legs but he recovers quickly, giving me his widest smile. I hand him the dress and he loads it into the washing machine.

I eye the bowls of tomato and basil pasta. 'Can I help?'

'Sure.'

He hands me a grater and a block of Parmesan. It's the fancy kind from a deli, not the shop-bought powder. When I look up from my task, I notice Gideon staring at my legs. He catches my gaze, smiles, looks away.

By the time we sit down, my mouth is watering. Aware that alcohol and an empty stomach is a terrible mix, I don't take a sip of wine until I'm halfway through dinner. We talk as if we're old friends. It doesn't seem to matter to him whether I'm delving into my darkest insecurities or chatting about my favourite Italian dish; he listens just as intently.

On the table is a traveller's guide to Indonesia. It's face down beside a half-finished, stone-cold cup of tea. I imagine he was reading it before he rushed out to meet me. 'You like to travel?' I ask.

He nods. 'I've been to a few places but I'd like to see more.'

He never mentioned this during our sessions, which I suppose is a sign of a good therapist. After all, he was being paid to listen to me, not the other way around. Now, though, something between us has shifted. The atmosphere is friendly, more intimate. I tell him about all the places I want to visit and admit the reason I never did was because of Oscar.

He sips his wine. 'And where's Oscar tonight?'

I swirl tagliatelle around on my plate without meeting his eye. 'We broke up.'

This admission hangs in the air between us like ripe apples. I feel him plucking them free, holding them up and inspecting them. He takes a bite. 'I'm sorry to hear that,' he says but I don't feel there's any sincerity in his words. When I look up and meet his gaze, I feel the heat of it all the way to my toes.

'I know he loved me but . . .'

'Some people can't love without destroying what they care for most,' he says.

I take another sip of wine and think about how, every day, Oscar and I snuffed out each other's dreams whilst clinging to one another with desperate, grasping fingers.

He clears his throat. 'Do you want to talk about what happened today? Why you called to meet me and almost got hit by a car in the process?'

My cheeks flush. 'I'll need another glass of wine for that.'

He grins.

We move to the living room. It's similar to his office, all dark wood and large rugs and brass hardware. We sit together on his cream sofa and I feel like I talk for hours about Oscar and his book, the wedding and everything that happened in the run up.

'You can't blame yourself,' he insists. 'You've been under a lot of stress. Break-ups are hard enough but his book complicates things for you and your family. You were bound to explode.'

I wince at the memory of me screaming during the ceremony. 'But coming apart like that at my best friend's wedding . . .'

'Olivia issued that warning the night before with the aim of shredding your nerves – your outburst occurred when you were operating on no sleep, no food and a broken heart – all of which Olivia was aware of, some of which she masterminded.'

'So you agree she planned it?'

'Meticulously.'

'But why? Why is she targeting me?'

'Only she has the answer to that question. Have you ever asked her?'

I think back. I'm not convinced I *have* ever been that direct with her. 'No,' I say. 'Not that I'm sure she'd give me the truth. I don't understand how the DNA test came back a match. She can't be the real Olivia.'

'Why not?'

'My sister would never hurt me like this.'

He sets his glass down on the coffee table before twisting to face me with an earnest expression. 'You feel responsible for not acting quickly the night she was taken. Is it possible she feels the same?'

'You think this is her revenge?'

He shrugs. 'Perhaps. She's jealous of you, Caitie.' I'm about to ask how he knows this when I remember he's her therapist, too. 'From the outside, your life looks almost perfect. When Olivia returned, she saw you had a house, a career, a fiancé, doting parents, a loyal best friend that was once hers. All the things of which she'd been deprived.'

Guilt knots my stomach. 'Because of me.'

He shakes his head. 'No, not because of you. No rational person would put blame at your door. But I don't think she's rational.'

I turn this theory over in my mind. It sounds plausible but only to those who never knew my sister. She wasn't vengeful. She loved me. *Really* loved me. We weren't siblings whose relationship was steeped in rivalry. The memory Florence shared about her buttercup-yellow dungarees encapsulates the girl I knew. The person she was. She was patient and taught me how to ride a bike. When our parents weren't looking, she would fork the broccoli from my plate and stuff it into her mouth even though she hated it, too. She never let me put myself down. She believed in me even when I couldn't believe in myself. That's my sister. Not someone poisonous and out for blood. I tell him so.

'But sixteen years is a long time, Caitie. She was away from you for longer than she was with you.'

I imagine her as an aureolin sunflower, growing straight, towards the sunlight, roots deep into the earth. I see *his* hand coming for her, yanking her from the ground and snapping her in two. Cut off from the earth, from her roots, she withers. Becomes unrecognisable. No amount of sunlight will repair the damage he's done.

Still, I'm struggling to come to terms with the idea that the woman who has taunted me, attacked my relationships, threatened me, is my sister. More than likely this imposter was held captive with the real Olivia – maybe by Simon Briggs – and that's how she knows so much about my sister's life. It's how she was in possession of the DNA sample she used to cheat the test. I'm sure. That's the only explanation. But what does that mean for my sister? Is she alive? Is it possible my sister killed Briggs? Poisoned him to save herself and the imposter, and now she's too scared to come forward? Perhaps my sister is the person behind the mask, observing us, trying to see if it's safe for her to return. Or maybe the imposter murdered Briggs, and my sister witnessed it. If she is dead, buried like I was told, it would make sense that the reason she was killed is to cover up a crime and to make it possible for the imposter to assume my sister's identity to escape police detection. But then, do I even believe the real Olivia is dead? The thought has grief curling cold fingers around my throat.

I take a breath and stare down at the rug. I start naming all the colours in it. Midnight blue, burgundy, mustard yellow.

'Caitie, are you OK?'

I drain my wine glass to soothe my nerves. I'll have to drive home at some point so this second glass is my last.

'You don't deserve any of this,' offers Gideon. 'And Oscar's the biggest idiot of them all.'

I tilt my face up to his. 'Why?'

'Because he let you go.'

It's simple. Effective. And from him, it is sincere. Something simmers between us. Something electric that makes me lean into it. Into him. When I breathe in, I taste sea salt and sage, lemongrass and clean skin. I run my eyes over his glossy, coffee curls, his long lashes, his stubble, and cleft chin. His broad shoulders and narrow waist. I want him. I want him, even though Oscar's scent still lingers on his pillow. Does that make me a bad person? I can tell by the way Gideon is looking at me that he wants me just as much. It's been so long since I felt desired. There's power in being desirable. In knowing you can turn the most confident, attractive man you know into a sweating, lust-fuelled animal.

I become all too aware of my own body. Of the soft T-shirt that rides up my thighs as I move, of my accelerated breathing, of how I am arching towards him. I think of flowers again, searching for light. Then I am reaching for him. Winding my fingers through his hair and pulling him to me. He presses his lips to my collarbone, my throat, and everywhere his skin meets mine, heat radiates. His teeth graze my neck and his mouth moves across my jaw. I part my lips, wanting to taste him, wanting to—

He pulls back. Gets to his feet. 'I can't.'

'Why?'

'Because if I start now, I won't be able to stop.'

I get to my feet, too. 'What if I don't want you to stop?'

'You're at a crossroads now, Caitie. What's happened to you, is *still* happening, feels like this awful thing, but it doesn't have to be. At least, not all of it. You wanted to travel. Now is your chance. I don't want to be the reason you don't go.' He scrubs a hand over his face as though he can't quite believe what he is saying. He takes a breath then comes to me. His fingers lace through mine, warm and strong. 'I want you to know, I'll be here when you get back. Whenever that is.' He smiles. 'Maybe I can even fly out and meet you, if that's what you want.'

'I can't just leave.'

'Why not? What's to stop you going right now? This mess isn't going to be fixed overnight. Aren't you tired of living your life for other people?'

He knows I am. *I* know I am. I want to be braver. The main character in my own life. A person who makes things happen. I have enough savings to go, and not many reasons to stay. Gideon's eyes are on my mouth. He wants me. It would be easy to fall into a life with him, like I did with Oscar. But Gideon isn't Oscar, he's doing the most selfless thing he can. He cares enough about me to encourage me to chase my ambitions, not to stand in the way of them.

'This is your opportunity to go and do something for yourself,' he tells me. 'And, if I'm honest, I want you as far away from this drama as possible and from whoever's been following you.'

'Is it right to run from your problems?'

'You're not running,' he says wryly. 'You're walking. Calmly. And into an airport lounge.'

Beneath the hesitation, a frisson of excitement is unfurling at the warmth of his faith in me. 'So I just send my parents a message telling them I'm leaving the country?'

'I'm old-fashioned. Personally, I'd suggest a handwritten letter.' His smile is a little sad. He touches a lock of my hair. 'But the sooner you're gone, the sooner you'll come back.'

41

Caitlin Arden

By the time I get home, it's dark. Still, I sit at my dining table and pen a letter to my parents explaining that I'm going to travel for a little while. I keep it short and to the point. I wonder if they'll be relieved when they read it. Out of sight, out of mind.

I send an email to my school, telling them that in light of my sister's return, I'll be taking some time away. I don't think they can argue with that, though they'll be furious it's only a couple of days before term starts. Even if they decide not to pay me, and I wouldn't blame them, I can still operate Wanderlust Illustrations from abroad. A few years ago, when I'd first pitched the idea to Oscar of taking some time out to travel, I'd found a company that can print and ship all my art to customers for a small commission, so I fire off an email to them now to confirm my plans. Knowing Wanderlust can generate an income on top of the savings I already have brings me peace of mind. As for the house, it might be best, and fairer even, for me and Oscar to rent it out until we're ready to sell – like Gemma is doing. I wouldn't have felt comfortable with him paying half the mortgage if he wasn't living here and I'd be resentful if it were the other way around. This way, we both win. I draft an email to him, too – it feels more formal than a text.

On a roll, I book a flight to Italy, leaving tomorrow night, and promise myself I'll leave my loneliness at the departure gate. I've always wanted to see the Colosseum, walk the Amalfi Coast, ride a gondola in Venice. I'm going to eat my bodyweight in pasta and gelato and use my time there to plan the rest of my travels.

The sensible thing would be to sleep on any big, life-changing decisions and act only once I've put some distance between myself and the events of today, but I can see my new life on the horizon and I want to seize it before it sinks below the shoreline.

The only task on my list that I can't bring myself to complete is writing to Florence. I write the words 'I'm sorry' at the top of the page. Then scratch them out. They aren't enough. No words will ever be enough. Or none I can find right now.

Unable to sleep, I go upstairs and turn on my phone. I'd left it here, at the house, when I went to meet Gideon. There aren't any missed calls – not even from my parents. Disappointment and shame curdle in my gut; I suppose this is confirmation that I am so far past the line, my family has given up trying to reach me. They're sure I'm beyond saving now.

I start adding to my overnight bag, carefully placing my passport in the side pocket. I'm just zipping it up when my phone vibrates. It's another withheld number. I answer, thinking it's Gideon.

'You were quite the entertainment today, little sister.'

I grit my teeth against Olivia's playful, mocking tone. 'What do you want?'

'To see you.'

'Why?'

'Because I have something you need.'

'Which is?'

Silence, then, 'Answers.'

My heart quickens. 'To which questions?'

'All of them. Who I am, what I want . . .'

Suspicion and doubt race to the forefront. 'Why would I trust anything you tell me?'

'Trust me, don't trust me, that's up to you. But if you ever want to see your sister again, you'll meet me.'

The phone almost slips from my fingers. 'She's alive?'

'Yes.'

'But you said—'

'I know what I said.'

Adrenaline replaces my blood, pint for pint. 'You lied?'

'Yes.'

I want to believe her, want to hold on to this sliver of hope so hard it will crystallise into a diamond, but diamonds, when squeezed too tightly, will slice deep enough to draw blood. 'Where is she?'

'My game. My rules. Agree to meet me – *alone* – and I'll answer all your questions, just like I said. Cross my heart. Do we have a deal?'

I don't trust her. Every fibre of my being is screaming at me not to trust her. 'Why now?'

'Honestly? I have almost nothing left to take from you. I have your friends, your parents, and, if I wanted, I'm pretty sure I could have your fiancé too. I could keep kicking you while you're down, but where's the fun in that?'

Snarling, feral, tar-black anger rages within me. 'This entire time, it's me you've been after—'

'Yes.'

'Why?'

'If you ask me one more question, I'll retract my offer.'

I clamp my mouth shut.

'I'd be stupid to agree to come alone.'

'I just want to talk in private.' When I don't respond, she sighs as though this conversation is painfully boring. 'If I wanted to hurt you, Caitie, I would have.'

Just because she hasn't physically attacked me up until now, it doesn't mean she won't. Sensing my hesitation, she says, 'As I see it, you have two choices. You either agree to meet me in exchange for answers and a chance to see your sister again. Or you refuse and we keep playing this game. One in which I am winning and you are losing. I'll ruin you, Caitie, and you'll never see Olivia again. The choice is yours.'

I didn't save Olivia that night, but maybe, if she's still alive, I can now. I think of her being led, a knife to her throat, down the stairs. How, even in her darkest moment, she lifted a finger to her lips, urging me to stay silent. Maybe that is the only reason I'm alive today. She was brave and selfless, even then, even as a child. So, no, I don't have a choice. 'I'll meet you.'

She tells me to go to the abandoned shed in the wood behind our parents' house. The one she shouldn't have known anything about if she really was my sister. But at least it's somewhere I know and it's within running distance of my family. I'm to arrive just before midnight, which is a little under an hour's time. I agree to leave my phone at home and have to prove this to her by downloading a tracking app so she can see its location. I was reluctant, claiming twice that the app wouldn't download, but she isn't stupid, and warned me she'd call the whole thing off if I didn't obey. Still, I plan to record our meeting so I can take whatever she says to the police later. I rummage through Oscar's study until I find his old work phone. I leave it on charge while I change, settling on an all-black outfit because in a dark wood, I'll be more difficult to see if I need to hide.

Olivia is convinced she's cut me off from everyone who cares about me. For whatever reason, her plans hinge on me being isolated, but she doesn't realise how close I am to Gideon. He is my best hope of getting out of this unscathed. I call him and tell him everything.

'Caitie, you can't go to the woods alone,' he insists.

'I won't be alone as long as you agree to come.'

'You need to call the police.'

'And say what? The woman I assaulted earlier today wants to see me? Meeting someone in the woods isn't illegal. She's untouchable, Gideon. The nation's sweetheart. No one believes a word I say, but everything that comes out of her mouth is taken as gospel. She's successfully painted me to be completely mad and now she has a crowd of over one-hundred wedding guests to back her up. If I have a recording of her admitting she isn't Olivia Arden or that she's been manipulating me and everyone else then maybe I'll be listened to.' I sigh. 'I have to go, Gideon, with or without you.'

But the idea of going alone makes me feel queasy with terror. He's quiet, that quick mind of his sifting through all the options. He soon arrives at the same conclusion I did.

'OK.'

We decide he'll get to the woods ten minutes earlier than me to take a look around. I give him the number of Oscar's old work phone and he says he'll call me if he thinks it's too dangerous.

If my suspicion that Olivia and the masked man are working together is correct, it's likely he'll be there, too. I open my mouth to warn Gideon, then close it again because I don't want to talk him out of coming. It's a selfish, reckless decision but I *need* answers. I won't be able to live with myself if I let a second opportunity to save my sister pass me by. Still, I go to the kitchen and take a small, sharp knife from the drawer. I make sure the safety sheath is secure and then slip it into my pocket.

42

Elinor Ledbury

Flynn had told Elinor that at weekends and between his university classes, he helped his cousin out at the music shop. She surmises that with Heath having quit his job, Flynn, kind, generous Flynn, would step in and offer a hand. Knowing there's a good chance he'll be there now, she makes her way through town towards it. If she's wrong, Elinor will ask Sofia to pass on a message or to lend her a phone so she can call him herself. She is nervous. So nervous, her stomach turns over.

She hovers at the end of the street. She's just worked up the courage to go inside when she sees Flynn leaving the shop. He is locking up and he is alone. Sensing her gaze on him, he looks up. Surprise darts across his face. She wants to run to him, to have his arms wrapped around her, but she is rooted to the spot, fearful of rejection. She drags cold air into her lungs and walks towards him on trembling legs. She tries to smile but it is strained. His brow furrows. 'What're you doing here?'

'I missed you.'

His face softens and she closes the gap between them but he backs away, pocketing his keys. If he notices the red mark on her face, he doesn't say so. She is not his problem anymore. 'Go home, Elinor.'

She wants to tell him she doesn't have a home. That it is as rotten as the corpse she helped put in the frozen earth. That Ledbury Hall feels like a stomach that is slowly digesting her, melting the flesh from her bones, dissolving her until she is nothing. She wants to crawl from its belly while she still has the strength, but only if he can help her to do it. The look on his face – stern and unyielding – makes her breath catch. He turns and starts walking away. She stumbles after him, knowing she must try because without Heath, Flynn is all she has left. 'What about South Africa?' she calls. 'I want to come with you.'

He stops. She stares at the back of his head, willing him to turn around. He does.

'You can't come with me.'

His words are like knives. She closes her eyes against the pain and searches for a way to fix it. 'Heath lied,' she tells him. 'I'm not fifteen. He was lying.'

A shadow crosses his face. 'It doesn't matter.'

'Doesn't it?'

'No.' He exhales. 'Heath came to see me after he caught us together. He warned me if I ever came near you again, he'd kill me. And I believe him.'

For a moment, she imagines Flynn's body on the study floor, eyes unseeing, blood covering his torso, ripped open and sticky with blood, and a scream pinches her throat. She reaches for him, wanting to feel his heart beat beneath her fingers, to reassure herself, but he knocks her hand away.

'Don't come looking for me again. Don't call me. Don't even think of me.' He is as cold as the frost that glitters on the cobbled stones beneath her boots. 'OK?'

She feels adrift in despair, as if there is a bottomless ocean of misery raging beneath her and she is in a tiny yacht with no sails. 'Flynn . . .'

Stiffly, he turns from her. Tears run rivers down her cheeks. She folds her arms across her chest and holds herself. The pain of losing her brother, of losing Flynn too, is physical.

He is getting further and further away, smaller and smaller. She opens her mouth to call him back but all that escapes is a strangled cry. Then, to her disbelief, he stops walking. He turns and makes his way back to her. The relief is absolute. She runs to him and then she is in his arms, sobbing into his chest. He holds her, squeezing her tightly. She clings to him, breathing him in. She is warm again. For the first time in weeks, she is warm. Once she has calmed, he pulls back and examines her face. With gentle fingers, he pushes her hair away from her tear-damp cheeks.

'Listen to me, Elinor,' he whispers. 'I meant it when I said we can never see each other again.'

She looks at him. Really looks at him. He is serious. Hope leaves her, like a light being snuffed out, plunging her into darkness.

'But . . . if there's one piece of advice I can give you, it's to get out of that house and away from Heath.' His fingers press into her shoulders. 'I know you think he won't hurt you, but you're wrong. He's dangerous, Elinor. You aren't safe with him.'

43

Caitlin Arden

The woods are pitch-black. I reach for the phone half a dozen times to use the torch but stop myself because I can't risk Olivia seeing it after I promised not to bring a device. I walk slowly, hands outstretched, palms scraping bark. I breathe in the sticky, humid air, and the smell of dry earth. I've lost all sense of direction and I'm not even sure I'm going the right way.

When we were little, Olivia and I would play blind man's bluff. I can still feel the softness of my father's tie covering my eyes as I staggered around, trying to find my sister. Fear-laced excitement that I'd smack into a table, but it was worth it for the moment I caught her. Now, as I stumble alone, searching, the fear is deep and lacerating. The stakes are higher, more than a stubbed toe or toppled vase.

The darkness seems to come alive on all sides of me, full of darting shadows and looming shapes. I have a feeling, as though eyes are on me. As my heart starts hammering against the wall of my chest, I tell myself it is Gideon. He's out here somewhere and he'll protect me, just like he did with that car today.

After a few more minutes of tripping over raised roots and crashing into trees, I stop. I'm lost and seized by an irrational, childish terror. Then I see a flash in the dark. A single twinkling light. I move towards it, a boat guided across a turbulent sea. The canopy above breaks and moonlight filters down, casting the shed in an eerie silver glow. Olivia emerges from it, stepping out into the night. I come to a stop, out of arm's reach. It's dark but I can see she's still wearing her bridesmaid's dress, though she's in flats and not heels. And is she wearing evening gloves? She's holding a phone I don't recognise but assume is the one she's been hiding. I watch as she turns off the torch, plunging us into a deeper shade of darkness, and places it on the window ledge.

The air between us feels charged and dangerous, a thin electrical coil, hissing and spitting.

'You have answers?' I ask.

'No small talk?' she says in mock disappointment. 'Fine. Let's cut to the heart of it. How long do you think I've known about Oscar's book?'

It takes me a moment to process her question, caught off guard by the mention of him. 'What?'

'He told you he'd confided in me about it recently. That was a lie. I've known about his book for years. We basically wrote it together.'

A thud of disbelief. 'No.'

'Yes.'

I close my mouth because my denial is like reflux, an instinct out of my control. Oscar lied to me our entire relationship, it's plausible he continued to do so, even at the end.

'All those late nights, work trips away . . . He was with me.'

The bottom of my world collapses and I am freefalling. 'He was having an affair with you?'

'No. He was having an affair with *you*.' Shock closes its jaws around me. 'I knew him before you did. It was me who encouraged him to get to know you in whatever way he needed so he could write that book.'

'Why?'

She laughs. 'Do you have any idea how much Harriers are paying him?'

I never asked. I was disgusted he'd betray me like that, I didn't care about the money. I still don't, because no amount would ever be enough for me to hurt anyone the way he hurt me.

'I can't take all the credit, it was *his* idea for me to pose as Olivia Arden. I mean, I look like her. The blue eyes, the blonde hair. He clearly has a type.'

I'm shaking my head. 'But the DNA . . .'

'When Oscar met your sister on that bus sixteen years ago, he gave her a bee journal but do you know what she gave him?'

She's quiet, a schoolteacher waiting for a particularly slow pupil to work it out. I don't.

'A lock of pretty, golden hair.'

I think of the silver tin I found in his drawer. The hair wasn't his. It was Olivia's. My breathing is coming hard and fast. My mind careens wildly like wheels over ice.

'Did you ever see Oscar and your masked stalker in the same room?' she presses.

I go from hot to cold and back again. 'No . . . I was on the phone to him when I was attacked. I—' But Oscar could've been in his office, on the phone to me, pretending to be out. It explains why there was no sign of a break-in. You don't need to force entry when you live there.

'After he got the offer from Harriers, they asked for a follow-up.'

This is ringing a bell; Oscar mentioned a sequel.

'So he masterminded it. A returned sister, a masked stalker hunting down the girl he left behind. Readers would go wild, don't you think?'

I can't speak. My throat is closing up.

'He was going to kill you. That was his plan. And in the wake of your death he'd have penned your story, as well as your sister's. He said we could be together properly, then. That your family and the media would accept our relationship. A mourning sister and mourning fiancé, bonded together in their shared pain.'

I'm shaking, my entire body trembling. 'Why are you telling me this?'

'Because you needed to know.'

The note delivered with the manuscript. It was her. She made sure I had a copy. 'How do you feel about your perfect fiancé now?' she asks. 'I did tell you I could find you a better husband.'

'I hate him.' The venom in my voice, pure and true, takes us both by surprise.

'Good.' She comes a little closer and her voice is softer now, the stroke of a feather. 'You deserve to be with someone who will really love you, Caitie.'

I stumble back. Confused by the sudden switch from taunting and cruel to caring and consoling.

'The fact that you believed all the tales I just spun about Oscar tells me you knew he was never right for you,' she says.

Tales? Lies. Another game. I'm so confused by what she is saying. 'Everything you just said, the affair, the book, the plan to kill me . . . you made it up?'

'Yes. Well . . . most of it . . . the lock of hair *does* belong to your sister.'

I am too perplexed to be angry. The *need* for the truth is a nettle beneath my skin. An itch only she can scratch. 'Why lie about Oscar?'

'You were so quick to believe the worst in him because he isn't who you're meant for.'

None of what she's saying is making sense. 'You promised you'd give me answers and instead you're toying with me.'

'And you promised you'd come alone.'

Terror cuts through me and despite the blistering summer heat, ice drips down my spine. '*Gideon.*'

She inclines her head a little and over her right shoulder, I see a heap beneath a tree. In the gloom it's easily mistaken for a pile of clothes but it isn't, is it? It's him. It's Gideon.

'You shouldn't have broken the rules, Caitie,' she chastises. And as she steps forward into a patch of light, I realise it isn't silk that covers her arms but dark, red blood, slicked over her hands and to her elbow like a pair of macabre evening gloves. I am too stunned to move as she brushes her fingers over my mouth and I feel the wet smear of blood on my lips.

'Don't worry,' she whispers. 'I broke the rules, too. I didn't come alone either.'

'Hello, Caitie.'

I whip towards the deep, velvety, unfamiliar voice at my back. I am nose-to-nose with the masked man. A scream wells inside me, a black insect scrabbling up my throat but before it can burst from my mouth, he lunges. One hand clamps the back of my head and the other rams a chemical smelling cloth into my mouth. My panic is muffled and weak. I fight him, scratching and punching. I reach for the mask but my arms and legs feel lead laden. Clumsily, I knock the mask to one side but his face swims and black sunflowers bloom across my vision. Then, I am taken by the dark.

44

Elinor Ledbury

Flynn calls Elinor a taxi and pays for it, too. He doesn't look at her as she gets into the car. She turns to stare out of the back window and watches as he walks down the street, his hands in his pockets. She wants him to look back at her, to prove he still cares. He doesn't.

Even though she feels like every bone in her body is breaking, she doesn't cry on her way back to Ledbury Hall. She focuses on what to do next. She is going to leave the manor. Leave her brother. Leave behind her uncle's ghost. All of it. She decides she will pack a bag and run. She will start over. Flynn is right, there are enough valuables in Ledbury Hall that she can sell them to get by. Then there are Heath's wages, his savings from the music shop that he keeps in his bedroom. She's going to be fine. She's going to be safe.

She expects Heath to have drunk himself into unconsciousness by the time she gets home but he is awake, waiting up for her.

'Where have you been?' he asks as she takes off her boots in the foyer. He reaches for her. She stiffens and steps away. He is stung. He swallows. 'I'm sorry, Ellie, I'm so sorry.' He sounds desperate. He has never sounded desperate before. 'I love you.'

Now the tears come. She cries because she is leaving and he doesn't know. He sweeps her tears from her cheeks with his thumb. For as long as she can remember, her brother has been there to catch her tears. His touch is gentle now. His fingers stroke her hair. He has always loved her hair. Those same fingers taught her how to tie her laces, have undressed her . . . Have pulled a trigger in cold blood. He is a killer. A murderer. She doesn't want to be his next victim. Or his accomplice. She longs for a life he can't give her, of uncomplicated kisses, of marriage, of children. A boring, ordinary life.

She loves Heath, she will always love him, but she has to leave.

'I love you, too,' she tells him. It is honest. The most glossy, precious pearl of truth.

He pulls her to him and kisses the top of her head. 'We have the same soul, you and I.'

He isn't wrong. She is sure she could find her brother in total darkness. Recognise him just by the rhythm of his heart. It is more familiar to her than her own. She has whiled away hours lying on his chest, listening to it. She is not sure she will survive without him, but she has to try.

'I killed him for you,' he says, voice feather-soft. 'For us.'

His eyes, which have always brimmed with confidence and challenge and wit, are now dark and haunted and pleading. She and Heath are alike, she realises, more than anything, they both just want to be loved.

'Am I forgiven?' he asks.

She doesn't answer. Instead, she moves her hands beneath his T-shirt and kisses him.

Later, Elinor opens a bottle of champagne. For every glass she pours herself, she pours him two. They do shots: his are vodka, hers are water. She leads him up to bed. They tumble into the first room they come across.

After, they lie entwined. She strokes his hair and tells him they will be happy together at Ledbury Hall. She tells him that he is loved. That they have an extraordinary life ahead of them. She murmurs soothing things until he falls asleep. Her vision blurs. She blinks the tears away. She stays with him a while longer and when she is sure he won't wake, she slips from beneath the covers and dresses quickly in the dark.

She takes Heath's money. She isn't proud, and promises herself once she has a job, she will post it back. She packs a bag with clothes and things that can be easily sold: the ivory chess pieces, old collector's coins, her father's watch. She feels like a burglar in her own home.

She wants to take the marble bust of Aphrodite, not because it is valuable, but because besides her mother's romance novels, it is her favourite thing in the library. It's too heavy, so she leaves it behind.

She is quiet and tense, her muscles coiling at every creak, every groan of the old pipes, terrified Heath will catch her. Bag slung over one shoulder, she dithers, desperate to go back up the stairs to the room where Heath is sleeping. She wants to go in and take one last look at him. To memorise his face. The sharpness of his jaw, the high slope of his cheekbones, his long, dark lashes. She wonders who he would've become if their parents hadn't drowned. When Uncle Robert beat Heath, he didn't just bruise his flesh, but his soul too. And in this moment, she is glad he is dead.

Knowing she can't see Heath without waking him, she decides it's time to leave.

She creeps from the library and into the hallway.

She freezes.

A figure, steeped in shadows, blocks the front door. 'Running away, little sister?'

Fear squeezes her throat. 'Heath . . .'

'You aren't leaving.' His voice is low and dangerous.

She feels her pulse in her neck. 'Please just let me go.'

'After everything I've done for you.' His voice breaks beneath the weight of her betrayal. 'I could've gone away to university. I could've left you behind but I didn't. I stayed. For you.'

'I didn't ask you to.'

'YOU DIDN'T HAVE TO!'

The tension is glass-sharp. 'Heath, *please*. If you ever loved me—'

'Love you? I dedicated my entire life to looking after you. You let me take beating after beating for your clumsy *fucking* mistakes,' he hisses. 'And you were going to leave me without even saying goodbye.'

'I should've run away with Flynn. I should've left the night you murdered Uncle Robert. I wish I had.' He steps forward, into a patch of moonlight, his face cast in a silver glow from the high, arched windows on either side of the front door. He looks so young. So incredibly harrowed. She is hurting him, causing him more pain than their parents' deaths, more pain than any slap or kick or punch their uncle inflicted upon him. Her confident, clever, conniving brother is a shivering, scared, lonely little boy, but she can't stay. She has to hurt him so he will let her go. 'I don't ever want to see you again. I mean it, Heath, don't follow me.'

'But—'

'Being loved by you is like being slowly crushed to death,' she says, her words hard and round, like bullets.

He screams as though he has been shot. She jumps back and knows she has made a fatal mistake. She has said too much. Taken it too far. Caused him too much pain. He flips the console table. It smashes onto the ground. The wood splinters and breaks. The glass vase shatters. There is no talking after that. She turns and sprints down the hall, through the dining room, smacking her hip on the table. He chases after her. She knows if he catches her, she is dead. She drops the bag and yanks open the back door. Then she is outside, the cold night air is sharp and welcome. It focuses her. She runs, runs, runs, across the grass. It crunches underfoot. She slip-slides on the dew. Hands seize her from behind and she is yanked to his chest. She catches his forearm with her teeth and bites down until she tastes blood. He shrieks and lets her go. Then she is running again. He screams her name. Over and over, like a siren.

Up ahead, she can see the pond, the stone lovers at its centre. If she can get around it, she'll make it into the woods. She can lose him there. Hide. She knows the woods better than he does.

But he is faster. By the time she reaches the pond, Heath has closed the distance between them. He slams into her. She is pitched to the side. Then she is falling, plummeting into the water. Into the dark. It is freezing and snatches the air from her lungs. Grabbing fistfuls of her coat, he lifts her from the pond. She is gasping, choking on murky, ice-cold water.

'Heath,' she splutters. 'Heath.'

His hands go around her throat and then she is forced beneath the surface again. She claws at any part of him she can reach. She is blind and she can't breathe. Water fills her ears and eyes and her open, screaming mouth. It washes down her throat. She cannot scream. Cannot beg. The hands around her neck squeeze harder and harder. She is dying. He is killing her. *Drowning* her. She hears a woman's voice:

You can love something so much that you hold onto it too tightly and crush it to death.

And then . . . and then . . .

Heath feels something snap. His sister goes limp. Still he cannot uncurl his fingers from her neck. His hands have become independent beasts. He holds her under the water until he is numb with cold. Finally, he lifts his sister's lifeless body from the pond and lays her on the ground. He strokes her wet hair back from her face. Her beautiful, perfect face. He stays with her until the sun comes up.

45

Caitlin Arden

I wake up handcuffed to a large brass bedframe. Metal clinks on metal. My head whips up and around to see my restraints, but when I shift, even a little, nausea rolls through me. Everything twists and blurs. I swallow and swallow again. I pull against the handcuffs but the metal digs into my wrists. The chain that connects them is a metre or so long, allowing me to prop myself up onto my elbows.

My throat is thick. My tongue too fat in my mouth. I can still taste the sharp chemical tang of the cloth used to drug me. This is when I become achingly aware of my own body. I glance down. My black T-shirt and jeans are gone. I'm wearing pyjamas – they're soft and feel new. The realisation dawns slowly: I was stripped while unconscious. I lie very still, making note of how my body feels, checking for torn flesh or pain. Other than the nausea and the taste in my mouth, I feel fine. Still, I think of the masked man, his hands on me, and my stomach lurches.

I force myself to stay calm and try to work out where I am. The room is unfamiliar. It smells of fresh paint. The walls are dark green. To my left is a door. It's open a little and I can just make out the tiled floor beyond and the porcelain base of a sink. At least my prison has an en suite. Not that I can get anywhere near it while I'm handcuffed to the bed. There are three large windows in a row but, from this angle, all I can see is the bright blue sky. The afternoon light stings my eyes. Opposite the bed is an ornate dressing table and chest of drawers, both distressed oak with gold hardware. In the middle of the room is a large rug in autumnal shades, laid over wooden floorboards. To my right is an enormous armoire. This bedroom is reminiscent of those found in exclusive boutique hotels.

In the farthest corner is another door. My heart races. I imagine a hallway beyond it. A flight of stairs. A door to the outside. To someone who will hear me scream. I pull against the restraints but the metal bites into bone. My entire body is shaking. I lie back down as another wave of dizziness takes hold. Very slowly, I look around the room for a weapon. If I can get free, I'll need one. I think longingly about the knife I'd tucked into the pocket of my jeans. There is nothing in this room I can use to defend myself. No mirrors I could smash. No glass frames. Not so much as a lamp to hit someone over the head with. I don't think for a second my lack of options is an accident.

I'm being kept in a house which means there must be other houses nearby. If I scream loud enough, I might be heard by a neighbour concerned enough to call the police. My captor could be nearby, but I can't let fear of what he might do stop me from trying to escape. So, I take a deep breath and let it out on a frenzied shriek. I shout. I clang my restraints against the brass headboard. I yell again but over-exert myself. The nausea takes hold and then I am vomiting over the side of the bed.

I hear the door open. I look up so sharply, the room spins, and I think I might be sick again. I wipe my mouth against the back of my hand and eye the woman crossing the room, carrying a wooden tray. She could easily be mistaken for the woman who's been impersonating my sister this summer: tall, blonde and beautiful. Wordlessly, she sets the tray down on the bedside table, glances at the puddle of vomit and then disappears into the bathroom. I stare after her, too stunned to speak. She returns a moment later with disinfectant wipes. I'm breathing deeply, trying to control the dizziness. She kneels and starts cleaning up the mess. 'You'll feel better soon,' she assures me softly. 'The drugs only made me sick for a day.'

I take in her pale blonde, waist-length hair and china-blue eyes. So much like Olivia. So much like the woman who pretended to *be* Olivia. This woman's lashes are long, almost touching her brows. She's thin – all bony shoulders and jutting collarbones and sharp jaw. Her skin is so white, I wonder when she last saw sun. She drops the soiled wipes into a cloth bag she pulls from the wardrobe and then tosses it towards the door. When she turns back to me, she eyes me pityingly.

I stare up at her and dare to hope. 'Olivia?'

She presses her lips together and shakes her head regretfully. 'Bryony.'

'Bryony.' I roll her name around on my tongue. 'Where am I?'

She smooths her hands over her white, ditsy-floral print dress. 'In your new home.' She looks uncomfortable, as though she had to force the word 'home' out of her mouth like a broken tooth. She glances towards the door and I get the impression someone waits on the other side, listening.

I lick my dry lips. 'Is this a cult?'

She almost smiles. 'No.'

I eye her. 'But you're not here by choice?'

She glances furtively towards the door and my skin prickles with dread. She gives a quick shake of her head. 'I've been here for seventeen years.'

My mouth falls open. Seventeen years. 'How old are you?'

'Thirty-one.'

She looks younger. I'd have guessed mid-twenties. Bryony was fourteen when she'd been brought here, only a year older than Olivia was when she was abducted. I sink into the pillows and stare up at the ceiling, heart thundering in my chest. If she's been trapped here for seventeen years and never managed to escape, what chance do I have?

'How long have I been here?' I whisper.

'Two days.'

Is that long enough for someone to realise I'm missing? But then, *who* would even be looking for me? I've burned all my bridges. It could be days before anyone attempts to contact me. I think of the note I left at home. If my parents think I'm travelling for a month, will they bother to look for me at all? I feel myself getting hot with panic. I jolt upright, struggling for breath.

Bryony hands me the glass of water from the tray, but I'm shaking so much it sloshes over the rim. I take a sip and my stomach roils.

I thrust it back at her. She reaches for the plate of dry crackers but I bat them away. 'Please,' I breathe. 'Help me get out of here.'

She glances nervously towards the door again, then back at me with wide, sympathetic eyes. I open my mouth to beg but she says, 'Your sister wants to see you.'

I blink. 'Olivia?'

She nods.

'She's alive?'

'Yes.'

Relief floods through me but drains quickly as doubt sloshes in. 'How do I know you're telling the truth?'

'I suppose you don't,' she says honestly. 'But I know your sister. I've known her for sixteen years.' Something like anger flashes across her face but it's gone before I'm sure. 'If you want to see her, you must agree to obey.'

My heart quickens. 'Obey what?'

'The rules of this house.'

I tiptoe into this conversation as though it is a snake-infested grassland. 'Which are?'

'Don't try to leave. Always follow his instructions. If you agree, he'll allow you to see your sister. Or you can refuse and stay locked in this room.' She gives me only a moment for this to sink in. Before I can ask who 'he' is, she says, 'What do you want to do?'

I don't know that she isn't lying, but escape is impossible if I don't at least get out of this room. 'I want to see her. I'll . . .' I trail off as the word 'obey' sticks in my throat.

Seeming to understand, she says, 'Obey?'

I nod.

'OK. I'll come back in a few hours to collect you.'

'For what?'

'Drinks in the library.'

'Drinks with who?'

She gives me a look.

'My captor?' I ask, outraged.

Her silence tells me I'm right. 'Olivia will be there, too.' She takes a small key from her dress pocket, reaches over and, to my astonishment, unlocks my handcuffs. I rub at the red marks on my skin. The urge to run for the door is almost impossible to ignore, but I'm still dizzy and weak, any escape attempt would be immediately thwarted. I need to know the layout of the house at the very least. So, I force myself to be patient.

'Eat the crackers and drink the water,' she instructs. 'It will help settle your stomach. Take a shower. You'll find everything you need in the dressing table.' She nods in the direction of the wardrobe. 'And wear something nice.'

She turns and starts walking towards the door. I don't want her to leave. I don't want to be alone in this prison. I have a thousand unanswered questions. 'Who is *he*?' I call after her. She stills, her hand on the door. 'What's his name?'

She glances over her shoulder. This time, there isn't just pity in her face, but fear, too. 'Heath,' she answers. 'Heath Ledbury.'

46

Caitlin Arden

Bryony is right, the crackers and water settle the nausea but they do nothing to alleviate the terror, the confusion, the rage. When I take a closer look at the windows, any hope I had of smashing them and jumping out, dissolves. The glass is thick and, in places, uneven. I think it's shatterproof and even if it wasn't, it wouldn't matter because on the other side are iron bars. I try the door hoping Bryony didn't lock it, and predictably, find she did. With no way out, I start frantically looking for a weapon. In the dressing table is a tiny compact mirror. It's so small, a shard wouldn't big enough to inflict damage. I dash to the bathroom, hoping to find a larger mirror. Of course, there isn't one. No razor, either. Nothing I can use as a weapon. Just another grand room. If this were a hotel and not a prison, I'd have melted into the freestanding, rolltop bath. Instead, paranoid Heath might barge in while I'm naked, I hop in the shower still wearing the pyjamas and wash quickly.

When I'm done, I wrap myself in the fluffy white towels and open the wardrobe. Inside there are dresses – *only* dresses – all in my size, all from my favourite shops and in my preferred colours. It's like this room has been waiting for me. Given how many clothes there are, they plan to keep me here for a long time. I browse the rail, looking for something that isn't restrictive so if I do get a chance to fight or run, I can. I settle on a cotton midi dress in navy and change quickly in the bathroom, one eye fixed on the closed door. I search for shoes but don't find any. Looks like I won't be taking a trip outside any time soon.

I dry my hair facing the door in case someone comes in. It feels surreal, dressing up to have drinks with my captor and the sister I haven't seen in sixteen years. I wonder where Fake Olivia is and how she fits in to all of this? Why have I been brought here? And what do they plan to do with me? Did my sister wake up in a room just like this? I try to imagine her, only thirteen years old, terrified and alone, sick and dizzy from drugs, being told to dress up for her masked abductor, and I feel nauseous all over again.

I go to the window. The sun is slowly sinking, spilling inky purple and deepest indigo across the sky. The grounds of this house are vast and green, mostly wild and overgrown. The only part that is carefully maintained is the area around the small lake. Bowed willow trees graze the water, and there is an island at its centre with a stone, weathered statue of a couple embracing, collecting just enough moss to look pretty. There are no other houses, though. Not one. Hope withers in my chest and I sink to the floor, pressing my knees into the hardwood. I didn't realise it is possible to feel claustrophobic in such a large space but the walls of this extravagant cage seem to close in on me. Either my heart is expanding in my chest or my ribs are shrinking. I fall forward, onto my hands and can't breathe.

I don't even hear the door open but Bryony kneels beside me, brushing sweaty strands of hair back from my face. She makes soothing noises and instructs me to copy her breathing. In and out. In and out. We sit like that until my pulse slows.

'It's the drugs,' she tells me.

'Not drugs,' I say. 'Fear.'

She's quiet after that.

'They're waiting for us,' she says eventually. It's only now, as I let her help me to my feet, that I notice the wedding band and sapphire engagement ring on her left hand.

'You're married?' I ask. 'To Heath?'

She frowns then looks down at her hand as if it doesn't belong to her. 'Yes.'

I blanche. Didn't Fake Olivia let slip she was married? Didn't she tell me she could find me the perfect husband? My stomach flips and flips again. Panic starts to rise, threatening to close over my head. She reaches for me and I see a shiny pink scar, snaking from wrist to elbow on her left arm. Did she do that or did Heath? Tears start to blur my vision. 'What's going to happen to me?'

She presses her lips together in a silent, pitying line. 'Right now,' she says softly, 'I'm going to put these on you.' She reaches past me to the windowsill where a pair of handcuffs wait. She must've set them down when she came in and found me mid-panic attack. The chain on this pair is only a few inches long. I shake my head and back away. 'No.'

She sighs. 'Caitlin . . .'

'No.'

She glances at the door. 'You won't be able to see Olivia if you don't let me put them on.'

My mind races. 'Pretend to do them up and then—'

She's shaking her head. 'He isn't stupid. And even if you aren't restrained, there are two of them.'

'Two . . .' I'm breathing too fast again. 'But there are two of us and my sister.'

She frowns.

'Please,' I say. 'Listen—'

'He'll kill me,' she says flatly.

I taste fear in the back of my throat but swallow it down and push on, knowing I have to convince her to help me. 'Bryony, please—'

'Put them on or don't,' she snaps. Startled by the sudden change in her demeanour, I take a step away from her. Gone is the patience and concern, replaced by something harder, something steely. 'Look, if I don't take you downstairs in the next few minutes, he's going to come up here and then we're both in trouble.'

Fear rises like bile. I swallow, weighing up my options. I don't want to be restrained but refusing means being locked up in this room with zero hope of leaving. Zero hope of seeing my sister. Decision made, I hold out my wrists.

As I'm led from the bedroom, I glance back and see the deadbolt on the outside of my door. We turn left and walk down the long, wood-panelled corridor. The light comes from either end where there are identical, enormous arched windows that overlook two sets of stairs. My gaze swivels left and right. There are at least seven bedrooms. Three, including mine, have deadbolts on the outside. One has a padlock. It's becoming apparent that I'm not just being held in a house, but in a stately home.

We descend the stairs to a large hall. In front of me is a sturdy wooden door, tall and broad, the kind you'd find in a castle or barn. The idea of making a run for it sets my heart skittering. I imagine myself fumbling with the lock, yanking the door open and sprinting from the house. I'd scream and scream and scream because even though no other houses were visible from my room, it doesn't mean there aren't any across the street. I step towards the door. Bryony grabs my upper arm, tearing my attention from it.

'Please don't,' she whispers in quiet terror. 'If you run, he'll blame me.'

Every instinct shrieks for me to flee but logic dictates that my chances of making it outside are slim to none. It's more than likely locked, so throwing myself at it won't help. I take a moment to tamp down the urge to try before nodding at Bryony. She gives me a tiny, grateful smile and leads me through a door on our left. In the sitting room are three patterned sofas in warm hues, expensive, dark-wood furniture and a fireplace so big I could stand up in it.

Bryony cups my elbow and guides me through another door. Three of the four walls house floor-to-ceiling bookshelves, complete with rolling ladder. I've never seen this many books outside of a public library. Ornaments and trinkets are sprinkled among the hardbacks: a globe, a marble bust, brass candlesticks. There's another lattice, an arch window and more mahogany furniture, a stone fireplace. At the centre are two navy-blue armchairs and a three-seater sofa arranged around a coffee table. In the corner is a fully stocked bar cart. Behind that is another door.

Bryony tells me to sit in one of the armchairs. Reluctantly, I do. She kneels.

'What're you doing?' I ask in a rush.

'Cable tie,' she answers, pulling one from her dress pocket.

I surge to my feet. Bryony looks panicked. She rises, too. 'Sit down,' she whispers sharply. 'You agreed to this.'

'I agreed to come down here to meet my sister. I was even mad enough to agree to the handcuffs. No one said anything about being tied to a chair.'

'Well, I didn't exactly have a terms-and-conditions document to hand for you to sign,' she bites. She rubs her forehead as though she's getting a headache. 'If you don't do this then Heath will come in here and escort you back to your room. I thought you wanted to see Olivia?'

'I do.'

Her patience has all the integrity of a threadbare carpet and my refusal to 'obey' is rubbing it ever thinner. I reason that my hands are already secured and useless so does it really hinder me any more if one of my ankles is anchored to the armchair? I can't spend even one night in this house knowing my sister is here without seeing her. Taking a couple of deep breaths, I sink obediently into the armchair.

Bryony exhales, relieved I'm complying. Once she's pulled the cable tie tight enough that it pinches, she stands. 'Try not to anger him,' she says quietly. 'It won't end well.'

And with her warning still ringing in my ears, she leaves, closing the door behind her. Of course the second she's gone I give the cuffs an experimental tug but the metal cuts into my wrists. My mind pendulum-swings between thinking about seeing my sister and plotting my escape. I'm wondering whether I can drag the armchair over to the window and reach up high enough to smash it when the library door opens.

Adrenaline floods my veins.

I twist in my seat. Our eyes meet.

She is silent, waiting for my reaction.

I open my mouth and I scream.

47

Caitlin Arden

She hurries to me, clamping her hand over my mouth to stifle my screams of fury. I've been deceived. I'm as angry with myself for believing I'd see my sister as I am at them for lying. 'Please, Kitty-Cate,' she begs. 'Take a breath.'

My throat burns and my head throbs and I am wild with rage, but I need answers so I stop yelling. In the quiet, she nods, and her hand slips from my mouth. I glower up at her. Up at the woman who has spent weeks impersonating my missing sister, who went out of her way to dismantle my life. 'Bryony promised I'd see Olivia,' I demand. 'Where is she? Where's my sister?'

She kneels in front of me and takes my hands. 'I *am* your sister.'

I whip my hands from her. 'No you aren't.'

'I am, Caitie,' she beseeches, those big blue eyes fixed unwaveringly on mine. 'How else would I pass a DNA test? Or know about the lock of hair and The Boy on the Bus? Or look like your sister? Like you? I *am* Olivia, Kitty-Cate, I am.'

She starts talking about the night she was taken. Our trip to the wildflower meadow. The popcorn and the movie we watched. How, at the top of the stairs, she'd seen me and pressed a finger to her lips, urging me to stay hidden. Things only the real Olivia would know.

As the fog of fury dissipates, I stare at her. Into her eyes. Glacial lakes and summer skies, forget-me-nots and bluebell petals. And I know, in the bright red of my blood, that she's telling the truth. A sob of relief, of joy, breaks from me but then . . . then it is swept beneath a river of confusion. 'But . . . you didn't know our cousin's name. You didn't remember Hathaway Cottage.'

'They were deliberate mistakes.'

I'm shaking my head, remembering more anomalies. 'The contact lenses . . .'

'Planted for you to find.'

'You even challenged me to discover who you really are. I don't understand.'

'It was part of the plan.'

'What plan?'

'To bring you here to Ledbury Hall so we could be together again. I told you in the restaurant I thought about you every day that I was gone. I meant it, Caitie. I came back to get you.'

'No, that isn't right. If you're my sister, why would you deliberately lead me to believe you aren't?'

She looks down, clasping her hands tightly in her lap. 'Heath said I had to. He said it was the only way to make everyone think you're . . . unstable.'

I'm quiet, trying to catch up. 'But why would you want people to think that?'

'I can't tell you.' Her eyes flick up to mine, pleading with me to understand. 'I can't. Heath will explain.'

'I don't want to hear it from him. I want to hear it from you.'

'Can't you just be happy we're together after all this time?'

'Happy? You lied to me. You made me hurt everyone I love. Then you helped abduct me. I've been drugged and locked up and . . . and . . .' The cocktail of grief and rage is heady, making it difficult to think. Whatever I was going to say is lost on a sob. Hot tears stream down my cheeks. Olivia reaches up to wipe them away. I whip my head to the side. 'Don't touch me.'

She is stung by the rejection, her bottom lip quivers. She looks so much like my thirteen-year-old sister that my heart aches. 'It's going to get better,' she says confidently. 'None of those people love you like I do.'

'That's not true.'

'Isn't it? Your best friend dropped you the second I returned.

Your fiancé was only with you because he wanted me first. Myles has barely looked your way in sixteen years, you said so yourself, and Clara smothers you so she can erase you, start over, redraw you in my image,' she says, aghast. 'That isn't love.'

'NEITHER IS THIS!' I yell.

She stands, all frustration and certainty. 'You were either betrayed or abandoned by everyone you cared about. *I'm* still here.' She throws her hands out. 'I've done all of this for you.'

'I didn't ask you to. You could've just come home, Olivia.'

'This *is* my home.'

'No, it isn't. You were snatched from your home. *Our* home.' She spins away from me and starts pacing. 'Olivia, please unlock these.' I pull my wrists apart as far as the cuffs will let me. 'We can get out of here together.'

She stops. 'No, Caitie, I love him. I love you both. I want us all to be together.'

'The psycho who kidnapped you?' I can't keep the disgust from my voice. 'Heath?'

'He isn't psychotic,' she says, voice riven with indignation. 'He's a devoted husband. He'd do anything to make me happy. When I told him I needed my sister, he made it happen.'

And there is the ugly, sad truth. My sister married her captor. I stare at her now and my anger slumps into pity. Heath has had her longer than we did. He's spent all these years twisting her out of shape. He's poisoned her against our parents – it didn't go unnoticed that she referred to them as Clara and Myles instead of Mum and Dad. She has Stockholm syndrome. She's sick and she doesn't even realise.

She sees that I am crying again. Her brow furrows and this time when she takes my hands, I let her. 'I was certain once he got to know you, he'd love you.' Her wide, proud smile makes unease ripple through me.

'I don't want to know him.'

Her face falls.

'You're going to hurt my feelings.' My head whips towards that deep, velvety voice. He stands in the doorway, as broad and as tall as I remember. The cuffs of his white shirt are rolled to his elbows, exposing his thick, muscular forearms. His navy trousers are an expensive cut. He, along with this house, reeks of grandeur. His face though, remains a mystery. He's wearing the mask again. Just the sight of it ignites fear.

'Heath!' Her voice is the delighted clap of a child. She gets to her feet and goes to him, taking his hand and tugging him further into the room. He winds his arm around her waist and presses her against his side. 'You know I don't like that mask,' she tells him with a sickening fondness. 'Don't play with Caitie. It's cruel.'

'It's theatrical,' he corrects.

She reaches up to remove it but he catches her wrist and slowly lowers her arm, their gazes locked. It's so intimate, it makes my skin crawl. Then he laces his fingers though hers and they walk towards me, stopping just out of reach. I become all too aware that I am sitting down and restrained.

I feel the weight and heat of his gaze on me and force myself not to shrink beneath it.

'Caitie,' he says my name slowly, as though it is an after-dinner mint to be savoured.

Leisurely, he lifts the mask.

My pulse races. I am lightheaded with trepidation.

Then he removes it completely.

And my world tailspins off its axis.

48

Caitlin Arden

He asks Olivia to wait for him upstairs. I can tell she doesn't want to leave. I don't want her to go, either, but I have been rendered silent with shock. She lingers at the door, her eyes on mine and then she is gone, closing it softly behind her.

He walks over to the bar cart and turns two crystal-cut tumblers the right way up. Then he pours whisky into them and returns, holding one out to me but all I can do is sit and stare up at him.

He smiles and tips the tumbler towards me. The amber liquid swirls. 'Going once . . . going twice . . .'

I grab it with both hands because actually, I think I need a drink if I'm going to make it through this conversation. He watches as I lift the glass to my lips and drain it in one. It burns my mouth, my throat, scorching my insides. I splutter and before I can launch the tumbler at his head, he takes it back. 'Why Irish?' I ask.

Gideon sets my empty tumbler down on the cart and then lounges against it, all long legs and arrogance. 'It's hard to resist the old Irish charm,' he says, easily slipping back into his Irish lilt. Then he drops the accent and returns to that deep, velvety, public-school voice. 'My sister ran off with an Irishman.' He looks down into his glass, but it's too late: I see the lie, the dark shadow crossing his face. He shrugs and it's gone, replaced by cocky amusement. 'That, and, if you ever talked about your Irish therapist . . .'

'It would never come back to you.'

He raises his glass. 'Exactly.'

Without his Irish brogue, seeing him speak is like watching a badly dubbed foreign film, the voice not quite aligning. 'But I thought you were dead. I saw . . .' What did I see? Not his body. A shape that only *looked* like a body which, in the dark, could just as easily have been a pile of coats.

'You thought I was dead because that's what I wanted you to think.'

'*Why?*'

'It was a contingency plan. If you had somehow managed to run from the woods, from me, you'd emerge rambling about a body that the police would look for and never find. Olivia would've washed the fake blood from her hands and denied the entire thing.'

'Adding to your narrative that I was insane. Why would you want anyone to think that?'

'So no one will come searching for you.'

I take a moment to pull all the pieces of this conversation together, but I'm still not getting the full picture. 'Why would my perceived insanity stop people from looking for me when they realise I'm missing?'

'As far as most are concerned, you've had a mental breakdown. It isn't too far-fetched to assume you might hurt yourself. After all, you've lost everything. Quit your job. Gone off the rails. Someone, perhaps the police, or a concerned member of the public, will find your phone and purse left on a bridge over the River Avon, and when your house is searched and your laptop is found, the police will discover a typed suicide note detailing your plan to drown yourself.'

My heart leaps like a hare caught in a trap. I don't move, sure that if I do, I will break into a thousand unfixable pieces. 'No one will believe that,' I whisper weakly, because even as I say it, I know I am wrong.

He raises one dark brow. 'Over a hundred people witnessed your outburst at the wedding, you said so yourself. You'll just be another tragically unhinged woman with a traumatic past who ended it all.'

The enormity of my situation settles around me like an icy fog. 'What about Olivia?' I retort. 'Surely, with the both of us disappearing, questions will be asked.'

He shrugs one broad shoulder. 'Doubtful. She wrote her own

letter, explaining she's left home because she couldn't bear her return upsetting the family.' His grin is wry. 'She's an adult, left of her own accord. Even if your parents report her missing, the police won't follow it up. Olivia will keep sending letters. I'll drive to different villages, different towns, and post them.' I ball my hands into fists in the face of his conniving arrogance, but my anger dissolves as I imagine my parents' heartbreak when they wake up to find both their daughters gone. I swallow around the knot of grief in my throat. Seeing this, he adds, 'Don't be down, Caitie. We've got years of fun ahead of us.'

I realise now that Olivia is the wife he claimed to be separated from. The one who encouraged him to see other people. To see me. Am I to be his next wife? The way he's looking at me with hunger and heat, makes revulsion slither down my spine. 'You aren't a therapist?' I ask, trying to steer the conversation on.

He sips his drink. 'No.'

It was Olivia who gave us Gideon Temple's card, claiming it was handed to her by the family-liaison officer. Obviously, that was a lie. I suppose that fraudulent card is gone now, torn into pieces, or burnt to ash.

He must've been the voice on the other end of Olivia's secret phone, though I have no doubt that me overhearing her call was deliberate. Rambling to anyone about a second device and snippets of whispered conversation was just another nail in the coffin of my perceived sanity. 'But I went to your office.'

'A friend of an acquaintance, Doctor Gideon Temple, needed a house sitter while he travels this summer.'

'Indonesia,' I say, remembering the guide I saw on the dining table.

'That's right. Handily, he kept a key to his office in the house.' He sips his drink. 'You know, I never even met the doctor.'

'What if you hadn't stumbled upon a therapist in need of a housesit?'

He shrugs, unbothered, as though he is a person for whom things always eventually come together. 'I'd have been a police officer, a reporter, an old friend of Olivia's.'

Anything to get close to me. Close enough to make me trust him. 'Why now? Why come for me now?'

'Olivia,' he says simply. 'She wanted her sister back.'

'Why not just kidnap me and be done with it? Why send Olivia home and go to all this trouble, all this risk?'

He starts idly browsing the shelves, picking things up and putting them down. This conversation of kidnap and mind-games handled as casually as one of summer holiday plans. 'I wanted to get to know you. See if you were a good fit.' He regards me. 'Don't get me wrong, you're beautiful, but you might've guessed you aren't my usual type.'

That much is obvious, with my dark hair and petite frame.

'But I fell in love with your determination, your loyalty, even to a man who never loved you the way you deserved to be loved, the grace in which you navigated your complex relationship with your family. Olivia was right, you're special.'

'Lucky, lucky me,' I quip.

He's looking at me in that way again, as though we are a couple during cocktail hour, anticipating a night of bedsheets and bare skin. Nausea rushes through me at the thought. He stands, comes close and kneels. Then, as smoothly as a magician pulling a rabbit from a hat, he removes a penknife from his back pocket. I coil tight with fear. His hands run down my bare calf, but his eyes never leave mine. His gaze is steady, confident – playful, even. To my surprise, he cuts the cable tie, freeing me from the chair. He steps back, an amused smile on his lips. He waits. Understanding this is some sort of test, that I am an animal under observation, I don't move an inch. Though my pulse thunders, I keep my tone light. 'Will you be removing the handcuffs next?'

That smile spreads wider. 'Unlikely. Let's start slow.' His low, velvety voice is too intimate, and needles my skin. He is thinking about us on the sofa together, my hands in his hair, pulling him towards me. He showed so much restraint, then. Now I know why, he wanted to unwrap his toy in his own home.

Frightened by his intentions, I smooth my bound hands over my dress and attempt to distract him with another question. 'But why risk Olivia never coming back to Ledbury Hall?'

'I wanted to test the boundaries of my relationship with her.'

'You mean you wanted to test the control you have over her?'

He regards me as though I am disappointingly uneducated. 'Love, *real* love, is trusting another person enough to hand yourself over to them completely. She trusts me and I trust her. Olivia had a choice to tell you and your family and the police all about me and Ledbury Hall, but instead she chose to come back. She chose me.'

He is bindweed, with roots too deep, wrapping himself so tightly around my sister, she can no longer see where he ends and she begins. I glower, despising every inch of him. 'You broke into my house. How did you get in and out?'

'Your parents have a spare key. Olivia gave it to me and I made a copy.'

'Did you break in so I'd report it and look insane in front of the police, or were you there to retrieve the manuscript?'

He smiles. 'Both. I knew about Oscar's little book weeks before Olivia returned.'

'How?'

'I've been watching you for months, Caitie.' I don't know why this shocks me, but it does. I run back through my memories, searching for him in my peripheral vision as I ran errands or made my way to work. I think of all the times I carelessly undressed with the curtains open, and my cheeks burn. 'I watched your fiancé, too, trying to understand what it was you saw in him. I even followed him to a couple of meetings with the editor from Harriers and sat a table away, listening in.'

I don't bother asking why he made sure I found out, Olivia already explained she wanted Oscar out of my life. I suppose, for Heath, I was a much easier target without a fiancé standing in the way. I remember Bryony's warning that there were two of them. When I was with Heath – Gideon – in the park that day, I saw the masked man. I know I did. Yes, it was in profile from quite a distance and it was only a flash, but that mask isn't exactly subtle. I ask him about it.

'That was your sister,' he tells me. 'Don't feel foolish. From that far away and in a busy crowd, anyone would've fallen for it.'

I look off to the side, my face reddening because I *do* feel stupid. I was so trusting. Too trusting. Surely *someone* will point the finger at him but, even as I think this, I know it's unlikely. When I mentioned to Florence about bumping into my therapist at the park, I didn't give her his name. The only thing Oscar knew about him is that the police gave us his details. I don't think Oscar is even aware that those details came through Olivia first. There is no way to link Heath to my abduction. When I visited *his* house, we used the back gate so we weren't seen. As the real Gideon Temple has no connection to any of this and isn't currently even in the country, no one would even *think* to question him about me or his house sitter.

'Is that it?' he muses. 'Is Question Time over?'

'And what about Simon Briggs?' I ask. 'How does he come into all of this?'

Heath's eyes glitter; he enjoys showing me how clever he is, how cunning. 'You can find all sorts of people at grief groups.'

'Vulnerable people.'

'People who need company.'

'Olivia's DNA was all over that cabin.' I suddenly feel ill at the thought. 'What did you make her do?'

'I don't share,' he says sternly. Then his gaze drifts down my body and I try not to shift beneath the intimacy of it. 'I scouted a few self-help groups, looking for the perfect candidate. I found Briggs at an AA meeting. He was trying to get off the drink. So, after, I took him out for one. He broke easily, of course. He was a weak-willed mess.' I imagine Heath, confident, witty, charming, befriending someone like Simon Briggs. A man whose life was in tatters after an affair with a student, his existence limited to a rural cabin with nothing but well-thumbed paperbacks and rats for company. He'd have felt chosen for the first time in years. I look at Heath's hands now. Ones that slipped up my bare back. Hands that scribbled notes on my innermost thoughts in the comfort of his stolen office. Hands that hauled me from the path of a speeding car. I imagine those same hands closing over Simon's like a sea creature over its defenceless, unwitting prey. Guiding him into a bar. Listening intently, making him feel more heard than he ever had in one of those AA meetings with their weak coffee and stale biscuits. 'I told him my sister, Olivia, needed a job, cleaning, cooking, gardening. He was enamoured with her.'

She's objectively beautiful. Of course Briggs would be infatuated, but from Heath's triumphant smile, that's exactly what he wanted.

'He tried to kiss her. Naturally, she rejected him, left the house and didn't go back. I stormed over, brimming with brotherly concern, and he apologised. I told him she wouldn't return, but I encouraged him to write her a note.'

Detective Grimshaw had mentioned a suicide letter, is that what he's talking about? 'What did it say?'

'The detective didn't read it to you?'

I shake my head.

He grins smugly and says in a West Country accent, '*I'm sorry, Olivia. For everything. Goodbye.*' He shrugs. 'Short and sweet with just enough melancholy to suggest suicide. Once he wrote it, I asked him to join me for a drink outside in the sunshine.'

'That's why they didn't find any other prints in the cabin.'

He nods, impressed I'm keeping up.

'I suppose you provided the drink?' I say, thinking of the thallium-laced bottle of whisky. 'He died alone. In agony.'

'He wasn't a good man. He was a predator.'

'So are you!' I explode. 'You took my sister when she was just a child. You ripped her from her family. From me.'

His anger flashes to the surface, contorting his features. 'I love her. I have given her everything. I didn't even touch her until we were married. Until she asked me to.'

A dark tide of contempt rushes through me. 'You're sick.'

He sets the tumbler down and eats up the space between us, then he grabs my forearm and yanks me to my feet, pulling me so close, all I can see is the jade-green of his eyes. His breath is warm on my mouth. 'You wanted me, too, remember?'

I spit at him.

His grip on my arm tightens so painfully, I cry out. At his furious, hateful expression, a seam of fear rips open inside me. I try to yank myself free but this only further infuriates him. He slaps me. I hit the floor and land hard on my side. My ribs burn and my vision blurs behind tears.

'Your fault!' he bellows, hauling me up. My shoulder screams in pain as I am wrenched upright. Then he is dragging me from the room and up the stairs. I trip but he lifts me easily, flinging me over one shoulder. One side of my face throbs like a second heartbeat. We're on the stairs, climbing higher and higher. I'm afraid if I struggle, he'll toss me down them. He marches along the hallway and I hear a door opening.

Olivia hovers, face ashen. She steps towards me but he barks at her to get back inside.

'Help,' I shriek. 'Olivia!'

'Inside!' he roars.

Reluctantly, she does as he says, closing the door behind her. His perfectly obedient pup. He sets me down outside the room I've been kept in and then traps me against the door. His body presses me into the hard wood and his hand closes over my mouth. He brings his face inches from mine. 'She's mine,' he says, voice low and dangerous. 'And so are you. And so is Bryony. You'll soon learn.'

Then he reaches past me, opens the door, and pushes me inside.

49

Caitlin Arden

I wore the handcuffs all night. No one came to unlock them. Even though tiredness burned behind my eyes, I didn't sleep. I sat on the bed, knees tucked to my chest, listening to the creaking bones of this old house. Now, I watch shadows move across the room. The sun has risen. It's sweltering again, the heat rubs against my skin like a hot, sweaty hand.

At the sound of the bolt being slid free, my heart drums against my ribs. Bryony steps inside holding a tray and gives me a small smile. She's wearing a blush-pink wrap dress, her feet bare, her hair pulled up into a high ponytail that swishes as she crosses the room. She sets the wooden tray down on the bedside table. It's laden with two paper plates of fruit salad, yoghurt-topped granola and two icy glasses of orange juice. I eye the flimsy, wooden spoons. Even if I snap one in half, it would be useless as a weapon. I haven't eaten anything substantial since the pasta that Gideon, or *Heath*, made days ago, but my appetite is lost.

'Got something for you,' she says, taking a small key off the tray. She unlocks my cuffs and I rub my wrists. They're ringed with blackberry bruises. 'I heard all the commotion last night, are you . . . OK?'

'Wonderful. I'm really enjoying my stay, actually,' I offer, voice thick with sarcasm. 'Though the food looks fantastic, the cutlery could do with an overhaul and the handcuffs are a little industrial for my liking.'

'But the host is so sane,' she deadpans.

Laughter bursts from me. It's a kind of shrill, nervous laugh that rises like hiccups. The reality of my situation is starting to settle in my bones like poison. The fact is, as far as the police are concerned, Simon Briggs, the man they believe is responsible for my sister's abduction, is dead. Killed himself. They aren't investigating anymore. And, thanks to Heath's meticulous planning, the police will follow the crumbs he has left and reach the conclusion that I've thrown myself in the river. A ribbon neatly wrapping up the tragic story of the Arden sisters. Heath managed to hold Olivia here for sixteen years and Bryony a year longer than that, without anyone ever suspecting him. I don't stand a chance. What will my life look like now, imprisoned in this house for the next ten years, the next twenty. I feel a rising helplessness, a mounting urge to cry that I give into. My laughter bleeds into sobs. Bryony climbs onto the bed beside me. She doesn't touch me. Just sits close enough to let me know I'm not alone.

'I wish I could tell you it gets easier,' she says quietly.

She isn't glancing nervously at the door this time, which means there's no one listening. I wipe my eyes. 'How did you end up here?'

She pulls the throw onto her lap and starts twisting the tassels around her fingers. 'I wanted to go to this party but my mum wouldn't let me. We argued. I snuck out. Walked there by myself.' She's shaking her head, as though she can't believe her own stupidity. 'I didn't realise he'd been watching me. Waiting for me to be alone. I never made it to that party. He came out of nowhere. All I remember is the hideous mask and then . . . nothing. I woke up here.'

I do the maths, as vague as it is. Heath is somewhere in his late thirties which means he was in his very early twenties when he took Bryony and Olivia. I'm about to ask Bryony what she knows about Heath's past when she says, 'I wondered if you knew anything about my family? If there was anything on the news or . . .' Her blue eyes are wide and brimming with hope.

'I don't think so,' I say gently. 'I would've been nine years old when you went missing. Things like that happened way above my head.' Her face falls and my heart aches for her. 'What's your surname?'

'Danvers.'

For a second, I consider lying just to save her feelings, telling her they're still looking. That there's a chance she'll be found. But I have suffered so many lies, and the pain of having them unearthed, it isn't worth it. I shake my head. Her shoulders sag. She seems to shrink beside me. 'What were your family like?' I ask, hoping talking about them will make her feel better.

'I came from a happy home. My parents are doctors. We played boardgames every Thursday. I was the best as Scrabble.' She smiles. Then she falls quiet. She has pulled a tassel thread so tightly around her finger, it's going blue. Her smile withers on her lips. 'I've lost my parents' voices now, though. It's like knowing the lyrics to your favourite song but forgetting the tune. I have a sister, too,' she says. 'She was three when I was taken. She'd be twenty now.' She looks up at the ceiling and I can see she's fighting back tears.

'I'm so sorry.' I lift my hand to lay it on hers, then stop myself, not sure she wants to be touched. She takes the plates from the tray and hands one to me along with the spoon. I'm not hungry, so I just push the fruit around. 'Heath says he has a sister.'

'Elinor.'

'You've met her?'

'No. And you won't, either.'

'She ran off with an Irishman?'

'No she didn't.' Her laughter is brittle and humourless. 'I don't think she ever left Ledbury Hall.'

'You mean . . . she's a prisoner here? In one of the locked rooms?'

She gives me a pitying look. 'I think he murdered her.'

Fear live-wires through my body. 'Why do you think that?'

'He has nightmares. He calls for her and when he wakes, he clings to me, sobbing like a child. Sometimes, when he's had too much to drink or he's coming round from another night terror, he calls me Elinor. Not surprising that he chose us because we look like her.'

'We? You mean, you and Olivia?'

She nods. 'There are photographs of his sister all over the house.' Bryony leans in. When she starts speaking again, her voice is low-slung. 'I think they were closer than siblings should be.'

Revulsion slithers into the pit of my stomach, followed by a surge of dread. 'He could kill me. Could kill any of us.'

'He works very hard to keep himself under control. He won't be happy with himself that he lashed out at you.'

'Why do you think he's collecting girls that look like his sister?'

'I think he regrets killing her. We're like his purgatory or maybe even proof to himself that he can love something without destroying it.'

After he rescued me from being hit by the car, he told me some people can't love without destroying what they care for most. Bryony's right, *that's* what this is about. The ultimate test of control.

Last night, I goaded him and he lost it. When Bryony and Olivia were brought here, they were just girls. Young and inexperienced, facing off against an adult man. He isn't used to dealing with women. With someone who is old enough to have lived, to know their own mind. He slapped me last night but he could beat me to death tomorrow. I have to get out. I have to get all of us out of Ledbury Hall. 'Do you have access to the kitchen?' I ask, eyeing the plate of food in my lap. 'To knives and forks? Anything we can use as a weapon?'

She pops a slice of mango into her mouth and chews thoughtfully. 'No. Olivia does though. She prepares all the food but he's banned her from coming to see you. Today she gave me this tray with both our breakfasts and told me to make sure you eat something. My room is just next door to yours.'

I put down my spoon. 'Is the door to this room unlocked? Could we run?'

'Olivia deadbolted it behind me. Even if it was left wide open, all the doors in this house are locked. You'd only be able to run along the hallway and down the stairs to the front door.'

'Which is also locked . . .'

She nods.

Despair opens up inside me like a trap door, dark and endless. I snap it shut, refusing to give up so soon. 'I saw the padlocked room, what's in there?'

'Elinor's bedroom. I wandered in there once, before Olivia was brought here, and he was furious. He locked it up after that.'

'Have you ever tried to run?'

She uses her spoon to cut a cherry in half. 'A few times. Never successful, obviously.'

'And what did he do?'

'Am I your crystal ball?' Her smile is rueful but there's an edge to it. 'Are you trying to see your future?'

'Yes,' I admit.

She's quiet for a while and I'm wondering whether she'll answer at all. I appreciate I'm not dredging up happy memories for her, but I need to know what he'll do to me if I'm caught. 'He was rougher with me than usual.' Her words hang in the air like a noose I am not willing to dip my head into. Still, fear cuts a valley from my throat to my stomach at the horrors both Bryony and Olivia have endured. What I might have to endure. 'He restricted my access to the house, too. Kept me locked in my room for weeks with nothing to do. No one to talk to. I was so lonely, when he eventually said I was allowed out of my room, I practically skipped down the stairs to the formal suppers.'

'Formal supper?'

She pulls a face. 'A Ledbury-family tradition. We eat together in the dining hall every evening. Though, I'm usually bound to a chair.'

'But Olivia isn't?'

'No.' Her tone is clipped. 'He trusts her because she's in love with him.' She stabs at a piece of nectarine.

'She's sick,' I say gently. 'She has Stockholm syndrome. It's when a captive develops an irrational bond with their—'

'I know what it is,' she hisses.

Her mood has darkened considerably at the mention of Olivia. This isn't the first time talking about my sister has made her angry. I get the impression if I ask her directly about the tension between them, it'll be like rubbing salt in an open wound. Still, I don't want her to blame Olivia for something she can't control. 'It's how she's coped with being held here. A survival technique.'

'Well her *survival technique* got me caught,' she says, sneering hatred in her voice.

'What do you mean?'

'Heath wears a master key on a chain around his neck. All the other keys are kept in a brass tin in his bedroom.'

320

'Are you sure?' My heart races at the thought of getting my hands on that tin. 'How do you know?'

'Over supper, Olivia asked if she could use the piano but it's locked away in the reception room. Heath, forever doting on her, told her where to find the key. It took me weeks to convince him I'd finally fallen for him. That I wanted him. I coaxed him into taking me into his bedroom.' She shifts uncomfortably. 'When we were . . . done . . . and he'd fallen asleep, I crept from the bed, took the keys and I ran. Then Olivia caught me halfway down the stairs and started screaming.'

Her hostility is palpable. And even though Olivia feels like a stranger to me now, I defend her because she's my sister and it isn't her fault that Heath Ledbury has crawled beneath her skin like a cancer. 'She's ill, Bryony.'

'I hate her,' she says, her words shot through with venom. 'I could've escaped this place seven years ago if it wasn't for her.'

I want to defend Olivia further but know it will only serve to aggravate Bryony, and I need her on side. 'Look, I can convince her to leave him. She'll help us get out of here.'

'That's never going to happen.'

'Tell her I want to see her.'

She drops her spoon too. 'No.'

'Why?'

'Heath forbade her from coming anywhere near you.'

'That's because he's afraid that if I spend time alone with her, I'll break the hold he has. Please give her the message. Tell her I want to see her.'

Her lips press together into a thin line of frustration. 'No.'

'Why not?'

'Because he'll kill my sister or, worse, bring her here.' She surges to her feet and slaps her paper plate down onto the tray. 'After he caught me racing down the stairs with his tin, he dragged me to my room and vanished for two days. When he came back, he had photographs of my sister. He'd stalked Lucy. Warned me if I ever disobeyed again, she'd suffer the consequences.'

She snatches the tray up with shaking hands. I lick my dry lips, trying to think of something I can say to convince her to help me.

I don't want to put her sister in danger, obviously I don't, but we have no chance of escaping unless we work together. 'Lucy won't be safe until we get away from Heath.'

She's staring at me, knuckles turning white around the tray, mouth working as though she is crunching on broken teeth. 'You know what is so maddening? I have done everything in my power to keep my little sister away from this hellhole but *your* sister has deliberately dragged you into it. She doesn't love you as much as she loves him. He will always come first.' Her scornful words spring at me like blades. 'Helping you and your sister means condemning mine. I won't do it. Ask me one more time, and I'll tell Heath you're plotting to poison his perfect doll. Then you'll never see Olivia again.'

50

Caitlin Arden

My mind is a murky pond, deep and brackish, questions muddying the water. Bryony resents Olivia. She's jealous of the freedom Olivia has in Ledbury Hall. She can't see that my sister is caught in Heath's snare. The only way we're getting out of Ledbury Hall is if the three of us work together. It's clear to me that Heath has deliberately driven a wedge between Bryony and Olivia, because dividing is conquering. I don't know how I can convince Bryony to help without her following through on her threat and raising the alarm with Heath.

With nothing else to do, I take a shower, wishing I could scrub this place from my skin. Wrapping myself in a towel, I pad back into the bedroom.

Heath is waiting for me. He stands by the window and surveys the view. He's dressed in jeans, and a black T-shirt that clings to his lean, muscular frame. His coffee curls are glossy in the sunlight. Slowly, he turns his square jaw towards me.

I want to run back into the bathroom and slam the door shut. Not that it would do any good. There's no lock.

'What do you want?' I ask, glad I sound more impatient than petrified.

'Did I frighten you?'

'Well you were *lurking* outside the bathroom.'

He inclines his head in a conciliatory gesture. His gaze lingers on the underwear I've left out on the bed, then roams over me. I draw the towel more tightly around me. 'What're you doing in here, Heath?'

323

He fixes me with a stare so intense, my insides knot. 'I came to apologise.'

'For drugging and abducting me? Or for losing your temper and hitting me?'

His jaw clenches and despite my show of bravado, fear thunders through me. 'I brought you these,' he says, stepping aside to reveal an enormous bouquet of flowers on the dressing table.

'White roses and—'

'Aureolin sunflowers.'

His brow quirks in a silent question I don't answer. 'Olivia picked those from the garden. She said they're your favourite.'

That day in the park when she called me to meet her feels like a million years ago now. I'd felt so proud that when she needed someone, it was me she turned to. Looking back, I realise it was a ploy to lead me into the café, where Oscar was meeting Samantha. All in the name of alienating me from those I loved.

Heath moves towards me. I scuttle backwards until my knees knock against the bedside table. He stares at me, his expression flickering first with frustration, and then with dejection. 'I'm not a savage, Caitie. I haven't forced myself on you.'

As though rape is the only qualifying factor. What's terrifying is that, though he presents as this educated, rational person, he doesn't see that what he's doing is wrong. 'What about Bryony?'

He glances away, just for a moment. When his eyes meet mine again, they are resolute. 'She's as attracted to me as I am to her.'

'And my sister?'

'My *wife*,' he says, as though pulling an ace from the deck, 'is in love with me. Surely you see that? You aren't blind. You aren't stupid.'

I lift my chin. 'She didn't have a choice.'

'She did. She chose me.'

My blood boils. I clench my hand into a fist and fight the urge to hit him. Breathing deeply, I step aside, and he lets me. To put as much distance between us as possible, I cross the room, feigning interest in the flowers. Seconds later, I feel him behind me. So close, his breath warms my neck. 'You wanted me before,' he whispers.

Slowly, I pivot towards him. 'No,' I lie.

'You felt it. You were hungry for it. If I hadn't stopped you, you'd have given yourself to me right there on that sofa.'

I swallow, remembering the throb of electricity between us, the power of feeling desirable.

'But I wanted to bring you here first.' He reaches past me and plucks a white rose from the vase. Slowly, he sweeps it down the column of my neck, along my collarbone, down my bare arm, leaving goosebumps in its wake.

'Did you think about me when you touched yourself? When you were lying beneath that deceitful, oppressive fiancé, did you wish it were me?'

With the back of my hand, I knock the rose aside. A thorn nicks my wrist and I wince at the sharp, sudden sting. He takes my hand in his and turns it over to inspect the small cut. For a moment, I think he might bring it to his lips. Instead, he catches the blood with his thumb. His eyes, jade-green and fathomless, burn into mine. 'I'm happy to have you here, Caitie,' he purrs. 'Enjoy the flowers.'

When he is gone, I pick the vase up and hurl it against the door.

51

Caitlin Arden

When Bryony brings lunch later that day and sees the mess of water and petals, she slaps the tray on the dresser and with a furious exhale, starts clearing up the chaos. I can't bring myself to help. I feel sick to my stomach that I ever let that man lay a hand on me. I sit on the floor at the foot of the bed, knees tucked close. She rights the plastic vase and stares at me.

'I take it Heath's visit didn't go well?'

'Whatever gave you that idea?'

Surliness forgotten, her mouth lifts in a wry smile. She picks the tray up and brings it to me. She sits down opposite, legs crossed, as though we are two friends enjoying a picnic in a grassy park. When I make no effort to take a plate, she pushes the tray towards me. 'Yours is the one with ham.'

'Not hungry.'

'You need to eat. You barely touched breakfast, and Olivia will have a fit if you don't finish lunch. She made your favourite.'

Curious, I lift a slice of the thick, farmhouse bread. It's filled with strong cheese and smoked ham, salad. Just like the ones we had on that last perfect afternoon in the wild meadow before she was taken. There's even a brownie and a glass of icy lemonade. Despite not having an appetite, I know it's important to keep my strength up if I have any chance of running from here. Sighing, I take a plate and rest it in my lap. 'I still don't understand why Heath brought me to Ledbury Hall.'

She takes a bite of her own sandwich. 'For Olivia.'

'He said that . . . but . . . why? He could've been caught.'

She scoffs. 'He already got away with it twice.'

'But still . . .'

She sets her sandwich down and gives me a long, sobering look. 'Olivia sinks into these depressions for days or even weeks at a time. And though she has free rein of Ledbury Hall, she shuts herself away in her room,' adds Bryony with a note of bitterness. 'She got worse during this last year, her low points stretching on for months. She told him the only thing that would make her feel better was you. It wasn't the first time she asked but it was the first time he listened.'

The depressive episodes surprise me. Olivia acts as though her life with Heath is like something from the pages of a romance, but clearly, on some level, she's aware her relationship with him is twisted and wrong. 'Why did he finally give in?'

'He was worried she'd do something to herself.' I glance down at the scar on Bryony's wrist. She catches me looking and quickly moves her arm out of sight. 'So, *voilà*, here you are. Her wish is his command.'

I take my sandwich from the paper plate and see a piece of paper folded beneath it. Without thinking, I pick it up, and read: *I miss you, Kitty-Cate x*

Then it is plucked from my fingers. Bryony's eyes widen. 'Olivia wrote this.'

'Yes,' I hiss and snatch it back.

She stares at me with childish glee. 'Perfect, obedient, Olivia.'

'Don't,' I warn, not liking her mocking tone.

'But Heath forbade her from coming anywhere near you.'

'She didn't come near me. She wrote a note.'

'Even so, I don't think he'd approve.'

And in this moment, I don't trust Bryony at all. She hates my sister but is she spiteful enough to tell Heath what Olivia's done? Panic flutters beneath my ribs. 'You can't tell him.'

Her eyes glitter. 'Why not?'

'Because this proves Olivia cares enough about me to disobey him.

So maybe I *can* win her round.' When she doesn't instantly disagree, I decide to test my luck. 'If you just tell Olivia I want to see her . . .'

Bryony turns this over in her mind, flipping a coin, weighing up her options. 'Fine,' she relents, 'but if this goes wrong, it's all your fault.'

52

Caitlin Arden

After breakfast the next day, when Bryony is gone, a shadow flits in the narrow gap beneath the door. I walk to it and press my palm against the cool wood. 'Olivia?'

Silence.

For a moment, I wonder if I imagined the shadow, but then her voice drifts through the oak, syrup sweet. 'I'm here.'

My pulse jumps in my throat. 'Are you coming in?'

'I can't,' she says, somewhere between a whine and a plea.

'Where is he?'

'Out. Posting another one of my letters to Myles and Clara.'

'You mean Mum and Dad?' I correct snippily.

Silence.

Heath's poison runs so deep, she talks about our parents as though they're mere acquaintances.

'You know they're going to be heartbroken that both of us have disappeared,' I say, the truth of it lodging in my throat like a piece of glass.

'They'll be fine.'

'They love us . . .'

'They were going to send me away. Did you know that?'

I frown. 'What?'

'Boarding school.'

I snap my tongue against the roof of my mouth in disgust. 'Did Heath tell you that?'

Silence.

'He's lying.'

'Our father went to boarding school.'

'And he hated it. He'd never have sent either of us away.'

'Heath showed me the brochures. Some convent miles and miles from you.'

I clench my fist against the door and struggle to keep the frustration from my voice. 'Olivia, that simply isn't true. He could've got those brochures from anywhere.'

She falls quiet again.

'What about Bryony's family?' I press. 'Don't you think they might want to see their daughter again?'

'She doesn't have a family. She was homeless when Heath brought her here.'

I shake my head, remembering what Bryony told me about them. 'Her parents were doctors. She has a sister.'

'They kicked her out. She was on the street for months. He rescued her.'

'I suppose Heath told you this, too?'

'No,' she says snippily. '*She* did.'

I'm about to call Olivia a liar then stop myself because she sounds so certain.

'Look at this house, Caitie. It's beautiful. Bryony's lucky Heath took her in. Do you know what happens to young homeless girls?'

'Nothing more terrible than what happens here!'

The silence on the other side of the door is icy. 'I'm not going to sit here and listen to you talk about my husband like this,' she says.

'Olivia—'

'And a word to the wise, don't trust Bryony. After all, *she's* the reason I'm here.'

Blood drains from me, replaced by hot nausea. 'What?'

'Goodbye, Caitie.'

I listen to her footsteps recede down the hall. When she's gone, I snatch a pillow from the bed and press my face against it. A horrible, primal scream is ripped from me. It's unlike anything I thought myself capable of. Rage, unlike anything I've ever known.

* * *

I pounce the second Bryony brings lunch. 'What did Olivia mean when she said *you're* the reason she's here?'

Panic floods her face but she composes herself quickly and sets the tray down on the dresser as though I haven't spoken.

I march towards her. 'Well?'

She pushes a loose lock of hair away from her face and regards me coolly. 'That's not quite right.'

I swallow around the lump of fury lodged in my throat. 'Enlighten me, then.'

She is tense, every muscle as taut as a violin string being pulled too tight. 'Though I *look* like Elinor, I don't act like her. For Heath, the fantasy of me never lived up to the reality. I was too wild, too angry, too disobedient.' She bites her lip, reluctant to go on. I keep quiet. I wait. 'I told him if I wasn't what he was looking for, he should bring another girl here and let me go.' Her cheeks redden and she can't meet my eye. 'I was just a child, Caitie. I didn't think he'd actually do it.'

I take several deep breaths as I try to work out how I feel. If Bryony wasn't everything he hoped, it's likely he'd have taken another girl even without her suggesting it first. 'It isn't your fault,' I say after a moment, and she visibly relaxes. 'Do you know how he even came across my sister in the first place?'

'She came to York on a school trip. He saw her in a museum.' I imagine him surveying her through a glass, display case with the intensity of a viper watching a mouse. 'He followed her all the way back to Bath. All the way back to her house. When he returned to Ledbury Hall, he couldn't stop talking about her. A few weeks later, she was here.' She presses her lips together. She wants to say more but her eyes dart to mine and then away again. I give her a small, encouraging nod. She sighs. 'If I'm honest, I was relieved because I wasn't alone anymore. I'd felt alone, desperately alone, for so long.'

I feel a pang of empathy because I know the sharp cut of loneliness all too well. This time, I don't hesitate, I lay my hand on hers and she squeezes it back. 'So what you told me about your family is true? They didn't kick you out?'

'No.'

'Then why did you tell Olivia that . . .'

'Heath made me. He wanted to paint himself as a hero.'

'And rescuing a homeless girl off the streets sounds much less villainous than abducting a happy teenager from her family?'

'Exactly. I don't know why she believed any of it.'

'Because it was easier for her to believe the man who'd taken her was a prince rather than a monster.'

She bites her lip. 'I have this horrible feeling.'

'What?'

And the way she looks at me makes fear rear up, visceral and wretched. 'We aren't all getting out of here alive.'

53

Caitlin Arden

The next morning, I am tugged from sleep by the soft, feather-light touch of a fingertip on my nose. When I open my eyes, Olivia is crouching beside my bed, and a wave of nostalgia engulfs me. This is how my big sister would wake me every morning when we were children.

She's smiling, but it doesn't reach her eyes. She's worried I'll turn her away but this is an olive branch I grasp with both hands. Responding the same way I always did, I try to kitten nip the finger. She yanks her hand back quickly. 'Too slow, Kitty-Cate.'

I grin. 'You came,' I say, voice heavy with sleep. 'I didn't think Heath would let you.'

'He doesn't know.' I feel a volt of shock that she's disobeyed him again. But this is a good sign, isn't it? My heart quickens with hope.

'Where is he?'

'Out.'

I sit up, pressing my back against the headboard as she climbs onto the bed to sits cross-legged opposite me.

'I didn't like how we left things yesterday.' She picks thoughtfully at her thumbnail. 'I knew this transition would be hard for you. Heath warned me to temper my expectations. I just . . . I'm eager to start our lives here together. I've spent years imagining what it would be like to have you at Ledbury Hall. Reading together in the library. Raiding the bar cart and mixing cocktails, sinking together into a boozy afternoon. Swimming in the lake. Heath says it's too dangerous but it doesn't seem very deep to me.' There's a dreamy, far away look in her eyes. 'I pictured us gardening together. We could grow *aureolin* sunflowers,' she teases.

'Fruit and vegetables, too?'

She nods.

'Vermilion tomatoes and amaranthine beetroots?'

She laughs. 'Yes! Exactly.'

We smile at each other.

'I imagined us growing old together,' she says. 'Wearing matching jumpers and talking to our potted plants. I have this really clear vision of holding your cool, wrinkly hand in mine, sitting in the garden, watching the sunset over the trees.'

On the one hand, I want to scream at her for imprisoning me here, and on the other, I want to fold her carefully in my arms because she does love me. Has loved me this entire time. She doesn't realise she has the clumsy good intentions of a child caging a small wild animal. Snatching up a terrified vole and housing it alongside a predatory tomcat, naïve to the inevitability that the tomcat will eventually kill it.

I don't know that it's possible to convince her that the life she's imagined for us is fantasy. I've been stripped of my freedoms and forced to live under the control of a sociopath. A rapist, despite his denial. That I will never love Heath Ledbury. That I will never thank her for persuading him to bring me here. It could take years to convince her that her *husband* is an evil bastard. She may never believe it. She's so desperate to have me here, she'll never help me escape. At least, not knowingly. A plan starts to form. 'Would you give me a tour?' I ask.

'Of the house?'

I nod.

She catches her bottom lip between her teeth. 'Heath wants to give you a tour after the wedding.'

I blanch. 'Wedding?'

She brightens. 'Of course. I told you Heath is a gentleman. He wants to do things the right way.'

Marry my captor in some deluded, farcical, fake ceremony?

Absolutely *not*. I'm careful to keep the horror out of my expression. 'I just . . . don't think I could marry him without seeing where I'm expected to live. It's not right, Olivia. I don't feel comfortable here. I've seen almost nothing of the house. You're right, it hasn't been an easy adjustment, but how can you expect it to be under such bizarre circumstances?' She mulls this over and, in a bid to sway her my way, I continue, 'Besides, *you* wanted me here, doesn't it make sense for *you* to show me around?'

'He'd never allow it.'

I give her a playful smile. 'Does he need to know?'

She shifts uncomfortably and glances at the door as though planning to leave.

Panic flutters in my stomach. 'I mean, I obviously wouldn't tell him.' If I have any chance of escaping, I need to get out of this room and I need to do it when Heath isn't here to stop me. I hold my playful smile in place, disguising the scheming beneath. Her eyes roam my face. She's on the verge of giving in to me. I can feel it. I reach out and take her hand. I squeeze it. '*Please.*'

And the second a smile pulls her rosebud mouth up, I know I have won. 'OK.'

I grin, alive with hope for the first time since I woke up here.

'He'll be gone for a couple of hours tomorrow,' she tells me. 'But Caitie, *don't* tell Bryony.'

'Why?'

'She hates me. She's jealous that I'm Heath's favourite,' she says. 'If it were up to her, I'd be dead.'

54

Caitlin Arden

Despite Olivia's warning, I tell Bryony everything when she comes that morning with my breakfast, because for my plan to work, I need her. I make her go over the layout of Ledbury Hall a hundred times, reciting it back to her when she comes again at lunch. She tells me exactly where in Heath's bedroom I'll find the brass tin of keys. During the house tour, I'll have to find a way to lock Olivia in a room to buy me enough time to free Bryony. Then the two of us will drag Olivia, kicking and screaming if we have to, from the manor. The plan is to find a road, a passing car, another house, any civilisation that can alert the police.

By the time supper arrives, I'm confident I know the layout off by heart. Though I don't entirely trust Bryony, I trust her enough to know she wants to be as far from Ledbury Hall as possible. We need each other.

I lie awake all night, too excited, too terrified to sleep. All the petrifying possibilities tomorrow bring spiders pouring from the crevices of my mind, until my head crawls with them. The thought of Heath catching me out of my room makes me sick to my stomach. What will he do? I think of his dead sister and wonder how he murdered her. *Why?*

The house creaks and groans around me. Old pipes, moaning ghosts. The walls are thick with secrets. I wonder if I press my ear against them, I'll hear the slowing beat of Elinor's heart, the dying hitch of her breath.

I wake to a long-lost chill in the air. After months of suffocating, sticky heat, September has arrived with a gust of autumn. The artillery fire of rain on the roof tiles fills the room. I get out of bed and stand before the rain-lashed windows. Dark, angry clouds swirl in the steel sky. A storm is brewing. When we were children, Olivia and I loved them. We'd wait with racing hearts and wide, eager eyes for the thunderous sky, counting between strikes of lightning. Waiting with bated breath for the next bolt of electric-blue. My heart races now, not for the upcoming storm, but with the wild-animal urge to flee from a trap.

I shower and dress in a white, cotton midi dress that's loose-fitting. Bryony brings breakfast but we eat in near silence. She glances continuously at the door and I know he's outside, listening. Before she goes, she gives my hand a reassuring squeeze.

By the time Olivia comes to my room, my stomach is in knots. She hums with a nervous, excited energy. 'Ready for your tour?'

My heart gallops. I smile. 'Absolutely.'

She holds open the door and I step into the hall. No handcuffs. No Heath. Even with two large windows at either end of the landing, the storm-darkened sky casts a dim, grey light. Unease skitters through me. Olivia bends down and scoops something from the ground. As my eyes fall on it, my pulse kicks. The brass tin. Of course. All the doors are locked, how else was she going to get into each room when Heath keeps the master key around his neck? I'm tempted to slap it from her hand and take it but force myself to stick to the plan.

'Let's start with the bedrooms,' she says.

I nod.

I pay very little attention as she leads me from one spare room to another, but when she pushes open the door to Heath's room, my curiosity spikes. It smells of him. Of sea salt and sage, lemongrass and clean skin. The walls are the dark, smoky grey of a storm cloud. The furniture is warm, bare woods. In the corner is a bookcase full of vinyl. A record player rests on the chest of drawers under the window. The focal point of the room though is the king-sized, four-poster bed. I imagine my sister entwined with him and anger bursts in my chest. I look away and that's when I see it. A large, framed photograph hanging on the opposite wall.

Gazing down at me is a girl, no older than sixteen, wearing a dress in a pretty shade of green. Just for a second, I mistake her for Olivia. Her face is in semi-profile, and she is sitting in an armchair, a smile playing on her lips. In her hands is an open book. It's as though she has been interrupted mid-read. Her hair is long and glossy and thick. Almost the exact shade of gold as Olivia's. Her eyes are a startling periwinkle blue. They are fathomless and intelligent, staring at the photographer with unmistakable affection. She's hauntingly beautiful, just like my sister.

'Elinor,' offers Olivia.

Heath's sister. Heath's murdered sister. Without looking at Olivia, I ask, 'Were they close?'

'Very.'

'What did he say happened to her?'

'Ran off with an Irishman.'

'And she's never come back?'

'No.'

'Don't you think that's odd?' When she doesn't answer, I turn to her. 'If they're so close, I mean?'

She lifts her chin but says nothing. She is wilfully ignorant.

'You look just like her,' I say, my eyes ping-ponging between her and Elinor.

Olivia's lips part and her gaze drifts up to the photograph. She has thought the same and wondered why. She clears her throat. 'Let's look at the other rooms.'

She leads me out and locks the door behind us, dropping the key into the tin.

Downstairs, I am led from one opulent room to another. It is only as I am taken into the sitting room that my stomach turns over. Hanging beside the fireplace is a wedding dress. Not just any wedding dress. The one I chose when I was with her. I reach out and touch the dainty, embroidered leaves.

Olivia is grinning, barely able to keep the eagerness from her voice. 'Are you surprised?'

I swallow. 'Very.'

Now I know why she wanted to go dress shopping with me. It

was never for my wedding to Oscar. It was always for my wedding to Heath. I take a deep, steadying breath, swallowing the burn of fear.

'This is pretty much it. You've seen every room.'

'What about the library?'

'You saw it that first day.'

'Not properly. It's all a bit of a blur,' I say. 'Isn't it through here?' I move towards the locked door. For this plan to work, I need to get into the library.

Olivia glances at the clock. 'I suppose so but we have to be quick.'

She takes a key from the tin and opens the door. My eyes dart around the library until they settle on the door tucked away behind the bar cart. The one Bryony and I discussed at length. I wonder over to it and grasp the brass handle. 'What's through here?' I ask, pretending I have no idea.

'Wine cellar.'

I feign surprise and then delight. 'I love wine. Can we take a quick look?'

She frowns. 'You want to look at dusty old wine bottles?'

'I actually know quite a lot about wine.' I don't tell her this is because of my relationship with Oscar. 'I love an oaky red.' I sweeten the suggestion. 'Maybe I could even pick one out for the wedding. You can tell Heath you chose it.'

Her gaze lights up at this, delighted I'm taking an interest in my looming marriage. 'Fine. But we have to be really, really quick.'

I nod.

She puts the key in the lock and opens it. Like always, she leaves the key in situ as we descend the stairs. Like always, I am ushered in first. I descend into yawing darkness. As I reach the bottom, a light flicks on overhead, and Olivia follows. I glance up, past her, to the open cellar door. In her hands is the brass tin of keys. I wander over to one of the shelves and slide a bottle of red free, blowing the dust from its label. I wiggle it at her.

'Nineteen eighty-two,' I say. 'Not bad.'

She takes it from me but frustratingly, she keeps hold of the tin. 'I prefer white.'

I roll my eyes. 'A heathen's preference.'

She puts the bottle back and I slide another free. Adrenaline courses through me as I try to work out how I can take the tin, get up the stairs and lock her down here. I don't want to hurt her. I glance towards the steps. She's closer to them than I am. I need to draw her deeper into the cellar. I slip the bottle I was holding back and move further along the shelves, pretending to browse. She follows, asking me questions about wine. I answer on autopilot, surprised by how much I absorbed from Oscar over the years. All the while, I am manoeuvring her further and further from the stairs. Once we are as far away as we can get, I pluck a bottle at random but I am shaking so hard with trepidation, I almost drop it.

'Caitie,' she admonishes. 'Be careful. If you break anything, he'll know we were down here.' She licks her lips, suddenly nervous. 'Look, you've seen the entire house, let's go back.'

But only one of us can leave this cellar. I could hit her with it. Knock her out. But even as I think it I know I'm lying to myself. I look down at the bottle in my hand, her warning not to break anything ringing in my ears. 'OK,' I say, and as I make to slide the bottle back into its holster, I deliberately drop it. It hits the concrete, shattering. Glass glitters in a seeping pool of crimson.

'Caitie!' she scolds. Setting the brass tin down, she kneels, picking pieces of glass from the floor.

I move around her. 'I'm so sorry.'

Then, while she's distracted, I snatch the tin from the floor and race across the cellar to the stone steps.

Olivia shrieks my name. She's fast, thundering quickly up the stairs behind me. She lunges, fingers snatching at my dress and yanking me back. I trip, smacking my knee against the lip of the step. I cry out in pain. Olivia's frantic, grasping fingers pinch at my skin, trying to get a hold of me. I kick out. My foot meets flesh and she yelps. But I'm free. I stagger up the stairs, still clutching the tin. Heart banging against my ribs, I reach the top and spin towards the door, slamming it shut. Olivia throws herself against it. I fumble with the key and snap it to the right, locking her inside.

Her screams are rage-filled.

'I'm so sorry,' I call to her, though I'm not sure she can hear over her own furious ranting.

Then, I turn and run.

Breathlessly, I slide the bolt free on Bryony's door but when I try to open it, I realise it's been double-locked.

'Caitie?' Bryony's voice drifts through the wood, voice so thick with disbelief, I can taste it. 'You actually did it? You got the keys?'

'Yes.' I open the box and tip the keys onto the floor then snatch one up at random.

'Where's Olivia?'

'Cellar.'

'Oh, my God, it worked!' she squeals. 'The plan actually worked?'

My cheeks colour, I am not proud of manipulating my sister or of locking her in a cellar. I turn the little plastic key fob over but my insides clench when I see it's labelled not by room, but by number. I drop that key and pick up another and another. They're all numbered. There's no way for me to know which of them unlocks Bryony's door. Olivia clearly memorised the corresponding rooms but then, she's had years of experience.

'Open the door,' says Bryony, giving the handle a little shake for emphasis.

'I can't,' I say, voice trembling. 'The keys aren't labelled "dining room" or "Bryony's bedroom", they're numerical.'

She's quiet. Then, 'You'll just have to try them all.'

I stare down at the pile of keys. There must be at least twenty. The only one that really stands out is an old-fashioned skeleton key in antique brass. Its ornate head reminds me of the key from *The Wizard of Oz*. It has to be for the front door. I slip it into the pocket of my dress and run my hands over the remaining keys.

'Caitie,' Bryony snaps. 'Can you please get me out of here?'

'I'm trying.'

I pick one at random. Though it fits the lock, it doesn't turn. I drop it back into the tin and take another. All the while, I can hear Olivia screaming like a banshee. I am terrified that Heath will return home any second and find me on the landing. As soon as he enters the house, he'll hear Olivia and he'll know. She said he'd be back soon. Imminently. My heart starts hiccupping in my chest. I am light-headed with terror. Olivia's screams are shredding my nerves. I make a decision. On my knees, I start sweeping the keys through the gap beneath the door.

'What're you doing?' Bryony snaps.

'You can try the keys from the inside.' I push the last one through the gap. 'I need to make Olivia stop.'

'Caitie, no!' she cries. 'Stay here. Help me!'

But I am already backing away. 'You've got the keys. Once you're out, meet me downstairs.'

My legs are shaking so hard, I almost tumble down the staircase. The key is still in the cellar door but she's so enraged that I'm afraid to open it. It will take both me and Bryony to drag her out of here. As I pace the library, trying to work out what to say to soothe her, the screaming stops. Cut off so abruptly, I stumble. There is only the howling wind and the rain that scratches at the windows. Has she fallen? Is she lying at the bottom of the stairs in a broken heap? The blood drains from me, replaced by icy nausea. My fingers clasp the cool metal key. I'm about to the open the door, to check on my sister, when I hear another key in another lock. The front door.

Heath is home.

55

Caitlin Arden

A fear like none I've ever known takes hold. An all-consuming, ravenous beast. It welds my feet to the spot. All I can do is stand and stare and listen. I hear a shoe hit the floor and then another. The rattle of keys being slipped into a pocket. Footsteps. I don't know whether Olivia hears it, too, or whether she is so connected to him that she senses his arrival, but she screams his name with such piercing, raw urgency, that I cover my ears.

Heath bursts into the room, skidding to a halt when he sees me. A kaleidoscope of emotion slides across his face. Panic for his wife bleeds into shock and confusion before crystallising into anger as realisation dawns.

Olivia is still calling for him. He charges at me. I lunge to the side, snatching a candlestick from the bookshelves and swing wildly. I can't let him get to Olivia. He jumps back and throws up his hands as though to ward me off.

'Caitie,' he says, struggling to keep the fury from his voice. He swallows hard, his Adam's apple bobbing, and levels me with a cold, poisonous stare.

He's wearing joggers and a soft grey T-shirt, as though he's been out for a run. He is so much broader, so much taller, so much stronger, than I am. The only thing between me and him is a few feet of space and a brass candlestick. I try not to think about what he'll do once he gets his hands on me.

'Caitie,' he says again, in the tone you'd use to soothe a wild animal. 'Put that down so we can talk.'

Olivia, hearing his voice, has stopped shrieking. I imagine her on the other side of the door, ear pressed against the wood to listen. It's possible Bryony is free from her bedroom. If she isn't, I need to buy more time. We have a much better chance of leaving here alive if we work together. I lick my dry lips. 'Is that what you told Elinor?'

He pales. 'What?'

'Your sister.' Then I see it. A ghost moving across his face. A long-buried memory. A scabbed wound. I pick at it. Push my fingers into the hot, wet gash. 'Did you tell her you just wanted to talk before you made her disappear?'

He freezes and I know I am right. There is no rush of triumph though, only a fear that tightens around my throat like a cord.

'Stop,' he growls.

I glance at the door behind him, praying Bryony will appear any moment.

'Did you kill her, Heath?'

He bares his teeth. 'Don't.'

'You can't do it,' I taunt. '*You* can't love *anything* without destroying it.'

'NO!' he roars.

But I can't stop. I have to keep him talking. If I'm honest, there is a burgeoning thrill at taking back power. At hurting him. 'Where's her body, Heath? The woods? The padlocked bedroom?' I raise an eyebrow. 'The lake?'

His eyes are ablaze with green fire. He moves so fast, he is a blur. I am slammed against the bookshelves. Paperbacks rain down on us. The candlestick slips from my fingers and clatters to the ground. Heath yanks me forward and then rams me against the shelves again. His hands close around my throat. My bare feet scrabble uselessly against the wood. He squeezes, cutting off my air. I claw at his arms. His grip tightens and my vision greys. I grope along the shelves for something, *anything*. My fingers curl around something hard and cool. It's heavy. I swing my unseen weapon. It cracks against the side of his head. I feel something give way. Bone breaking free from bone. His grip slackens and then falls away completely. Blood pours from his temple. He stumbles, making low, guttural noises. Then he collapses. I stare down at the bust in my hand, blood smeared across the white, pale marble of a woman's face. It slips from my terror-numb fingers and thuds onto the rug beside him.

I sink down and with a trembling hand, I roll him onto his back. His eyes, fixed wide and unseeing, stare up at the ceiling. Blood pools, spreading thickly across the rug, soaking into it. I turn my face away from the hole in the side of his skull and vomit.

56

Caitlin Arden

I struggle to my feet. The room whirls around me. I keep Heath's lifeless body in my peripheral vision, worried that if I see the gaping hole in his head again, I'll be sick for a second time. After taking several deep breaths, I stumble to the cellar door. This isn't over until I get Olivia out of Ledbury Hall. I turn the key and open the cellar door. She tumbles into the library, eyes searching. I stand in front of her, eclipsing his body from view.

'What happened?' she gulps. 'Are you OK?' She is smoothing hair back from my face, her touch soft and reassuring. Then she sees the blood splattered across my skin and her hands still. 'Where's . . .' She trails off as her gaze finds him.

'Olivia,' I sob, but she pushes past me.

She stands over him. Rooted to the spot. Then something inside her cracks open. An overburdened rain cloud. The noise that breaks from her is gut-wrenching devastation. She drops to her knees. Then her hands are on him, touching his face, smoothing over his chest. 'Heath? Wake up. *Please* wake up.' She balls his T-shirt up in her fists. 'Please,' she begs. 'Please wake up.' Her entire body is overcome with thick, clotted sobs. Her mourning is ocean-deep, the pain as real as a blade across soft flesh. I go to her, hovering, keeping my gaze fixed on her so as not to catch him in my sight. Olivia chokes down the last of her sobs.

'We have to get out of here,' I whisper. 'We have to leave.'

Slowly, she raises her eyes to mine. There is an eerie stillness in her gaze. A frozen lake in winter. 'You killed him.'

I swallow. 'I didn't have a choice.'

'He's dead.' She rises. 'You killed him.' His blood is on her hands. She looks down. Sees it. She is trembling all over. 'He's gone.' Her fingers curl into talons. 'You *murdered* him.'

'Olivia—'

She opens her mouth and screams in a brutal, bloody way. Then she throws herself at me, knocking me to the ground. She's on me, talons in my hair, slashing at my throat. I kick out and struggle and buck. I throw her off. She tumbles to the right. I flip onto my stomach and push to my feet. Then I am running.

I smack into the door frame on my way out and catch my shoulder on the next. In the foyer, instinct makes me swing left and propels me up the stairs. I sprint along the dark landing. All the doors are closed. Bryony is still locked inside. Vaguely, over the blood that pounds in my ears, I hear her yell that the lock is stiff, but there's no time to stop. I glance over my shoulder. Olivia is behind me. I pick up my pace, doors blurring as I pass. I reach the second staircase, the one beside my room, and realise it doesn't go down. It goes up. I take the steps two at a time until I reach a door at the top. It's bolted shut. I fumble and manage to slide it free. A moment later, I am spat outside. The wind shrieks, pulling at my hair with frenzied fingers. The rain pelts down, a thousand tiny needles against my skin. I spin around, trying to get my bearings. I'm on a roof terrace. There's nowhere left to run. Behind me, the door swings open.

Olivia, blinded by grief, overcome with rage, flings herself at me. We tumble to the ground, rolling over and over, only stopping when we hit a stone balustrade. She straddles me. Her fingers curl around my throat and squeeze. I am choking, gasping for air. Her hair is plastered to her face in rain-soaked clumps. She is feral, screaming. I dig my nails into her wrists, knowing I have only minutes left to live. I am crying, rain mingling with my tears. But then her screams weaken, withering into great, hiccupping sobs. Her grip loosens. Our eyes meet. My sister, *my* Olivia, slowly returns. Like the sun rising after a long, dark night. And she sees me. *Really* sees me. The tension seeps out of her. She frowns down at her hands as though they don't belong to her, and then she gapes at me, mortified and repentant. Tears stream down her cheeks. She opens her mouth in what I know will be a plea for forgiveness. But I never get to hear it because in the next instant, she is flung aside. Knocked off me. And then she is gone. Disappearing over the balustrade. Swept away like a leaf on the wind.

Still lying on the ground, my gaze swings up and around.

Bryony stands over me. She is glassy-eyed and expressionless. I roll onto my side and crawl to the wall. I use the slick, wet stone to pull myself up. I stand on quivering legs.

Then I look down.

I look down at the broken marionette figure that lies on the gravel driveway below. Arms and legs splayed at unnatural angels.

Olivia.

Blood pools around her head in a macabre halo. 'No.' It is a whistle of grief. An impotent denial. 'No.'

Then I am shoving past Bryony. I am running, down, down, down. In a heartbeat, I am at the front door, taking the key from my dress pocket. I yank it open and then I am outside. The rain is heavier now. A sheet of water. I stumble down the steps and drop to my knees beside her. The sharp, wet stones dig into my skin.

The panic and the terror carved into her face is absolute. She makes a noise, as though she is suffocating, drowning. She can't breathe. Her lips turn blue. I scream. It comes from the very bottom of me. From the darkest, farthest corner of my soul. I don't know what to do. How to save her.

I take her face in my hands, leaving scarlet smears against the clammy grey of her skin. If I hold on to her, if I touch her, she'll stay. She won't leave me here alone. 'I love you,' I tell her. I say it again and again, like a prayer, like a healing spell. 'You're going to be OK.' I don't know if she can hear me. If she understands. 'Don't go. *Please*, don't leave. Don't leave me. I need you, Olivia. I need you.'

But my sister's eyes, those brilliant blue eyes, ones that always made me think of glacial lakes and summer skies, forget-me-nots and bluebell petals, ones I have known since the day I was born, are sightless. Empty.

She is gone and I am alone.

57

Caitlin Arden

Dear Olivia,

My beautiful, brilliant, bewitching sister. As an adult, I've never written in a journal. I wasn't sure how to start but 'Dear diary' felt too Jane Austen so, instead, I've decided to address it to you.

Something I have come to understand in this last year is that there are universal truths we live by. The sun will always rise in the east and set in the west. Everything that is born, dies. No one will ever know you the way a sister does. There's a special type of magic in being born to the same two people. Of growing up together. In knowing the blood that courses through my veins is the same as the blood that coursed through yours. What I'm trying to say is, I miss you. Losing you is like a thick soot that has settled over every surface of my life. For the first few weeks after you died, I poured all my energy into trying to scrub that soot away. Desperate to erase the grief so I could breathe clean air again. Now, though, a year on, I realise it is not soot. It is glitter. It is every shining, sparkling moment I had with you, sprinkled all around me. Everywhere I look, I see you. Sometimes you are the girl queueing for a coffee in front of me. A smiling face in a crowd. I find you in my own reflection, in the blue of my eyes and the slope of my nose.

Harriett assures me it's all a part of grieving you. Of remembering. Harriett's my new therapist. Don't worry, she's a *real* therapist. I checked. And checked again. It was her idea to write to you. She suggested letters to seal up and keep but then I thought of your gold-bee journal and how much you loved to write. I whiled away hours in stationery shops, looking for the perfect one. It's hardback and the colour of aureolin sunflowers. Harriett's office is a summer house at the bottom of her garden. It is surrounded by roses and forget-me-nots, wild daisies, and sunflowers, too. For the rest of my life, I won't be able to look at one without thinking of you.

Everyone wore yellow to your funeral. Aureolin. And everywhere, everywhere, were sunflowers. Oscar turned up, sheepish and remorseful, but Mum and Dad sent him away. They read his book. Much to my bitter censure, it's a best seller. Mum raged. Dad even threatened to sue. I told them not to bother. That whatever he wrote doesn't matter because he didn't know you. To him, you were only ever a girl on the bus. A childhood crush. And later, a project to exploit. I choose to remember you not as the person he needed you to be to sell books, but as a sister who was not only willing to share the limelight, but to thrust me into it, spinning me into the praise of our parents even when I hadn't earned it. As the little girl who announced to a room full of taunting children that buttercup-yellow dungarees were cool. A special type of nicotine electricity.

There has been so much loss. Not just of you, but of friends, too. I have seen almost nothing of Florence this last year. Even though Bryony corroborated my story, explaining Heath's instructions for you to paint me as paranoid and delusional, Florence has never forgiven me for ruining her wedding. I don't blame her. It's a sad truth that you were the twine that bound us but, with everything that happened, it was easier to snip the thread than it was to sit and try to untangle it. I'm at peace with it now.

Despite his attempts, Oscar and I haven't spoken. Though he wasn't bold enough to try and see me again after being exiled from the funeral, sometimes in the dead of night, I'm woken by my vibrating phone. No one speaks when I answer, but I once heard a woman say crossly, 'Oscar, who the hell are you calling at this hour?'

I live with our parents now which has been good. Healing. Things between me and them are different. Better. A week before Christmas, I was in the kitchen making mince pies. There was ice on the ground, and everywhere was festooned with twinkling Christmas lights. I was rubbing butter into flour, just as Mum taught us, when Dad appeared by my side. Wordlessly, he started cleaning around me, wiping down the work surfaces and stacking the bowls I was no longer using.

'Olivia's disappearance wasn't your fault,' he told me gravely. We were side by side. 'It was mine.'

I was quiet, letting him fill the silence with whatever it was he needed to say.

'The night he . . . took her, we'd arranged for a babysitter, but she cancelled last minute. Your mother wanted to stay home. I didn't. My boss was hosting, you see. I knew it wouldn't sit well with him if we didn't attend.' He dipped the brush back into the melted butter. 'So, against her better judgment, your mother agreed to leave Olivia in charge.'

I glanced at him. Saw the slight tremble of his hand, the tightness in his jaw, the sadness and guilt that swirled beneath the gaps of him. 'I don't blame you, Caitie. I blame myself. I'm sorry you overheard that argument between me and your mum. I was grieving and I was wrong.' He shook his head. Put the brush down. 'The truth is, every time I looked at you over the years, I saw all the ways in which I'd failed you. Failed Olivia. Seeing you all alone, without a sister, was a constant reminder that I'd let both my girls down in the most *unthinkable* way.'

I stopped rubbing butter into flour and I turned to him. 'It wasn't your fault, Dad.' I told him what I knew of Heath Ledbury. That once he had you in his sights, Olivia, he'd stop at nothing until he possessed you. That if it wasn't for that opportunity, he'd have created another. The second he set eyes on you; you were his and your fate was sealed. No one, not even our father, could have protected you.

'I love you, Caitie,' Dad whispered fiercely.

I flung my arms around him. He didn't seem to care his shirt was covered in raw ingredients. He peppered the top of my head with frantic kisses, just as he did when I was a little girl.

I haven't been back to Ledbury Hall since my escape. It's up for sale now. I don't know who'd buy it after what happened there. I'd happily see it burn to the ground. The police found your gold-bee journal and returned it to us. They found Elinor's journals, too. Like you, she loved to write. Maybe that is why Heath took it the night he abducted you. I stayed up reading it, devouring each page, each word, tracing them with my finger. Over the years, you felt the sharp cut of loneliness just as deeply as I did. My heart ached for you. For the poison Heath fed you. As well as journals, the police found human remains buried in two places across the property. One was unearthed in the woods. A middle-aged man believed to be Robert Brent, the Ledburys' uncle. The other was, of course, Elinor. Heath buried her a few feet from the lake, facing the stone statue of two entwined lovers. Both were murdered two decades ago.

Bryony and I were lucky to escape with our lives. Just last week, I saw a photograph of her in the paper. The long blonde hair Heath loved so much is short now and dyed auburn. In the photo, she was holding the hand of a young woman and they were looking at one another with so much joy. Lucy. Her sister. And I couldn't help but think, *that should have been us*. Just as I was cleared of Heath's murder, Bryony was cleared of yours. Extenuating circumstances, they said. Given all Bryony was subjected to at the hands of her captor, they were lenient. In her witness statement, she claimed she believed I was in mortal danger. Claimed she didn't know you had halted your assault on me. She was lying. You were right, Olivia, she wanted you dead. I didn't listen. I trusted her. So maybe your blood is on my hands, too. Maybe I am as much to blame as she is. I confided this fear, one that has left me haunted by night terrors, to Harriett, but she told me a person is only ever in control of their own actions. That I did the best I could with the information I had. That there was no shame in trying to save everyone, but I need to come to terms with the fact that not everyone deserves to be saved. Or, like you, not everyone *wants* to be saved.

I've decided to focus on my future. To make plans all of my own. I'm taking the money from the sale of my home alongside my earnings from Wanderlust Illustrations, and I am travelling for the next six months. Gemma is back in England now, but she's going to meet me in Norway in a few weeks.

I think you would be proud, Olivia. I think you would want me to step out of your shadow and feel the sun on my skin. To forge a path all my own. Losing you has forced me to create a life that is bolder, braver and more vivid than the one I merely existed in before.

As I write this, I am sitting in a departure lounge, waiting to board my plane. Our parents offered to drive me but I knew if they did, I might back out of leaving. Six months is a long time but they've promised to join me for Christmas. It's only eleven weeks away.

Besides, there was somewhere I wanted to visit before I left. The taxi trundled along the winding roads of Stonemill. I watched our hometown drift by. I could see us, two sisters, two young girls, heads bowed close together, dipping into the farm shop to buy our sandwiches and then racing down the street with our haul.

The taxi pulled up at our destination and I got out. Paid the driver to wait. I hadn't been to the meadow, to *our* meadow, since the day you were taken.

It is unchanged and looks exactly as it did that balmy, July afternoon. I stood among the flowers and thought about death. Because I did not just lose you once. I lost you twice. I lost you the night Heath entered our parents' home and led you from your bed. And then again when you fell from that roof and broke your neck. The belief I had the night you were taken, the one I felt in each beat of my heart, in every breath, even in the bright red of my blood, was right: you were never coming home. Not really. What returned to us after sixteen years was what Heath made you. There were moments, diamond-bright glimmers of my sister, but that's all they were: glimmers.

Even now, at twenty-seven, I know people whose loved ones are all alive, who've never experienced the deep, lacerating grief that accompanies loss. I wonder what it feels like to be blissfully ignorant to that pain. Blissfully ignorant to death hovering, ready to snatch everything from you at any given moment. This used to be a bitter, jealous thought but, as I stood in the wild meadow, it was merely a sad one.

Now, as I wait in departures, a wave of anguish engulfs me and I let it. I let the knowledge that you won't be at the airport to greet me when I return to England after my travels, wash into my ears and eyes and nose and mouth. You will never get to hear about my next heartbreak or my last love. You won't stand beside me on my wedding day. Or feel the weight of my first child in your arms. We won't grow old together like you hoped. You will never feel my cool, wrinkly hand in yours. The years which we have lost and continue to lose, lie like thorns in my palms. But I pluck them free. Toss them aside. And choose to focus on the years we did have, letting them blossom inside my mind like new roses. Like sunflowers.

Back in the meadow, I'd closed my eyes, turned my face up to the warm light and thought, *I do not love you sloppily or lazily, Olivia. I love you with a pounding, visceral certainty.*

When I opened my eyes again, there you were. A young girl. Waiting for me. Your profile against the lit sky. I will see you forever like that. In the balmy glow of the evening light, you performed a seamless cartwheel across the wildflower meadow. All long, tanned limbs and flawless symmetry. You flipped your golden hair back from your face and our eyes locked.

Glacial lakes and summer skies, forget-me-nots and bluebell petals.

I wanted to wrap my arms around you, as though that would stop you from leaving me again. But you are gone. You are already gone.

'Goodbye, Olivia.'

You smiled a slow, lazy, radiant smile. 'See you, Kitty-Cate.'

Then you turned and walked away, towards the sun that was sinking below the hill.

For years, without you by my side, I felt loneliness as keenly as a blade beneath my skin. Cold and unyielding. But now I know better. You glitter in the bright red of my blood. *Our* blood. We are sisters. We are aged twenty-seven and thirteen years old. I will *never* be alone.

Acknowledgements

Many thanks to my agent and friend, Thérèse Coen, for believing in me first. Gratitude to Una and everyone at Susanna Lea Associates for your support.

I am incredibly lucky to be published by the innovative and dynamic Embla Books team. Thank you to Anna Perkins who I adore, to Hannah Deuce and Marina Stavropoulou for all that you do. An extra-special thank you to my kind and patient editor, Cara Chimirri, for all the hours you have poured into this story. I hope it makes you proud.

Thank you to Lisa Brewster for another gorgeous cover – my favourite so far. You are wildly talented.

To my readers – you are a fervent, generous, wonderful community. Your love for *One Small Mistake* and *The Perfect Match* was overwhelming and much appreciated. I cannot thank you enough for your continued support. A special thank you to those of you who leave reviews and send me messages of encouragement. I hope you enjoyed reading this story as much as I enjoyed writing it.

Thanks to Dr Rebecca Annis, Dr Matthew Stuttard and Dr Wesley Dean for your medical wisdom and for taking my morbid research questions in your stride.

Thank you to my KES colleagues for cheering me on. Especially to Binny, to Andrew, and to the members, past and present, of the L.G.

To Rachel Rowlands for listening and understanding.

Infinite thanks to author and friend, Rachel Delahaye-Lefever, for furiously championing this book. Your belief in this story, your love and your excitement for it, was like a healing spell. I love you dearly.

To my mum for devouring my third book with as much vigour as all the ones that came before. Thank you for instilling in me a love of stories and a belief in myself that I could achieve anything.

And to Lucy Perkins for making the time to read this story even as you studied for your master's degree. Your outlandish plot theories kept me entertained and your unwavering confidence in me kept me motivated. Thank you for your encouragement, your thoughtful nature and your ability to make every day brighter. I am never more myself than when I am with you.

Thank you to my husband for every park-walk, for your patience and your creative input. For having faith in me even when I don't have faith in myself. I am lucky to be loved by you. And love to our girls, Ivy and Maple, the waggiest, most adorable writing companions.

This book is dedicated to Mel, my oldest friend and long-term therapist. I could not have written *The Wrong Daughter* without you. You were the first person to fall in love with this story. Your feedback and theories shaped this book. Your enthusiasm and wisdom helped me to write it. It's rare to meet someone who loves you long enough to know you as a girl and as a woman. Together, we've graduated university, got our master's degrees, bought houses, become dog-mothers, got engaged, got married, got book deals – I am so proud of the lives we've built. Two decades of friendship behind us, a lifetime left to live.

Exclusive Interview with Dandy

Q: How long did it take you to write *The Wrong Daughter*? Is this your first book?

The Wrong Daughter isn't my first book. It's actually my third! My first is *One Small Mistake* and my second is *The Perfect Match*. *The Wrong Daughter* took a little longer than usual to finish, as I suffered a concussion while writing it which was far from ideal. I think the first draft was completed in about nine months!

Q: What drew you to writing in the thriller space versus other genres?

It was a total accident. I started off writing young adult fantasy, but those books were (very fortunately) rejected by editors for being too twisted and too dark for a younger audience. My wise and wonderful agent, Thérèse Coen, encouraged me to write a book for adults and so, during lockdown, I penned *One Small Mistake*, which is a story from my soul about a woman so desperate for a book deal, she agrees to fake her own abduction to write a best-selling novel. I wasn't sure what I'd written but my agent gleefully informed me it was in fact a domestic thriller! Luckily for me, my dark and twisty stories found the perfect home at Embla Books.

Q: What was the inspiration for *The Wrong Daughter*? and what was your favourite part about writing it?

I listened to a true crime podcast about confidence trickster Frédéric Bourdin, who pretended to be Nicholas Patrick Barclay, a 13-year-old boy who went missing in 1994. While listening to this story, I wondered what would have happened if the missing person had truly returned? How would years spent with a captor change them? What impact would their return have on the family? Who in that family would doubt this person and who would accept them with open arms? That was the seed from which sprouted the idea for *The Wrong Daughter*. My favourite part about writing it was spending time with Caitlin and exploring the complexities of her relationship with Olivia, as well as those around them. At its core, *The Wrong Daughter* is about sisters and how the love and loss of them shapes you.

Q: Did you always know you were going to be a writer and what appeals most about it?

I had always *dreamed* of being an author – writing stories from the moment I could hold a pen or sit at a keyboard – but as I grew up and explored it as a career option, I became painfully aware of how challenging it is to get published. With the glowing support of my parents, I studied Creative Writing at Bath Spa University, the first in my family to attend, and after my master's degree, I signed with my agent. Even then, I worried publication wasn't on the horizon for me and it took a few years and a lot of tears and determination before I eventually signed with the brilliant Embla Books.

What appeals most to me about being a writer is the opportunity to immerse myself in someone else's world—exploring their thoughts, feelings, relationships and motivations. It's a deeply fulfilling experience to bring a character to life. I love the variety too. As an author, you're not just creating characters; you're also a costume designer and a location scout. There are so many components and the sense of accomplishment when everything clicks together is incredibly rewarding.

Q: When you're not writing what do you like to get up to?

Writing is a pretty sedentary occupation, so I make sure to stay active. I walk my two bouncy cocker spaniels, do aerial hoop, spin classes and (with a little encouragement from my husband) spend time at the gym. But I'm also about those cosy days at home – blankets, candles and board games are my perfect way to unwind. I love interior design, often losing track of time on Pinterest but, for me, it's important to feel inspired by the space in which I live *and* work. I also adore hosting family and friends. My cupboards are practically bursting with serving bowls, ready for the next get-together!

Q: What is the one thing you love most about being able to connect with readers?

Receiving so many gloriously kind messages! It's wild to me that people take time out of their busy lives to read my books and reach out to share their thoughts, and I'm deeply thankful that they do. Putting a book out into the world is nerve-wracking – you pour so much of your soul into each story – and you don't want to disappoint anyone. So, when a book is well-received, it's an enormous relief. I'm endlessly grateful for the generous, compassionate community of readers who help make my dreams a reality. None of it would be possible without their support.

Q: If you were to share one life lesson with your readers what would that be?

Never give up on your ambitions. Surround yourself with people who tell you that you can. People who believe in you. Those people are the rays of sunlight that break through a drizzly sky. Bathe in them.

Q: What can readers look forward to next?

More murder, mystery and complicated women. My next book *The Wedding Vow* follows Verity Lockwood. A year after the brutal, unsolved murder of her husband Linden, Verity discovers he'd been having an affair. Everyone is a suspect—her neighbour, her best friend, her assistant, even her cousin. Verity is determined to expose the other woman before she joins her husband in the morgue. The story is told from the perspectives of both the wife and the other woman, which made it tricky to write as the other woman's identity is kept a secret until the final page. I think readers will love trying to unravel the mystery of who killed Linden Lockwood and trying to figure out the identity of the other woman!

One small mistake. One deadly consequence.

Elodie Fray wants to be more like her perfect sister, Ada, the one her parents are actually proud of. When she decided to quit her job and pursue her dream of becoming an author, she thought it would be her time to shine, but a year on nothing has happened. And she's getting desperate.

When Elodie makes one small mistake on a drunken night with a friend, things quickly spiral and suddenly everyone believes she has a book deal. Unable to find a way back from her little lie, her perfect dream becomes a perfect nightmare – and desperate times call for desperate measures.

Meanwhile, everything is not as it seems in Ada Archer's perfect life. When her sister suddenly disappears, she questions everything – from her marriage, to the man who's been charged with Elodie's abduction. The papers say it's him, but the more she digs into her sister's life the less convinced she is. Ada will do anything to discover the truth, even if it kills her.

No one knows what happened to Elodie Fray, and now her only chance of survival is her sister.

You can listen to the audio narrated by Georgia Maguire & Daphne Kouma now!

Scan the QR code below to order

She loves him, but can she trust him?

When I meet **Henry** by chance at a wedding, it is love at first sight. He's charming, handsome and successful – everything I've ever wanted.

When he proposes, it seems like all my dreams are coming true.

But **Ivy**, my best friend, isn't happy for me at all. She tells me I am making a huge mistake and accuses Henry of something unthinkable.

I know it can't be true. But why would Ivy lie to me?

Now someone is dead and I need to find the truth, whatever it costs me. Before I lose everyone I've ever loved . . .

You can listen to the audio narrated by Helen Keeley now!

Scan the QR code below to order

She is the perfect wife.
Is he the perfect liar?

Verity and **Linden Lockwood** vowed to spend the rest of their lives together, for richer, for poorer, in sickness and in health, till death do they part. Five years later they›ve kept their promise to never let their love die, to never slip into becoming one of *those* couples . . . .

But a year after Linden is brutally and inexplicably murdered in their picture-perfect home, Verity's world shatters again. They're not the golden couple she thought they were. Linden betrayed her: he had been having an affair.

Determined to uncover the identity of the other woman, Verity delves into her husband's life. Everyone is a suspect: her neighbour, her best friend, her assistant . . . even her cousin. But as she unearths Linden's shocking secrets, Verity realises she didn't know her husband at all and the truth might be more dangerous than she realises.

Can Verity expose the other woman before she joins her husband in the morgue?

You can listen to the audio narrated by Tuppence Middleton now!

Scan the QR code below to order

Keep reading for an exclusive extract . . .